THE CHAPEL OF BONES

THE CHAPEL OF BONES

Michael Jecks

headline

First published in Great Britain in 2004
by HEADLINE BOOK PUBLISHING

10 9 8 7 6 5 4 3 2 1

Cataloguing in Publication Data is available from the British Library

ISBN 0 7553 2295 9

Typeset in Times by Avon DataSet Ltd,
Bidford-on-Avon, Warwickshire

Printed and bound in Great Britain by
Clays Ltd, St Ives plc

Headline's policy is to use papers that are natural, renewable and
recyclable products and made from wood grown in sustainable forests.
The logging and manufacturing processes are expected to conform
to the environmental regulations of the country of origin.

HEADLINE BOOK PUBLISHING
A division of Hodder Headline
338 Euston Road
London NW1 3BH

www.headline.co.uk
www.hodderheadline.com

This book is for Don and all the Mortons.

In affectionate and loving memory of Mary.

Also for Keith Aylwin.
A kind, considerate, and generous friend.
He's missed.

Glossary

Accounts
Medieval accounting was very simple compared with today's bookkeeping. The accounts were kept yearly on rolls of parchment sewn together, top-to-tail, and recorded simply charge and discharge, with totals carried forward each year.

Annuellar
Priests appointed by the Dean and Chapter of a cathedral to service a specific **chantry** and participate in certain tasks.

Approver
The medieval equivalent of 'Turning King's Evidence'. A felon could confess and thereby postpone his execution; this often meant that he, the approver, would have to stand in combat against his former partners in crime.

Calefactory
A 'warming room' in a monastery or nunnery in which a good, blazing fire was kept going during the colder months.

Canon
Exeter Cathedral had a large **Chapter** of some twenty-four canons – men who had chosen to live together under the Church's rules. They controlled the income of the Cathedral and mostly lived in the Close in their own houses.

Chapter
The Cathedral at Exeter was ruled by the **dignitaries** – Church officials who possessed separate endowments.

Chaunter
An archaic term for the next most senior **Dignitary** after the Dean. More recently (and commonly) known as the Precentor.

Choir
The full body of men who served the Cathedral, including the **canons** and the **minor clergy**. The word also refers to the part of the Cathedral where their stalls were located.

Common Fund This was the fund through which all the running costs of the Chapter were maintained – prebends for **canons**, monies for food and drink and so on. The two Stewards, both **canons**, received money into the exchequer for the Common Fund (which did not include the Fabric monies) and then allocated it to salaries and expenses.

Dignitaries The ruling body of the Cathedral, comprising the Treasurer, Chancellor, Precentor and Dean.

Fabric Fund While the Common Fund dealt with the general Chapter running costs, the Fabric handled all the actual Cathedral building expenses. The Warden of the Fabric received and dispensed the money for supplies of timber, iron, wages for the workers and all other aspects of the works.

Minor Clergy Four groups consisting of the **Vicars Choral, Secondaries, Choir** and **Annuellars**. The minor clergy had a pleasant, sociable life with access to good food and drink, and a certain amount of personal freedom.

Secondaries Appointed by the Dean himself, these were usually young men between the ages of seventeen and twenty-four. Many were choristers whose voices had broken.

Treasurer One of the four 'dignitaries' of the Cathedral, the Treasurer was responsible for the general Chapter costs. At Exeter this did not include responsibility for the Fabric accounts – as far as we can tell. Instead there were two Wardens of the Fabric, one of whom was the Master Mason and the other a member of the Chapter. In 1300 and beyond, this was a vicar.

Vicars Choral The personal servants of the **canons**. Each was appointed by his own canon, to whom he rendered personal services in exchange for benefits. He had lodgings in the canon's house, meals at his table, and accompanied his canon to the Cathedral. In 1300 these men were paid between two and three pounds each year in cash, but of course they also received free board and lodging.

Warden of the Fabric The Chapter member responsible for the Fabric accounts and who worked with the Master Mason – also called the Clerk of the Works.

Cast of Characters

	working with his companion Joel for many years.
Mabilla Potell	Henry's wife is a stolid, dependable woman in her middle years.
Julia Potell	Their daughter, and of marriageable age, Julia is a noted beauty and is pursued by some of the men in the city.
Udo Germeyne	A German, Udo arrived in Exeter many years ago and decided to make the city his home. He desires Julia for his own wife.
Joel Lytell	A successful joiner, who makes the frames on which Henry Potell builds his saddles.
Maud Lytell	Joel's wife. A rational and calm lady.
William	An Exeter man, William came to the notice of the King after the murder of the Chaunter. A notable member of Edward II's household, he has recently been installed as a corrodian (pensioner) at the Priory of St Nicholas.
Saul	A well-known mason, Saul is a strong stone-worker and earns a good wage.
Sara	Wife to Saul and mother to his boys, Elias (three and a half) and Dan (eight), Sara is a stranger to Exeter.
Ralph of Malmesbury	A notable physician, Ralph is known to those in the city who can afford his services.
John Coppe	Wounded by pirates many years before, John has lost one leg and his face is fearfully scarred. He now has to beg at the gate to the Cathedral.
Vincent	Apprentice to Joel.
Wymond	Vincent's father, a tanner on Exe Island.

The Cathedral

Chaunter Walter   Walter de Lecchelade was the Chaunter murdered in Exeter Cathedral's grounds in 1283.

Dean Alfred   The Dean conceals a sharp mind behind his bumbling manner.

Treasurer Stephen   A canon who has invested much of his working life in the rebuilding of the Cathedral, Stephen is devoted to ensuring that the works are completed successfully (even though he knows he won't live to see them finished).

Matthew   The Warden of the Fabric, Matthew is responsible for much of the accounting for the building works.

Friar Nicholas   Once a novice at the Cathedral, Nicholas was dreadfully injured while trying to save his master, Chaunter Walter, during the fight when Lecchelade died. He has recently returned to the Friary.

Janekyn Beyvyn   The porter at the Fissand Gate of the Cathedral Close, Janekyn is popular with the beggars of the city, all of whom know him to be a kindly, generous soul.

Prior Peter   Peter was once a member of the Chapter of the Cathedral, but after his part in Lecchelade's assassination, he was evicted. Now he has become acting head of the Priory of St Nicholas until a new Prior is elected.

Robert de Cantebrigge   A famous Master Mason from Kent, Master Robert is supervising the rebuilding of the Cathedral as well as several other projects.

Author's Note

This story has been in my mind for some time, ever since I first heard of the strange murder of the Chaunter at Exeter Cathedral.

The tale has all those elements which a novelist would love: intrigue, hatred, jealousy and murder, all occurring within the supposedly calm and contemplative environs of a Cathedral Close. Naturally I was drawn to it.

A good friend of mine, Susanna Gregory, author of the excellent Matthew Bartholomew series of medieval murder stories, has commented that at a time in which almost a third of the male population of the country was directly or indirectly employed by the Church, it would be astonishing if some of them weren't unpleasant, murderous or plain mad. Well, if events at Exeter in the 1280s are anything to go by, there were many men in the Cathedral who were 'mad, bad, and dangerous to know'.

The story really began with the arrival of Bishop Quivil in 1280. He would appear to have been a thorough and responsible Bishop, who was notable for spending a lot of his time in the saddle travelling about his diocese and making sure that people were well-served by his men. Unlike Exeter's Bishops before and after him, Quivil devoted his time to the souls under his jurisdiction, and would appear to have largely ignored the country's politics. Sadly, though, he managed to make his Archbishop angry even before he had won his post.

Archbishop Peccham refused to consecrate Quivil*, sending him a curt letter that read: *We should desire personally to confer on you the rite of consecration in the Metropolitan Church of Canterbury on the Sunday before St Martin's Day; but, finding it* a little inconvenient *to be present in our own person* . . . Thus Peccham found it too much of a trial to attend the installation of one of his top men in his own church at Canterbury.

This was a poor start to Quivil's rule, but matters were soon to deteriorate.

Although Quivil appears to have been an exceptionally mild-tempered Bishop for his time – he rarely excommunicated anyone, tended not to call

*A History of the Diocese of Exeter by Rev. R.J.E. Boggis MA, BD (1922). See pp. 142–5.

in the secular arm of the law to chastise the disobedient, had disputes neither with laymen and clerics nor the priories and abbeys in his territory – yet he still had a series of problems with one man: John Pycot.

The Archbishop installed John (also called John of Exeter) as his Dean under Quivil. From the records, John would appear to have been 'an unscrupulous though plausible worldling' (Boggis). Although Quivil fought against his appointment, John had the full weight of Peccham behind him, and eventually became Dean on the death of Dean John Noble in 1281. Quivil unsuccessfully appealed to the Pope against his installation on several grounds.

The actual reason for their enmity has been lost; however there are some clues. Nicholas Orme in *Medieval Art and Architecture at Exeter Cathedral* ('Transactions of the British Archaeological Association', 1985), points out that Pycot was already the Treasurer of the Cathedral, but that alone hardly seems reason enough for Quivil's violent dislike of him. There must have been some other grounds for Bishop Quivil's refusal to accept Pycot as his Dean.

For whatever the reason, Quivil would have nothing to do with him. He refused to acknowledge Pycot's position, and then, when it was apparent that he was getting nowhere, he installed his own Chaunter, Walter de Lecchelade, who made it his business to obstruct the Dean whenever he could. He took over the Dean's stall in the Cathedral, the Dean's residence, and his income, as well as taking on all the rights pertaining to the office of Dean. As Chaunter, he had second-in-command status after the Dean, and would take control in the Dean's absence. The fact that he was put in post in the same year in which John Pycot was elected to Dean seems to support the view that Quivil was looking to counterbalance the Dean's authority.

In any case, two years later a terrible event took place in the Close. On 9 November 1283 – W.G. Hoskyns in *Two Thousand Years in Exeter* (Unwin, 1960) gives the date as 5 November – Walter de Lecchelade was murdered. He had attended Matins at the Cathedral and was walking the short distance home at between one and two in the morning, when he and his men were set upon by an armed gang. Lecchelade's body was discovered early the next day, lying in the mud.

This set in train the events which I've outlined in my story. There was no resolution between the Dean and the Bishop, and relations must have worsened, because by 1285, two years later, the Bishop was asking the King to come and hear the matter.

King Edward I arrived on 22 December 1285 with his Queen, and they installed themselves in the moderate comfort of the castle. That was a Saturday. The next day, the royal couple attended Mass in the Cathedral, and on Christmas Eve they started hearing the case.

There were twenty-one men accused. Eleven were clerics, and as such were spared the risk of death, but were confined in the Bishop's gaol. Dean John Pycot was one; the Vicar of Heavitree, John de Christenestowe, and John de Wolfrington, Vicar of Ottery St Mary, were two others. Among those who had nothing to do with the Cathedral were two main citizens of Exeter: the Mayor, Alured de Porta, and the porter of the South Gate. The reason for this was that the gates had been left wide open all through the night of the killing. The Bishop contended that this proved that the city had conspired in the murder of his Chaunter.

The trial was halted during Christmas Day, naturally, and continued on Boxing Day. On this day, Alured was taken out and hanged, along with the porter at the gate. Later, the churchmen were convicted by the Bishop's court and Dean John was imprisoned.

This wasn't quite the end of the affair. Archbishop Peccham interested himself in the fate of his ally still, and tried to have him released along with his ten associates. It didn't work, though, and Pycot stayed in the ecclesiastical prison until 1286, at which time he was banished to a monastery – we don't know which one.

This was obviously an extreme case of violence in a Cathedral's Close, but when we look back through history at the behaviour of our ancestors in the Church, we find many other examples. Men were, in the words of Henry Summerson, 'aggressive, vindictive, acquisitive and suspicious'*. For example, when there was an argument between a group of churchmen in 1271, the parson of Quantoxhead threatened Master Thomas de Graham that he'd be 'revenged on him within three days'. Clearly a man in a hurry, the parson saw to it that Master Thomas was murdered the very next day. The poor fellow was attacked at Thorverton by men who slaughtered both him and his groom, cutting out Master Thomas's tongue as well – presumably because the insult given had been verbal.

The point is, the members of the clergy were as likely to draw a sword as any other man. Perhaps more so than the average peasant, because so many of the clergy had been raised in noble surroundings, and many would have trained with their older brothers as warriors before being sent into the Church.

Clergymen saw no problem with girding themselves with a sword. They would protect themselves and their churches with steel, if necessary, and many who were of nobler birth would have no compunction about defending their honour with a blade. *These were not the sort of men to turn the other cheek.*

Crown Pleas of the Devon Eyre of 1238 (Devon & Cornwall Record Society, 1985)

*   *   *

Those who have some knowledge of the rebuilding of Exeter Cathedral may be surprised at my sudden improvement of the schedule of works. So far as I know, the section east of the towers was largely completed by 1310, and in 1318 there was some remodelling (increasing some parts from two storeys to three for coherence of the whole) and presumably the rest of the works were internal finishing. The impressive – in fact, quite alarming – Bishop's throne was made between 1313 and 1319. Thomas of Witney may have designed this, and was appointed Master of the Works around 1316. He was almost certainly responsible for the pulpitum (1317–25) and the presbytery sedilia (1316–26). We know that in 1324 Thomas was ordering huge quantities of stone from Caen, as well as from more local quarries in Silverton, Salcombe and Beer among others, in order to build the new nave. At the same time he ordered fifteen poplar trees for scaffolding, as well as a hundred alder trees, forty-eight 'great' trees from Langford, and assorted loads of timber. The Bishop bought 13s 6d worth of timber in London.

The materials for the west front were being purchased in 1328. In 1329 the nails were bought with their fittings for the door, hence much was finished by then – although not the fabulous image screen which we see today. That was started in about 1346 (so far as I can learn – it may have been begun a little earlier), and wasn't finished for a hundred years.

To be entirely honest, though, I'm not sure how far advanced the rebuilding would have been in 1323. I have assumed that at this time the old walls were being thrown down, in preparation for the new walls to be erected. Sadly, because of time constraints, it has not been possible for me to learn precisely how much had already been done. I think that my guess of the topmost courses being removed is probably not too far out, though.

There is one last point I should mention for those who wish to look up any references to these events, and that is the spelling of the names.

In this period there was no consistency of spelling, and this is particularly true with the spelling of people's names.

For example, Alured de Porta I have found as Alfred of Exeter and Alfred Duport. Likewise, Walter de Lecchelade is also Walter Lechlade and Walter Lechdale, while Bishop Quivil is also recorded regularly as Quinil. I have tried to take the middle road, and have stuck to what seems best phonetically, while retaining a little of the 'feel' of the period where I can.

Naturally, as always, any errors are entirely my own responsibility.

Michael Jecks
Northern Dartmoor
April 2004

Map of Exeter in Early 1300s

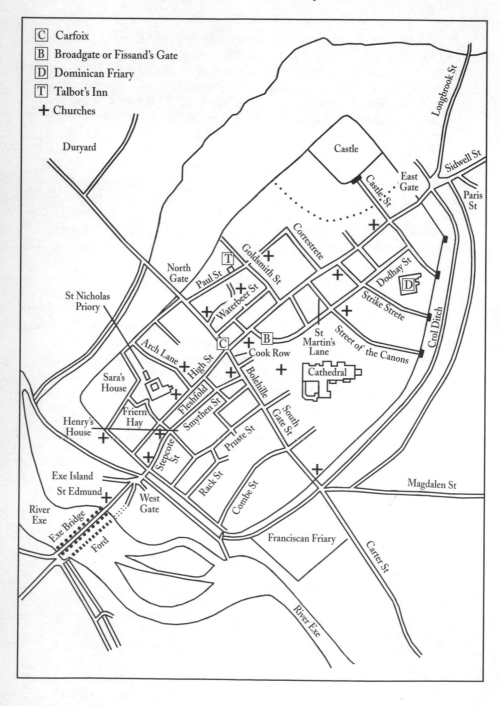

C Carfoix
B Broadgate or Fissand's Gate
D Dominican Friary
T Talbot's Inn
✝ Churches

Duryard

Longbrook St

Castle

Sidwell St

East Gate

Castle St

Paris St

Correstrete

North Gate

Paul St

Goldsmith St

Dodhay St

St Nicholas Priory

Waterbeer St

Strike Strete

Crol Ditch

Arch Lane

C

High St

Cook Row

B

St Martin's Lane

Street of the Canons

Sara's House

Fleshfold

Cathedral

Friern Hay

Smythen St

Bolehille

Henry's House

Stepcote St

Pruste St

South Gate St

Exe Island

Rack St

Magdalen St

St Edmund

West Gate

Combe St

River Exe

Exe Bridge

Ford

Franciscan Friary

Carter St

River Exe

Map of Cathedral Close

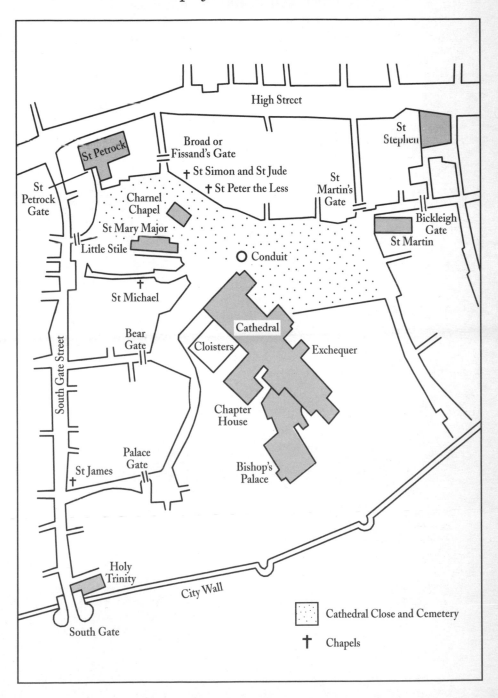

High Street

Broad or
Fissand's Gate

St Petrock

St Stephen

St
Petrock
Gate

† St Simon and St Jude
† St Peter the Less

St
Martin's
Gate

Charnel
Chapel

St Mary Major

Bickleigh
Gate

St Martin

Little Stile

○ Conduit

†
St Michael

Bear
Gate

Cathedral

Cloisters

Exchequer

South Gate Street

Chapter
House

Palace
Gate

St James
†

Bishop's
Palace

Holy
Trinity

City Wall

South Gate

:::::: Cathedral Close and Cemetery

† Chapels

Chapter One

Saul died because of the ghost.

It was a clear morning, with only a few wisps of cloud passing overhead, and Thomas had been whistling happily, stripped to his waist, his long hair bedraggled with sweat.

As a mason, he preferred building work to demolition, but in order to erect the new Cathedral, first they must throw down this old one. Starting at the south-eastern corner of the wall of the nave, Thomas and his men had climbed up the scaffolding and were gradually levering loose the old rocks, attaching iron bolts to them so that they could be lifted out by the cranes. It was backbreaking work, with the Warden of the Fabric, Vicar Matthew, often peering over their shoulders to ensure that the stones were damaged as little as possible. He wanted them reused.

Thomas was terrified that at any moment Matthew would see through his thick, salt and pepper beard, his long hair, and know him, but so far there had been no flicker of recognition. Perhaps after forty years Matthew had forgotten him; perhaps he paid little attention to a mere labourer.

To avoid meeting Matthew's eye, Thomas turned to face the Bishop's Palace gate. That was when he spotted the brown-clad figure of a friar, stooped and obviously weary, entering the Close. From his high position, Thomas saw the ghost immediately. He felt as though he might totter and fall, so great was the shock.

There was a leather bag and rolled blanket on the ghost's back; a thin, clawlike hand gripping the thong that bound them together at his shoulder. Thomas recognised him immediately. He had seen those features in his mares, especially at nights, so often in the last forty years. Forty years – and in all that time he hadn't forgotten the man whom he had once been happy to call his friend – his *best* friend.

Thomas was an experienced mason, and he should have been concentrating. Afterwards, he knew that Saul's death was his fault, but at that moment he couldn't drag his eyes from the man down there in the Cathedral's Close.

The poor, misshapen figure, clad in the garb of a Grey Friar, looked as if he had been tortured and discarded, a living warning to others. He dragged his left foot, his left arm was obviously all but useless, and he walked bent low, like a man who carried a heavy load. Only when he reached the little chapel did he halt suddenly and look up in wonder. As well he might, for the Charnel Chapel was quite new, built at the instigation of Dean John before he was exiled from the Cathedral. Thomas himself had been surprised to see it there, built where the Chaunter's house had stood.

The ghost stared at the chapel, his tonsured head set to one side as though to hide the dreadful scars, and Thomas gave a moan, retreating, trying to hide from that terrible gaze. Without thinking, he released his rope, covering his face with his hands, shutting out that hideous view, when he *should* have been watching the crane.

Yes. It was the ghost. If it hadn't been for the friar, Saul wouldn't have died.

Long afterwards, Thomas would still be struck with that appalling guilt as he recalled the terrible event that followed. At that moment, when the massive block shifted, he was incapable of thinking. The rock was like a vast creature, its movements thrilling through the twisted planking of the scaffold, tremors clutching at his feet. When he glanced at it, he saw the great lump start to slip, ponderous and terrible; and although he grabbed the thick hempen rope, he knew he could do nothing. His rope was positioned to pull the rock from side to side, not keep it up. He sprang back, eyes fixed on it.

'Wait! 'Ware the stone!' he cried, but it was too late. As he opened his mouth, there was a sudden snap like a whip cracking, then a roar, as though God Himself had torn apart the ground beneath their feet. The rock plunged down, crashing through the planking and tearing four-inch spars apart, ripping them to splinters; and then the rope snaked through his hands before he could release it, scouring the flesh from his palms, and there was a gravelly noise like leather being torn as the rock slid down the wall to the ground, striking it with an earth-shaking roar.

For a moment Thomas felt relief that no one was hurt as he stared down at the billowing clouds of rock dust.

'Christ Jesus!' he moaned, his breath sobbing from his breast as though he had run a mile carrying that rock on his back. The damn thing was so huge, it was astonishing to think that it had ever been lifted up here.

They were enormously high up. From here, he could see over the houses that encircled the Close, over the new walls erected in the last twenty years, over the High Street and beyond, up the hill to the red stone castle directly north, west to the great Priory of St Nicholas and south to the new Friary of the Franciscans, opened only fifteen-odd years ago.

Some men looked terrified when they clambered up the lashed poles to this giddy height. Thomas could remember the first few times he'd been up scaffolding like this; he'd been petrified too, but the view was the compensation. And men didn't often fall from here. It was too far up for people to forget when they were new to the job, and when they were experienced enough to forget the height, they were able to walk around with balance and without fear. Thomas had only seen one lad fall from a scaffold in the last forty years since he started out as a mason.

Today, though, the view couldn't keep his attention. He stared down at the lump of masonry crumbled at the foot of the Cathedral's wall, but his eyes wouldn't stay there. Gradually, unwillingly, he felt himself forced to turn back until he was gazing down again upon the Charnel Chapel, hoping against hope that the ghost had gone.

It had. The brownish-grey-clad friar was nowhere to be seen. Thomas thought, just for a moment, that he caught a flash of grey up at the Fissand Gate, but it was gone in an instant, and he could breathe more easily.

Relief flooded into his veins, and he rested a hand unconsciously on a scaffold-pole at his side to support himself, flinching from the pain in his raw palm. A group of men had gathered about the rock below. Workmen would always gawp at a fallen piece of masonry, he thought. No matter.

Vicar Matthew, the Chapter's Warden of the Fabric who spent so much time up here trying to save money, was only a matter of feet away, and he stared at Thomas for a long moment – so long that Thomas wondered whether he too had seen the ghost of that novice, or still worse, recognised him from that other time, that other life.

'You let the stone fall,' Matthew whispered.

Thomas shrugged. 'Sometimes it'll happen.' There was a lot of noise from below, and he wondered at that for the briefest of seconds before a leaden feeling of dread entered his belly.

Down below he could see the Master Mason staring up at him, his mouth wide in alarm. There was a semi-circle of workers about the stone, and something else.

'Look what you've done!' Matthew hissed. 'You have *killed* him, Tom!'

And Thomas could only stare at him uncomprehendingly, then down at the rock, with the fat red stain that now marked the dirty ground beside it.

Friar Nicholas felt his right cheek. The tingling was there again. It often came on like this when the weather was cooler or damper, and here in Exeter in October it was rarely otherwise. He left the new chapel and shouldered the small leather sack containing all his possessions: a small bowl, a cup, some material to wrap about his throat when the weather was at its most inclement, and a spoon.

Here there was always noise, he supposed, standing at the Fissand Gate and casting about him. The Cathedral might be in the process of being rebuilt, but that didn't stop men meeting and discussing their business. There was more money spent and snatched by greedy businessmen in that yard than in the marketplace, he thought with contempt. Men all about, shouting and calling, and the unchanging clamour of the damned workmen. Fine, they needed the workers there to get the Cathedral expanded, but he hated it. It hurt his ears. The din was deafening, especially since he suffered from his affliction; his hearing was unreliable, and when there were too many noises at the same time, his head began to ache.

It was many a weary year since he had last been here. After that evil night, he had been taken away to recover, and it was a long time before he could stand and speak. By then, of course, his master was gone, and he had no home at the Cathedral. Or so he felt. It was as though his life had been ended, his family slain about him. When Bishop Quivil visited him in the infirmary, he could only agree with him that it would be more expedient for all, were he to leave Exeter and find his peace in another city. Bishop Quivil had been kindness itself, as he should have been. After all, Nicholas had almost been killed while trying to protect the Bishop's own man.

It had been for the best. He didn't regret the decision to leave. When he was well enough, he had taken the cloth of the Grey Friars, living first in London, then York, and now at last he was returning to Exeter, to the city of his youth.

By God, it had changed, though! The Charnel Chapel had given him a surprise when he caught sight of it. It was built on the place where the Chaunter's home had stood, just by the spot where he had died and where Nick himself had won this fearsome scar.

Recollecting, he had to close his eyes a moment: the boy's screaming figure running at him, Nicholas grabbing for his dagger, then sweeping it across the fellow's throat before he could attack anyone, the gush of blood as he fell at Nicholas's feet, his eyes already clouding, his heels striking at the mud with a staccato rhythm as he drowned in his own fluids – and then the full onslaught of the ambush. Christ's Pains, but it was an evil night.

As he stood pondering the past, and what might have been, a great shout went up, and shook his head to clear it. Irritably he told himself that there was no need for that kind of noise. It reminded him too much of that awful night.

Turning away, he began to limp off towards the High Street, not seeing the men who threw down their tools and pelted over the Cathedral's Close to help remove the stone from the broken body of Saul Mason.

Udo Germeyne could hear the roaring from the Cathedral as he sat in his chair, but although he glanced up at the window in his hall, he didn't go and see what had caused the noise. He had lost interest in everything since the accident. All his plans had gone to pot, simply because he had tried to impress the wench in a moment of foolishness.

This was the cost of love, he told himself. All he had wanted was a little companionship, and instead he was here, a prisoner in his own hall. *Mein Gott*, but this shoulder hurt!

Women. They were unreliable, weak creatures – but, no matter. He could love, he was sure. A man of fifty – well, five-and-fifty, then – a man like Udo craved companionship. He had lived here in this strange country for many years, ever since he'd come seeking a new life with a parcel or two of skins and an enthusiast's determination to make money. And his enthusiasm had paid off. He was a successful merchant.

Yes, he was no different from other men. He wanted a woman he could call his own, a woman who would cleave to him and make him whole. She would have a good life with him, and when he died, she would have a marvellous dowry; he would see to that. And by the time he died, he would leave a woman who was mature, educated, and who knew her own mind.

It had been some little while since he first had this idea, that he would like to be married, but it had taken firm hold. Udo was not a man who believed in prevarication. He made a decision, and stuck to it. Udo was lonely, he had much to offer; naturally he should hurry and find a wife. And so he did.

Ach! She would have to have been a fool not to recognise how he felt! He had done all he could to demonstrate his interest in her. Yes, Julia Potell must know that he loved her. At least, her *father* Henry must, anyway – and he would surely have told her.

Not that it could help Udo since that damned fall two days ago. He winced as he tested his bruised arm. At least it was improving since the physician's visit. Ralph of Malmesbury charged a small fortune for his treatment, but he was good.

Udo had seen Julia first in the market, when she was still a foolish, gangling creature, all coltish and clumsy. He had glanced at her, but there was nothing there to desire. Nothing that could make him wish to take her to his bed.

Since then, he had seen the girl more regularly. Her parents brought her to his church. Henry he knew moderately well. He was a saddler, with a thriving business and a good head for profit. Yes, a man whom Udo could admire. Strong in his beliefs, and respected among the men of Exeter, Henry was a useful potential father-in-law. His wife, Mabilla, was one of those strong, quiet women whom Udo rather liked. She watched and witnessed much, but saw no need to open her mouth and chatter inanely all the while. With luck, her daughter Julia would follow her in this quiet attitude. Although in middle age, Mabilla was still handsome, and she had the carriage of a much younger woman. A man would be proud to have her on his arm.

But Julia. Julia!

God, but she was lovely. The gauche young maid had grown into a beautiful young woman with the fair skin and hair of his homeland. She had stopped tripping and stumbling; now she glided like an angel. And her smile was the most seductive he had ever seen.

He was besotted.

Which was why he had bought the damned thing from her idiot father in an attempt to inveigle his way into the family. What better method to get to know them than by purchasing a saddle? He needed a new one anyway.

He had walked to Henry's hall by way of Ham's cookshop. There he bought some of Ham's finest little pastries and cakes. Tarts filled with flavoured custards were the ideal way to win the heart of a maid and her mother. It was little gifts like these which made the difference between a failed negotiation and a successful one. He entered the hall, he spoke at length to the saddler, discussed the leathers and decorations, and agreed the deal. Only then did he offer the basket of cakes for the saddler's wife and daughter with no further comment, merely a stiff nod, and, 'May I present these for your lady wife and your daughter with my compliments?' as he left the shop.

There. All done; all easy. They must wonder at his motives – but not for long. A logical man like Henry would soon discern the thinking behind the gift.

Two days ago a messenger had come from the saddler. Henry had asked to see him and his horse to try out the new saddle, and so Udo took his best rounsey over to Henry's hall, binding the reins to the ring in the wall before knocking.

The saddle was magnificent. Supple, soft, it felt like he was sitting on a cushion. He mounted as soon as the horse was grown accustomed to its weight, and tried it out, trotting up the road, then turning and riding back a little faster.

'How do he feel?' Henry called after him in his thick Devon accent as he passed the man's hall again, but Udo didn't speak. To him, this was one of the most wonderful sensations in the world, riding a good horse with a fine saddle beneath him. He glanced about him, then gave a short twitch of his rein-end to his rounsey's rump, and cantered gently down the hill towards the wall. Reining in at the bottom, he snapped his horse's head about and set off back up the hill towards Henry.

And it was then that the devil tempted him.

Udo was a good horseman. He knew that. There was hardly a horse he hadn't managed to bring to his command in a short time, and this rounsey was one of the best pieces of horseflesh in the city, so when he saw the object of his affections in the window to the upper chamber of the hall, he spurred his mount on, just like any churl who sought to impress his young woman.

He galloped up the hill, cobbles sparking where the flying hooves caught them. Up, up, and then, as he drew level with the hall, he wrenched the horse to a halt. There was a crack, a ripping sound, and suddenly he wasn't in the saddle any more. Something had happened behind him – he couldn't tell what, but suddenly all support had gone – and then he felt himself sliding sideways and backwards, over the horse's backside. With a final despairing wail, he toppled, and had just enough good sense to throw out his arms and break his fall before his head slammed onto the cobbles.

The pain was instantaneous. A thrust of agony shot from his shoulder to his throat, and for an instant he thought he must be about to die, but then mercifully it abated somewhat, and he could pant cautiously, trying to keep his shoulder still.

'Master! Are you all right?'

'No thanks to you, *verdammtes Idiot! Scheisse!*'

'Have you hurt your head?' Henry asked with panic.

'No, my shoulder. Call a physician, man! Your damned saddle could have killed me,' Udo roared, and then winced. 'My God! This is terrible.'

'I'll call the best doctor . . . and of course I'll pay for him,' Henry said miserably, bellowing for a servant.

'You'll pay for more than that!' Udo swore.

So that was why he was here, broken in spirit and body in his hall when he should have been out adding to his treasure. He had been tempted by a maid; the temptation caused him to buy a saddle; and the saddle caused him to dislocate his shoulder.

The whole incident had cost him dearly.

When Prior Peter heard of the mason's death, it served only to lighten his mood a little.

Peter was not unkind. He had no feelings of hatred or anger towards Saul. In fact, the man's life or death were immaterial to him. A mason was a necessary fellow, no doubt, and useful when there were buildings which required his services, but any misfortune which happened to strike that damned Chapter was pleasing to Peter.

He heard of Saul's death in the small open area south of St Nicholas's Priory. The gatekeeper had sent a novice for him, and he inclined his head as he listened to the short lad. Peter was a tall man, grey of hair but with startlingly black eyebrows. His face was worn, and somewhat lugubrious, but there was a steely glint in his eyes that spoke of his intelligence. As he listened, the long fingers of his right hand tapped pensively on the wrist of his left – a strange mannerism which some whispered he had learned while in the Bishop's gaol at the Cathedral. Peter neither knew nor cared what others said: it was merely a habit which he found comforting.

'A man has been killed at the Cathedral? What of it?' he enquired coolly.

'Prior, he was a mason, and the man here, he wants to find the mason's wife – to tell her he's dead. Only no one knows where he lives.'

'He doesn't live any more,' Peter said, his attention going to the little gate which led onto the High Street. The gatekeeper was there already, his hand resting on the door's handle, and through the open way Peter could see the panicky face of the man sent to tell the wife that she was become a widow. 'Tell him that I can't help.'

The novice was quiet a moment, then, 'May I ask the Almoner, Prior? He may know her.'

Peter glanced down at him dismissively. 'If you wish, yes. Now leave me to consider.'

'Yes, Prior,' and he scampered away.

Peter continued walking around the open area. It had been his custom to walk about the Priory from the first moment he arrived here. Those years in the Bishop's gaol – damn Quivil's memory! – had made him feel uncomfortable in small rooms for any period. As soon as he was released, he had taken to walking, morning and afternoon, out in the open. It mattered not a whit whether it was raining, snowing, or the sun shining. All he knew was that he had a compulsion to go outside and breathe the clean air whenever he had an opportunity.

The boy had called him 'Prior'. It was rather pleasant to be so addressed, although 'my lord Prior' would have been better. Alas, Peter wouldn't ever be given that salutation.

All because of the evening so long ago when he had helped his companions to attack and kill the Chaunter. It was a grievous price he had paid since then. Some had been forced to suffer still more, and he honoured them, but others had survived, living out their years in comfort, without the penalties which Peter had endured. Even now some were rich merchants in this city, wallowing in their wealth like hogs in the mire. Repulsive people!

Peter had been looking at a successful career when disaster struck. He had thought that he would be able to move up the ranks of authority within the Cathedral, perhaps one day winning his own Bishopric, if he built enough support for himself along the way. There was no chance of that now. Since his punishment, when he had been thrown from the Cathedral's Chapter by those hypocritical dogs the canons, he had been forced to renounce all possessions and income. He had been made a monk, had taken the vows, and sent to moulder at Battle Abbey, far from here. There he was expected to live a life of penance for the murder.

Penance, indeed! The other members of the Chapter well knew what was happening. It was the Bishop's fault. Quivil had created the hatred and mistrust that had led to the Chaunter's death, not Peter. Peter was simply one of those who responded to Bishop Quivil's idiocy by removing his ally.

It was fortunate that he had been able to return here. Battle Abbey was a hideous place, and when he heard that there was a post here at its daughter house in Exeter, he had pressed to be allowed to return. He had been born here, he knew the area, he knew the air; fortunately his

Abbot was an amiable, generous-hearted soul, who looked at the misery on Peter's face and felt compassion. He agreed, and Peter was given leave. He would never have authority, but he was a good, reliable monk, and he could live out his days in the monastery outside whose walls he had played as a child.

And then the Abbot at Battle Abbey died. Prior Roger from St Nicholas's Priory was chosen to rule the Abbey, and when he left Exeter, a new Prior was due to be selected. However, the election was contested, and as there was no clear winner, Abbot Roger asked Peter to caretake the role. So here he was in the position of full power, without the possibility of keeping it.

All because of the malicious treatment he'd been given by the Cathedral's Chapter forty years ago, and their vindictive Bishop – may he rot in hell!

Chapter Two

Thomas was still feeling that odd juddering in his belly, as if a load of moths were fighting in there. Vicar Matthew had seen his shock, and gave him a little wine to calm his nerves after he'd helped Thomas down from the ruined scaffolding. However, Master Robert de Cantebrigge was entirely unsympathetic, even when he saw Thomas's raw hands.

'Look at him, you prick! You dropped a ton of rock on the poor bastard, and killed him! That's criminal carelessness, that is!'

'Christ's Bones, Master, I didn't mean it to happen . . . I don't know what—'

'You don't seem to know sod all, do you?' Robert spat. 'You can call on Christ as much as you want, but it won't bring back a bloody good mason, will it?'

'Master, I didn't mean to . . . I'm sorry, it was an accident.'

'Oh no, it wasn't, Tom. You *killed* him – it was sodding negligence, that's what. Don't try to get out of it that way. This was no bleeding accident, laddie – it was near as buggery pure sodding *murder*!'

The Master Mason was almost screaming at him, the spittle flying from his mouth, and Tom averted his head. Unwise move – for doing so made him catch sight of the corpse, and that in itself was enough to make a man heave. Sweet Jesus! Saul had no head left, no upper torso. The rock dropping a good thirty feet straight onto his head had completely removed every vestige of humanity above his belly. It was merely a repellent smudge of blood and flattened muscle, with a few yellowish cartilaginous lumps that made Tom want to puke. At one side he saw a single tooth, snapped off and not quite destroyed, but the rest of Saul's face and features were gone. It was like a chalk picture smeared away with a damp cloth. That was all Saul was now: a smear.

'I can't bring him back,' Thomas said sadly, and he could feel the tickling of tears behind his lids. Matthew shouted for linen bandages as he said quietly, 'I would if I could.'

'No, you can't, can you? *Cretin*! Where am I going to find another decent mason like him? God's Ballocks! What a fucking mess!'

'He was married,' Matthew said, his voice hushed. He put a comforting arm about Thomas. 'We should tell his wife.'

'His *widow*!' Robert rasped. 'That prickle can do it. He took her husband from her, let him be the one who explains it to her. I'm damned if I can understand a word he's said about how he managed to lose the block, myself.'

Thomas looked back up at the pulley at the top of the crane. Still lashed to the hook was the metal wedge that should have remained inside the block, while whips of rope were tossed from side to side in the wind, their ends frayed where they'd broken. That was the first crack he had heard, when those ropes snapped under the weight of the rock. One, he saw, was still blackened with his own blood where he'd tried to hold it. His hands were raw, the flesh stripped from the palms, and he'd covered both with pieces of linen he'd hacked from his own shirt. They'd be dreadfully painful for days, he knew.

His rope and the others weren't supposed to support all that ponderous mass. It should have been the iron wedge that took the weight. How could it have slipped out? He couldn't have thrust the wedge in properly. That was the only explanation. Robert was right: his negligence had killed Saul.

Poor Saul. Thomas had known him slightly. There were so many men working here on the rebuilding of the Cathedral that it was hard to get to know even all the stone-workers, let alone the members of the other crafts. Saul was a foreigner, Thomas remembered hearing. One of those who'd been working on some other project with Robert de Cantebrigge and had been brought here with him. That was how Master Masons made sure that their work was up to scratch. They kept a stable of good workers with them, taking them from one job to another, so that hopefully when the Master Mason had to go to another site, he could leave his men working together, knowing what he would expect them to do.

It was a hard life, building churches and cathedrals. Saul had been too young to know the misery associated with growing older in the trade: the bones that ached in the mornings on a winter's day, the sudden cramps in the legs, the back that locked and wouldn't move, the weariness at the end of a summer's day when every moment of daylight had to be used to the full; no matter that your fingers were scratched and bruised, the nails ripped out from the last falling rock you tried to lift onto the wall, nor that your arms refused to lift another pebble, they were so exhausted. The work was the thing. Any man here on the site must work as quickly as possible to bring to fruition the creation that men would look on for evermore, thinking, That, that is God's House.

But a Master Mason didn't only have one project on the go at a time. He was a skilled engineer, hence much of a man like Robert de Cantebrigge's life was spent on horseback travelling from one city to another, monitoring each of his building projects and making sure that they remained on target.

Saul had been with him longer than Thomas. That was the thing. It was why Robert would probably never forgive Thomas. He had taken away one of Robert's best, youngest, strongest men, and finding a suitable willing replacement would prove a considerable headache.

And now Thomas had come to see the Almoner at St Nicholas's Priory, to trace the whereabouts of Saul's wife.

'You wished to know where a certain woman lives?'

The Almoner was an austere-looking man who listened gravely as Thomas explained his mission.

'What a tragic event,' he said when Thomas was finished. 'I knew Saul slightly. A good man – he often gave to the poor. And his woman seems good, too. They have two children. Little boys, both of them. This will be grave news for her, poor Sara.'

'I would do anything I could to escape telling her,' Thomas muttered. 'Even if it meant taking his place. It's not right for a boy to grow without a father.'

'It's not right for a man to consider self-murder, either,' the Almoner said sharply. 'I hope you are not speaking in earnest. Saul is dead because God thought this was his time; when it is *your* time, God will call you too.'

'I wouldn't kill myself,' Thomas declared. 'But I wish he wasn't dead.'

'That is good. You shouldn't hanker after the death of another, no matter who he might be,' the Almoner said approvingly.

He began to give directions. Apparently Saul and his wife had lived in the easternmost corner of the city, in the area vacated by the Franciscans when they moved to their new six-acre site down outside the southern wall.

'As soon as the friars were gone, a small army of the poorer elements of the city took it over, building their own sheds from dung and straw and roofing them with thatch. Now they live there in their own little vill, made by themselves for themselves.'

'I have never been there,' Thomas admitted. 'I live at the Cathedral while the works go on.'

'You have a local man's accent, though,' the Almoner noted.

'I used to live near here, but I left when I took up my trade,' Thomas said quickly. He still feared being discovered. For all he knew, he could still be taken and hanged.

The Almoner was too rushed with other work to notice his defensiveness. 'Well, go back to Fore Street, take the first street on the right, and follow that all the way to the end. That will bring you to the friars' old compound, and you'll find all the huts there. I think that Saul and Sara's was the third on the left as you bear round to the right, just before the left-hand turn in the road. She used to have a door of limed oak – but I don't know if she still has. A door like that is expensive, and many up there would be keen to filch it, I don't doubt. So remember to count.'

'I thank you, Master Almoner,' Thomas said, respectfully ducking his head low as he set off.

As the man had said, it was easy to find the place. Where the Friary had been, the workers had removed all the building material, razing the old house and leaving nothing but a wasteland. It was here that the poorest of the city had taken up residence, throwing up a series of hovels, each one room and no more. The stench was overwhelming, for although there was a drainage channel cut into the lane leading up, the area itself was relatively flat and, rather than walk to the gutter, people threw their wastes into a huge malodorous midden that lay just to the left of the entrance to the place.

There were two dogs fighting over a bone as Thomas arrived, with four men idly watching them and gambling on the winner. He didn't wish to speak to them. Instead he walked along the road, hoping that the Almoner was right about the location of the woman's home.

The third house on the left was a sturdy enough looking place, and the door was whitened timber. Thomas closed his eyes a moment, then took a deep breath and crossed the yard, past the scanty little vegetable plot with its yellowing cabbages and stunted leeks. He rapped hard on the door.

'Sir?'

The voice came from behind him, and he almost sprang into the air with alarm. Turning, he found himself staring into the laughing green eyes of a woman who was almost as tall as himself. She had hair the colour of burnished copper, and skin that was pale and freckled, with almond-shaped eyes and a tip-tilted nose. She smiled, showing regular teeth that shone. 'My apologies, master. I didn't mean to terrify you. Do you want me?'

'I was looking for Saul's wife,' he said, and as he spoke the last word, his voice died away. He looked at her silently for a moment.

She returned his gaze and gradually her smile disappeared. 'Has something happened to my husband?'

'Mistress, I wish I could . . .' he croaked.

'Is he dead?' she demanded.

'I . . . yes. I am sorry.'

She didn't seem to hear; she made no movement for a moment, and then he saw her eyes roll upwards, and he had to leap to catch her as she fainted.

The saddler was drunk.

That fact was unarguable, and more than a little amusing, Henry reckoned, as he slumped back in his chair, blearily staring at the mazer on the table before him. With a burp, he smacked his lips and reached cautiously for the wine.

'Husband, haven't you already had enough?'

'Enough? When there's still a little more left in the jug, my dearest? Of course not!' He chuckled to himself, repeating his words a couple of times to gain the fullest humorous benefit from them.

Mabilla's face swam into focus at the other side of the table, and he waved a hand at her in a vague gesture of dismissal. 'Woman, leave me in peace!' he pleaded.

'I will not leave you to ruin yourself and us,' she stated flatly. 'You are drunk again. This cannot continue, Husband.'

'Don't seek to rule me,' he growled, but then his eyes popped open as she leaned across the table towards him.

'And *you* don't seek to tell *me* what I can and cannot do, Henry Potell!'

'Am I not master in my own home!'

'You need to ask me that? What is making you behave this way? You never used to get so drunk. Is it something serious?'

'Oh, it's serious, madam!' he said, assaying a light giggle. It appeared to fall flat.

'Henry Potell, you will ruin us all. *That* is very serious. I won't have you destroy everything you've built up. What will you say to your daughter when you are dead in the gutter and she has no husband nor means to find one?' Mabilla snapped.

Henry snatched the mazer before she could remove it, and defiantly lifted it in a mock salute before draining it once more. 'She will be all right. So will you,' he said thickly. 'There's enough money saved for you both.'

'And what of you, my husband?'

Her tone was softer, he noticed, and was relieved that the spat was probably already over. 'My love, I don't know. Just now I can't think straight.'

'The wine won't help you.'

'It may not clear my head, but it eases the pain,' he slurred.

'What pain? Are you suffering?'

He looked at her, but couldn't answer. The pain he had was a forty-year-old guilt, and he had never heard of a cure for that.

Vincent the apprentice joiner stretched his arms high over his head and yawned.

'Oi! Get out here, will you, you lazy shite! It's Master Ralph come to see his frame.'

Vincent grinned to hear his master speak like that. Master Joel Lytell always made a loud noise to let his customers feel that he was jumping to satisfy their every whim, and today was no different. When a customer appeared, Joel bawled at his apprentices without pause, determined to create the right impression.

Picking up the heavy demonstration frame, Vincent carried it out from the workshop into the main hall at the front of the building. There he found his master talking to a shortish figure, well-padded, with bright blue eyes and an easy, smiling appearance. Vincent had seen him before about the city. He was a physician known as Ralph of Malmesbury.

Vincent took the frame over to the two men, and set it on the tall bench which had been made to display this and other works for clients. Standing back, he watched as Joel led the man to the frame, pointing to the strengthening points, pulling at the joints to demonstrate how firm they were, and how sturdy the entire saddle would be.

'I'm known as the best joiner in the city,' Joel finished with pride.

'Really? And I'm the King's physician,' Ralph said disdainfully.

'I am! I build the frames for Master Henry, and no one can buy better than his saddles, master,' Joel said with a hurt tone.

'Ha ha! And you think that might be a recommendation? I've only just treated the last of his clients.'

Joel's smile grew a little fixed. 'What do you mean?'

'Udo the German's saddle broke when he was testing it the first time, and he was thrown onto the cobbles. A terrible dislocation. Very unpleasant. So don't tell me that selling your frames to Henry is any sort of endorsement! Christ's Bones, maybe I oughtn't to be here after all. I'd heard your equipment was better than that.'

'Ah well, Master, I can assure you that my frames *are* the best in the city, and if one of Master Henry's broke, no doubt he bought it in as a cheaper piece of work from someone else for a poorer quality saddle,' Joel said smoothly. 'Perhaps this Master Udo didn't want to pay full price for one of Henry's top quality saddles.'

'I wonder. I'd want to know that the workmanship on this would be as good as it could be,' the man said.

'I would have my best man build it,' Joel said.

Vincent preened himself. He knew he was the best joiner in the shop out of all the apprentices – probably better than Joel himself.

'Hopefully not that little runt, then,' Ralph said, peering at Vincent with a look of contempt on his face. 'He doesn't look like he could put a simple stool together!'

When Henry was young, he'd never have thought that the crime could affect him so much so late in life. Here he was, damn it, almost in his grave, and he'd hardly ever given a moment's thought to the night when he'd trailed across the city with the others, huddled close to the Chapel of St Simon and St Jude, waiting until that terrible moment when a crack of light appeared in the door to the Cathedral and the men poured out.

And now that moment had returned to haunt him, for he knew that his life couldn't last much longer, and when he went to God, he wanted no risk of rejection just because he had once aided one man against another. By St Peter's beard, this was a mess!

'Is it the German? Is that why you're worried?'

He could hear the concern in her voice, but he had no power to ease it. Udo Germeyne's threat was a real one: Germeyne could certainly cause havoc with their finances. The man had every right, too, Henry thought, scowling at the mazer. 'That bastard! He thought he could pull the wool over my eyes, did he?' he snarled.

'I don't think Master Udo tried anything of the sort, Husband,' Mabilla said soothingly. 'You've been drinking too much.'

'Not him, woman! That ox's arse Joel. He fobs me off with ballocksed frames, and when a customer comes and takes a tumble, he leaves me in the shit.'

'I am sure Joel didn't mean anything of the sort. Have you told him about the fall?'

'Not yet. Haven't had a chance.' Henry belched, reaching for the jug and topping up his mazer.

'Then tomorrow, when you are sober, go and speak to him. Joel has been one of your oldest friends, hasn't he? Talk to him and see what he has to say. I am sure he'd not want you to be unhappy. He's supplied you for donkey's years.'

'He won't any more,' Henry declared stoutly. He stood and lifted his mazer, declaiming, 'Here I state that I'll go to any other damned joiner in the city rather than him!'

'Oh!' his wife exclaimed. 'If you're in that sort of a mood, I'll have done with you. Let me know when you're sober again, and I'll speak to you then.'

He watched as she raised her hands and dropped them again in despair, then she flounced heavily from the room, her gorgeous crimson skirts flaring.

The sight was enough to bring a smile to his face. His Mabilla still loved him, and she was a woman any man could love in return. She looked barely forty – five-and-forty at most. Still had that soft, pale flesh that a man associates with a much younger woman. There was none of the harshness of old age on her, nor the pain or lines of fear. No, she was a delicious woman still. God, but he was lucky to have her. They'd married more or less despite her parents, who weren't sure that this young saddler, who so recently had been an apprentice, was going to be a powerful enough figure to protect their daughter, but he'd shown them! Yeah, he'd shown them.

First he had saved his money carefully, rarely getting into the normal occupations of apprentices and vomiting or pissing his money away on wine and ale. No, Henry had a plan even then. He wanted to be a wealthy fellow in his own right, and everything he did was aimed at that one target. He made saddles from the finest materials and presented the very best workmanship to those who could afford it. While others spent their days knocking together cheap stuff to make workaday equipment that a modest fellow could afford, Henry concentrated on buying in the most elegant decorative pieces, beautiful ironwork from the best smiths, enamels from old Jack in the High Street, silken threads and soft padding. His saddles gained a reputation for being the most comfortable, distinctive examples of his craft; works of loveliness as well as function. His reputation had grown as had his purse, and soon everyone who had a pair of pennies to rub together wanted one of his saddles.

And now all that was at risk because of bloody Joel Lytell.

Stephen, Treasurer of the Cathedral, stood staring at the body with a feeling of revulsion. The victim had been so cruelly disfigured by the lump of stone, it was hard to see that the upper part of the torso had once belonged to a man.

'The mason should not have died', Stephen said. He had been down here at a trestle table, arguing with a lead dealer when the screams and shouts had disturbed him. Men must die in a project like this, of course. Men would always die in the cause of great tasks, and there was nothing greater than the construction of God's Own House. It was crucial that this wonderful Cathedral be built as quickly as possible to God's praise. Yet it was sad to see a man like this mason die unshriven. Perhaps he would receive special recognition in heaven for his works down here on earth. It was sincerely to be hoped. Stephen would pray for him.

And poor Matt. He had already suffered enough in his time. That was why Stephen looked after him, because Matthew was deserving of honour for his role in that fight so many years ago. His integrity was proved at the same time as Stephen's own was destroyed. He supported and helped Matt because he hoped that it would reflect well on him.

But for now the vital thing was to clear up this mess and get the builders back to their work. The Cathedral mustn't be delayed, not even for death.

Joel Lytell showed his client out through his front door with a respectful bow before shutting it quietly and breathing, 'What a little shit!'

'He was a right smarmy churl,' Vincent agreed.

'I didn't ask your opinion,' Joel snapped. 'Take that frame back out to the workshop, and don't be cheeky about your betters, boy.'

Vincent said nothing. It was rare for his master to be in a bad mood, but Vincent felt sure that this was the beginning of one. He had no wish to be in the vicinity when Joel was angry. Since he had been apprenticed here, Joel and Maud had been like Vince's father and mother. Especially since his own mother had died some years ago. She had been on her way home from the Cathedral, where she had been helping to brew ale for the canons and their servants, when a clerk racing a companion on horses rode by at the gallop and knocked her down. Two hooves struck her, and she was dead almost before the clerk could ride back to her. Vince had hardly known her, which was why he loved Maud and respected Joel.

Now he ran to the table, took up the frame and hefted it out to the workshop, past the pile of fresh, green wood that had been delivered a few weeks ago. It was too young to use yet. Put to use on a saddle frame or decent piece of work, and it would twist and crack, ruining the workmanship. Only well-cured wood could be used for frames. Of course, much of the older wood had been used up now, and the possibility of finding more that had been dried out and kept under cover for long enough was a problem. Recently, even Joel had . . .

No. That was daft. Vincent set the frame on the table at the back of the workshop, and moved away to gaze about the room. The light was beginning to fail now; the sun had slipped beneath the roofs of Joel's house and the houses opposite on the High Street. At this time of year, Vince had to work much of the time in the comparative dark. That was why they had a large bill for candles during autumn and winter. Still, it wasn't dark enough yet to light a candle, so Vince set to with his adze, trimming wood ready to be jointed to make a table-top.

It wasn't a bad life here. Vincent was a keen worker, and was proud of the results of his efforts. His stools and chairs were highly regarded.

He only had another two years of his apprenticeship to run. After that he could leave and establish his own business, where he could build his own saddle frames, and then join forces with a saddler to finish the work and sell it on. There weren't enough saddlers in the city to cope with demand. Sure, there were some like Henry who could sell the really expensive ones, and there were quite a few who could sell cheap ones which would almost cut a man in half over a long journey, but there was a need for strongly constructed saddles which weren't as grossly over-priced as Henry's. And Vince reckoned he could make them.

His plan was similar to Joel and Henry's arrangement. Vince's father was a tanner, and he had a friend who would take the tanned hide and work it into useable leather. Then there was another apprentice, Jack, who worked with one of the cheaper saddlers up near the East Gate. With all of them working in conjunction, they could make saddles that would be ideal for the merchants of Exeter . . .

'Vince? What the hell are you doing in there? Get a move on!'

Joel was really in a foul mood. Vince left his daydream behind and began working again, making the chips fly. Yes, one day he would be a known face in Exeter. He'd be a man with money.

Chapter Three

Dean Alfred of Exeter Cathedral was by nature a quiet and introspective man, better suited to studying than vigorous effort, but today he felt he should go outside when he heard that a mason had been crushed.

The weather was as clement as usual in late October, which was to say it was cold and the air damp. He felt the chill on his tonsured head. The spare fringe of white hair did little to keep him warm, and he pulled on a woollen cap before he left his chamber and made his way down the stairs.

'Dean. Good of you to come so soon.'

The voice belonged to Brother Stephen, Treasurer to the Cathedral. He was a taller man, stooped and somewhat drawn-looking, with deep trenches of disapproval gouged at either side of his mouth.

'Oh . . . ahm . . . yes, Treasurer?' The Dean knew that his mannerisms irritated Brother Stephen, but this only spurred him on. For some reason the Treasurer got on his nerves. He appeared to think figures were more important than the souls they were all supposed to be saving.

'Ah – yes – hmm. I came as soon as I could,' the Dean murmured happily. At the first clearing of his throat he could almost hear Stephen's infuriation. His eye took in the ruined body, and he automatically crossed himself. 'My dear fellow! How could this have happened?'

'This man was walking along here,' Stephen said in a cold tone, 'while another mason was up on the scaffolding removing a stone from the wall.'

'It was a sad accident,' Robert de Cantebrigge stated.

'It was either incompetence or an act of malice,' Stephen countered.

'Ah?' the Dean enquired.

'You know how they lift the heavier blocks . . .' Stephen began, but then he caught sight of the expression of baffled amiability on the

Dean's face and gritted his teeth. Stalking to a block nearby, he pointed. 'Look! All the masonry has to be taken down from the wall.'

'Yes. I – ah – thought so,' the Dean agreed affably.

'Except: how to lift them?'

'They use a crane, do they not? Hmm?'

'But the stones are too heavy to lash to a crane safely, so each has this channel cut into it,' Stephen said.

The Dean peered. Where the Treasurer was pointing, a deep curiously-shaped hole had been carved. From above, it looked like two slots, joined to each other on their longer edges. Above was the shorter, below the longer, which overlapped its neighbour at either end by about two inches. Looking into the hole, the Dean saw that both slots had the same base. That with the narrower entrance still had a ten-inch base deep inside the stone, but its sides sloped inwards towards the entrance-hole. If the rock were to break where this hole was dug into the stone, that part would look like a dove's tail, the Dean thought wonderingly.

'This is how they lift them,' Stephen said. He picked up an iron bar. In section it was a trapezium – like an isosceles triangle with the topmost part of the narrower angle cut off. It had a base of almost ten inches, and was some two inches thick. In cross-section, it was the same shape and dimension as the dove's tail shape inside the rock, the Dean guessed. He was right. 'This bar drops into the larger slot,' Stephen said, plunging it in. 'And then it's shoved over into the recess carved to fit it,' he grunted, twisting and rocking the metal until it slipped sideways and sat in the narrower recess. Pulling on it, he said, 'The space at the top of the hole is too small to allow the base of this iron bar to be pulled out. While it stays in the hole, the rock is secured to this piece of metal.'

'And how would you – um – retain it there?' the Dean enquired.

'A two-inch thick wedge. It fits into the wider slot and prevents the bar from sliding sideways, which would allow the rock to fall. Except some fool today forgot to put the wedge into its hole.'

'Are you sure? That is a – ah – serious allegation, Brother.'

'If it wasn't there, the iron could move, and then the rock would fall,' Stephen said, folding his arms. 'As it did.'

'It was an accident, I say,' the Master Mason repeated. 'I saw my man setting the rock ready, and he'd already taken off the first three courses from this wall. He knows his job.'

'You weren't there to watch?' Stephen asked.

'No, but I know Tom. He's no fool.'

'Who else did see him?' Stephen demanded.

The Master Mason stared at him from lowered brows for a moment, then he glanced over his shoulder. 'Your vicar there,' he said at last. 'He saw it. He was up there with Tom.'

'Matthew, come here, please,' the Dean called.

The Clerk of the Fabric Roll looked as though he was still suffering from shock, but that was only to be expected.

'I was up on the scaffold, Dean,' Matthew began. 'It was terrifying. I thought we must all die when it fell . . .'

'Why did this wedge of iron move in its slot? Did you see?'

'Yes. The rock was ready to be hoisted just as the others were, and it seemed solid enough. But I think that the iron block you're holding there, Treasurer, is so heavy that it dropped and slackened in its slot. The hole in the rock, perhaps, was not the right size? For whatever reason, I think that the wooden wedge holding it in place got loose. Then, when we were about to lift the stone and swing it from the wall, the wedge was squeezed out. Instantly, the iron block moved sideways and the rock was released. When that happened, all that restrained it was the rope about it, and that wasn't strong enough.'

'There – ah – Stephen,' the Dean said. 'It was an accident. Very sad, I am sure. We must do something to honour this poor fallen hero. He was here to help us complete our great work, and has died trying to see our vision realised. It is a terrible thing to have another death on our hands.'

The Master Mason Robert rubbed his forehead. There was something about these canons that raised his hackles. The Dean seemed to walk about in a daze most of the time, while the Treasurer watched Robert as though expecting him to take off with the church plate. 'Dean, we've been very lucky so far. We've had very few deaths,' he said tiredly.

'Which is how I want it to continue,' the Dean shot back, and the Master Mason was surprised to hear how sharp his voice suddenly grew.

'Now – ah – Stephen. Please see to it that this poor fellow is cleaned up and made a little more presentable. We shall – ah – hold a service for him,' Dean Alfred said, his affable manner returning. Then, with a quick look down at the ruined body. 'Perhaps we should buy a small coffin.'

'Certainly won't need a big one,' Robert muttered under his breath with a look at the half-sized corpse before him.

Thomas was relieved to be able to settle the woman in her hut with her children and three of her female neighbours to look after her.

There was nothing he could say. His only consolation was, he had done all he could. At least poor Sara had been informed now. It would have been cruel to leave her unsuspecting. Thomas had seen that before on other building sites where the Master Mason was less caring than Robert, and widows had been left without even the courtesy of a message to tell them of their husband's death. Robert's bark was much worse than his bite, and today he was mourning not only a companion of some years, but one of his best trained and experienced masons.

On his way to the hovel today, Thomas had spied a small shop with skins of wine for sale. He hurried away and bought one, carrying it back less swiftly, hoping that she might have recovered. Hers was the sort of face he'd have liked to see smiling, not full of grief. When he first saw her, wearing that sweet and mischievous smile, he had felt that he would like to see her smile like that for ever.

She was awake, lying on her palliasse and shuddering with grief, when he gently pushed at the door and peeped around it. As soon as he did so, a matron of his own age, sixty or so, rose with a glower and thrust a hand against his breast, almost knocking him over.

'Mistress!' he cried.

'Shut up. You've done enough harm already, bringing the maid this news. Do you go, now, and leave her to recover. Go on, clear off!'

'Mistress, I have brought her this to soothe her spirits. Please tell her I'm very sorry.'

'Sorry won't buy bread for her and the boys, will it?' the woman said caustically, snatching away the wineskin and closing the door in his face.

*   *   *

Henry Potell belched as he tipped the jug one last time. There was a small trickle, then two drips, and that was his supply of wine finished. He slumped back in his chair, polished off the remaining dregs, and stared moodily at the far wall.

Joel. *He* was to blame. It was all his stupidity that had led to this disaster. Soon Henry would hear that the pleader had been instructed, and then he'd be called to the court to explain his mistakes. Not that there was any excuse for what had happened. He'd simply trusted Joel, that was all. He'd been buying his frames from Joel since he first set up his shop. If he was to be sued now, he'd sue Joel as well. There was no reason why he should be held responsible, when it was another man who had built the blasted things.

'So, Husband. You're still here, then? Are you going to try to drink all of the wine in the house?'

Mabilla's sarcasm was of little consequence to Henry. He had made up his mind. He stood slowly and, so he felt, magisterially. 'I'm going out.'

'Out? Oh, no! You can hardly place one foot in front of the other, Henry. Please, stay here and have a rest. We can talk about it again later, when you're sober.'

'Woman, I am as sober as I need to be for this!' Henry exclaimed, and strode purposefully to the door, grabbing his thick, fur-lined cotte as he passed the chest.

Outside, the sun was harsh at the limewashed houses opposite, and he winced as the brightness stabbed at his brain. Here, on his side of Smythen Street, all was in shadow; the low wintry sun couldn't reach his front door, and all along his walk he had to keep his eyes narrowed. There was a cacophony of noise as he went, hawkers shrieking, horses neighing, dogs whining and barking – all conspired to erode whatever calmness there had been in his mind. As he passed by yet another female huckster selling apples from a great basket, he almost bellowed at her to be silent. God, he thought, grabbing hold of a table outside a shop, if only these damned people could be quiet for a moment!

Joel lived at the corner of Goldsmith Street where it met the High Street. The place was not as large as Henry's own house, but it was comfortable, and it had the advantage of a great yard behind it where Joel could store all his timber.

Henry staggered to the door and pounded upon it with his fist. He had a slight light-headedness, he found, and he had to take some deep breaths of air as he stood there, contemplating the crowds hurrying past. The town seemed unaware of his predicament. Some folks did indeed cast a glance in his direction, but for the most part, all scurried along like so many rats in a sewer. Except this sewer was of their own making. *His* own making. That made his predicament all the more terrible.

'Yes? Oh, it's you, Henry.'

'Yes, Joel, it's me,' Henry said, shoving his old friend out of the way without further ado and stomping through into the hall.

'You look unwell,' Joel remarked in concern. 'Do you want some wine?'

'Why not. Yes, broach your best barrel, Joel. You never know, you may not have time to finish it,' Henry said nastily.

He slumped on a stool while Joel first stared and then hurried from the room.

The joiner's hall was well-proportioned, with a wealth of pleasant carvings. Henry knew that Joel often relaxed with a baulk of timber and a set of chisels, and carved decorations for his own amusement when he had time; this hall was a testament to his skill. It was lovely, and it made Henry feel unutterably sad. He had no such tribute to leave behind him. All he had was his family, when all was said and done, and a certain amount of money. All he had made, his saddles and bridles, were owned by others. He had nothing – not even a simple harness of his own. He had no need: he didn't possess a horse. There was little point, when a man could hire a mount when he needed to travel.

Looking about him now, he felt that his own life was lacking. Even though he had the love of his dear Mabilla, and his daughter was a model of perfection, there was an emptiness at the core of his life. And that life would not go on for ever. He was over sixty years old, in God's name!

'Come, Henry, tell me what the matter is,' Joel said as he returned to the room. He held a quart jug and two cups, and as soon as he reached Henry, he poured a good measure into the first cup, passing it to his old companion.

'Where's Maud?'

Joel's eyebrows rose at that. He was a portly figure with a thinning crop of pale hair, not quite light enough to be fair, not dark enough to be mouse-coloured. His face was rounded and comfortable, more prone to laughter than rage, and the crow's feet at his eyes proved that he was cheerful company. 'My wife is out at the market, I think – why?'

'I wouldn't want her to hear me like this,' Henry said.

Joel sat and sipped his wine. 'Tell me what this is about, Henry.'

'One of my bloody saddles broke last week, Joel. Hadn't you heard?'

'Well yes, I had heard something about that.'

'And it was the frame that broke. It happened right in front of me – in front of my own house, Joel! The customer was reining in, and the cantle broke. I saw it with my own eyes. He plunged down to the cobbles headfirst, and I was sure he must die . . .'

'Terrible.'

'Yes, pretty damned terrible. And then he demanded that I pay for his physician, and told me he'd sue me for damages. He lost a lot of money that day, Joel.'

'I'm very sorry to hear that.'

Henry saw the sympathy in his eyes, but that wasn't good enough. 'Not as sorry as I was. But that frame was one of yours, Joel. It was one that you sold me. You told me you only had good quality wood, but it snapped. You rooked me, you bastard! What did you do, put together green wood knowing I wouldn't notice?'

'You've known me long enough to realise I wouldn't do that to you.'

'Do I? That saddle frame was lousy, Joel.'

'I'll repay you for the frame, if you like, old friend.'

'You're damn right you will!'

'Is that all? There's something else eating at you, isn't there? Come on – get it off your chest.'

Henry set his cup on the floor, then put his head in his hands. When he spoke again, it was a whisper. 'Joel, I can't go on much longer.'

'Come along, old fellow, you're as hale as I am!' Joel said heartily.

'Perhaps I am, but I had a visit last week. From the madman.'

Joel's face set as though it had been carved from stone. 'What do you mean?'

'Who did we always mean by that?' Henry sneered. 'William is back in the city. He's a corrodian at St Nicholas's Priory.'

'Sweet Mother of God,' Joel mumbled, looking away.

'He dropped in to see me,' Henry continued. 'At first he only had eyes for my daughter, but then he wanted to chat to me about the good old times. Not only that, he was happy to tell me all that he has done in the last forty years. God in heaven! Joel, the stories he told . . . you wouldn't want to hear them, let alone believe them. The men he has killed . . .'

'I never thought to see him again,' Joel said.

'Nor I. Yet here he is. He has served the King and the King's father well, it seems. Well enough for his master to buy him a pension at the priory of his choice. So he is here, and he visits my house almost every day. I tell you, Joel, it makes me sick to hear him. Sick! I had to sit and listen to him snigger to think of poor Nick's injured face, then boast about how he slaughtered the Chaunter himself, and then how clever he was to divert attention from himself and get the Mayor and gatekeeper hanged.'

'That was how he found his patron,' Joel agreed.

They both remembered the old story. When King Edward I, the present King's father, arrived in full panoply to determine who should pay for the murder of the Bishop's man, it had been William who pointed out that the Southern Gate to the city had remained open all night. The King had decided to execute those responsible, even if they couldn't find the true murderers. Then he rewarded William by taking him into his host. William had never looked back.

'What of it? He'll probably die soon enough,' Joel said. 'He was that bit older than us.'

'I don't know that I can continue to live with the guilt,' Henry said. 'My life is scarcely worth a candle. I am to die before many years are out. I'm lucky to have survived so long already. Before I die, I have to make my confession to the Cathedral.'

'Now wait, Henry,' Joel said hastily. 'There's no need for anything rash. Think of the risk if you do that: the Bishop may decide to haul you into his gaol and hasten your end, rather than show compassion. Never trust a man who has power of life and death over you.'

'I have to do something. That is just what Matthew said, but I do have to do something. This guilt is eating at me.'

'You told Matthew?' Joel asked with astonishment.

'I thought I could rely on him at least. I've known him so long,' Henry said. 'But he was very kind. He said that he had forgiven all those involved many years ago. In fact, he argued that this was such an old issue, it wasn't worth raking up the embers again.'

'I think he was very intelligent to say so,' Joel said.

'You none of you care, do you?' Henry asked sadly. 'That man died, with all his *familia* about him, and for what? To bolster the career of a man who was himself ruined. What was the point?'

'To try to help the man who promised us much,' Joel said.

'Just as we should all try to help other Christians,' Henry said bitterly. His heart felt as hollow as the empty cup on the floor beside him. 'I don't know. I think I should tell the Bishop.'

'Well, I think you shouldn't. Indeed, you mustn't.'

'Do you remember that first lad? The one who ran to the Chaunter to warn him? What was his name? Ah, it was so long ago. And then the Chaunter's own man cut the boy down, thinking he was another assassin. That was the beginning of the slaughter. All so unnecessary.'

'It may seem that way to you now,' Joel said soothingly. 'But it *was* necessary.'

'Oh, damn you and damn Matthew! I must do what I think is right!' Henry exclaimed. 'I can't carry on like this. Prior Peter on one side telling me I ought to confess before I die, and you two seeking only . . .'

'Henry, don't bellow like that, not in my hall,' Joel remonstrated.

'Oh, to hell with you, you old devil! I'll have nothing more to do with you,' Henry said, rising heavily to his feet. There was no anger in him now, only a kind of dull resignation. 'I'll decide what I'm to do. In the meantime, if Udo Germeyne decides to sue me, I'll sue you in return. I won't be left damaged by your shoddy work.'

Joel followed him out to the door. 'Friend, be easy. I'll return your money for that frame.'

'You'll do more than that, Joel Lytell – you'll take back *all* the frames you've sold me, and you'll compensate me for the damage done to my business by this fiasco.'

Henry glared at Joel as he pulled the latch and threw open the door to the High Street, then stumped away in a semi-drunken state of misery.

It was as he was approaching Carfoix, past the Fissand Gate in this busiest street in Exeter, when one man's features suddenly stood out: the cold visage of a man he had thought dead many years ago – a man with a livid scar that slashed through the whole left side of his face from temple to jaw. That eye was clouded, the other was brown and intense, glittering with the fervour of the religious fanatic.

'Sweet Jesus! Nicholas!' Henry swore, a hand rising to his throat, but in that moment the figure was gone.

He felt entirely alone in the middle of the crowds, like a foreigner with no knowledge of the language or customs. The past was vivid before him, and his throat closed up in dread.

Chapter Four

The Clerk of the Works was relieved to enter the Cathedral and take part in the service after the shocks of that morning.

The way that the rock had moved had brought home to Matthew just how immense was the weight of stone used to build this great place. He glanced up nervously at the walls and ceiling as he knelt, thinking how easy it would be for one of the massive blocks to tumble down and leave him as a splash of crimson on the tiled floor. It was a sickening thought. God could do it with a snap of His fingers, if He so wished, and there was nothing that a man could do to prevent Him.

He offered up a prayer of his own for the spirit of Saul. Matthew was a conscientious canon, and it was his task to pray for the souls of all those living or dead.

Service over, he walked through to the frater and sat with his bowl of pottage and hunk of bread. While the voice of the reader droned over all, he stared down at his food.

The rock had gone so quickly, he had hardly registered its progress. He'd noticed Thomas's distraction, of course, and had tried to see what the mason was staring at so intently, but he'd had to lean over to peer around Thomas, and couldn't see anything out of the ordinary. And then the rock fell, and it didn't seem so important any more.

That noise would forever reverberate in his ears, like the machines of hell preparing for the final battle between good and evil; and he was sure he'd heard a short scream, like that of a petrified quarry before the fox's jaws clamped and life was extinguished. Only a few moments before, Matthew had seen Saul hard at work below, happily shaping a block and gauging whether it would slot into its neighbour. The next moment, he was dead.

Matthew sighed. There was a slight twinge in his shoulder, but that was normal. Whenever the weather began to change, that old pain came back to pester him.

'Matthew?'

'Treasurer. Please, take a seat.'

Stephen nodded and took his place beside Matthew on the bench. 'Is it your shoulder?'

Matthew nodded. He had gained this wound on the night that the Chaunter, Walter de Lecchelade, had been assassinated. Matthew was a member of his *familia*, living under Walter's roof, and he had been struck down by the murderous devils who killed his master. Fortunately, he was unconscious from early on in the fight. Others hadn't been so lucky. In fact, only he and one other survived the defence of their master: Matthew with a broken head that took months to mend, and Nicholas, a man marked with hideous wounds to remind him of the honourable attempt to protect Chaunter Walter.

'It is always bad when the weather changes,' he said simply.

'If you wish, I can arrange for a period of retreat. Perhaps you should go and build up your strength – visit one of our possessions and rest for a while? Colebrook has a pleasing church and there is a large Seyney House there.'

'It is kind of you, Treasurer, but I shall be fine. My work keeps me occupied, and that is sufficient for me.'

He could feel the Treasurer's eyes upon him, and heard the gentleness in Stephen's voice as he said, 'God bless you, Matthew. You must be cautious, though. You mustn't ruin yourself in the cause.'

Matthew smiled. 'But the cause is just: to build God's greatest House here in Exeter – that is enough for any man, surely? I would be pleased if I could only see the work ended in my lifetime.'

Stephen nodded, but his face was marked with a little sadness. 'Ah, I should like that too – but I fear we are too old to hope for it, Matthew. The building work was started more than forty years ago, and it'll be another forty-odd before we are finished. You and I shall both be long in our graves by then.'

'But at least we can go to our graves knowing what a legacy we have left,' Matthew said.

'That is true,' Stephen said, but the clerk was surprised to see a furtive expression appear on his face.

Matthew left him soon afterwards, going out into the cloisters, then returning to the building site. He walked to the smudge of blood on the ground near the wall and stared down at it, shaking his head slowly from side to side. They must find a new mason to replace Saul, he told himself with a frown. There was another twinge in his shoulder, and he instinctively glanced back at the Charnel Chapel, the spot where he had gained the wound.

The sun passed behind a cloud, and as the Close plunged into greyness, Matthew's attention was transfixed by the grim mausoleum and he felt a flood of revulsion at the sight. That place was terrible – a remembrance of an abomination. Thank God there had been no more serious rifts among the members of the Chapter since then. Pray to God there never would be.

In the High Street, Nicholas found himself standing near one of the larger gates to the Cathedral Close. He eased his roll and bag from his shoulder and glanced about him hopefully. When he had lived here before, it was the main entrance into the Cathedral's precinct, because it was so wide and gave straight on to the western doors. A man could wander along this street unsuspecting, and then suddenly find himself in the main Cathedral yard, with that broad expanse of turf leading to the magnificent edifice.

Today, though, he wasn't here to marvel, but to see whether he could win some alms. In the Cathedral there was a Clerk of Bread who supervised the production and distribution of the loaves for the canons, vicars, annuellars, choristers and workmen, but all his food would be long gone by now and the clerk probably dozing after his hectic morning. Up at midnight for Matins, then the other services, and as soon as they were done, he must rush to his ovens and begin bread-making for the new day. As soon as the loaves were baked and had cooled a little, they'd be sent to all those who had a right to them; by lunchtime, most of them would already be consumed. He'd be dead on his feet by noon. If only Nicholas had arrived here earlier, he might have been able to plead a loaf, but not now.

At least here, though, in the Fissand Gate he would be able to beg a little from the passers-by. Perhaps someone would give him a coin.

There was a sour-looking old clerk at the gate chatting to a one-legged beggar with a twisted face. The beggar set his head to one side. 'Friend friar, please join us here.'

Nicholas hobbled to their side, slumping on the stool offered by the clerk. 'Thank you.'

'Pleasure,' the porter grunted unemotionally. He snorted, hawked and spat, then muttered about the weather being cold before disappearing into his little room.

'Don't mind him,' said the old beggar.

'A man who gives me a stool can be as grim-faced as he wishes. Anyway, his presence detracts from our prettiness, friend,' Nicholas muttered with a chuckle.

'Ha ha! You speak the truth there! He's always a miserable-looking sod. Still, he's spent time as a soldier in the King's host before he came here, so he appreciates bold fighters like me. I daresay he's readying a brazier to warm us both even now. Friend, I am called John Coppe. The porter there, he's Janekyn Beyvyn.'

'I am Friar Nicholas. How did you win your injuries? You say you were a fighter?'

'Pirates. Used to be a sailor, and the bastards caught me and my ship. A big, brawny bugger with an axe took off my leg and then swung at my face.' Coppe shrugged. 'But I'm alive, and apart from the looks some women give me, life's not so bad. What of you?'

Nicholas's gaze passed down towards the Cathedral Close. 'Many years ago, I was attacked in there and left for dead.'

The porter had returned, and he set a brazier before them. Returning to his shed, he brought out a pot filled with spiced wine, and set it on top. Passing them cups, he ladled wine into each. 'You were hurt in here?'

'Yes. I was with some companions when our master was attacked, and I won these wounds.'

'You were with the Chaunter?' the porter exclaimed.

'Aye. My name is Nicholas. I think I was the only man to survive that attack.'

John Coppe looked up at him, then over at the porter. 'I've never heard of this before, Jan. How long ago was this?'

'Before my time,' Janekyn said with a sniff. He held out his hands to the brazier.

'You are a local man, then?' Nicholas asked.

'Yes. So's Coppe here.'

'I understand, good Porter. I'll go and find another place to sit,' Nicholas said, and rose.

'No, Friar Nicholas, wait,' Coppe said. He looked from one to the other with dismay. 'What's the matter with you two?'

Nicholas glanced at the porter. 'You tell him, Master Janekyn.'

He shouldered his pack again and set off away from the Fissand Gate and off up the road towards the High Street. There at the top he stopped. He reached into his pack and brought out his wooden bowl, holding it out to passers-by. When he had some coins, he bought a little loaf from a baker's in Cook Row, then slowly continued on his way towards the old Friary.

Henry reached home in a muck sweat. He thrust the door wide, and then slammed it shut, resting against it while he stood panting, close to puking, his eyes squeezed tight shut.

That can't have been Nicholas! Sweet Jesus, but he had left Exeter so long ago . . . and yet could there be two men in the kingdom with that fearful wound slashing down the side of his face and destroying the eye? It was unlikely. Good Christ! To think that the man was here. It was terrible!

He was shaky on his legs. Forcing himself upright, he stumbled along the passage and into his hall. He wasn't proud that his first feeling was one of relief that his wife was not in the room already, and when his bottler appeared, making sure that this wasn't some stranger from the street essaying a little investigation of a wealthy man's house, he barked out for some wine, and forget watering it today. He had need of some sustenance.

However, it was not the bottler who brought the wine, but his wife. She walked in with a set face, and when she spoke, she was decidedly shrewish.

'So you want more, do you? From your breath and the look of you, I should have thought you'd had plenty, Husband! You look as though you might empty your stomach all over the reeds at any moment.'

'Woman, be still for five seconds!' Henry snapped. He was in no mood for a confrontation and yet, when he felt her gently pressing a cup into his hand again, he looked up and realised what he must do.

'Mabilla, my love, there is something I have to tell you,' he said, and as he started his tale, his voice broke at last, and for the first time in many years he wept; not for himself, but for all those men he had killed or helped to kill.

If there was one man who was more responsible than most for Henry's grief and pain, it was Peter, and yet the temporary Prior of St Nicholas knew no happiness himself. If he had been certain of Henry's feelings of remorse and guilt, it would have helped him overcome his own sense of simmering rage at the injustice done to him.

After the murder, Peter had returned to his room and sat on his bed. Even forty years later, he could remember that. He'd sat there for a long while, his body exhausted, two little scratches on an arm and his belly, but they really were just minor wounds. The Vicar of Heavitree had a worse wound – a knife-cut in his shoulder that could have been quite dangerous. He was advised to get it seen to at the earliest opportunity, when the others crowded around to take a look in the flickering light of a torch.

It was astonishing how easy the attack had been. They had massed there in the gloom before midnight, men arriving in ones and twos. Peter had been at the bottom of what was now called the Fissand Gate, while the rest stood at the other entrances. Men were waiting at the Bear Gate, and more at the Erceneske Gate and St Petrock's, just in case the man managed to escape the initial assault. To prevent their weakening, the Dean had seen to it that there were men among them to stiffen the feeblest resolve – the Vicar of Heavitree was at the Bear Gate, the Vicar of Ottery St Mary at the Erceneske, and William was with Peter at Fissand. They were all in their places soon after the bells tolled for the start of Matins, the blood thundering in their veins as they waited to execute this interloper, Chaunter Walter de Lecchelade.

There were many different reasons for the men to be there. Some wanted the simplest reward: money. Others were looking to the future, when that fool Quivil was dead and John of Exeter, their Dean, naturally took the post. John was the obvious choice, after all. He was clever, witty, and a local man; he understood the people in his parishes, and he was bright enough not to try to enforce damn stupid rules that wouldn't be accepted. Unlike Quivil, with his lunatic schemes.

Peter shook his head. It was so long ago now, he couldn't even remember the reasons that Quivil gave for wanting the Dean out of there. There must have been something – it can't just have been the age-old complaint that he was holding several benefices in plurality. Not that it mattered. As far as Peter was concerned, although the Dean and Bishop were at loggerheads, it was clear to him that the Dean was in the right. While the Bishop refused to speak to John or even call him 'Dean', the Primate Archbishop Peccham scarcely spoke to the Bishop! Even when Quivil was elevated to the Bishopric, he refused to confer the rite of consecration, explaining that it was a mite inconvenient . . . that studied insult was never going to be forgotten or forgiven, but as far as Peter was concerned, the opinion of the Primate was all that mattered.

He could remember thinking that as he stood there that night, William beside him with his teeth shining in the torchlight, fiddling excitedly with the blade of his sword. Rather than the cold and the damp and the fact that they were there to slaughter a man who had interposed himself between two powerful factions in the Cathedral, Peter's mind was fixed upon the glorious future he would enjoy. As soon as John of Exeter realised that Peter had been there and put in his own blow, Peter would be able to count on the Dean's support for any promotions. The Vicars were fine, they could get the money and power that they craved, but the Dean had the ability to reward his own friends more liberally in the Cathedral.

And then there was the chink of light as the congregation threw open the great doors, and the Chaunter walked out, his black cloak and gown flapping about him like the wings of an enormous bat, his *familia* trailing along behind him; and then came the shout of warning that stopped them all in their tracks.

The Chaunter never stood a chance. Even though that damned idiot Vincent ran down to him, shouting that he was walking into a trap, it was too late. The boy was struck down almost instantly by Nick, one of the Chaunter's men, thinking he was one of the assassins.

He might as well have been. As soon as the novice had fallen, the rest of them piled over the muddy grass, weapons ready, and bellowing their war cries. All apart from William. He simply smiled as he rushed onwards, eager to be in at the beginning. William always enjoyed the feel of a sword in his hands, and the idea of hacking at another man was appealing to him. All Peter could remember of William was a kind of high-pitched manic giggle as he stabbed at the men before him.

The one who'd killed the novice, he went down fairly quickly. Then a second was killed by Henry. The latter was still riven with guilt over that, the fool. What he had to complain about, Peter didn't know. He wasn't even arrested.

Yes, Peter could remember every part of that night: the tension while they waited, the raw thrill of hurtling over the mud, and later the strange emptiness as he stood with the others, staring down at the bodies. There were no apparent survivors at that stage. Peter himself certainly didn't realise that two of the men were still alive. Not that it would have changed anything. William might have executed them on the spot for sheer devilry, perhaps, but that was all. The two left alive couldn't identify any of the attackers, not that that mattered. All knew exactly who had been there, including the Bishop.

Which was why two years later Peter was taken and held in the Bishop's gaol: a terrible punishment. His livings were stripped away and he was left destitute, until he could join the monastery.

If he now wielded the power of a Prior, it was no more than he deserved. He had carried out the wishes of his Dean and of his Primate. The only man who disagreed with the action taken was Quivil!

Thomas wasn't drunk. Not quite. After the morning's events, he didn't think he could be completely drunk, no matter that he wanted to forget all that which had passed. The sight of that poor, lovely woman lying in a faint was so sad that he could have thrown himself on the ground with guilt. Her sorrow and despair were all his doing.

If only he hadn't seen that figure, he thought – but he had. The ghost of the man he had once called friend, and whom he had then severely wounded.

The sun was bright, and warm enough to dry the ground. Only the mud in the roadways was still moist, kept so by the horses, oxen, cattle and dogs that trampled through the filth and straw. Tonight the rakers would come along again and cart off the worst of it, most to be taken to the fields and spread for fertilizer. The streets were not clean, and yet Thomas had seen worse. He dawdled along. The tavern where he had stopped after seeing Sara and leaving the wineskin at her hut was a short way up from the road leading to her section of the city. It was time for him to return to the Cathedral, except he didn't want to. It would remind him of the man whom he had killed by accident today. As though in reminder of his guilt, his palms started to tingle and sparkle with fresh pain.

And seeing Saul crushed beneath that rock made Thomas think of Vicar Matthew. It was enough to slow his steps. When he had first arrived back here, he had thought that his beard, long hair and age would make him all but unrecognisable. Surely most of those whom he'd known in the Cathedral would have died long ago. When he first realised that the Vicar in charge of throwing down the old walls was Matthew, he had been tempted to bolt – and yet Matthew showed no sign of having recognised him. Curbing his desire to fly had been difficult, but then Thomas started to feel a little more settled. If even Matt didn't realise who he was, surely he was as safe here as anywhere in the realm.

Still, he didn't want to go back to the Cathedral and see Matthew just now. The Vicar would stare at him if not accusingly then somewhat pityingly, and Thomas wasn't ready to suffer that. He carried on to Carfoix, the great crossroads where the main east-west and north-south streets all met. There were a great many people there: men and women, horses, dogs and cattle, all vying for space while tranters added to the din, shouting their wares. Thomas took one long look at them all, and headed south.

He hadn't been here since his return. Well, there wasn't much point in coming here. He had no need to travel, and the Southern Gate was only useful for those who had to go down towards the coast. All the things that Thomas was likely to need were already available at the Cathedral. He didn't need to even look this way usually.

But just now, after the shock of Saul's accident and the wretchedness he had caused that beautiful woman, he felt the need to go and see the gate again. Just once more, he told himself. He'd never have to come here again after this.

The South Gate to the city was a massive affair, with two square towers set in the wall presenting a daunting view to those approaching from outside. From the interior, they were scarcely less alarming. A large building lay beside the roadway, with lodgings for the porter, as well as rooms for a guard. There was a room beneath in which all those whom the porter considered dubious could be held, too. Thomas could remember that place only too clearly, the foul odours, the sobbing of men or women as they waited for the guards coming to take them away . . . and the never-ceasing drip of water from somewhere. No matter what the weather, that cell always seemed wet.

Looking to the left, he saw the church, Holy Trinity, where he had been baptised and took Mass until he left. Beyond it was the wall where he had played as a child. It was huge, a rising rampart supporting the masonry, and as a mason himself he could only wonder at the labour that over the years had created this enormous ring of stone about the city. The wall was crenellated, and must have been eleven feet thick at the base, narrowing to perhaps six or seven at the top. It was a wall that could hardly have been bettered by any other in the land.

But it wasn't the wall which attracted his attention. He could not stop his eyes from moving back to the gate to take in the three wizened, blackened shapes hanging up by the gate itself. They were good and high, so that they should be out of reach of people attempting to move them, but positioned where all could see them, for these were men who had been accused of treachery to the King after the most recent wars, the fights between the Lords Marcher and the King's friends, the Despensers. There were only the three, all of them knights, and each of them a loyal servant of his own master, whoever he might have been. Up and down the kingdom there were similar hideous shapes hanging or stuck on spikes. They would remain there until they had disintegrated, so that the King's justice could be seen by all.

The King's *justice*, Thomas sneered to himself. It was an amusing concept, here where a King could choose a man's fate, whether he should live or die, on a whim.

Still, at least his own father wasn't there any longer. His body would have rotted and fallen away many years ago now.

Chapter Five

Sara woke to a miserable morning, feeling as though the cold had penetrated her very marrow. She wriggled further under the scratchy fustian blankets. They smelled of the damp, of cats' pee, but it was better than rising. Outside, the rain was sheeting down. There was a growing puddle by the door, spreading slowly across the floor and curving back towards the wall, and she watched it dully for a few minutes. The idea of going outside to fetch water and empty her bladder was unappealing.

A widow must shift for herself, though. She embraced her boys, pulling them to her. Eight-year-old Dan was reluctant, as though such behaviour was too immature for him now he was the master of the house, but three-year-old Elias was enthusiastic, as always, and his arms gave Sara a strange feeling of comfort; she had found herself desperate for the little boy's hugs since Saul's death. He wanted as much of her warmth as he could take, and he happily snuggled closer. Then, when Dan had already risen and was trying to strike a spark from his flint and dagger, Sara finally eased herself up and pulled her old cloak about her, tucking the bedclothes in around Elias. She kissed him, then went to the door and peered out.

Rain was falling like spears, pelting into the mud about the huts. All was so wet, it was like staring at the sea. She shivered and pulled her cloak tighter, and hurried outside. Behind her hut was a little lean-to shack with her wood neatly stored on either side. Here she squatted over the hole Saul had dug for them when he built this little home for his family, and cleaned herself as best she could with a damp rag. Grabbing a bucket, she ran out to the walls near the West Gate, filled it with water and carried it back home up the hill, careful not to slip on the wet cobbles. Manure lying on the streets could make walking hazardous in this weather.

She was soaked. Still, at least Dan had managed to light the fire. The room was already filled with smoke as the dry tinder caught and started to singe the bits and pieces of wood shaving he'd put over them. He was still crouched on all fours, arse in the air, head down, like a puppy begging to play, when she entered.

Tipping a little water into her ewer, she rinsed her face, then grabbed a reluctant Elias and washed his face too. Dan would do his own later. Her children were always hungry. It was not something that would improve, she knew. So many children died too young to have ever known a full belly. Of all her friends about this city, not one hadn't lost a child. All knew the pain of loss, just as she did herself. Her only daughter, little Claricia, had died just before her second birthday. It had been a close thing for Elias, too.

'Oh God, let us find some food today!' she murmured under her breath.

It was two weeks since Saul's death, and still she found herself willing him back, as though he had gone travelling and must soon return. Somehow, she couldn't quite believe that she'd never see him again.

Dan was coping with the loss. He was a little rock, he was. Strong, he had nodded when he was told, and then sniffed a little, before declaring that he would have to start breaking up the firewood as his father always had before. He felt the responsibility of being master of the family very strongly. Bless him, he'd even borrowed old Jen's hatchet, since he couldn't lift Saul's axe.

Elias was too small to understand. He had seen dead men before, of course, but he somehow thought of them as something else. His own father couldn't have gone. Sara had seen the disbelief in his eyes as she told him. He'd listened as she explained he was dead and couldn't come home again, and then he'd asked for some food, and while he chewed his bread, he said, 'It's all right, he's bound to come back soon.'

The funeral was a blur. She'd seen little, her eyes were so fogged with tears, and when they carried her husband's pathetic half-body outside, the heavens had opened again. There were inches of water in the grave, and a man nearly fell in as they were settling his body in his hole. Sara had stood there staring down at him, trying to remember his smile, his kind brown eyes, his mouth fixed in that half-smile he always wore. She tried to remember his hands about her waist, on her breasts, how his arms felt as they pulled her towards him in one of his great hugs – and found that all these memories and more were already fading. He was gone: the staunch defender of her and their children was dead, and there was nothing she could do to change the fact.

Elias looked terrible today. The rain was abating somewhat, and in the feeble light, she could see that his face had a sickly tinge to it, and she sighed as she mixed the greens into her bowl for pottage. He needed more sustenance – meat and eggs, not a weak broth of Good King Henry, Alexanders, some peas and a handful of beans. It wasn't enough to keep a lad together.

She would go to the Priory again and see if she could beg some food. A rich fishmonger had died, so she had heard, and part of his bequest was a great donation of food from the gate of the Priory of St Nicholas, bread and fish from the Almoner. If she could get a little fish and bread, it would make all the difference to her boys. They needed their food so desperately. She would go and plead with the Almoner.

Nicholas was already out. He had visited a church to preach, but the priest had refused him entry, and Nicholas was left to kick his heels outside. Rather than do that, he decided to go and have another look at the Cathedral. A keen urge prompted him to take a look at the Charnel Chapel, even though the rain was still falling steadily. It didn't bother Nicholas much. He was used to all weathers.

It was a strange little building. Dedicated to St Edward the Confessor, because it was built in honour of King Edward I who had come to hear the trials after the murder, Nicholas thought it a peculiar place. Of course, all cemeteries had the same problem: if the religious establishment had been there for a while, when new bodies were ready to be interred, the pit-digger would keep coming up with old bones, and where should one store them? Bones took so long to rot down compared with flesh and blood. The favoured route was to put up a little chapel like this with a large storeroom beneath in which the bones could be installed, while above prayers were said for all the poor dead.

This was an innovation since Nicholas's departure. When he had lived in the Cathedral's grounds, he had truly lived *here*, on the spot where the chapel now stood, when this place had been the home of Walter de Lecchelade, the Chaunter.

No one had said what had happened to the old house. Presumably it was an accident: a fire had razed it to the ground, or a supporting beam had collapsed. It was of no importance. The place was only a building, when all was said and done, whereas this little chapel was significant. It protected people, giving a shelter to their remains while annuellars prayed for their souls.

It was as likely that after Walter's murder the Chapter decided to remove the memory by eradicating his house. And they honoured the King while so doing.

Naming it after King Edward was fair, Nicholas considered. After all, if it weren't for him, the guilty might never have been punished.

This was the first chance he'd had to take stock of the Cathedral since he had arrived, and now he studied the place with interest.

When he was living with the Chaunter, he had been prone to walking about the works, and he had been fascinated by the way that the workmen had gone about their tasks. Of course in those days they were working on the eastern range of the Cathedral, whereas now that end was completed and the men were attacking the nave and western front, bringing it up to the same height as the rest. It meant that scaffolding and equipment were standing apparently all higgledy-piggledy about the main entranceway. Also, the masons, smiths and carpenters had brought all their tools so as to have them closer to where the work was being conducted.

While he wandered about the Close, the rain stopped at last, and now there was a bright sun peeping between the rents of tattered clouds. Warmth began to return to him as his garments soaked up the heat, and he could smell the wet-dog odour as his woollen clothing steamed gently. It was a smell that spoke of comfort to come when he was dry, and he relished it.

There were so many men here, scurrying about like ants in the presence of this massive building. All no doubt knew what they were doing, but to Nicholas it looked as though they were all witless. There seemed to be no logic he could discern.

Walking closer, he saw men hauling on ropes, and he stopped to watch them. With his head and back so bent, it was hard to turn his head to gaze upwards, so he simply assumed that they were lifting something up to the wall and continued on his way.

'Friar! Friar! Stop!'

Nicholas paused in the mud and moved his head this way and that, but couldn't see the man who had called.

'Please, stop there. A little while ago a man was squashed to death right there! Wait!'

'If people want to talk, why do they conceal themselves?' Nicholas muttered to himself as he waited. Soon a pair of legs appeared encased in the black of a clerk's tunic, and Nicholas let his eyes ride slowly upwards. 'Well?'

'I . . . my God!'

Nicholas always felt a slightly perverse satisfaction when people first took in his appearance. The scar inflicted on him that night had ravaged what had before been rather good looks. His assailant had used a long-bladed weapon, perhaps a sword, or a very long knife; whichever it may have been, it had torn into his flesh at the temple, pierced his eye and ruined it, and then continued downwards, ripping away the flesh from cheek and jaw, opening the whole side of his mouth. He was told that when they found him that morning, the two annuellars on their way to prepare for the first of the day's masses in honour of patrons and dead canons, the Bratton's Mass, had come across the bodies and thought all must be dead. Nicholas himself had most of his head simply a mass of blood, and with all the exposed bone, they had thought he couldn't survive, until one noticed that there was a bloody froth coming from around the wound. He was breathing.

'My visage shocks you?' Nicholas asked nastily.

'Is it really you, Nicholas?' the man gasped, and Nicholas peered up more closely.

'Matthew?'

Henry heard the banging on his door soon after he had gone through to his counting room, and groaned inwardly. 'Another damned fool asking for a saddle he can't afford,' he grunted as he listened for his bottler's steps. Soon he heard the steps return, and he sat up a little more smartly in his chair. For all his cynicism, a man couldn't afford to shun any client, especially when he was in the process of waiting to hear from a dissatisfied customer who might well sue him and ruin him utterly.

'Master, it's . . .'

The bottler was shoved from the doorway, and William entered, his face wreathed in smiles. 'Master saddler, it's good to be here again. Bottler, bring me a jug of wine, and one for your master,' he added, prodding the man with his staff. He hopped over to a stool and sat, rubbing at his calf. 'Fucking wound. You'd have thought fifteen years would see it off, but the bleeding thing comes back each winter. Hurts like a sodding burn under the skin. All because of a poleaxe some arse shoved at me when I was fighting a man on the stairs above me. I killed him slowly when I caught him, I can tell you! Ha! He squealed for a good three hours before I got bored!'

Henry surveyed him despairingly. 'What do you want here, William? I'm very busy.'

'Ach, God's Balls, man, you're always busy. I thought the idea of being a rich man in this city was, you could take more time off to enjoy yourself, eh? Well, this is your opportunity. I fancy getting lashed today. You can come and help me.'

'I can't just drop everything to go and drink with you!' Henry protested. 'I've got a business to run here.'

'What's the point of a fucking business if you can't tell them all to poke themselves and have some fun?' William asked reasonably. 'Anyway, the market's open and the bulls will be baited soon. We could go and have a drink at the alehouse on the corner, then on to the baiting pens for a wager or two, and back to . . .'

'I cannot possibly. That is ridiculous.'

'Why? You too grand to enjoy a drink with me any more?' William asked, his grin broadening. 'Time was, you were happy for a few cups of ale with me.'

'I don't have time for this,' Henry muttered.

'What's the matter? Have you forgotten all the fun we used to have? Eh? Come on, grab a cotte and a hat and let's go.'

The bottler returned with the wine and William slurped a half-cup in one gulp.

'I can't. I have work to do,' Henry said, looking away.

'There something wrong? Something wrong with me?'

Henry looked back quickly. He recognised that tone. It was the voice of the other William, the man who would draw steel and stab a man for an imagined insult. 'No, old friend.'

'Then what is it? You ashamed to be seen with me?'

Henry felt his shoulders sag. 'Will, I am worried. A customer has threatened to sue me.'

'Tell me who it is, and I'll see he doesn't,' William said reasonably.

'You can't fix everything with cold steel!' Henry blurted.

'I don't know anything you can't,' William smiled.

'I'm still suffering from the night we killed the Chaunter. I feel such guilt . . . it is heavy on my soul.'

'Him? Christ Jesus, that was such a long time ago,' William exclaimed in genuine astonishment. 'I haven't counted the men I've killed since then. Why on earth does his death worry you?'

'Because it was murder, Will: murder! We set upon him, we bribed others to help us, and we murdered him,' Henry said wearily. 'It was a foul deed.'

'Pah! It was nothing.'

'I am going to be dead soon, and before I die, I want to confess my crimes.'

William shrugged. Then he leaned forward, and the other grin was on his face again, the cold, dead grin of the murderer. 'That's fine; you do that. But don't recall any other names, will you, Master Saddler? Because if I heard you were trying to fix *me* at the same time, I'd see if I could keep you screaming even longer than my record. Eh? You understand me? For you, a confession will hurt a bit, but for me, it could mean me being thrown out of the Priory. I don't want to lose my corrody, Saddler. So keep my name out of anything like that. You understand me?'

John Coppe watched his friend the porter. They were at the gate again, and Janekyn was busying himself about the place, watching all those who were passing through, ever alert to the sight of known cutpurses or men or women of ill-fame who might enter either to rob or solicit for business.

Janekyn was a remarkably calm man. Sparing of words, he was nonetheless kindly, and to men like Coppe who had suffered in battles, he was generosity itself, always sharing his meagre supplies of food. Yet there was something about the friar which had unbalanced him. At the time Coppe had seen this, and decided that he wouldn't probe and upset his friend, but that was some days ago now. Jan had had enough time to get over whatever it was that the fellow had said. Even so, Coppe was reluctant to broach the subject . . . but his fascination was being fed by the air of mystery.

'You remember that friar? I saw him again earlier.'

'Ah?'

'Yes. Down there near the Charnel Chapel. He met up with one of the Treasurer's clerks – the one in charge of the works.' There was no response. 'Come on, Jan, what's the problem? He said something about there being a murder, and then you and him went all quiet. He asked whether you were a local man, said that was that then, and buggered off.'

Janekyn shrugged slightly, his eyes still on the passing folk, and then he pursed his lips, shot a glance at Coppe, and jerked his head to beckon his assistant. When the lad was standing in his place with a heavy ash staff in his hands, Janekyn went inside and came out with a couple of thick fustian blankets and a jug that steamed in the cool air. 'Who needs cups when the weather's like this?' he grunted rhetorically, and took a swig before passing it to Coppe. It was heavily spiced and sweetened wine, and Coppe could feel the warmth soaking down from his belly to his toes – even to the toes of the leg that had gone so many years ago.

'There was a murder, right enough. It was November, a week and two days after All Souls' Day.'

Coppe nodded. That would be the ninth, then.

'The trouble had been brewing for ages. I was only a lad, but I can remember it still. It cut up the city. The Bishop was a foreigner, a man called Quivil, who was arrogant. Wanted everything done his own way. Under him the Archbishop put in a Dean who was a local man, John Pycot – everyone called him John of Exeter. The Archbishop was determined to see Pycot grow in importance and fame. There were rumours spread about him – that he was greedy, took benefices wherever he could, and never did a stroke of work apart from what would benefit him – but they came from the Bishop. That was the sort of man Quivil was. Always putting down those he couldn't get on with. All the city respected the Dean. We liked John Pycot. The Bishop refused to accept him, and never even acknowledged his position, but couldn't get rid of him. So he put one of his own men in as Chaunter, to sort of keep Dean John at bay the whole time. The Dean was cross, and it led to a fight. The Chaunter got killed. And that's about it.'

'Why the coldness towards the friar, then?'

'He was there; he helped protect that damned Chaunter against the good Dean's men. That friar saw what the Bishop wanted him to. Useless. No, any man who knows this city would agree that the Dean was the better man.'

'Is he dead now?'

'Don't know. He was gaoled for a long while in the Bishop's cells, then forced to take up the vows and go into exile in some monastery or other. No one will hear from him again.'

'Don't you think that the friar has paid for his actions?' Coppe said, thinking of the dreadful wound on his face that all but matched his own.

Janekyn gave him a steady look. 'Sorry, John, I know you feel sympathy for a man like that, but I can't. He fought on the side of the man who helped create a rift in the Chapter. For that I hope the Chaunter rots, and I don't care to drink with those who tried to save him, neither.'

After William's departure, Mabilla entered the counting room. 'I saw him leaving,' she said quietly, nervously fingering a thread on a tapestry.

'He told me I mustn't confess,' Henry said heavily. His wife, he could see, was very scared. She seemed unable to meet his eyes, as though she feared his emotions might force her to break down in sympathy.

Sympathy was a commodity he could not summon up for others. He sat drained, his face twisted and his eyes moist; he could have wept. Both forearms lay on the table before him, and Mabilla felt that William had sucked the energy from him. Even the will to live was gone.

'Oh, my love,' she said. She went to his side and took his hand in her own, kneeling and gazing up at him. 'My love, don't look so upset. The man was only demanding that you protect him.'

'He said he'd *kill* me. I think he threatened not just me, my darling, but you and Julia too. I need some wine!'

'My love, no! Keep your head clear just for a little longer. Don't think of me or of Julia. We are strong enough. Think of yourself. If you allow him to threaten you, it's your soul he'll harm. Don't let him do that. We can always seek protection. There are men you can hire.'

'Darling, he threatened . . .'

'All he can do is perhaps try to hurt you, but we can stop that. We'll get men to guard you, if you want. But his threats are nothing compared to the risk to your immortal soul, Henry. Think of that: your *soul*! If you feel you must confess your sin, then do so.'

Henry turned his head and looked at her. 'I wish I knew what to do for the best.'

'Look into your heart, my love.'

'It's not just my heart, darling. Peter, the acting Prior at St Nicholas's said I should confess, too.'

'Then you must do it, my love. It's your eternal soul. Don't let him risk that.'

'But if I speak to any of the canons or vicars, they'll be bound to tell someone else. The Cathedral is no repository for secrets. They gabble away all the time like old women. If only I . . .'

A face returned to him. A face he had seen in the streets, the ravaged features of the man he had last seen sprawled in the mud at the side of his master. Friars could hear confessions, he reminded himself.

'Perhaps there *is* one man I could speak to,' he said.

Sara was early at the gate to St Nicholas's. She and Elias were waiting for the bread to be distributed, and she lifted and pushed her little son before her, trying to maintain their place among the people who crowded the narrow street.

It was a blessing that the good monks at St Nicholas's Priory issued their alms. Without their generosity many of the poor of the city would die, Sara among them.

No! The boys were reason enough to continue the battle. She might have lost her man, but she wouldn't lose her boys too. And if that meant queuing at the gate to St Nicholas's, she'd be here all night if necessary.

Just then, the bell tolled out, and now she could hear the chain and latch being pulled. That meant the Almoner had brought food for the poor. She'd be able to get something into her belly, with luck. But there were so many people about, she realised, glancing from side to side. What if there wasn't enough food for her, for Dan and Elias?

As she looked and felt the others pushing her forwards from behind, she noticed that the ring of people before the gate was contracting: men and women were forcing their way towards the gate from either side. The crush on all sides was so tight that it was impossible to move her arms, and then her breasts were bruised as she was shoved painfully into the backs of those in front. They retaliated with elbows and backward kicks, and her shins were barked by the boot-heels of the man in front of her as he shouted for people to stop their 'infernal fucking shoving!'

It was alarming, most of all because she knew that Elias was at her side. He had her hand in his, and he was wailing already. She couldn't pick him up, though. He was terrified, and so was she as the mass of people pulled her inexorably on. And then the fellow in front wasn't there. He simply disappeared from sight, and as her mind tried to absorb this, her feet were trapped. She couldn't lift or press them onwards, and the weight of hundreds was at her back. With a scream of dread, she felt herself topple; her son's hand was ripped from her grasp, and she tumbled down with her ears seared by the sound of his screams.

Chapter Six

Henry Potell was sunk deep into thought as he walked from his house. He knew that he ought to confess his offences before God before he died – but he was concerned that he would be hastening his death, were he to try to speak to Nicholas Friar and William got to hear of it.

Mabilla was convinced that he must confess, and she seemed confident that William would pose no genuine threat. Henry had wondered at that for a moment. She had once known William very well, when she was younger . . . but there was no point doubting her. She was his wife; she'd been loyal to him for years.

'Christ!' he muttered. The prospect before him was not one to inspire cheerfulness.

Still, he must persevere. Fear of William's retribution was one thing: his fear of God's wrath was infinitely more pressing. He would find poor, scarred Nicholas and beg forgiveness – but first he would go to the Cathedral and offer a prayer to show how sorry he was to have participated in the murder. It couldn't hurt.

He stopped at the entrance to the Fissand Gate and peered down at the Cathedral. It looked so forbidding, he was tempted to turn around and go straight home again. The scaffolding which rose about the truncated walls looked eerily like giant polearms, as though God had sent a force of great angels to capture him and harry him down to hell. The thought was enough to make the saddler feel sick.

Right in front of him was the Charnel Chapel, a plain block, pointing towards the Cathedral's western front, with a pair of doorways. One gave into the chapel itself, while the second opened onto a flight of steps which led down to the undercroft where the bones were neatly stored.

Henry shivered with revulsion, not because of the remnants of the dead, but because this undistinguished charnel block was the site of his greatest sin.

At the time it had seemed so simple, so straightforward. John Pycot the Dean was a local man, from Exeter, and Henry had believed him to be the better judge of what was best for the Cathedral, rather than some outsider like Quivil. Just because he'd been made a Bishop didn't make the man infallible. And anyway, everyone knew perfectly well that he didn't even have the support of his own Archbishop. It was only natural that when Quivil went and installed Walter de Lecchelade as his henchman and spy to counteract the beneficial influence of Dean John, that Lecchelade himself should become the target.

For Henry it was a matter of his personal belief in and allegiance to the Dean. John was an endearing man, the sort of fellow who could easily instill trust in a youth. He was interested in Henry, treated him with politeness and respect, which wasn't normal for an apprentice saddler. Usually they were granted a level of disdain which fell only slightly short of contempt.

It was that easiness in the presence of other Exeter folks that endeared Dean John to so many, although others were keen to help him from less worthy motives. Henry knew that some, like Peter, were determined to slaughter Walter Lecchelade to further their own ambitions, aware that they'd be more secure if they helped their Dean to put this foreign Bishop firmly in his place.

Even those who sought political advantage were preferable to the others, who were only in it for the money; they repelled Henry just as they must any man with a conscience. He had no dislike of money, naturally enough; money was essential for any man, but some would betray their own master for financial gain.

As he had this thought, he swallowed his anxiety and forced himself onwards. At the gate itself he saw the beggar, John Coppe, sitting at his accustomed post; he threw him half a penny, as though that small donation could in some way redeem him for the harm done to Nicholas by his companions while the Friar was trying to defend his master. It was a strange coincidence, that Coppe too had lost his right eye in a sweeping blow which had raked down his face from temple to jaw.

The darkness of the narrow gateway always gave Henry the curious sense of some gloomy region that wasn't quite of this world; entering the tall houses on either side prevented the sun from reaching the cobbles. And then suddenly he was out in the wide expanse of grass which was the Close, confronted with the mass of the Cathedral itself. It was an exciting moment, and just as he always had been, Henry was impressed. Even with the scaffolding about the sections of wall that were still being erected, even with the mess of builders and masons and all the labourers lying at its foot, the Cathedral was a marvellous, living entity, a symbol of God but also a growing proof of Exeter's own importance.

As he strode along the grass among the workmen, he heard a voice address him.

'Master Saddler! I *am* pleased to see you again.'

'Udo . . . I am glad to see you, too,' Henry said with a sinking heart.

Thomas was at an inn when the commotion began.

There was a clear, tinkling noise like a bell, and then he heard voices shouting. A bellow roared out, followed by a scream and then a rumbling noise . . . He quickly downed his quart of ale and went out after the other patrons into the street.

The row seemed to be coming from the entrance to the Priory. As Thomas hurried up Fore Street he joined a gang of children who were capering along too, and some women. Even a few hawkers who apparently had little better to do were giving in to their curiosity. All those with more urgent things to do were already over beyond Carfoix, Thomas said to himself moodily.

Further up the street, the crowd increased, and soon Thomas could not see the Priory gate itself for the press of men and women thronging the path.

The screams were much louder now, and made the blood run cold. Necks craned, there were confused shouts and then the press of people parted as the first of the wounded appeared – a girl, eyes wide in terror, arms outstretched, pushing and wailing, desperate to get away. Thomas grabbed her arms and tried to calm her, to get her to explain what had happened, but she only mewed like a cat, and as soon as she could, pulled away and bolted past him.

People were suddenly melting away, and Thomas barged on-wards, not certain why, but convinced that he must get forwards, to the front.

Later it became clear what must have happened, but at that moment, when he reached the Priory's wall, he gasped in shock as he, and those around him, found themselves confronted by the pile of bodies.

So many, he found it hard to believe. Some at the top were still twitching, but those beneath were still, their eyes open, blood dripping from scratches and scrapes, hands and feet mingled in a hideous mound of death. All about there was a strange, tragic silence.

Thomas doubted that there could be any survivors in that monstrous heap, and yet someone must make sure. Reaching for the first, he tentatively pulled at the scrawny ankles until the thinly dressed figure of a girlchild of maybe nine years fell on the cobbles before him – a pretty little waif, with round face and fair hair. 'My God!' he exclaimed, his throat constricted with the horror, and reached for the next. '*Help me*!'

Other willing hands were soon at work, and they began hauling bodies aside. Some were still breathing, and these they set apart, but the dead were the larger group, and it was easy to see why. They were all malnourished, the children with rickets, the adults with the yellow or grey skin that spoke of illness and hunger.

It was when he had pulled the fourth body from that obscene mound that he found Saul's wife, poor Sara.

Udo extended his hand and nodded to the saddler.

'I . . . er, I'm pleased to see you so well,' Henry stammered.

'Ja, well, your physician is very good,' Udo said with a grimace. 'He bled me twice, and assures me I can expect to have a full recovery.'

'I am very glad to hear it!' Henry said effusively.

Udo glanced at him. 'It was exceedingly painful,' he noted.

God in heaven, but how painful he could never describe. The physician, Ralph of Malmesbury, had arrived with two assistants, both carrying large leather bags filled with the tools of their trade. Almost as soon as he entered Udo's hall, he subjected the room to a cursory investigation, and only when he had noted Udo's silver plate and the pewter jug and goblet on the table at his side did he show any desire to study the patient himself. Blasted physicians always wanted to make sure a man could pay before bothering to exert themselves.

'I understand you fell from your horse?' Ralph began. He was a chubby fellow, with bright blue eyes set rather too close for comfort, and hair of a faded brown, like a fustian cotte that had been washed too many times. His chins wobbled softly whenever he nodded his head, which he did a great deal as though everything Udo said was merely confirming his initial opinion.

'*Ja!*' Udo had grunted, the pain still overwhelming. 'The *verdammte* saddle broke!'

'I see. You put your arm out to break your fall, of course? Yes, as I concluded. It is a simple enough case, then. It is either a broken arm or a badly dislocated one. There is no bleeding?'

'Not that I've noticed.'

The physician was nodding and looking bored, as though this matter was so simple and lacking in professional interest as to be almost beneath his skills. He motioned to his assistants. 'Remove his shirt.'

At least these two were gentle enough. They gradually tugged the shirt from his shoulders and eased it from him until Udo was bare-chested. He glanced at his shoulder and saw how swollen and sore it looked. 'Can you—'

'My dear fellow, a barber could mend this!' Ralph smiled. 'Now, we shall need a good strong piece of wood. A lance would be ideal, but anything of that dimension would be fine.'

Udo could remember the rest of that day with perfect clarity. Apparently the operation was most straightforward. That was what the physician said. They had set Udo kneeling on his table, one assistant in front, the other behind, both holding a long wooden pole over their shoulders, which passed beneath Udo's underarm. The physician gripped his wrist, and then, eyeing his patient speculatively, he yanked down with all his weight while the assistants pushed upwards. Udo shrieked with the agony of it, trying to stand and wrench his wrist from the damned physician's grasp, but he could do nothing while the assistants raised the pole under his arm. And then, suddenly, there was a strange, painful, and yet noticeably *right* crunch. Something slipped sideways or backwards, or something, and although there was a sharp stabbing for a moment, instantly he felt indescribably improved. '*Mein Gott!*'

'I felt that!' the physician smiled, leaving go his hold.

The pole was removed and Udo flexed his hand. There was a sensation of pins and needles, but the feeling was already returning. His shoulder was painful, yes, but already he could move his arm a little without agony.

'Very good, master. I am glad to have been able to help you,' the physician said. 'Now, is there anything else I can do for you? I specialise in hernias and haemorrhoids,' he added hopefully.

Udo shook his head slowly, unwilling still to jolt his renewed arm. 'I need nothing more. You may present your bill to Henry Potell the saddler.'

'So he informed me. Very well. I thank you.'

Ralph had gestured to his assistants, who had packed their bags and taken them and their pole away. Soon Udo was left alone in his hall, flexing his hand and wondering how much that short course of treatment would end up costing the saddler.

There had been plenty of time to muse over his misfortune that day. He had gone to buy the damned saddle only because he wished to get to know the Potell family better, and introduce himself to their daughter Julia; instead he had hurt himself, scared Henry with talk of suing him, and probably petrified his wife Mabilla and the girl into the bargain! Udo had several times thought of going to the saddler's house in the last days to put things right, but somehow he had never quite summoned the courage.

This appeared a perfect time to talk to Henry. They were both away from home, there was no reminder of that disastrous day, and Udo could perhaps hint at his interest still in Henry's daughter. Yes, that was surely the best approach.

'I have not seen your delightful lady for some days.'

Henry stiffened slightly. 'I suppose your shoulder was too painful to be able to go out,' he said drily.

'Your physician was most competent. I have no complaints. He has mended me well.'

Henry was still apparently reticent. His eyes, Udo noticed, kept flitting towards the Charnel Chapel.

'Henry – Master Saddler – I should like to talk to you about a matter of delicacy.'

'You mean to ruin me?'

There was a depth of sadness in that question and in Henry's eyes as he uttered those words which Udo felt compelled to ease. 'Master Saddler, I have no intention of pursuing you. Any man can,' he swallowed, 'be unfortunate enough to have an accident. It was surely not your intention to see me hurled from my horse, so how could I prosecute you? That would be the act of a cruel man.'

Henry appeared stunned. He stopped dead, and turned to Udo with an expression of complete bafflement. 'You mean you won't sue me?'

'I have not instructed a pleader, no, and I shall not, I think. No, I believe that you and I should become friends.'

'I'm sure that'd be good,' Henry stammered. 'But, how can I thank you?'

Udo cleared his throat. 'There is one way . . .' he said hesitantly.

Without realising that she was the subject of a discussion between Udo and her father, Julia wrapped a neckerchief about her shoulders and pulled it tighter as she walked into the hall. Her mother was already there, sitting at her favourite place on a stool before the table, near to the fire. Against the cool of the afternoon, she was wearing her cote-hardie and a blanket wrapped about her, but Julia was sure that it was not the draughts but the family's straits that chilled Mabilla's blood.

'Mother, may I fetch you some wine?'

Mabilla glanced up at her and gave a smile. 'No, I am fine, dear. Just waiting for your father to return.'

'Where has he gone?'

'He has some business to attend to,' Mabilla responded slowly.

'It's nothing to do with that odious man, then?'

'You mean Master Udo?'

'God, no, not him! That revolting old pensioner, Will. I hate him, Mother. He looks at me like a man staring at a piece of meat on the butcher's slab. He has no compassion or sympathy for others. How could Father have grown to know him? And how can he let a fellow like that in the house?'

'You shouldn't speak of him like that,' Mabilla countered, but without anger. 'Your father knew Brother William a long time ago.'

'I've never seen him before. It must have been a very long time ago that he left here.'

'No matter. You should know your father better than to think that he would desert his friends just because they've been away for a long while.'

'Will that German seek to ruin us, Mother?' Julia said after a moment's silence.

'He may not, Daughter. Let us hope not.'

'I had thought . . .'

'Yes?' Mabilla pressed.

'The way that he stares at me in church . . . like a man besotted. And when he asked for the saddle, I felt he was considering making an offer for my hand,' said Julia. She hadn't broached the subject before with her mother, and now she could feel her cheeks flush as she spoke.

Mabilla eyed her. 'You mean you'd consider taking his hand? A man so very much older than you?'

'He would be experienced of things that I'd know nothing about, and he'd be able to look after me.'

'For a while, perhaps. But he would be certain to die, wouldn't he? And then what would you do?'

Julia lifted her chin. 'I should have thought that he would be able to protect me after he had died. I would be able to count on at least a third part of his estate even if there was a child, according to the law, and he might settle more on me if he wished.'

'I don't think there is much likelihood of his wishing to settle anything on you now, dear,' her mother said sadly. 'I had no idea you guessed his intentions. I only realised myself when your father told me of the gift he brought for you and me. Then I wondered. We hardly know the man, after all, and there was no need for him to bring us cakes, but then it seemed so obvious.' She sighed. 'I shouldn't think he'd want to treat us like that again.'

'Perhaps . . .' Julia was hesitant, running the fingers of her right hand over the top of the table, avoiding her mother's eyes. 'I mean, if I were to signal my interest to him, maybe he'd be prepared to think me a worthy prize? Instead of harming Father's business, might he not consider taking me and a dowry?'

'Possibly,' Mabilla said, but now her voice was harder. 'Yet think on this, Julia. If a man was to take you not from love or affection, but because you were a prize won at another man's expense, or rather, you were another man's prized possession, and he took you in compensation instead of another reward, just ask yourself how well he would treat such a woman. Would he cherish you, or merely own you like any other chattel? As your mother I should be wary of letting you enter a bargain of that nature, child.'

It was all too true, Mabilla thought bitterly. A man could take a woman without care, without thinking. If he desired her, all too often he would have her, promising her love and adoration for life, and then disappear the moment any proof of his commitment was needed. Yes, Mabilla knew that well enough. Yet at least Julia was not keen on William. That would have been too demeaning and degrading to consider.

'To live as the unloved wife of a wealthy man would not be so very hard,' Julia continued. 'Especially if the alternative was to live in dire poverty without a husband.'

Mabilla bit back her anger. 'You would be happier living in luxury with your father's enemy, rather than remaining with us if that same man sued us and ruined us?'

'I didn't mean that!'

'It's what it sounded like.'

'No, Mother.' Julia took a deep breath. 'I was only thinking that I should prefer to live with him as his wife if that was all it cost me to see you and Father living in comfort. If the alternative was to see you both impecunious, obviously I'd prefer to marry him.'

'He would be taking you for the wrong reasons.'

'I don't know,' Julia said, and now she stood at the great window, pulling her neckerchief about her again in the draught. 'He was keen enough before. I believe he loved me. Who can say how his heart is today? Perhaps he would still make me a good husband. It's worth thinking about, isn't it? I know how worried you are.'

Her mother grunted, staring back into the flames, but Julia was sure that Mabilla would consider her words. It did make good sense, after all.

'Well? And what is your feeling about this?' Udo asked as he completed his offer.

It had taken him time to work out the best means of presenting his suggestion. First, he had thought that he should perhaps threaten the man, saying that if he didn't agree to let him take Julia, he would continue with suing him for damages – but on reflection, he felt that threatening a fellow in order to be able to take his daughter's hand in marriage might not be the ideal approach. No, it was better simply to present himself as a keen groom to the daughter, and ask for her hand as would any hopeful swain.

Henry stood gazing at him blankly, and Udo felt a rising irritation that this man had not jumped at the opportunity of having him as son-in-law. He had made his case as best he could, after all. He was surely not such a poor catch, was he? This man's gormless stare was insulting. He should be glad that Udo had not threatened him with ruin! Udo had gone to some lengths to explain that he had desired a wife for some while, and felt sure that Henry's daughter would serve him well. She was young and desirable, Udo was old but wealthy. They would make a good match.

Henry cleared his throat. 'You are asking me for my daughter? You want to marry Julia?'

'Of course. It would be a good arrangement, so I think.'

'You expect me to sell my daughter to a foreigner?'

'I have lived in Exeter for many years, Henry. I am more of an Exonian than many others who are members of the freedom.'

'I would have to think very hard. And ask Julia.'

'I am sure she would agree with your advice. She is a dutiful woman, I think.'

'Perhaps she is, but I wouldn't tell her to marry against her own feelings.'

'This would be a good marriage for her. I can support her better than . . . than most.'

'You mean, "Better than you, Henry Saddler".'

'No, not at all. I was thinking of the other men who could ask for her.'

Henry chewed at his inner lip. He was unsure of the best course. Right now his mind was focused on the friar and what he must say to him in Confession. His eyes wandered over the Close until they reached the Charnel Chapel again.

It was a foul little place. Henry could see again the anguish and naked terror in the Chaunter's men's eyes as the first fellow hared down to them screaming that it was an ambush, only to be struck down by the man at the Chaunter's right hand. He fell without a further sound, tumbling down like a rag doll, by a small depression in the grass. Staring about him now, Henry could see that depression again. If he was of a melancholy disposition, he might have considered that it looked like a grave. Poor devil: to be slaughtered like that when all he was trying to do was save them all.

'Come, now. I want your daughter. Will you not accept? I promise to make her happy, wealthy and wise.'

'She's not a piece of property to be bought and sold. She's my flesh and blood.'

'You are a stubborn man, Saddler. I expect you to persuade her, though, yes?'

'I will not force her,' Henry said, allowing a little testiness into his voice. This foreigner was persistent to the point of annoyance. There was a figure near the chapel, he saw, talking to the Annuellar. A tall, thoughtful man clad in a friar's greyish-brown robes, his head concealed by a hood.

'My God,' he breathed. The figure was stooped, one hand ruined, a mere claw, yet he reminded Henry of . . .

'I do not demand that you force her . . .' Udo continued.

Henry listened with only half an ear. The man's clothing was worn and stained from many years of use, but there was something about him. Was he the man who had been attacked, who had been so dreadfully hurt during that night of blood? The friar with the terrible scars whom Henry had seen after leaving Joel's house? It made the blood still in his veins. This was the man he must talk to! If no one else, that friar could give him absolution. If he could hear the confession of the man who had inflicted those dreadful wounds, Henry could be saved. Damn William, he thought. I will tell the truth at last!

'Come! All I ask, then, is that you speak to her kindly about me. She must know I am wealthy. After all, you have been worried, I expect, that I would bring a suit against you.'

Henry had not been listening. Now, suddenly coming to the present once more, he was surprised to realise that Udo was still talking. Then his surprise turned to anger as he absorbed Udo's words. 'So that is it! You mean, I would be better off if I sold her to you, rather than suffer the risk of you ruining me!' Henry spat. 'I would rather see her die a spinster or a nun, than force her into a marriage just because I was being blackmailed!'

'I did not mean that,' Udo stated firmly. His own temper was darkening.

'Leave me! Sue me if you wish, but I won't help you to steal my daughter just to save myself from your threats!'

'I do not threaten. Listen to me, Master Saddler.'

'Leave me alone, Germeyne! I have business with others.'

'Damn you! If you don't listen to me, man, I'll destroy you!' Udo bellowed as Henry stalked away. He watched as the saddler turned. Slowly and deliberately, Henry bit his thumb at him, and Udo felt the blood rush to his face with his anger as he registered that insult. 'I'll destroy you!' he repeated, more loudly.

Henry closed his eyes, shook his head in a brief, dismissive gesture, and stalked off.

It was tempting to grab his sword's hilt and hare after him, but Udo swallowed his anger. His face was mottled with his fury, but gradually as he calmed, he saw the other people standing and staring at him. There was a friar up ahead, a couple of labourers behind him, and a pair of the Cathedral's canons. One he recognised as the Charnel Chapel's Annuellar, who stood quivering with anger for a moment before launching himself at Udo with the speed and ferocity of a rock hurled from a trebuchet.

'What is the meaning of this? You dare to threaten a man's life here in the Cathedral Close, man? You will apologise to the Dean and Chapter of this holy place!'

'I am leaving. It was not to upset you,' Udo said with what hauteur he could muster.

'Remember, fellow – I heard you threaten that man. All of us here did,' the Annuellar said, waving a hand at the group nearby. 'If any harm comes to Henry Potell, I shall see you brought to justice. I hope that is clear. You had best pray that he remains safe!'

Janekyn, the porter at Fissand Gate, heard the curfew bell with enormous relief. 'At last,' he grunted to himself, shoving the heavy doors closed and dropping the huge timber plank into place in its slots.

'That's it! You want some wine, Paul?' he asked.

The young Annuellar from St Edward's Chapel had arrived to help with the gates. As usual, he looked rather drawn, Janekyn thought. Maybe the fellow needed a break from his routines. He had the appearance of one who fasted too often and too rigorously. Janekyn often used to offer food and wine to the choristers who seemed to need it most, and tonight he was tempted to do the same for Paul.

Paul shook his head. 'I'm off to the calefactory. It's bitter tonight.'

' 'Tis cold enough to freeze the marrow in your bones while you live,' Janekyn agreed.

Aye, it was ferociously cold, and the stars shining so merrily in the sky hinted that it wouldn't get any warmer. The porter had often noticed that when the clouds were up there, they seemed to behave like a blanket over the world, keeping the area a little warmer, but that was a forlorn hope now.

'Are you well?' Janekyn asked gently as the Annuellar stood as though lost in thought.

'Yes. I think so.'

'What is it, then? Your face would curdle milk.'

'Is it that obvious? Well, I'll tell you. Earlier I saw the German arguing with Henry the Saddler. They were rowing about young Julia, I think.'

'Udo wants her?' Janekyn pulled the corners of his mouth down. 'I can't blame him. Who wouldn't?'

'When Henry parted from him, Udo said he'd ruin Henry – no, not that – he said he'd *destroy* him. I was quite angry to hear such words in the Close.'

'Did Henry strike him or anything?'

'No. He left soon afterwards, walking off with a friar – you know, that man with the terrible scars?'

Janekyn nodded slowly. That description fitted only one person.

As the youth left him, Janekyn finished the last of his chores. He set his brazier back in the middle of the floor, snuffed the three candles at his table, leaving only the one in his bone-windowed lantern, and tidied his room, unrolling his palliasse and spreading his blankets over it. He had a pottery vessel, which he now filled with hot water from the pot over his fire, stoppered it and put it amongst the bedding to keep it warm. Then he settled down with his last cup of wine, and sipped the hot drink.

He had consumed only half when there was a splattering of gravel at his door, and a hasty banging. 'Jan, come quickly!' shouted a voice.

Suspiciously he opened his door and peered outside. Recognising Paul, he demanded, 'What are you doing back here?'

'Help, Jan! Please come and help me!'

'In God's name, what is the matter, boy? I'm ready for my bed!' Then his eyes widened as he saw the blood that clotted the boy's hands and breast.

'It's Henry! He's been murdered! Oh God, a murder in our Close! Jan, what can we do?'

Chapter Seven

Dean Alfred eyed the body unhappily. 'Ahm – what was the man doing here, Stephen?'

'If we knew that, Dean, we'd perhaps be able to guess why he was dead,' the Treasurer commented with a degree of asperity.

'But someone must have seen him come in. Who is he? He seems familiar.'

'He's the saddler from Smythen Street,' Stephen said. He stared down at the body again, shaking his head. In God's name, the last person who should be in a position of power was the Dean. If only the Bishop were here. The Dean had done well enough over the unpleasant matter of the murder of the glovemaker* some while ago, but this was a different affair, surely.

The Dean stepped delicately around the body. 'My heavens, but it is cold in here, isn't it? This – ah – Charnel Chapel makes a man think of death just by feeling the chill.'

Stephen glanced at him with distaste, then turned back to Janekyn. 'Porter, the Annuellar found him here, did he?'

'Yes, Treasurer. It was Paul here, wasn't it, lad?'

The fellow was not an impressive sight, shivering in the doorway, but Stephen couldn't fault him for that. He had been given the shock of his life when he found Henry's body. 'Tell me again what happened.'

'I had helped Jan to lock and bar the gate, and was on my way to bed. It took me past the chapel here, and I saw that the door was ajar. I . . . I didn't want to enter, sir.'

'That is understandable,' Stephen said drily. Not many would want to pass through the graveyard itself after dark and alone. No matter how often a man taught logic and common sense, local men would

* See *The Boy-Bishop's Glovemaker*

continue to believe the old superstitions; ghosts must wander about the world. The worst place was this charnel house with its concentration of mouldering bones. No doubt the older members of the Choir had been enthusiastically dinning terrible stories into all the others until they'd only go out at night in gangs of two or three. 'Yet you did. Why?'

'I thought that if someone had been in to steal the cross or plate, I should make sure that the Dean was told as soon as possible, sir.'

'Most commendable,' Stephen said. The fellow might be telling the truth at that. Or he might have gone in there to steal a gulp of Communion wine. It wasn't unknown.

'When I entered, I tripped over him, sir. It was dark and I just fell over him,' Paul said, his eyes moving once more to the body which lay only a few feet from the doorway.

'Quite – ah, yes,' the Dean said at last. 'Hmm. And that is how you got his blood on you?'

The Annuellar looked like he was going to be sick. 'Yes.'

'So how could this have happened?' the Dean murmured to himself. 'We shall have to investigate.'

'The Coroner has been summoned, but I understand he is off at another death,' Stephen said. 'He may be away for a day or two.'

'A sad loss,' the Dean said.

There was no flicker of amusement on his face, but Stephen knew why his tone had such a depth of irony. The Dean and the new Coroner had never seen eye to eye. The Cathedral had its own rights and liberties, but the Coroner, who had been given his position to replace poor Sir Roger de Gidleigh, who had been killed during a rising early in the year, was ever trying to impose the King's rules on the place. Issuing commands was no way to persuade the Dean that cooperation was to their mutual advantage.

'Perhaps, then, we should be entitled to ask for assistance from another quarter,' the Dean mused, and Stephen was struck, not for the first time, that when the Dean wished it, he could speak quite normally without his damned annoying hmms and hahs.

He eyed the Dean shrewdly. 'What are you plotting, Dean?'

'I plot nothing. I just – ah – wonder whether we ought to aid the good Coroner by asking for help from people who have already proved their use to the Church.'

'You mean the Keeper.'

'He did – um – help before,' the Dean agreed.

When the call came, Sir Baldwin Furnshill was already in a foul mood, and the messenger who found him grooming his rounsey at the stableyard behind his little manor house was somewhat shocked by his reception. Baldwin was not by nature captious, but when the messenger arrived he was not his usual self.

That morning his wife Jeanne had in jest accused him of watching one of their servants over-closely, and he had denied it angrily – and guiltily. The young servant-girl had reminded him so much of the woman he had met while returning from pilgrimage in Santiago de Compostela in Galicia, and the shame of his adultery still poisoned his soul.

It wasn't his wife's fault – he knew that. In God's name, his crime was entirely his own responsibility. No one else could be blamed – certainly not poor Jeanne. Baldwin had been close to death, and when he recovered, he had seduced the woman. She was married, as was he, but they had both been lonely and desperate – she because her man was incapable of giving her children, he because of his brush with mortality. Both had taken comfort in the way that men and women will.

That was Baldwin's view, after rationalising his behaviour over the weeks, and he was not of a mood to reinvestigate his motives just now, so when Jeanne joked at his apparent interest in the new maid, he had responded with anger sparked by his own shame.

'What?' he had shouted. 'You accuse me of trying to get the wench to lie with me? I've been gone all these months, and now I'm home you seek to watch over my every gesture like a gaoler?'

He should have gone to her and comforted her, hugged her and reassured her of his love for her. That was what he would have done before, but today, even as her eyes reflected her shock and hurt, he could not do so. That would be hypocrisy, for he *had* been comparing the new girl with his lover, and the thoughts of her, with her long dark hair like a raven's wing enveloping him as she gently moved above him were still too sweet. He couldn't embrace Jeanne while thinking of another woman.

So she had turned and left the room with pain in her eyes that he should have sought to wipe away, and he, foolish and clumsy in his shame, went out to take comfort in the only way he knew, riding his horse until both had built up a powerful sweat and he had exorcised his guilt for a while. Now he was grooming the mount, swearing to himself under his breath while he wondered how to ease his wife's feelings of hurt.

The relationship of a man with his mount was much more easy than that of a man with his wife. A woman could be demanding, petulant, irrational. Horses needed food and drink, but beyond that were biddable and easy to understand. How could a man understand a wife? Even Jeanne, the most quick-witted, intelligent and loving woman he had ever met, was still prone to ridiculous comments.

No, that wasn't fair. Baldwin knew he was just trying to excuse his own behaviour. It was he who was at fault, not Jeanne. And suddenly he had a flare of insight as he brushed at the rounsey's flank, and his brush was stilled in his hand.

'Great, merciful heaven,' he breathed.

When he had first met Jeanne, she was a widow, but she had often remarked that she never missed her first husband, because he was a bully and had lost his affection for Jeanne. He berated her, insulted her before his friends, and had taken to striking her – all because their marriage wasn't blessed with offspring. Suddenly Baldwin understood that her pain this morning was because she thought that he might grow like her first husband, and with that thought he was about to go to her and apologise, beg forgiveness and plead with her to understand that he adored her still, when the clatter of hooves announced a visitor.

'Yes, I am Sir Baldwin,' he repeated testily when the rider held his message a moment longer than necessary.

'I am sorry, sir. I had expected to find you in your hall at this time,' the fellow said, eyeing Baldwin's scruffy old tunic doubtfully.

Baldwin grunted and snatched the letter from him. Just then, a stableboy who had heard the noise, ran out to see who had arrived but slipped in a damp pile of leaves and fell on his rump on the cobbles.

'Let that be a lesson not to take too much interest in matters which don't affect you,' Baldwin said as he slowly read the page. 'In the meantime, fetch a broom and clear the leaves before a horse falls and breaks a leg.' He read on. 'Why does the good Dean ask me to attend on him in Exeter?'

'It is a murder, Sir Baldwin. A man has been killed.'

'I see,' Baldwin said, and he had to make an effort not to show his relief at the offered escape. 'Well, I shall have to loan you a fresh horse.'

'This one will be fine to take me back to Exeter in a little while, sir.'

'Yes, but you'll need a fresh mount to get to Tavistock, lad.'

Simon Puttock, a tall man of seven and thirty with the dark hair and grey eyes of a Dartmoor man, slammed the door behind him and strode out into the chill air, pausing a moment to stare out over the harbour.

It was a typical Dartmouth morning in late September. The rain was coming in from the sea. He pulled his cloak more closely about his shoulders as he surveyed the ships sheltered in the harbour, the men loading or unloading cargo, the heavy bales of merchandise almost bending them double. Some carried spices, some dyes, others hauled on ropes operating the hoisting spars, lifting heavier goods, the barrels of wine and salt from the King's French possessions. The port was a thrusting little township with its own charter, and the scurrying men down there at the waterfront proved that the town was thriving financially.

Which was all to the good, because that meant more money for his master, the Abbot of Tavistock.

It was many years since Simon had first joined the Abbot. He had previously worked at the Stannary castle at Lydford, acting as one of the bailiffs who struggled to keep the King's Peace over his extensive forest of Dartmoor, preventing the tinminers from overrunning every spare field, diverting every stream, thieving whatever they could in order to win more tin from the peaty soil, or simply threatening to use their extensive rights to extort money from peasants and landowners alike. One of their favourite games was to say that they thought they might find tin under a farmer's best piece of pasture; only desisting when offered a suitable bribe.

Those years had been his happiest ever. He had seen his daughter grow to gracious maturity; he had buried one son, Peterkin, but his wife had conceived and now he had another to carry on his name. Yes, his life at Lydford, while busy and at times taxing, had been very rewarding. Which was why he now suffered like this, he told himself ruefully.

'God's Ballocks!' he muttered, and turned to stride along Upper Street until he came to an alleyway. Here he turned and trod over the slippery cobbles down to Lower Street, and along to the building where he could meet his clerk.

The room where his clerk awaited him was large, and the fire in the middle of the floor was inadequate for its task.

'Oh, Bailiff! A miserable morning, isn't it, sir?'

Andrew was a Dartmoor man too, but there was no similarity between them in either looks or temperament. Simon was powerfully built, his frame strong and hardened from regular travelling over the moors. He was only recently returned from a pilgrimage to Santiago de Compostela with Baldwin; during which period he had lost much of his excess weight. In contrast, Andrew was chubby. He looked much younger than his sixty-odd summers, and still had the twinkling, innocent eye of a youth, whereas Simon's expression was more commonly sceptical, having spent so many years listening to disputes and trying to resolve which of two arguing parties was telling the truth.

This clerk was born to write in his ledgers – and how he adored them! It was enough to drive Simon to distraction sometimes, the way that Andrew would smooth and clean each sheet before setting out his reeds methodically. He had been taught and raised as a novice in the Abbey, and his loyalty to Abbot Robert was not in doubt, but Simon wished that he could have had a more worldly-wise clerk instead of this stuffed tunic. He would have liked a man with whom he could dispute, who would have had new ideas and on whom Simon could have tested his own, but Andrew appeared content to be a servant, never offering advice or commenting on Simon's decisions, merely sitting and scrawling his numbers and letters.

It was the latter which entranced him. Whereas Simon would admire a pretty woman, or sigh with contentment at the taste of a good wine, Andrew knew no pleasure other than forming perfect, identical figures. His numerals were regular in size and position, the addition always without fault, yet he strove constantly to improve. Simon could read and write, after his education at Crediton with the canons, but he saw these skills as means to an end. Records must be kept, and the only effective manner to store records was on rolls. But Simon didn't like the idea of spending his entire life trying to make his letter 'a' more beautiful. If it was legible, that was enough. No, Simon was happier out in the open than sitting here in this draughty, smoke-filled cell with this pasty-faced, rotund clerk with his reeds and his inks.

'This weather is nothing,' Simon responded shortly, and then felt a wave of guilt wash over him at the hurt in Andrew's eyes. The man was only doing his best to be sociable, yet Simon snapped at him like a drunkard kicking a puppy. Andrew was necessary, and he was going to remain with him whether Simon liked it or not.

He was silent a moment, seeking some means of repairing the damage, but then, irritable with himself, he knew he couldn't. There wasn't the understanding in him to be able to make Andrew a friend. He was a servant, nothing more. Simon beckoned the clerk and led the way outside and down to the harbour itself, all the way cursing his miserable fate in being sent here.

What really stuck in his craw was the fact that he was only here because his master had wanted to reward him.

Lady Jeanne de Furnshill was stoic when her husband announced that he was going to have to leave again. 'It hardly feels as though you have been home at all, my love,' she said quietly. 'Richalda shall miss you. As shall I.'

'Yes, well, I suppose it is a part of the duty of a knight in the King's service,' Baldwin said shortly. He looked at her and smiled with as much sincerity as he could manage. 'My love, I will be home before long.'

'I understand,' Jeanne said, with complete honesty and a simultaneous shrivelling sensation inside her breast. She'd known the loss of love before, and now she was to face it again. Perhaps it was something wrong with her?

Her first husband had been a brute and bully; convinced that she was barren, his love for her turned into loathing, and with that, he started to beat her regularly. At the time, Jeanne had sworn to herself that she would never tolerate another husband who raised his fist to her. Of course, Baldwin had not shown any indication that he could do so yet there was a new coldness in his manner towards her, and she was sure that his love for her was fled.

Her sense of unease had been growing, and was confirmed when she joked about his interest in the pretty young peasant girl. His surly response then had shocked her, and she knew that things were no longer the same.

Rationally, she knew that 'love' was a commodity which was greatly overrated. A man like Baldwin would naturally find his feelings withering over time. It was perfectly normal for a man to seek younger, more exciting women when he had an opportunity. That was presumably the reason for his need to go to Exeter.

Yes, rationally she knew all this, and yet . . . she had thought that *her* man was different. She'd thought he still loved her.

He had only been home a matter of a few weeks. Before then, he and his friend Simon Puttock had been on a pilgrimage, during which they had encountered more dangers than Jeanne could have dreamed of. She had expected risks from sailing, from footpads, from the occasional burst of foul weather, but not all three – plus fevers, shipwreck and pirates as well.

When Baldwin returned, she felt as though her soul had been renewed, as if she had been waiting with her life suspended in his absence. She had missed him terribly, and when he walked in through their door, she threw down the tapestry on which she had been working, and hurled herself at him. She saw his eyes widen in surprise, then he staggered backwards as she thumped into him.

That evening had been wonderful. It was all but impossible to realise that he was truly home again, that she had him all to herself. He looked so happy, so brown, healthy, warm, kind and content, especially when he saw his daughter again, that Jeanne was entirely free from anxiety. Her man was home and she still possessed his love. There was nothing more that she desired. Nothing she *could* desire.

And yet soon afterwards, within a day or two, she grew aware of a reticence on his part, and that distance had gradually grown into a gulf. The man whom she loved and with whom she wanted to spend the rest of her life had slipped away somewhere.

She felt as though her heart would break.

*   *   *

Joel was in his workroom when Mabilla came storming in.

'Joel!' she burst out, her face red and tear-stained. 'Was it you? Did you kill him just to stop him suing you?'

'Eh? Wha—?' He was in the process of cramping blocks of wood together in the tricky form of a war-saddle, where the seat rested some inches above the horse. Her sudden eruption into his workshop was an instant disaster. The second block fell from his hands, and the glued edges, gleaming nicely, fell into the grit and sawdust that lay all about on the floor.

'Now Mabilla, what is the matter?' he asked with a long-suffering sigh. 'Oi, you lads, get that wood up and clean it outside. Go on, you nosy gits! Leave me and the lady alone. Vince, get a damned move on!'

'Henry – did you kill him? Who else could have done it! Oh God, what will become of us?'

Joel saw her red eyes and the trickle of moisture that trailed down both cheeks. 'What on earth are you talking about, Mabilla? I don't understand.'

'Why was he left there, in the chapel?'

Joel bellowed for his apprentice to bring strong wine, and then spoke softly to her. 'Look, Mabilla, I've heard about Henry. I was going to come and see you and give you my condolences as soon as I could. I know his death was a terrible shock – I can scarcely comprehend it myself – but *I* had nothing to do with it! He was my friend, for God's sake! One row couldn't turn us into enemies. Look, I was here all night – you can ask the apprentices if you don't believe me. I didn't leave the shop once.'

'You swear? I thought, because he threatened litigation . . .'

'It wasn't me,' Joel repeated.

'Who else could have killed him?' She turned her bloodshot eyes to him. 'Joel, you were his oldest friend, please help me! I don't know who to trust. Oh God, can I trust *anyone*!'

She was staring about her as though expecting an assassin to leap upon her at any moment. When Joel moved to put a comforting hand on her shoulder, she recoiled as though from a red-hot brand, and he lifted his hand away at the last moment, not actually touching her. She looked like a fawn startled by a circle of raches, petrified with terror.

'Mabilla! I am terribly sorry to hear of his death. You know Henry was my best friend in the world.'

'Even when he threatened to sue you? He told me all about it, that he came here and threatened to do so if the German sued him.'

'He was an old friend. Old friends don't kill each other over a matter of business.' He smiled sadly. 'I am terribly sorry, maid. You know that. I shall miss him dreadfully.'

'You will miss him? *I* shall miss him – and so will Julia! She is in her bed still, paralysed with grief, and there is no one can help us. No! Get away from me! Don't touch me!' she shrieked, slapping at him with both hands when he approached her.

'I only want to help, Mabilla. That's all.'

'Oh God!' she said with a broken voice. 'What shall become of us?'

'What was he doing over there anyway, in the Cathedral grounds?' Joel wondered aloud.

'He was going to confess. He told you he wanted to confess, didn't he?' she said, and then suspicion flared afresh. 'And you didn't want that, did you? You've avoided censure from the Cathedral all these years, and then Henry threatened to bring it all out into the open – your murder of the Chaunter with him!'

Joel almost put a hand over her mouth. 'Hush, woman! Look, I had nothing to fear. When he came here, he threatened me, yes, but he was drunk, maid. I didn't think much of it. For the last time, Mabilla, he was my oldest friend. We've worked together for forty years.'

'Ever since the Chaunter's murder,' she said, her eyes blazing. 'Yes, you were there with him, weren't you? Was that why you killed him? You thought he could implicate you – just as William did!'

'Oh, shit.' Joel felt a sickening tug at his heart. 'Poor Henry. He didn't tell William that, did he? He didn't tell William he was likely to confess to his part in the murders? Because if he did . . . that bastard Will would kill his own mother for the price of a pie, let alone to protect himself. *Did* Henry tell him?'

She looked at him again then, eyes raw from weeping, lips moist and swollen. 'Oh God, yes, he did!'

Chapter Eight

Stephen the Treasurer strode along the cloister with a face as black as his gown, and it was some while before Matthew could make his presence known.

'The fabric rolls, Stephen. You have to check them.'

'I can't, not now. You'll have to do them yourself. There's too much going on just now, what with this murder.'

Matthew reluctantly took back the proffered rolls. His canon had never before shown such distress and inability to concentrate. Certainly it was shocking to find a body in the chapel, but murder wasn't so rare, as he himself knew. That the Treasurer should be so alarmed was strange. He threw a look over his shoulder towards the Charnel Chapel. 'No one can think straight today.'

'No. It is appalling to think that the man was lured here to his death.'

'Lured?'

'Why else should he have been here in the Close? Someone must have tricked him to come here,' Stephen said.

'He could have been here because of some business with other people, or maybe he was taking a short cut, or wanted simply to see the rebuilding works,' Mathew replied reasonably.

Stephen stopped and looked at him with keen eyes. 'See the rebuilding? Everybody of any age in this city has seen the rebuilding works all their lives. We of the Chapter are the only people who truly care about the works, Matthew. And as for a short cut – he lived out on Smythen Street, I'm told. This wouldn't have been a short cut in any direction.'

'Then he was here for business,' Matthew said. 'After all, who could have wanted to lure him here, as you suggest? You are not suggesting that a member of the Chapter was so angry with a faulty saddle that he killed him, are you?'

'No,' Stephen said, 'but why should he have been killed here if it was nothing to do with the Chapter?'

Matthew shrugged and was about to turn away when the Treasurer clutched his arm. 'I have just had an awful thought! He was found at the Charnel Chapel, the very place where John Pycot's men killed Lecchelade . . .'

'I know,' Matt said unemotionally.

'My apologies – I forgot you were hurt in that attack too.'

'It is nothing. I recovered well enough. Now, what of this saddler?'

Stephen's face was paler than usual. A man who adored his ledgers and accounts, he was already pale, but now as he glanced at Matthew, he seemed almost translucent. He shook his head emphatically, a hand going momentarily to his brow. 'Nothing, nothing. It's my shock at this killing. Nothing more. No.'

Baldwin went up to his solar as soon as the messenger had set off again, and stood at his chest for a long time before he could work up the enthusiasm to open it.

He had wanted only to return here, but his infidelity had made his homecoming a hollow reward after his travels. All the time in Galicia and Portugal he had looked forward to once more being able to hold his wife in his arms, but then he had almost died, and his arms had embraced another. It shouldn't have affected him, but it had. He felt as though his marriage had been shredded by that one act.

His sword was on top of the chest, and he pulled the blade out partway to peer at the cross carved into the peacock-blue steel. The smith had used a burin to etch the shape, and then hammered gold wire into it. It formed a Templar cross, to remind himself always of where he had come from, and the men with whom he had lived.

Baldwin had been a *Poor Fellow Soldier of Christ and the Temple of Solomon*, a Knight Templar, almost from the moment of leaving Acre when it fell in 1291, until 1307 when the knights were all arrested on the orders of the French King. It was the injustice of the capture, torture and murder of his companions which had led to his returning to England afterwards, determined to seek a quieter life in the Devon countryside and avoiding contact with any men in positions of power. He detested politicians after the French King's betrayal of the Templars purely for his own benefit, and he couldn't trust even the Church, for the Pope himself had left the Templars to rot in gaols, then aided the King in stealing all their possessions.

That was, perhaps, the guiding treachery which lighted his path thereafter. The Pope had been the ultimate leader of the Templars. They owned fealty to no man, no man on God's earth, other than His vicar, the Pope. No baron, earl or King could command a Templar knight; only the Pope himself. Yet he had deserted them to their fate. The accusations levelled against the Order were so vast and all-encompassing that few of the men could present a case for their defence, yet they were not permitted the advice of even one lawyer. Their destruction was assured.

So Baldwin returned to learn that his older brother was dead, and he was the owner of the small manor of Furnshill near Cadbury in Devonshire. Except he was not to be allowed to wallow in his feelings of hurt and misery. Soon after his arrival, he met Simon Puttock, and shortly thereafter he was given the post of Keeper of the King's Peace as a result of Simon's lobbying.

He had been content here in Furnshill, he had been happy as a Keeper; yet there was something that now, when he looked back over his life, seemed to be gnawing at him. Partly, he supposed, it might be due to his marriage.

When he had joined the Knights Templar, he had taken the threefold vows. The Knights were warrior monks, and although they lived as men-at-arms, they also lived apart from the secular world. They had a Rule which had been written for them by Saint Bernard himself, and Baldwin had adhered to it. He had sworn before God, accepting his Order's harsh demands of obedience, poverty – and *chastity*. When he had left the Order, that had been the most difficult to adhere to, but he had recognised his loneliness, and he felt that in the absence of a Grand Master to obey, his other vows might equally be considered redundant.

That was fine, but still he had qualms. And these had magnified a hundredfold since his adultery. It made him feel less a man, more a beast. If only he had resisted . . . but he had not. And now, perhaps, he should confront the whole sin.

His marriage, although built upon love and, until now, mutual trust and respect, was surely foul in the eyes of God? Other Templars had managed to escape the fires and find their ways to alternative Orders, some joining the Benedictines or Cistercians. Provided that they went to an Order whose Rule was more stringent than the Templars' own, they were permitted, once the French King had raped their treasury and stolen all he could from their preceptories, to go into another House. Those who refused and lived were likely to be found begging on the streets of Paris.

He loved Jeanne, but how could she love him, if she were to discover that he had been so false to her?

Hearing a step behind him, he turned and saw his wife entering. 'Jeanne.'

'I wanted to know if I might help you to prepare for your journey.'

He saw, with a stab in his heart, that she had been crying. 'My dearest, my Jeanne, I will not be gone for long,' he said.

'Of course not, Husband,' she said. 'I shall wait your return. And I shall always hold my love for you deep in my heart.'

He thrust the sword back into the scabbard and began to bind the belt about his waist. Unaccountably, her ignorance of his behaviour, and her sweet acceptance of his treatment of her made him feel a sudden anger, as though she was being unreasonable in the face of his own offence.

'Sir, have I upset you?'

Her voice, so low, so level and yet so brittle, as though she was about to break down into tears of despair, made him glance at her again, and this time his anger was washed away by his guilt, but also his recollection of his love for her. 'Oh Jeanne, Jeanne, come here!'

He put his arms about her and buried his face in her shoulder, eyes squeezed tight shut, and muttered, 'Jeanne, don't worry. There's just something . . . I need to think about it, that's all. I am not another Liddinstone, Jeanne.'

She stiffened to hear the name of her first husband, but then she seemed to melt into his embrace, and he felt her arms reciprocate his hug. 'Come home soon, Husband. I will miss you.'

'I know,' he whispered, hardly trusting his voice.

'I love you,' she said quietly. 'Don't leave me.'

He felt his treachery like a blade in his throat.

*   *   *

'What is it, Joel?'

He was still sitting in his great chair staring at the fire when his wife Maud entered, and he didn't hear her at first.

'Hmm?' he grunted, then smiled. 'Oh, it's you. I was miles away.'

'So I saw,' she chuckled. She was a contented woman. Although their marriage had not been blessed with children, she and Joel had been together for almost six and thirty years now, and while she was feeling her age at all of four and fifty, and he no longer looked like the fresh-faced joiner she had married so many years ago, her affection for him had only deepened over the years. He saw to her needs, providing her with money and clothing, and in return she saw to it that his household was managed well and that his table was always overflowing with food.

'Miles away? Leagues, more likely, Husband,' she murmured. She was carrying a handful of scented herbs for their mattress, but catching sight of his expression again, she paused, then set them down on the table. 'What is it?'

'Henry. It's such a shock.'

'The market's full of the news of it. He was found in St Edward's Chapel, wasn't he?'

'Yes. Look, I didn't tell you this, but Mabilla came here and accused me of killing him.'

'What! That's ridiculous!'

'Of course,' he said.

But there was something in his voice that made her look more closely at him. 'You wouldn't have hurt him, would you?' she asked slowly.

'My dear, of course not!' he said more emphatically, and he smiled into her eyes, but when she returned his smile, she saw a blankness there, a space where once there would have been conviction, and she was suddenly aware of a sense of fear.

Thomas had taken Sara straight to her house, carrying her in his arms like a child. She weighed scarcely more than a girl. She clung to him while she sobbed, her face buried deep in his throat.

'I don't know what to do! I can't continue like this!'

'I'm so sorry about him . . .'

They had found Elias's body very close to Sara. The child's arm had been outstretched, as though in his final moment he was reaching out towards her. Thomas had tried to cover the little face, but he was too late and he heard her give a sudden intake of breath, then the low, animal moaning as she shook her head from side to side in frantic denial of this latest horror.

'Sara, I'm so sorry,' was all he had been able to say. The boy's arm was snapped cleanly in two places, and the blood dripped like a viscous oil from the second gash above his elbow where the bones were thrust through the thin sheath of flesh. Yet there was no mark of suffocation about his face, and no sign of pain or anguish, just a terrible vacancy in his dead eyes.

In the end it took Thomas and two other men from the street to pull the young woman away from her trampled child, Thomas himself carrying Elias's slack form off to the Cathedral.

They were most kind in there. Janekyn Beyvyn; the porter at the gate, directed them to a priestly-looking canon, and Thomas recognised the Almoner. This fellow took Sara to a house nearby, in which a midwife lived, and she drew Sara indoors immediately, to give her comfort and a soothing draught. That was last afternoon, and now Thomas was taking her home again after the funeral.

'You have no family here?'

'None,' she whispered. Her voice was rough and raw from weeping, and Thomas found his own breast spasm as though he was about to weep at any moment. He felt appalling guilt that she should have been reduced to this.

When he first saw her, only a fortnight ago, she had been a beautiful young woman. And then came the miserable accident that took her man away from her, reducing her status to that of a widow, and depriving her two sons of a father. The fact that there was no money in Saul's purse when he died meant she had to rely on the alms given by the Priory. Her son's death was a direct consequence of Thomas's negligence in killing her husband. This woman's misery was entirely his responsibility.

They reached the house and he kicked the door wide. Sara moved hardly at all in his arms, and he set her down on a stool while he unrolled her palliasse and spread blankets over it to make her bed. Then he took her up and placed her gently upon it.

'Where is my son?' she asked pathetically. 'Where is Dan?'

'He's down the way,' Thomas said, putting his sore palms under his armpits. 'I sent a man here last evening to find him and see to his safety. He should be all right. Now, I am going to leave you a while and find a little food for you. All you need do is wait here.'

She looked at him. Her eyes were red, her mouth a vivid gash, and her whole manner that of a woman who had lost everything. 'Just send me my son . . . my only boy.'

Thomas nodded, then fled.

First he went to the woman's hut where Dan had been installed. He saw that the boy was well and fed, then hurried to the market, buying pies and wine with the few pennies he possessed. When he arrived back, the same woman who had last thrown him from the place was there again, but this time she was less severe, telling him her name was Jen and even smiling once or twice.

'Thank you for helping her,' she said in a low tone when Sara seemed to have fallen asleep with the exhaustion of despair. 'Sara will need all the help she can get after the last two weeks.'

'I'll do anything I can,' Thomas said. 'But . . . I don't know what I can do to help. I can try to bring food and drink . . .'

'That'll do for a start.'

'She told me she has no family here. I thought her accent was strange. Is there no one?'

'No. You know what it's like for these workers on great buildings. Saul was a good mason, and he followed his master from one church or cathedral to another. This was the latest of the great buildings he'd worked on. Their families are somewhere else. I don't know where.'

'So she has no one she can rely on?'

'No one.'

Thomas nodded, staring at the woman on the bed for a long moment. He would do anything to bring the smile back to her face. That lovely, radiant smile: the one he had erased for ever, just as his rock had wiped away her husband's face.

William stood in the entranceway of the tavern, leaning on his old staff.

The room reeked of sour ale and wine and shit from the privy too, the stench only partly tempered by the little fire in the hearth at the middle of the room. Its smoke removed the worst of the smell, but the acrid fumes attacked the nostrils and throat.

He checked the place. It seemed safe enough. He stepped down from the doorway onto the six-inch block of wood that served as a step, and then strolled over to a bench. A grizzled man, probably only in his thirties, although he looked more like fifty with his pallid complexion and bloodshot eyes, was sweeping up some rushes. The stained and filthy towel tied about his waist showed he was the master of the place, just as the sagging flesh of his face spoke of his fondness for the ales sold there.

'Ale,' William said.

The man turned and surveyed him, nodded, and ambled unhurriedly to the back of the room where a pair of barrels were racked against the wall. He drew off a large jugful and brought it to William, together with a green-painted drinking horn made of pottery.

William watched him as the innkeeper moved about the place. His slowness was a studied insult to a man like him who was used to the swift service of esquires and heralds in the King's host.

It was a long time since he had been free of the trappings of the King's service. Starting out from Exeter with King Edward I in 1285, he had thought that he might, if he was fortunate, manage to eke out some sort of existence within the royal household.

Of course, that was the present King Edward II's father, Edward I, and life was different in those days. The old man was alarming back then – in his mid-forties, tall, imposing and severe; you were well-advised to keep to the right side of his temper. When the mood took him, he was a vicious bastard. He even ripped the hair out of his son's head in handfuls, so it was said, when they had one of their rows – probably over that vacuous bolster-head Piers Gaveston. Most of their later quarrels were over him.

The old King was a real man. Strong, quick to take offence, slow to forgive or forget, and he could scare any of the barons in the land. He was utterly ruthless, and the devil with any man who stood in his way. Still, for William he had been a good master.

He had noticed William when the latter had explained about the South Gate to the city and how it had been left open. That was during the trial of the Chaunter's murderers, and the implication was obvious to the meanest intelligence: the city was complicit in the assassination. Only with the connivance of the city's oligarchs could the killers have had the gate opened in order to guarantee their escape after curfew.

Standing up like that in his own city to denounce his neighbours, that had taken courage, and the King had seen it. He admired it, too. A man who'd stand against all his past friends to help the King, that was a man of loyalty . . . or greed. Either way, it was enough to make him useful to the King.

Soon after the ending of the trial, when the King left Exeter, he took Will with him. He joined the King's host, and climbed the ladder of opportunity whenever he could. Under King Edward I he became an infantry constable, a post with which he was well-satisfied, and when King Edward II took the throne in 1307, within two years Will found himself a Royal Yeoman. He never was too sure what had led to that, because he hadn't got on very well with the new monarch, but he supposed it was something to do with Edward's needing allies. Everyone seemed to dislike him. He had begun his reign in a promising way, taking over the realm to general acclaim and delight, because he was a tall handsome lad, and people were sick of the austerity of his father's rule. All military clothes and no style – if it wasn't practical, Edward I wasn't interested. The young Edward, however, wanted *fun*!

Actors, jugglers, singers, troubadours . . . all came to see and entertain him, and when he was particularly enamoured, he'd join in and perform with them. At first, this pleased some of his subjects but then a sourness started to settle. His frivolity angered the churchmen, who muttered about his excesses, and his barons looked on him disrespectfully, comparing him unfavourably with his father.

Then came the ignominious disaster of the invasion of Scotland, and Robert Bruce's repulsion of the English at Bannockburn.

Ach, William could remember that well enough. He'd been one of the hungry foot-soldiers there, standing with his pikemen at his sides, waiting, and seeing the knights all go down in the pock-marked swamp. They did not stand a chance. The Scots bastards stood back and fired at them with their bows, then formed into groups of pikemen, the points outthrust like a hedgehog's back, and none of the knights could penetrate their defence. Not that many of them got that far: most fell in the mud and drowned or were slaughtered where they lay, incapable of rising in their armour, their mounts thrashing at their sides with their legs broken in the pits dug by the Scots. It wasn't a good battle. Will and his men had been lucky to escape without a serious mauling.

After that, his star waxed full marvellously. King Edward had granted him the custody of Odiham Castle with the men-at-arms who resided there, twenty-one squires and their pages, even though William wasn't of knightly rank. And there he'd remained, occasionally answering the King's calls to go to war, once falling out with the King when he tested his skills by using a writ of the Privy Seal to thieve a manor from the widow of a knight. He'd won, though, in the end. The King had need of trained fighters, especially men who could be trusted with a company behind them.

War had been good to Will. He'd made his fortune several times, and if he lost it afterwards, well, that was what money was for. He wasn't going to complain.

Still, when he realised that his sore joints and scars were making him unfit to fight, the idea of coming back here to his old home was attractive. Even if there might be one or two who still bore him a grudge because of the way he had fingered Alured de Porta, the city's Mayor, and the Southern Gatekeeper, pointing out that only their incompetence or their active support could have led to the gate being left wide open for the killers to escape. So Alured was taken out and hanged on the feast of Saint Stephen, the day after Christmas. A shame – he was a pleasant enough fellow. But when the murderers had all escaped, apart from the vicars and novices in the Cathedral of course, the King had to pick someone who could be punished symbolically on behalf of the whole city. The Mayor was the best and most fitting victim. Nothing personal.

Will filled and drained his horn three times while he waited, considering again his long life and the many battles in which he had participated, the men he had killed. Some had died in the angry heat of warfare, while others had expired more quietly in little green lanes when they had least expected it – and when their deaths could benefit him most directly. All those bodies were in his memory, available instantly to be called to his mind, and he smiled as he recalled some of them: the weaker ones who pleaded with him; those who tried to flee; those who brazened it out, lying to him in order to secure their freedom.

Some of those were the most memorable. All had helped him. While he removed their lives, he also took their purses.

Only when the third horn was empty did he hear the door open and, glancing up, see the figure he expected. 'At last.'

'I can't drink that stuff. I need some wine.'

'You look as though you need more than wine,' he said fondly.

Mabilla stared at him, and her expression froze his blood. It was a look of pure, intense hatred.

'Why do you look at me that way?' he almost stuttered. 'It's me, your William . . .'

'How did you think I should look?' she hissed malevolently. 'I'm a widow now, because of you! It *was* you, wasn't it? You murdered my Henry!'

Chapter Nine

Baldwin had made his journey with a joy-filled heart, glad to be out and working again. It felt so good to ride the muddy roadways, smell the fresh, damp soil, feel the warmth of the sun on his flank, the sensation of swaying with his rounsey as the massive beast moved with him – and yes, to be away from the petulance and confusion of married life.

He rode down the road south to Thorverton, and here was tempted to cross the river at a convenient ford and approach Exeter from the north, but he changed his mind when he saw the Exe. He hadn't realised how full the river had become recently, and the sight of the broad floodplain told how foolish he would be to try to cross so far north. In preference he headed south to Brampford Speke. Here the river was a little lower, and he could test it, but he wasn't happy with the angry, grey look of it, nor with the fast-flowing waters, and continued south and west.

The River Creedy was less engorged when he reached that, and he decided to follow the road that led west of the Exe and approach Exeter by the great multi-arched bridge that led to Exe Island and the city beyond. With this in mind, he clattered through the Creedy and on. With his delays at the rivers, it was well past noon by the time he breasted the last hill and could see the bridge ahead.

Exeter's bridge was a wonderful feat. Before this great stone thoroughfare with its eighteen arches had been constructed, there was only a wooden footbridge, so Baldwin had heard, which had been appallingly dangerous in winter, and which only permitted people on foot. Carts and horses must take their luck with the ford. In summer this ford was safe enough, but the river had a very powerful current which would often wash travellers away. So Nicholas Gervase and his son built the bridge with funds which they raised from the county, and when Nicholas died, sadly before the bridge was completed, they buried his body in the Church of St Edmund on the eastern end of the bridge.

The structure was massive, and Baldwin always rather enjoyed riding so far up above the river on the sixteen-feet-wide roadway. Today the waters swirled angrily about the pillars below, however, and he was uncomfortably reminded that only solid rock, placed there with human intelligence, was keeping him up. He had never understood why an arch should support a great weight over its gaping emptiness, and now, peering over the side of the bridge, he felt a faint queasiness at the sight of the roiling water. He swallowed hastily and continued on his way.

Having almost reached the city, he wondered again about the Dean's message. A man had died; his body found lying somewhere in the Cathedral's Close. He was not a member of the clergy, so Baldwin assumed that the death could be a cause of some embarrassment – still, he wondered why the Dean should have asked him to come and look into the matter. Surely there must be a new Coroner by now?

As he reached the eastern end of the bridge the stench was foul, due to the tanners' yards on Exe Island; Baldwin spurred his mount onwards to be past it. The skins were left in the sun, soaked in urine in order to remove the hairs, and in the next stage, the leather was left soaking in vats filled with a mixture of bird droppings or dogshit. How any man could wish to become a tanner was quite beyond Baldwin, other than the fact that there was always a demand for leather.

When he looked over towards the nearest works, he saw in among the great vats and pots, a large man with a bow. The fellow stopped, crouching slightly, and then nocked an arrow and drew it smoothly. He paused, his muscles straining, and then released the arrow. As Baldwin watched, it shot off swiftly up towards the river, and the man relaxed. He trotted off after his arrow, and Baldwin saw him pick it up. It had passed almost completely through a large rat. The fellow jerked his hand, and the rat was flung from the arrow, over the fletchings, and into the river. It sank, leaving only a small swirl of crimson. He slowly made his way back towards the bridge.

Baldwin nodded to the man, who acknowledged him with a cheery wave. 'A good shot, Master.'

'Aye, well, a man has to keep them down.'

Baldwin stopped and rested his forearms on the crupper of his saddle. 'It's been very wet.'

The man nodded seriously. 'Miserable weather. Makes the rats all come out, otherwise they'd drown in their tunnels. If I killed one each minute of the day, I couldn't get rid of them all. There are thousands down here.'

'They are foul creatures.'

The tanner grimaced. 'My wife used to hate them.'

'She died?'

'Many years ago. She fell under a horse – a proud clerk rode her down. He apologised and helped pay for a nurse to look after my boy, but it didn't bring her back. Miss her every day,' he added, staring away up river.

Baldwin was struck by his attitude. There was a stoical sadness about him, like a man with a grim understanding of grief who must yet continue with life. He might recognise his loss, but he must accommodate it, not allow it to colour his entire existence.

With the odour of faeces strong in his nostrils, Baldwin chose to ride on. Offering the man a respectful 'Godspeed, friend,' he trotted on. It was with relief that he saw the great square tower of the West Gate appearing before him. He trotted past the church and all the works on Exe Island and hurried up to the gate where he acknowledged the surly-looking porter, before continuing on his way towards the Cathedral Close.

Reaching the entrance to the Fissand Gate, he felt a sudden sinking sensation. The last time he had been here, it was at the time of the Christmas celebrations, and he had been in the company not only of Simon Puttock, his old friend, but also the Coroner, Roger de Gidleigh. Roger was dead now, and Baldwin regretted his passing. The man had been a good, sturdy investigator, as tenacious as Baldwin could have wished. His death was a sad loss, and not only to Roger's wife. Baldwin missed him.

He swallowed, cleared his throat, and spurred his mount onwards. At the gate itself, he beckoned the porter and swung himself from his saddle. 'I'm here to see the Dean. Tell him Sir Baldwin has arrived.'

*   *   *

Mabilla closed her eyes against the headache that threatened, so it seemed, to make her head explode into shards of red-hot bone. It was hard to believe that Henry really was dead: the man who had been the rock of her life, who had protected her, who had given her three children, only one of whom had survived.

Hearing faltering steps, Mabilla groaned to herself. The very last thing she wanted right now was her daughter wandering about the room with her eyes all red and bleared with misery.

Seeing William hadn't helped, either. The man seemed to think that now Henry was dead, he, Will, would be able to step in and claim her again.

'Come on, girl! You wanted me before him, didn't you? It was only when I left the city . . .'

'You expect me to come to you as soon as you kill my husband?'

'Mab! You don't really think I'd do a thing like that? Just remember the good times we had before I went.'

'When you deserted me, you mean. You wooed me enthusiastically, but when you bethought yourself well-enough acquainted with the King's temper, you chose to fly off with him.'

'What else would a man do?' he demanded innocently, his hands outspread, palms uppermost in a gesture of openness. 'It was a career for a man like me. I went there with the King's father, who gave me money and honours. The new King even bought me my corrody, when I was too old to continue in his service with all my wounds. He respected my service to him and his father.'

'And you left *me* all alone. You had sworn yourself to me, and when you'd had your fun, you sought other women. You went off with the King's host and abandoned me. You didn't care what happened, did you?'

'I knew you'd be all right,' he said, the twisted grin returning to his face as he sat back and studied her. 'And you were, weren't you?'

'I was fortunate to marry a good, decent man,' she said. 'Henry . . .' Her eyes filled with tears, and a lump appeared in her throat. A moment passed before she could continue in a low hiss, 'And you killed him! You murdered my man, just so that you could try to claim my body again!'

'I love you, Mab,' he said, but then something glittered in his eyes that was nothing like love. 'But don't accuse me of things like murder in a public room. I won't permit it, woman.'

'You wanted me back, didn't you? Thought I'd be a comfort to you in your old age.'

'I'd *like* to be comforted by you,' he grinned.

That was what made her stand and leave. It was that expression of his, as though nothing bad had happened. He didn't – he *couldn't* – understand her devastation. There was nothing malicious about it, it was just that he had no comprehension as to how others might feel.

Walking along the High Street afterwards, Mabilla had a sudden, terrible thought. She had to stop and grip an upright pole, panting as though she had run a great marathon. *Will hadn't denied killing her man*. He had no sense of empathy with her, because to his mind, Henry was merely a body which had ceased breathing. To him, that was all other people were: animals that walked and talked. Equals or targets. There was nothing else in his simple world.

It was appalling. She was as sure as she could be that William *had* killed her man – and she wanted to denounce him, but daren't. William had no feeling for others. He had killed her man, presumably hoping to win her back, but he would have no compunction in killing her or Julia, were he to view them as a possible threat.

And now she had accused him, that was exactly how he viewed her: as a threat.

Joel stood before his window and gazed out into the street.

Maud was out again, seeking for sweetmeats and other morsels to tempt his appetite. He could have told her not to bother, for there was nothing which could calm his spirit at the moment, but having her out of the house meant he could drop the mask for a while – the mask of a man who was in control and ready for anything. He was Joel the Joiner, in God's name: Joel Lytell – a man of substance. Yet Maud could sense that he was worried and upset. Christ's Cods, it'd take something dramatic to make him lose his love of wine and good foods, but since he'd heard of Henry's murder, he'd had no appetite at all.

That ungodly bastard William! The murder had all his marks on it. Killing Henry in the Charnel where they had murdered the Chaunter

just when Henry was going to confess his part in it . . . William couldn't
bear the thought that his crimes might be uncovered at long last. He
was evil.

It was all because of that damned night so long ago, just as Henry
had said. Forty years ago now. Joel had thought that the matter was all
done and dusted. When they hanged the wrong men, it was plain as the
nose on the hangman's ugly face that the affair was over. The men in
the Bishop's goal languished there for a while, but not overlong. And
by the Fall of Acre, everyone had more important things to worry
about. The Cathedral didn't want to rake up old enmities when they had
the news of Moors attacking and capturing the Holy Land. As though
that weren't enough, that appalling famine followed – when so many
people died. Joel knew four families which had faded away and expired,
the whole lot of them. The Pieman family in particular were sorely
missed. Lovely little girls, they were. Four of them. And they all starved
to death because Hal Pieman hadn't any savings to rub together. The
cost of flour and grain rose so sharply, Pieman was unable to buy the
ingredients to make his pies, and his poor young family suffered. In the
end he hanged himself. He was discovered the next morning by his
apprentice. His children and wife were all dead by then. Someone
reckoned that almost half the population of Exeter died.

No, so many lives had been lost, so much water had passed down the
Exe, there was no reason to suspect that some silly arse might refresh
people's memories about those far-off times. Yet someone had. And
now, Joel felt doubly threatened. There was the story about his part in
the killings, and the fact of Henry's death; if the matter of the broken
saddle were to come to court now, it might well be against him that the
German directed his ire. After all, it was the frame that broke. Joel's
frame.

'Master?'

Joel didn't hear the first calls. He was still standing before his
window, unaware of the breeze that blew in and ruffled the tapestries
and hangings. Such rustling and whispering of material was a constant
feature of life in a pleasant little hall like this, just as the whistling and
chattering of birds and other wild creatures was in a forest. Thus it was
that when Vince spoke his name again, he was startled, and span on his
heel, eyes wide with alarm. He was off-balance, and had to grab at a

curtain to save his fall, and as soon as he had regained his posture, he bellowed at his apprentice.

'*Don't you ever dare to creep up on me like that again, you little shite*! Sweet Christ, it's enough to give a man a heart-attack! You prickle! What did you think you were doing?'

'I wanted to ask if I should make a start on that new saddle for Master Ralph, sir?'

'When I want you to do something, I'll tell you. Get out of my sight! Just go and clear up the workshop. I'll bet you've left it in a sodding mess again, haven't you? Go and clean it all, and I'll come and inspect it. You leave the bloody saddle to me!'

'I was only trying—'

'Shut up! By God's Honour, one more word out of you, and I swear I'll take a strap to your arse! I've never done it before, but so help me, I could beat you to death just now and not give a damn! I'll bet it was you who used green wood to make the frame for Henry, wasn't it? I ought to kick your backside all the way around the outer walls of the city for that, you cretin! Go on, get out!'

Vince scampered off as quickly as he could until he reached the relative seclusion of the workroom, and only then did he turn and stare back the way he had come in bafflement.

Joel had never beaten him, nor even threatened to. And as for the green wood used in the frame – well, Vince wouldn't have used that if Joel himself hadn't told him to.

Henry was lucky: he could buy in a saddle frame from Joel quite cheaply, add some leather to it, fit it out with the choicest decorations, carve and print and paint the leatherwork, and make a vast profit when he sold it. For Joel, though, there wasn't enough money per frame. He couldn't live on that. So instead, he had taken to making cheap frames to sell to some of the other saddlers, the men who were closer to the thin line between legality and illegality. He had Vince manufacture many cheap frames for them.

'Oh, no!'

He couldn't have made a mistake and sold a green wood frame to Henry, could he? The lad winced at the thought. Christ in heaven, if he'd done that, and his saddle frame had broken, he wouldn't be surprised if his apprenticeship was about to come to a sudden end.

* * *

For the Dean, it was a welcome relief to see the tall, dark-haired knight in his Close. He hurried over to Baldwin's side. 'Sir Baldwin, I am so glad to – ah – see you again. It has been – um – far too long. Yes, far too long. Now, may I offer you some hospitality? A little of my – ah – store of wine, some bread and cheese?'

'Dean, that would be most welcome,' Baldwin said, and the two fell into step as they crossed the Close towards the Dean's residence. 'Where is the body? May I see it?'

'It's in the chapel where it was found. Poor soul. I think it is too late to go and see him now, surely,' the Dean said, glancing up at the sky. 'Come and eat and we can discuss what we should do.'

'He was murdered in a chapel?' Baldwin exclaimed.

'Yes. Whoever killed him committed a dreadful act, polluting a holy chapel like that. It shall have to be reconsecrated.'

'Can you tell me what has happened?'

'Hmm. Let us wait until we reach my house. All I need tell you is that the body was found in the Charnel Chapel. I have left it there until the Coroner may come to view it. There are guards about the body, of course.'

'So you will not contest the right of the Coroner to view?' Baldwin asked innocently.

The Dean gave him a mild smile which didn't fool Baldwin for a moment. The knight was quite certain that the Dean had one of the brightest minds in the whole Chapter. Whereas other canons tended to be entirely devoted to their studies, their praying, or their bellies, Dean Alfred was a different man. Used to power, he knew that the most effective means of getting things done as he wished was by ensuring that there were as few interruptions as possible; that meant removing all potential causes of dispute with the city. He was above all a devious, intelligent politician.

'I didn't think that the last Coroner would choose to make an enemy of me, and yet he was strangely – ah – determined to impose his will upon me.'

'He was a good man,' Baldwin sighed. 'He'll be missed.'

'Aye. I feel you are right. His widow has left the city – did you hear? No? She didn't come from here originally, and she has gone to Sidmouth, where her brother lives.'

'Simon too lives on the coast now,' Baldwin said.

'Really? And what does he do there?'

They had reached the Dean's house, and now the Dean stood aside to permit Baldwin to enter.

'He is the representative of the Abbot at Dartmouth. It is a terrible job, from what he has told me. He dreaded being sent there in the first place, because he was so comfortable with the moors and the ways of the mad devils who live up there, the tinners. I had always thought him so sensible a fellow, too. Yet when he was told that the Abbot would prefer him to go to Dartmouth, I don't think Simon realised just how confused and difficult the new task would be.'

'Is it so – ah – terrible?'

Baldwin threw him a sideways look. 'The traitor.'

'Oh!'

There was no need to say more. As both knew, no one could afford to pass comment on the recent events in London. The King's spies might be listening. Yet the whole country knew that the King's household was living in fear. The Lord Marcher, Roger Mortimer, who had been captured as a traitor for raising arms against Edward after a glittering career in his service, had been thrown into a cell in the Tower of London. Astonishingly, as soon as the sentence of death which was to have been passed on him became known, he was rescued.

Baldwin had no idea how he could have made his escape, but escape he had, and the King's men were panicked. Messengers were sent to all corners of the realm from Kirkham, where the King was staying when he heard the news. A small host rode to the ports with Ireland, where Mortimer had allies, while all other ports were instructed to check all men trying to leave the shores. That was the first set of instructions. More recently, Baldwin had heard that there were clear signs that the man had escaped and fled the kingdom, passing into France or some similar land.

This could have been cause for celebration in the King's household, were it not for the fact that Mortimer was reckoned the King's own best General. If Mortimer could summon a force about his banner, thousands of Englishmen would probably rally to his cry. And there were many disaffected men in Europe waiting for just such a call. Men who had been deprived of their livelihood by the King – or, rather, as Baldwin knew, by his friends, the Despensers.

'I think that there are many issues for Simon in a good port like Dartmouth,' Baldwin murmured. 'Both to guard against men who would leave the country, and to prevent others from entering.'

'Hmm, I see. Well, at least *you* are here,' the Dean said as he grabbed his black tunic and hoisted it up over his lap before sitting. 'Please, take a seat.'

A servant entered and brought wine and bread with some cheeses. Only when he was gone did the Dean look at Baldwin seriously again.

'Well, Sir Knight, this is a pretty mess which I have had arrive before me. I am not sure what to do about it.'

The Dean was a lean, ascetic-looking man, once he allowed that habitual expression of amiable confusion and his bumbling manner to drop. This was a man in control of vast estates, as well as one of the largest building projects in the country and many hundreds of men. The Bishop was theoretically in charge, but Bishop Walter was a politician, and he spent most of his time with the King. No, it was the Dean who dealt with all day-to-day matters.

'Who was the murdered man?' asked Baldwin, cutting some cheese. 'Was he to do with the Cathedral?'

'No. He was a saddler.'

'And he was found in the Charnel Chapel? How was he killed?'

'Stabbed. Anyone can find a knife during a dispute.'

Baldwin nodded. 'And you think that might be what happened?'

'It's the only explanation I can think of.'

'When was he found?'

'Last thing at night. The porters had locked their gates, and an Annuellar happened to notice that the door to the chapel was open. He tried it, found the body, and called for help.'

'Did anyone see the saddler enter the Close? You have many gates here.'

'Janekyn up at the Fissand Gate reckons he might have seen the man enter, but he must see hundreds every day. He couldn't swear to Henry having passed him yesterday.'

Baldwin ruminatively chewed at a piece of dry bread. 'There appears little for me to go on. If a tradesman is murdered, any number of men could have killed him – a fellow who felt that he had been unreasonable in a negotiation, a man who wanted to remove a competitor, perhaps a simple cutpurse whose theft went wrong . . . the possibilities are endless. I don't honestly know that I can be of much aid.'

'I should – ah – be most grateful if you could look into the matter nonetheless,' Dean Alfred said. 'This body was found on Cathedral land. I don't want a Coroner to come blundering about my Close, accusing all and sundry of murder, without my trying to discover the truth first.'

'I should be pleased to do all I can to help the Dean and Chapter of the Cathedral,' Baldwin said with an inclination of his head.

'Thank you. It would be an unpleasant thing, to have a heavy-booted Coroner galumphing about the place,' the Dean mused, picking at a chip on his cup. 'They are – um – rarely conducive to prayer, in my experience.'

William made his way back from the Talbot Inn to the Priory, slipping on a small turd at the entrance to an alley as he cut through towards Water Beer.

'Damn all brats,' he muttered, scraping it off, and had to stand still a moment while the shaking overtook him.

He hadn't always been like this. When he had first gone into battles, he had been scared. Of course he had! No one without a brain could first enter the fray without appreciating his danger. It was one thing to stand face to face with some bastard whose sole desire was to shove an eight-pound lump of sharp metal into your face when you were alone in a road or field, and quite another when the two of you were yelling and screaming at each other with thousands of others on either side. It was only worse when arrows and crossbow bolts rained down on you from the sky, and the roar of massed destriers' hooves could be felt through the thin leather of your boots and you wondered whether the fuckers were behind you or in front, and you didn't care, you couldn't take your eyes off the wanker in front, because as soon as you did, his sword would open you up like a salmon being gutted.

War wasn't fun. Will could talk a good story, but at the end of it all, a winner was the man who ideally lost marginally fewer men who were still capable of chasing after the enemy and slashing and cutting them to pieces as they tried to flee the field. That side was the winner. And to them went the spoils – which were usually a couple of boxes of coin, which would go nowhere towards satisfying warriors who'd lost their mates in the last mêlée.

Still, after a while, when Will got to be in charge of a small force, it became safer, and anyway, he got used to it all. And it was fun. And Christ's Balls, it was a good life. All that time in taverns and alehouses and pillaged halls, drinking until everyone was fit to burst. Yes, those were times worth living for. There was nothing like it. The rush as you realised that your side was victor again, the thrill of finding the wine and the women and taking them both until you were sated; that was living, boys. That was life.

He'd had many good times, and even when there was a disaster, he'd invariably managed to be safe from real danger. The only time he'd been close to harm was when the Queen had been left to her own devices, and the Scots had invaded again, sneaking round behind the King's men and threatening to cut off their defeat.

Will had been with the King during that campaign in the summer after Boroughbridge. For some reason, Edward II, who was intelligent and brave enough in his own right, was an abject failure whenever he tried to attack the Scots. Will couldn't understand it at all. Still, there it was. When Edward was flushed with his success at Boroughbridge, and all thought he couldn't fail so long as he had his men at his side, just then, the Scots surprised him at Blackhow Moor, and the King and his favourite fled. Isabella, Edward's wife, was deserted at the Abbey at Tynemouth, and she had to make her own way past the Bruce's men to escape. Luckily, Will had been there with her, and he had been able to join her on her boat which threaded its way past the blockading Flemish craft there to support the Scots.

The Queen lost two of her ladies-in-waiting during that flight. It was a sore grief to her, and Will saw her weeping over them long into the night, but that was nothing compared to what might have happened had they been captured. When Edward I, the King's father, had invaded Scotland, he captured the Bruce's sister and his mistress. Both were held in wooden cages for three years, on the walls of Roxburgh and Berwick Castles. Isabella knew, as well as any of the men and women with her, the sort of fate she could expect, were she to be captured by the Bruce. At the very least she would be humiliated and shamed.

William knew that she had seen how little her husband cared for or about her during that flight. That he made no effort to save her was shameful, and it proved to her beyond doubt that her man considered her as nothing more important to him than a chest of gold with which to buy influence. She was, after all, the daughter of a French King.

It was soon after that war that Will had developed this strange malady. He'd been bled for it often enough, but still it would come back. It was a weakness that sometimes affected him when he had taken a shock. The first episode occurred after a brisk fight just before he boarded the ship with the Queen, when a mace caught him on the helm, and he was felled like an ox. Another man from his force found him and took him off to the boat, throwing him aboard, still stunned. It saved his life.

But since then, and he assumed it was caused by that blow, he found that if he had a sudden shock, his heart started to race, his breath grew short, and his head felt light – dizzy. It was damned strange and inconvenient, but he must learn to cope with it.

That had been the first motivation for him to consider leaving the King's service. A warrior with such a handicap must surely die. There was no possibility of his surviving.

Not if slipping on a child's turd could make him feel so weakly.

He bared his teeth and forced himself to carry on along the alley. Only a short while ago he had been a warrior who could instil fear into the heart of any opponent, but now he was just a sad old man, no good for anything.

The alley stopped and he walked out into the street, along to North Gate Street, and thence to Carfoix. As twilight took over the city, it grew astonishingly dark between the tall houses, and he slipped again on half-seen obstacles. Soon, though, he was approaching the main entrance to the Priory. He should hurry, he knew, because the gate there would soon be closed and barred, and if the corrodian was not there, that was no concern of the gate-keeper.

Hurrying his steps, Will found himself limping a little on his bad leg. He could see the open gateway, and was about to call out, when there was a tinny clatter to his side. As soon as his mind registered the noise, he had just enough energy to hurl himself sideways as the next arrow flew at his throat.

He crashed to the ground, tasting the bile of fear once more, crawling to the relative safety of a rotten barrel and pulling his cloak about him. In a moment the street disappeared, and he was back on the miserable bogs of Scotland.

In his ears he heard again the shrieks and agonised cries. Arrows wailed and hissed through the air, to strike flesh with a damp slap, or to pock at steel armour. Mail rattled and chinked, men fell, hiccuping or screaming, and William waited for the next bolt to strike him, pushing himself into the edge of the lane as though he could re-form his body to fit the cobbles and hide. Appalled, terrified, he expected to die, and he *wasn't ready*!

There were no more arrows. Only the rasp of his breath, the smell of terror in his sweat and the sound of footsteps running away on the cobbles; and then, as the noise faded, so too did his petrification, and he found his soul swamped with vengeful rage.

He would find this would-be assassin, no matter who it was, and he would see him sent to hell with as much anguish as one man could inflict upon another.

Chapter Ten

Simon awoke early enough, but his mind was fuzzy after the wine and ale of the night before, and he lay back in bed, his eyes resolutely shut, demanding that sleep should once more overtake him.

Yesterday had been another day much like all the rest. He had woken, got up and dressed, walked to the hall to meet that pale reflection of a human, Andrew, and continued with his work.

God's Bones, but it was tedious. They added figures, checked the tallies of tolls taken compared with the ships that had come to dock, and more or less busied themselves with little problems all the long day. It was detailed, painstaking work, and Andrew was as meticulous as he could be.

Halfway through the morning, Andrew looked up with a smile to hear the hail falling outside. 'It sounds as if God is throwing His pebbles again, does it not? A terrible time to be out on the moors in this weather. Are you not glad to be indoors with a good fire roaring?'

Simon could not speak. He had listened to the hail with the lifting spirits of a man who remembered that there was a real life out there, beyond the walls of this dreary chamber. He had crossed the moors more than a hundred times, often feeling those icy balls striking his face with the fruitless desperation of a toddler beating at an older sibling. Yes, sleet and hail and snow could grind a man down and put him in his grave, were he unlucky enough to succumb, but Simon thought of hail as only a mild threat. He knew all the places to which he might run in the event of the weather closing in, and all the safe paths which would lead him to a warm fire and spiced wine or ale.

He couldn't even look at the happy clerk who sat scratching with his damned reed all day. Instead he had muttered an excuse and left the room. There was an alehouse three doors away, and Simon entered to find some refreshment. He had a couple of good, meaty pies, with three quarts of strong ale to wash them down, but even that didn't improve his mood. The town was fine; in reality it was moderately more comfortable and pleasant than his last home, with access to food, drink and luxury items which were never seen in Lydford, and yet the work was dull in the extreme, his companion was a pedantic, boring old woman, and . . .

No. It wasn't Andrew's fault. Simon knew that before he'd started his second quart. Rather, it was Simon himself and Simon's family that were worrying him.

Meg was a good, loyal wife, and she'd never have held Simon back, but she was most unenthusiastic about moving all the way down to the southern coast. She had taken a while to get to know anyone in the small, insular community of Lydford, because the folk there had viewed her as a foreigner, and worse, the wife of the stannary bailiff. Nobody would trust a woman who possessed the ear of the man who could have any of them thrown in gaol. It had taken all her skills of diplomacy to wheedle her way into the homes and some hearts at Lydford, and the idea of having to do so again here in Dartmouth was daunting.

His son was no trouble. Peterkin, or Perkin, depending upon Simon's mood, loved the idea of living by the sea. Any boy would want it! What, turn up the chance of meeting men who'd been abroad, who'd seen strange monsters and endured all that the sea could throw at them? They were romantic, exciting men, these sailors. That was what Peterkin thought. Given the chance, he would have been leaping about on boats, chatting to sailors, learning all the crafts to do with the port and generally getting under everyone's feet in the process. Sadly, though, his sister Edith hated the thought of coming here. She was a young woman now, and her fiancé, Peter, a young apprentice, lived not far from Lydford. She had no wish to be farther away from him than necessary. That was why she'd wailed and moaned and complained about the prospect of being sent into exile so far from her home. Peter couldn't go with them – he was apprenticed to a successful merchant, Master Harold – so that was that.

Which was why Simon was so lonely. He had spoken to Meg and they had discussed the move unemotionally and come to the only sensible conclusion: that it would be better for them all if Simon were to come to Dartmouth alone for a short while, to see what he thought of the place, to make friends if he might, and prepare the way for his family to join him. Perhaps Edith would break with her lover and be glad of a change of scene, perhaps Simon would meet other families with whom Meg might strike up friendships – and perhaps Simon could conceive of a means of depriving his son of too ready access to the shipping that lay in the port. The last thing he desired was for Perkin to find an ally who would let him travel to Guyenne or beyond without Simon's knowledge. Sailors could be a dangerous breed.

He rolled over in his bed. There was a growing rebelliousness in his gut, and he remembered the rest of the day with sudden clarity.

After his lunch, he'd returned to his work, but boredom had served to sharpen his mood. He was incapable of listening to the clerk without snapping in response; no matter what Andrew said, Simon couldn't like him, and his temper was not improved by the fact that he knew he was being unreasonable. In the end he grunted an apology, claiming his bowels were giving him trouble, and he walked out. But he couldn't face the empty house where he was living, so he returned to the alehouse.

It had been filled with sailors and lightermen, all the human detritus that would wash up in a port's drinking rooms, and Simon was shouldered roughly as he entered, although a sharp whisper that passed about the place soon stopped that. When people realised that this was the man who could impose harsher tolls, or who could order that an entire cargo be pulled aside and held until he had inspected each and every bale of goods, they were happier to leave him in peace.

He hated this job, as he hated his loneliness. Already this year he had spent months away from his wife during his pilgrimage, and being apart from her again was terrible. He wanted to see Peterkin, to see Edith, and especially to have his wife with him once more to warm his bed. This separation was the worst thing in the world.

It was also leading to this lethargy. His lying abed was not merely the result of too much wine and ale last night, it was also the reluctance to return to that cell-like room, listening to the scritch, scratch of that blasted clerk Andrew's reed.

The work was weighing down his spirits. He would give anything – even most of his treasure – to be back home again at Lydford with Meg and his children. Here in Dartmouth his mind was turning to mash and his heart was losing all sense of proportion. He found it difficult to break out of his torpor, and he hated himself for his idleness. It was so unlike him.

When he heard the cheerful whistle from the hall beneath him, he tried for a moment or two to cover his head with his arms, but then he had to admit defeat as the smell of smoke started to fill his little chamber. Reluctantly, he rose, pulled on his shirt, tunic, cote-hardie and a thick lined cloak, heavy woollen hosen and boots, and made his way to the ladder.

'Morning, Master Simon.'

'Hello, Rob,' Simon sighed. Rob was a young servant whom he had hired on arriving here. A merry fellow with sharp eyes that spotted everything, Rob was dressed in a faded tunic with a leather jerkin. His head was encased in a hood that surrounded his throat, always a good idea in this chill weather.

'Did you sleep well, Master?'

'I slept,' Simon grunted.

'I heard your snores would have woken a sleeping dragon!'

'Then it's lucky there aren't any dragons around here,' Simon snarled. 'Now get me some bread and stop wittering!'

'You had a good evening in the tavern?' Rob asked innocently. He was stirring at a thick broth of oats over the fire, crouched down and keeping his eyes on the pot, but Simon was suddenly sure his whole attention was on him.

'Who told you I was there?'

'All the people here know it. They say you're in need of some company.'

Simon grinned briefly. It was not the first offer he had received since moving here: a couple of sailors had offered their sisters, another, perhaps more enterprising, his wife, if only Simon would turn his back while certain vessels arrived in the port or nearby. Simon had made it clear that he had no need of women. He was content with his wife.

'Tell them to mind their own sodding business,' he said harshly, and maintained a diplomatic silence as Rob ladled some of the porridge into a bowl for him.

*   *   *

Wymond was at his tanner's yard first thing in the morning, same as usual, and he inhaled deeply as with a broad smile he surveyed his little empire.

There were pots and great chambers cut into the ground, filled to the brim with his leathers. He was proud of his rise from impoverished child to this position of importance. Even the members of the Freedom would deal with him as an equal. There was no one else who produced such good quality leather as he, because no one else had such a splendid area for the work.

Exe Island lay at the western edge of the city, and the river flowed all about it, which gave access to a plentiful supply of water. Others had set themselves up as tanners, but some had done so in the daftest places. Old Mart up in the High Street, for example. He had to spend a fortune every year to get water hauled up to his shop in carts. What was the point? He fancied himself important, living up there in the middle of the town, but all it really won him was the passionate hatred of all his richer neighbours, who couldn't stand the smell of him, or the worse stinks that permeated his hall and seeped out to annoy all and sundry. It was mad to work as a tanner in the middle of a city like Exeter.

Whereas out here, away from people, you didn't upset anyone and you had as much water as you could wish for. And all tanners needed lots of it.

He walked about his estate and chose which pits he would work on later. There were some hides which had been resting in his warming shed. They'd been sprinkled with urine before being folded up together. They were left here to help the hair roots rot so they could be scraped off more easily. He checked them, and rubbed a couple with the ball of his thumb. Only a few hairs came away: they could do with at least another day.

Shutting the door to the shed, he walked off to the next skins. In the bating tanks, where the leather went after scraping, the skins were immersed in a warm mixture of dogs' dung. Some tanners swore that birdshit was the best softener, but Wymond was sure that it was the dogs' dung that gave his leathers their natural pliability. All the leathers he'd seen which had used chicken muck tended to be a little more brittle; not quite so pleasant to handle. For his money, he'd stick to dogshit – it wasn't as if there was any lack of it!

The last area of his domain was the tanning pits: it was here that the final result was stored. The first pit was the handling pit, where the fresh leathers would be turned and stirred for days in a weak oak solution, until they reached a uniform colour. Then they were taken out and stored in the other pits, the great ones, where the leathers rested in a fresh solution for at least a year and a day, before being removed ready for smoothing with a setting pin – a long, blunt knife – and then dried slowly in a dark shed with a free flow of air. Tanning was not a fast process.

There were several jobs to do today. He had some skins ready for the handling pit, and he'd get his apprentice to start the stirring and mixing process. First, though, Wymond had a fresh cartload of cattle hides to clean. They'd been brought from the butchers after the slaughtering yesterday, and he had to immerse them to wash away the loose blood and dung. If any had been brined, the salt would also have to be removed. He busied himself with that, feeling the thickness of the pelts, pulling away odd lumps of fat from the skins, before thrusting them into the Exe's fast-flowing waters. Down here he had constructed his own little leat, and at the far end he had installed a metal grate. The skins went into the river and were caught by the grate. There he could pummel them with a club, like a washerwoman with her linen, until the worst of the dirt and muck was cleaned off.

He was finished, and was reaching into the chilly waters to rescue his skins, just as his son appeared.

'Vin, what are you doing down here?'

Vince glanced at his father with a half-apologetic smile. 'Maybe you'd offer me a job if I needed one?'

'No, boy! You're going to be the big master at the city, you are,' Wymond said loudly. He reached out to his lad and ruffled his hair affectionately. 'You'll be Mayor, or master or somesuch! You learn your joinery, lad, and when you have, we'll buy you a small shop to start trading, and get you working to make as many saddles as will fill the whole of Devonshire. There won't be a place for anything other than my son's saddles! Ha ha! With my leather, your wood and Jack's work to finish the saddles, we'll all be rich, eh?'

'I hope so.'

'There's something the matter, isn't there, boy?' Wymond said.

He was a medium-height, thickset man with deep brown eyes that were mostly hidden in among the wrinkles about his eyes. Looking at him, Vince suddenly realised how old he was. Although Wymond still worked as hard as ever he had, his black hair was turned grizzled, with wings of white at either temple. His face was as square as Vince's, but the jowls drooped on either side like a mastiff's, and his face was as brown and rugged as his finished goods. As he put his arm about Vince's shoulders, the boy tried not to pull a face as he caught the smell of old flesh, rotten meat, dung and urine. It was the odour he had grown up with, and he had never been so grateful for anything as he was for the chance of leaving that stench behind. He recalled with a shudder all those days when, as a lad, he'd been sent out before the rakers to find any decent-sized lumps of dogshit, bringing them back in his old bucket, carrying it two-handed because it was so heavy and he was so small. The smell of dogs could still make him want to heave even now.

'Did you hear about the German who fell from his horse?' Vince began.

'Yeah. Showing off, I heard. So what?'

'Well, I think it was one of my saddles that broke. It was one of the cheaper frames that was supposed to go to—'

'You sold off a duff one?' Wymond said sharply. 'Christ, what were you doing? Flogging off crap to your mate Jack so you could make a few pennies at your master's expense?'

Vince glowered. 'No! I was told to make them by Joel himself. He was selling them to all and sundry to get hold of some extra money. I had to knock them up, and then take them round to Jack's master for him to make up. But they were supposed to be sold off for market. They shouldn't have affected anyone in Exeter!'

'What does your master say?'

'He threatened to thrash me, said that the saddle frames were my responsibility and that I must have sold the wrong one to Henry.'

'Then you deserve a thrashing, you arsehole,' Wymond said, and he slapped Vince about the cheeks with a brawny hand. 'What the hell did you think you were doing, playing at being a master, when you're still an apprentice? You need your head bashed to get some God-damned sense into you, do you?'

'Stop it!' Vince said, putting his forearms up to protect his face. He couldn't force his father to stop – Wymond was stronger than him – but he didn't have to take so much punishment. 'It wasn't me, it was him. He's been an arse just recently, since Henry visited.'

'Henry? Someone told me he was dead,' Wymond said.

'That's right. Some bastard shoved a knife under his ribs in the Charnel Chapel – the one dedicated to St Edward.'

Wymond's eyes narrowed, and he looked away. He rested his arm on his son's shoulder again as though nothing had happened. 'That sodding place,' he said. 'Nothing good can ever come out of there.'

'Why?'

'Because my brother and others died there, Vin. My brother, your uncle, was murdered there, and they built the chapel to try to atone for their crimes, but they couldn't. It's builded on shame and lies and the blood of decent men.'

Baldwin had been relieved to find himself back at the Talbot Inn before curfew the night before. Curfew might not mean that all men must be at their homes any longer, but it did mean that the hour was late, and it was the time when certain people with sharp knives and hard cudgels would take to the shadows, preparing to knock some sound financial sense into those foolhardy enough to walk without protection and with over-filled purses. A city like Exeter attracted people of all sorts, and along with the legitimate businessmen were always some who'd be looking for an easier means of earning their income.

Among these, he always felt, were the beggars, and when he walked back to the Cathedral the following morning, he noticed with interest the one-legged figure squatting at the side of the Fissand Gate entrance. He recalled the fellow from the last journey he had made to Exeter, investigating the murder of the boy-Bishop's glovemaker. At the time, he recalled that his wife had been impressed with this man.

His wife. The thought of Jeanne drove everything else from his mind, and he walked past the begging bowl without noticing.

The sun was feebly trying to penetrate thick clouds overhead, and the gloomy light lent a dreary aspect to the Close. At other times, it must have appeared bright and cheery, Baldwin considered as he glanced about him. The houses along the Canon's way were all limed oak and whitewashed cob. Flags fluttered near the Fissand Gate entrance, there was a pleasing colour to much of the reddish-brown stonework and those, together with the green turf, would have been delightful on a bright summer's day; especially when the Cathedral's western front was complete, with all the saints and patrons of the Cathedral carved in stone and set in niches about the wall. Their painted figures would brighten the whole area, with marvellous crimsons and greens, yellows and golds. Baldwin had no idea what the image screen would look like when it was done – and it would not be completed for many years after his death – but he had seen enough at other cathedrals to know how it would likely appear.

Today the place was grey and dismal, however. It wasn't only the lack of bright sunshine; there was a pall that hung over the area, as though the dead man's soul had permeated every stone with his misery and pain, and was calling out for revenge.

It was not just an impression of supernatural despair; the building looked depressed with its cloak of scaffolding, the spars and timbers projecting upwards like the exposed ribs of a putrefied corpse. Where there should have been good pasture, now all was trodden mud, and the whole of the precinct was a building site, with rocks strewn liberally about the place, and masons gradually forming sense from chaotic hunks of stone. Working benches, saw-pits, smiths hammering at red-hot iron formed a fiendish din, and Baldwin felt as though he would like to turn around and leave the place.

But he couldn't. He squared his shoulders and strode to the Dean's house. Dean Alfred was already waiting for Baldwin at his door, and he welcomed the knight politely, if solemnly, before leading the way to the chapel.

A porter was at the door, and he stood aside on the Dean's signal.

'We have to keep it guarded for the Coroner,' Dean Alfred said, and pulled a heavy key from beneath his robe. He slipped it into the lock and turned it. His eyes lifted to meet Baldwin's. 'I wish you luck,' he said quietly. 'We must find this murderer, Sir Knight, before he can kill again. Godspeed.'

Baldwin nodded, thrust the door wide and stepped inside.

* * *

As Simon reached the hall, he could already hear the scritching of the clerk's reed as he stood at the door.

It would be so easy not to enter. He could walk back to the house, pack, hire a horse, and simply go home. See his wife and children. My God, but it was tempting. Anything rather than enter this place and spend more time with that moron Andrew. Christ's Teeth, was there no way out of this miserable existence without upsetting and insulting his master, the Abbot?

Simon felt like a trapped rabbit. He could see safety beyond the circle of destruction that closed in upon him. A rabbit would see the teeth of the hounds approach; Simon could see the years stretching out ahead of him: lonely years of boredom and counting. It was a future to strike horror into his bones, and he felt almost sick at the thought of all that time sitting on his arse, when he could have been out dealing with the stannary's miners on the moors.

'Oh God, please save me from this!' he prayed, and as he finished, he took a deep breath and opened the door.

Andrew looked up from his writing. 'Godspeed, Bailiff. Um . . . there is a message for you from the Abbot.'

'What is it?' Simon asked as he slumped into his seat and eyed the pile of papers unenthusiastically.

'You are summoned to Exeter to help the Dean and Chapter,' Andrew said with a tone of respect. 'You should ready yourself to leave immediately.'

Simon felt a broad grin spread over his face. 'You mean it?' he demanded as he sprang to his feet and crossed the floor. He snatched up the paper and read it with glee.

'Yes, Bailiff. The letter explains it clearly enough. There has been a murder at the Cathedral and the Dean has asked that you go to help him.'

'Wonderful!' Simon enthused, and then wiped the smile from his face as he saw Andrew's scandalised expression.

'Yes. Well, the Abbot has sent a note to say that you shall board a ship here and take it to Exeter. It'll be faster than a horse.'

'A ship?' Simon repeated, his face falling. 'Oh God. Not a ship.'

Joel was pleased with the morning's business as he showed his last client out before calling a halt for some lunch. He bowed and smiled as

Ralph of Malmesbury nodded to him – then walked off without acknowledging the joiner's outstretched hand.

'Arrogant prickle!' Joel muttered, but very quietly. He couldn't afford to upset customers with purses so well-filled as that physician's.

As he finished speaking and turned to re-enter his hall, a forearm snaked across his throat and a leg slammed at the back of both knees. Suddenly he was suspended like a hanged man, all his weight held by his neck, and he reached up to claw at the forearm with desperation, trying to speak or cry out.

He was thrust forwards into his hall and a foot kicked the door shut behind them, before he was hurled to the ground.

'Right, Joel, old friend,' Will said without a glimmer of amusement in his glittering grey eyes. He wielded his staff and brought it crashing into Joel's flank before using it to stab two-handedly at the other man's belly. 'I want to talk to you about assassins who try to kill poor defenceless old corrodians in the evening. And I hope you have some sensible answers for me, because I'd hate to have to kill you.'

Chapter Eleven

Udo had prepared himself as best he possibly could. He wore his finest linen shirt, with a crimson gipon over the top. This was the best he could find in Exeter, a tight-fitting, rather uncomfortable garment, but padded throughout. Over this he had his best cote-hardie, low-necked, with sleeves that ended at his elbows so that his gipon's buttons (which extended all the way to his wrists on both arms, a hideously expensive and rather ridiculous fashion, so he felt) were displayed. At his throat and hems all was lined with beautifully soft squirrel fur, which complemented the pale russet colour of the cote-hardie itself. And then he had his new headgear, a blue felt hood with a long liripipe that curled about his head as though there was a snake resting there.

As he gazed at himself doubtfully in his mirror, he was forced to consider how much foolishness a man must endure to prove himself worthy of a young bride. Take this new idea of a hat with a liripipe. What on earth was the point of a length of material bound about the head like a moor's turban? It served no useful purpose, other than persuading an idiot of a buyer that he should purchase at least double the length of material which was actually required to keep his head warm . . . and that was the whole point of a hat, wasn't it? It was something to keep the chill off a man's forehead and ears, when all was said and done. Perhaps the old King, Edward I, had been right when he had restricted the sort of clothing people could buy. There was little in the way of laws against what a man or woman could wear, but in his day there wasn't much need. People knew what he liked and what he didn't. He liked his men to be dressed soberly, with simple haircuts and no beards. Women he liked to see dressed modestly – until he got them into his chamber, no doubt – although Udo had heard that Edward I was not like most Monarchs in that he was devoted to his wife, and after her death he appeared to have little interest in other women.

Perhaps Udo would feel the same about his own dear wife. If he won her, that was.

The note from Julia had arrived the evening before, and he had read it three times before realising that there was a message hidden beneath the bald prose.

On the face of it, the note was a simple request to meet with Udo in order to discuss the sad matter of the saddle. Udo read that with some anger, for it seemed a bold comment after the way that Henry had treated him, with that bitter refusal even to consider the match of Udo with his daughter. It was an insult that the women should now decide to plead for his mercy, when he knew that Julia's hand was to have been refused him. What did they take him for?

But then he had another thought and read it a fourth time. As he did so, his brow grew furrowed. And then he realised: Henry had died before he could go home and explain his angry words with Udo that afternoon! Suddenly the letter made sense. The women were desperate for a protector, and they now saw Udo as their only hope.

'She knows of my affection for her,' he told his reflection once more in the mirror. 'She holds a regard for me, for otherwise she would not consider speaking to me after the death of her father. Surely his death has had an impact on her – she must possess a deep trust in me to have decided to ask me to attend to her.'

Perhaps, but then again the hard-headed man of business would keep reminding him that at the time of her father's death, it was Udo who was threatening to destroy Henry's business. He had said he might sue him, which could leave Henry's widow and daughter with no means of personal support.

The two ideas: her love for him and his cynical suspicion that she only wanted to guarantee that she had a roof over her head, vied for his attention all the time that he completed his toilet, checked his reflection one last time, and walked along the roadway to her house.

Before knocking at the door, he took a diversion.

As he left his house he could smell the fresh bread from the bakers further up the road towards the Carfoix, where the four main roads met. The odour made him consider: he could scent beef from the pie-maker's at Cook Row, and the odour of sweet almonds from the cakeshop where the still-warm cakes were being snatched up by all those who could reach them. Warm cakes were such a pleasure. Infinitely better than cold. They were a treat to be treasured, Udo thought, and suddenly he beamed. He'd buy some for the ladies. No woman could resist a warm tart filled with flavoured custard.

No sooner had he made his decision than he set off up the hill. Cook Row was at the top of Bolehille, and continued in a straight line towards the Carfoix. Here the shops were set up to display all their wares. Each morning the shutters were dropped from the great shop windows, some hinged down to rest on a trestle, or removed entirely and set out like a table just in front of the shop, in order that all their goods could be spread out to their best effect.

Udo bought a small pie and ate it as he eyed the merchandise in the road, but his mind was already made up. The shop he wanted was the small one halfway along the road with the door gaping; no window, just a wooden board with a rough painting of a cake on it hanging above, and a plain table made from two planks laid over a couple of barrels. A green sheet was spread somewhat lopsidedly over this, and on it were set out the finest cakes in Exeter. That was not Udo's opinion alone. Already a small queue of people trailed from the doorway out into the street.

'Small' was hardly the word for this shop. In another street it would be called a stall, and that would be a compliment. Only five feet wide, it was always hard to get inside, because the customers filled it when Ham opened up. Luckily Ham knew Udo well, and winked when he caught sight of the German. He was a large, satisfied-looking, brown-haired fellow with arms like a labourer's: massive, with short, square fingers. He had the sort of face that Udo associated with brewers – relaxed and comfortable. He knew his job inside out, and loved the work and the end result. Contentment radiated from him like warmth from the sun. Although he was busy, he bellowed to the back of the crowded shop for his apprentice, and soon Udo was collecting a selection of flavoured custard tarts and sweet *dowcettes*, flans filled with jellied fruits. With his purchases made, he nodded to Ham, who winked again and commanded a small boy to take the basket and carry it for Udo.

With the boy in tow, Udo set off down Cook Row and turned right, down the hill, towards Julia's house.

It wasn't far down that alley, he knew. The place was one of the larger shops, not like the cook's, but at least twelve feet wide and a good fifteen deep. That was the difference between a cook and a saddler, he thought to himself. A saddler of Henry's quality would always make good money, although it seemed as though Henry had not recently been quite so successful. Udo was adept at reading a man's status in the city. It was a necessary skill for a foreigner, and to his eye, this place had been in need of maintenance for some little while.

The timbers had been limed, and the plaster covering the wattle and daub between the frames had been whitewashed, but that was plainly a long time ago. Now the building appeared to be in a state of disrepair. The whitewash hadn't been renewed this year, and the timbers had darker patches where the damp had seeped beneath the lime. It was good oak, this wood, and would last many years, damp or no, but Udo knew that the appearance was all when it came to selling a property, and right now, this place was falling in value. It could hardly do anything else.

Udo felt certain, looking at the dilapidated building, that the women here must be delighted with his offer. He hardly need bother to honey his words. He was a man of wealth and status, and his desire to help them was untarnished with greed – it was based upon his desire for companionship, and the result would be a good education for his wife, and a home for her mother. Surely no impecunious women could turn down his generous offer – especially when she herself had asked him to come and visit her.

He glanced at the boy, who was eyeing the basket of cakes with more than mere professional interest, and then rapped sharply on the timbers with his stick before clipping the lad about the ear. 'Keep your eyes and your fingers off those cakes, boy!'

Thomas had watched the men approach the Charnel Chapel. 'Who're they?' he wondered.

Matthew was there with his roll and a reed. He glanced up from his calculations. 'Hmm?'

Thomas pointed with his chin. 'Them at the chapel. There's the Dean and a couple of Chapter men, but who's that knight?'

Matthew stared along the mess of the building site towards the little chapel. 'Oh, him. He's a friend of the Dean's. When we had a murder here some little while ago, the Dean asked him to come and help discover the killer. I suppose he's here for the same reason. That saddler's still in the Charnel Chapel, you know. The Dean wouldn't let us move the body until the Coroner had seen it.' He sniffed distastefully. 'I was surprised at that. Far better, I'd have thought, to bring the body out and store it somewhere else, and have the chapel reconsecrated. It is a great shame to have it polluted with shed blood in this way.'

'Aye. Not pleasant for poor Henry Saddler, neither.'

'You knew him?' Matthew asked.

There was a sharpness in his tone which warned Thomas to be wary. 'Who doesn't get to know a man like him? He was famous for his workmanship, wasn't he? It's only a small city, when all's said and done.'

'I just wondered,' Matthew said. 'There was something about you . . .'

'What?' Thomas asked, feeling the ice settle at the pit of his stomach.

'No, it's nothing,' Matthew said, but then he set his jaw. 'It's just that I had reason to hate him, you see. Henry was one of the men who attacked my master and killed him.' He stared back at the chapel. 'They nearly killed me too. So anyone would look on me as the murderer. I must be the clear candidate for guilt in their eyes.'

He faced Thomas once more, and the recognition which Thomas had feared for so long was in his eyes today. Yesterday there had been nothing, but now, Thomas knew, Matthew recalled him from all those years ago.

Thomas had fled this place, and when he returned, he knew that there was a risk that someone might have remembered him. He hadn't thought that Matthew posed a risk, but poor wounded Nicholas had arrived here, and suddenly all Thomas's careful attempts to disguise his voice and his features seemed pointless.

He had made it his task to ensure that he knew always when the friar was likely to be in the Cathedral Close, and then he avoided the place. He daren't risk being seen by him, for Nick would be sure to denounce Thomas if he saw him. How could he *not* accuse him – the man who had so cruelly scarred him all those years ago and blighted his life?

Thomas found his eyes dragged back to the chapel. A man was hurrying away, and Thomas wondered where he was going in such a rush. That was the trouble with the body appearing there just as Nicholas returned to the city: it meant that men's thoughts were once more on the evening nearly forty years ago, when the Chaunter was killed. It brought the events back to life, in some way. The fact of Henry's body being discovered in the chapel had made Thomas's life here dangerous. If he had a brain, he'd pack his tools tonight, and take to his heels. He'd always be able to find work, and he could maybe explain himself to the Master Mason. Robert de Cantebrigge was going to leave before long, to go and inspect another building site he was managing. Thomas could tell him that he was sick of this city and persuade his Master Mason to take him too, when he left. It would be the best answer.

Except he couldn't. Beforehand he had had little feeling for this city. He'd been away too long to remember it with a child's golden memory of delights and pleasures. Instead he had the one vision in his mind: his father's body swaying in the breeze by the South Gate. That was no reason to remain here. Yet now he found he had another fetter that prevented his escape.

Sara. She had not yet recovered from the death of her husband and child, and Thomas felt a deep guilt that he hadn't managed to ease her pain even slightly. He had given money, and he'd provided food, but that wasn't enough. Whether he liked the fact or not, and in reality he hated it, he had a new responsibility in her. When he killed her husband, he caused the death of her son as well. Elias had died because he, like his mother, was desperate for food.

At least she still had the other son. Dan seemed a strong lad, from all Thomas had seen of him. Perhaps Dan would soon be able to find some form of work and help his mother. Then again, he might well leave her to her fate. Other boys did. And then what would happen to Sara? Thomas could guess all too easily. She'd a pleasing face and body, and if there was nothing else available, she would become just another member of the oldest profession.

Thomas didn't want to see that. He wanted to make her smile again, give her back some self-respect and dignity. He would buy some more food with his money today and take it to her, he decided. It would be good to see her face light up at least for a short time.

*   *   *

It took a little while for Baldwin's eyes to grow accustomed to the dim interior. 'Dean, could you have a man bring me a lighted torch? It is very gloomy in here.'

While he waited, Baldwin studied the room with the door wide open. It felt like little more than a cell.

The body lay on the ground before him as soon as he had walked inside, and that fact gave him pause for thought. 'Dean, do you know if anyone has touched the body? Could someone have moved it, for example?'

'Not that I know of, no,' the Dean replied. 'Oh – ah – here's a torch for you.'

Baldwin took the sputtering torch and held it aloft. Tutting, he called to the novice who had fetched the thing, and ordered him to hold it up while he investigated the man's body.

Clearly he'd been stabbed in the back; there was no doubt of that. There was a neat tear in the material of his cloak and cote-hardie, and when Baldwin lifted the material and peered underneath, he could see the blood. Whoever had stabbed this man had managed to hit the right mark with the first blow: the blade had entered below the shoulderblade and must have punctured the heart at the first attempt. There was blood, but not much, and Baldwin was reminded of bodies he had seen before; when the heart was stabbed, often it would stop profuse bleeding, as though without the heart the body ceased to function.

Without moving the body, Baldwin studied the ground all about. There was dirt on the floor – hardly surprising given the amount of mud outside. No man could entirely clean his shoes before entering. Some of this now had formed dust, and Baldwin could see that there were the marks of many others. It would be impossible to tell which belonged to the killer or killers, and which had already lain there before this fellow had died. Then again, probably many Cathedral men had come in here to view the body. They too would be responsible for making their own prints. The dust couldn't help him.

He crouched and studied the dirt nearer the body, wondering whether the man could have been killed elsewhere and brought here – an unlikely possibility, but Baldwin preferred to reject no idea until he had evidence to justify its dismissal. Studying the ground nearer the body, there was nothing other than the mess of footprints and scuffmarks.

Rising from all fours to squat, Baldwin sighed. There was no possibility of learning anything from this corpse. Too many men had been here over the last couple of days, probably first of all making sure that he was truly dead, more entering to gawp and speculate. He'd seen it all too often before at murder scenes; people couldn't resist coming to see what had happened. All he could hope was that the man who found the body would be a more or less reliable witness. The body had been moved several times, probably, and Baldwin would like to know how the corpse had lain when it was first found. Looking at the way the man was lying now, he wondered if he had been like this, face down, feet pointing back to the door, head in the chapel itself.

Time, he thought, to study the dead man, and he rolled the body over.

He was perhaps six or seven years older than Baldwin himself, about sixty. His belly was proud proof of his wealth if nothing else. His stomach was well-rounded, and his jowls would have made a blood-hound jealous. For all his girth, he was not an unattractive fellow, from what Baldwin could see. Although his eyes had closed as though he was sleeping, Baldwin could see that his features were pleasingly regular and there were laughter lines at either eye, making him a cheerful companion. And yet there was also a set of wrinkles at the side of his mouth and at his forehead which spoke of recent worries. It was possible that Baldwin wouldn't have seen these if he had studied the face in daylight, but here with the flickering yellow torch flame, the man's face was thrown into stark relief. Clearly he had been worried about something before he died. Concern was etched onto his face like a pattern carved into leather.

Baldwin stood, staring down at the dead man. He glanced at the novice with the torch, a slightly green-faced youth who appeared to be gazing with fascination at a point on the wall some feet above Baldwin's head.

'Sir Baldwin?' the Dean called. 'Have you – er – discovered anything?'

Baldwin decided not to offer his observation that the man was certainly dead, and instead walked out to join the Dean.

'He was definitely murdered. He could not have inflicted such a wound on himself with any ease.'

'Of course he was murdered!' snapped a voice.

The Dean gave the speaker a rather irritated look. 'You – um – remember our Treasurer, Sir Baldwin? This is Stephen.'

'I recall you well, Master Treasurer,' Baldwin said smoothly. He hadn't liked the Treasurer on the previous occasions they had met, and saw no reason to alter his opinion now.

'Did you learn anything useful in there?' Stephen demanded.

'I should like to talk to the First Finder,' Baldwin said after a moment. 'What sort of a man is he? A stable sort? Intelligent, or prey to fancy?'

'It was a fellow called Paul. I do not think that he is – um – prone to fancy, no, although I have to admit that he is new to his role as annuellar. Perhaps he could be a little . . . ah . . . unreliable? We are fortunate, however, because he called for help as soon as he found the body, and the man who – um – went to him was Janekyn Beyvyn, our porter from the Fissand Gate. *He* is not prey to dark imaginings. A more sensible fellow you could not – ah – hope to meet.'

'I am glad.'

'Do you think you can learn who actually committed this terrible crime, though?' Stephen blurted out. 'It's revolting to think of that poor soul's corpse in there waiting until the blasted Coroner can be bothered to make his way here. The man responsible should be made to pay for this dreadful abomination. To slaughter a man in a holy chapel! It beggars belief!'

'I agree,' Baldwin said, but he felt, as he looked at the men before him, that he could not and should not deceive them. He sighed. 'Yet I fear that even were Simon Puttock with me, this matter could prove to be beyond our powers of investigation. There is nothing in there to show who might have killed him. Perhaps I can learn more from the man's family. Was he married?'

'Yes, with a daughter, I fear,' Dean Alfred said.

Baldwin shook his head slowly. It was one of his constant fears that he would die too soon and not see his child Richalda grow to graceful maturity. All he hoped was that, should he die, she would at least hold fond memories of him. As would his widow. That thought suddenly sprang upon him, and he had a sense of complete loss, perhaps a recognition that he had already lost Jeanne's love. The idea was appalling. 'I . . .'

'You are well, sir?' the Dean asked solicitously. 'You have blenched.'

'I am fine,' Baldwin stated firmly. 'Very well, then I must speak to this novice and the porter you mentioned, and then, perhaps, you could have a man guide me to the widow?'

'Of course.'

'I sent a messenger to Tavistock to ask the good Abbot whether he could release Simon for a few days to help me here,' Baldwin started tentatively. 'I do not suppose you have heard anything from Abbot Champeaux about that? A messenger could have arrived here by now, I should have thought.'

'No, I have heard nothing. Ahm – perhaps someone will come here later today?' the Dean said hopefully.

'Perhaps,' Baldwin said. He glanced at the chapel a last time and unaccountably felt a shiver pass down his spine.

A Charnel Chapel could hardly be thought of as a friendly, welcoming place: it was a storage area for those remains which would not naturally dissolve. The bones of many men and women lay inside there, under the ground, all higgledy-piggledy. It wasn't surprising that the place should acquire a strange atmosphere all of its own. Of course Baldwin knew full well that he was not in the slightest fanciful, not like Simon; Baldwin was no romantic fool who heard ghosts and witches at every turn.

Yet he was aware of a curious shrinking sensation as he looked at the chapel, as though it was truly built upon death, and death would come here once more.

Chapter Twelve

The German should be with them some time soon. Mabilla took a deep breath and rubbed her temples.

'Mother, this is the right thing to do,' Julia said once more.

'Yes, yes, yes,' Mabilla responded testily. She looked at her daughter again and gave her a weak smile. 'I am sorry – I know you are as sad as I am today, but it is so hard . . .' She could feel the tears welling again on seeing her daughter: so tall, so elegant, and so terribly distraught, her eyes red from weeping. It was a testament to her beauty that the desperation and grief which so ravaged her features did not devour her attractiveness. In many eyes her terrible anguish only added to her appeal.

They had both sat up late discussing their plight since the sudden shock of Henry's murder. Their situation was doleful. Mabilla had gone through the ledgers with an experienced clerk whom Henry had oftentimes used before, and the result was not reassuring. Henry was owed a considerable sum from other members of the Freedom of Exeter, and Mabilla knew that she'd have to start implementing court proceedings to gather even a small part from most of these fellows.

In the meantime, the house was their sole real asset, and the two women must shift for themselves in any way they might.

'It's the only way, Mother.'

Mabilla closed her eyes. The shock of Henry's death, followed so soon afterwards by the veiled threat in Will's words, was almost more than she could bear. Will had been so malevolent in his manner and speech: that alone had convinced her that she and her daughter both urgently needed a protector.

Seeing William had forced her to face the truth about the man. Will had been her lover many years ago, and even as she had accused him she had been aware of his masculinity – not because she wanted a lover straightaway, but because old attractions died hard. If she was honest, her accusation was not intended to provoke a confession – it was an invitation for him to *deny* his guilt.

But his manner, his coarseness and brutal disinterest, revealed his true character. He was more than capable of murder; he had very likely killed her Henry.

Julia saw the need for protection as clearly as she, and it only served to make her determined to win Udo as a husband before it was too late and he found another woman to his liking.

When her daughter was born, Mabilla had dreamed of the day when Julia would marry. She had thought of the dress, the gathering crowds at the church door, the admiring faces, the jealous mothers and daughters who bitterly saw that they had missed out on this splendid match because their daughters were not so beautiful as Julia. She had expected Henry to be there, with his wealth exhibited on every side; and now, here she was, plotting with her child to install Julia in the first available man's house, in a financial arrangement to guarantee both of their futures. And such a short time, such a very short time, after poor Henry's death, too. It was enough to start the tears springing again.

'I am sure he will make me happy,' Julia said confidently. At least Udo would save the two of them from ruination. 'We must find a husband for me so that we can be safe.'

Aye, her mother thought, and so that I can be safe from the man who said he used to love me and now threatens to murder me. And again her mind turned to Will, and to wondering whether he really had murdered her husband.

'Oh, God! My poor Henry!' she wailed suddenly, and fell to her knees, her face hidden in her hands.

What should she do? What else *could* she do, other than sell her daughter?

Sara was getting over it. She must: she had another son to think of. The bodies had been taken away to the church, and all waited there now for the Coroner's arrival so that he could comment on the deaths, and when that had been done, her Elias could be buried.

It was only three days ago, and yet it felt like a year of suffering. She'd hardly got used to the idea that she would never see Saul again, and now she must wait for the Coroner once more. Her poor Elias! Her darling little boy! All he did was try to find some food from the Priory, and he had paid for it with his life.

She might have died too, had it not been for the kind mason. The man Thomas had appeared as though from nowhere again, and grabbed her from the dark sea which was gradually carrying her out on the tide towards death. At that moment, it had been a welcome journey, and his intervention unwelcome, but as soon as she began to breathe and could think, and realised that her son was in there somewhere too, needing to be rescued, the will to live had flooded her body. Then she had seen her little Elias's ruined frame being picked from the mound of corpses, his eyes open but unfocused, his mouth slack, head dangling, his body crushed. It took one glance to see that he was dead.

She had sunk to the ground with Elias in her lap, weeping and wailing, pulling her hair, mixing dust and ash from the ground in her long tresses, utterly bereft. It was only the feel of the hand on her shoulder that helped her to come to her senses. That and the words Thomas muttered: 'Be strong, girl. It's terrible, but you must be strong for your other boy. Think of him.'

That gruff, sad voice had hauled her back from the edge of despair like a rope. She still had Dan. And he deserved to have her alive and whole to protect him as best she might. It would avail nothing, were she to die of misery and leave him alone in this cruel world.

And so she had remained sitting there while the men about her, Thomas included, pulled bodies from the pile, gave them a cursory glance, and then either set them gently at the wall's side to rest until they could be helped, or joined the larger pile ready for the Coroner to view before they might be interred.

Like many of the men there, Thomas was crying as he joined in this terrible task. Those who were helped to the wall to sit upright were all in the topmost layers of bodies. As the men released them from the press, they began to find fewer and fewer who were still breathing. So many were dead, that they had to start a second pile for all the corpses. The crowd had shoved forwards on a wide front, and when people began to fall, they collapsed from the front, up to six deep in places, where those behind had tried to clamber over the bodies in front in order to escape the terror, only to fall and be smothered in their turn by others. Now this long line of three-and-forty people was being broken into a series of smaller piles.

Thomas couldn't remain until the finish. When he was sure that there were no more people living in that hideous mound, he walked to Sara and helped her up. They took Elias back along the roadway which she had entered all those hours before, buoyed with the hope of a filled belly at last, and Thomas led the way to the Church of St John Bow, where he asked the shocked-looking priest whether they could carry her child into the church. The priest nodded his head, his own eyes full of tears. They carried Elias into the church and set him down gently before the altar. Elias was the first body there.

Recalling those moments, Sara wiped her eyes. He had been a rock to her, this Thomas. She was sure that he must be a kind man. Since the disaster, he had appeared with food and drink for her each day, and she had forced herself to eat under his sternly compassionate eye, reminding herself that she had to remain strong to protect Dan.

The older boy had taken the news of his brother's death badly. He had sworn aloud to hear that Elias was dead, and his anger had not been assuaged when Thomas tried to calm him. His words were directed at Thomas, but Sara knew that his true rage was targeted at himself. He was the master of the family, and he had failed his brother; it should have been him, Danny, in that queue, not his mother and his feeble sibling.

She was expecting the tentative knock when the light was starting to fade. The masons and labourers worked longer hours in the summer, but when the sun dipped earlier, they were allowed to have a shorter day, although the Cathedral reduced their pay accordingly. Thomas always came here as soon as he stopped work, and usually brought either food he had saved from the Cathedral's contribution – because all the workers were entitled to their own supply of ale and bread at the Cathedral's expense – or, if that wasn't available, he'd buy more food for her and Dan on his way to them.

He was a generous-hearted man, she thought. When she was at her lowest ebb, he was there to collect her and renew her spirits. He had certainly saved her life that day outside the Priory, and since then he had kept her and Dan fed.

Yes, it was him. He stood in the doorway when she pulled it open, his bearded face smiling apprehensively, as though he half-expected her to launch herself at him and tear him to pieces. She had the impression that if she were to attack him, he would do nothing to protect himself.

It was a weird idea. She was nothing to him, just as he should be nothing to her – but she could feel a tie between them. Just as he must have accepted responsibility for her in some way for saving her life, likewise, she was ready to accept his presents. Perhaps it was nothing more than the kindness of a co-labourer and mason for the widow of another. She knew that there were little clubs which allocated a sum of money to cover the funeral expenses of the less fortunate workers who died at the Cathedral so that their families shouldn't have to suffer that expense just as they were coming to terms with their grief; but sadly she also knew that Saul had never invested in such a fund. If the other masons knew of her plight, maybe they had thrown some money into a cap to help her, and since Thomas knew her slightly, after bringing her the news of her darling Saul's death, perhaps they thought his face would be more acceptable to her.

Looking up at him now, she reckoned that if that was their thinking, they were right. She liked his rough, untended beard with the grey flecks and sandyish hairs about his bottom lip. It was a perfect frame for his kind eyes, which watched her always with that faint hint of anxiety, as though he was convinced she'd show him the door the instant he began to speak to her.

'Thank you,' she said as she took in the sight of the food he held in his arms. He smiled as though relieved to note her welcoming tone, and then she gestured him inside, taking the items from his arms and setting them on the table.

'Dan not here?' he asked as she almost pushed him down into a seat.

'No, he's gone out. A friend called for him.'

Sara was fascinated by Thomas's changing expressions. It was hard to read any emotion in his face. His mouth could smile without affecting his eyes, yet sometimes she saw that his eyes were laughing, although his mouth was set in a firm, pursed line. Although she had no intention of dishonouring her husband's memory, she found herself attracted to this powerful, big-hearted man.

'You are too kind to me,' she breathed as she discovered a slab of meat, dripping with blood. It was only very rarely that she and her husband had been able to afford meat, and the sight of this made her belly rumble alarmingly.

He looked away with embarrassment. She put the meat into her cooking pot, added water from the bucket and set it over the fire to stew. Neither spoke for what seemed a very long time, and then she looked up and found his eyes upon her. There was an infinite sadness in his face, and she set her head to one side with sympathy flowing through her veins. She said gently, 'Tell me what upsets you so much, Thomas.'

He looked away. 'I was just thinking – I never had a wife nor children, and I realise how much I've missed.'

'It's not all easy,' she said. 'Sometimes you hate your family.'

'I don't believe that of you. You loved your man, didn't you? And his children.'

She could feel the tears begin again. The mere mention of Saul and Elias could make her throat constrict. 'I never regretted marrying him,' she said in a choked voice. 'I couldn't.'

'You are fortunate.'

'Did you never want to settle with a woman of your own?'

'There were women I admired from a distance, but when I set out on my trade, I never stayed long enough in one place to settle down. By the time I had slowed down enough to appreciate what I was missing, it was too late. I was too old. Look at me! A wrinkled husk of a man with little to recommend me.'

'There's enough. You have a good soul.'

He looked away again at that.

'Your voice,' she said after a moment. 'You sound like the men of this city. Did you use to live here?'

'Yes,' he whispered. 'But I had to leave.'

'Why?'

His head drooped, and he glanced at her from under his brows. 'Many years ago, when I was a wild youth, I got into a fight. A man died. Then because of one man lying, someone else was captured for the murder, and he was executed. He died for what I'd done.'

'That's terrible! So you felt so sorry to know that an innocent man had died, that you left?'

'The innocent man was my father,' Thomas said, and his shoulders began to leave with silent sobs. It was the first time he had ever spoken of his guilt, but now his life was changing again. Matthew was sure to spread news of his presence.

After all, Thomas had helped kill Matthew's companions, and almost killed Matthew himself.

Baldwin had spent the afternoon uselessly waiting to speak to the Annuellar Paul who found the body, but Paul's canon had several duties for him that day and the lad couldn't be found until it was almost time for Vespers.

Baldwin caught up with him as the fellow walked towards the Cathedral. 'Paul? I must speak to you,' he said.

The Annuellar was tall and lanky, with a mop of tallow-coloured hair and a pasty face which showed off an explosion of acne to best advantage. He shot a look at his canon, a short, thickset man with a glowering demeanour. 'May I just speak to this—'

'It's time for Vespers, boy. Get a move on. We don't have time to stand and chat with everyone who wants our company!'

Baldwin felt his jaw tighten. 'That is fine. I have travelled ten leagues to be here at the request of your Dean to help the Cathedral before the Coroner returns because of the shame and embarrassment the dead man's body will bring to you all. I have already been forced to wait the afternoon, so I suppose you do not wish me to learn what has happened. I shall take my leave, Master.'

'Where are you going?' the canon asked suspiciously.

'To apologise to your Dean. And to write to your Bishop. I haven't seen Bishop Walter for some weeks, but we are well-acquainted, and I should be sorry to leave here without putting in a commendation for your deeply religious approach in this matter. Clearly Vespers is very important, Master, and it is your duty to see that all the services are correctly attended. God forbid that one should miss a service, when the only alternative would be that a man's murderer, who shamed the whole Chapter, might be discovered.'

'Wait! Oh, very well, Sir Knight, but hurry with your questions, and don't forget, God watches over us, and if you prevent this lad from performing his duty, God will punish you for your temerity!

Paul, go. But hurry to the service when this . . . person has finished with you.'

Baldwin watched the canon hurrying off self-importantly, his black gown and tunic flapping, his *familia* – novices, choristers and servants – streaming behind him in a haphazard line. Farther up the Close, more canons were emerging from their houses, each again trailing streamers of hangers-on, while the bells tolled for the service.

'Is he always such a fool?' Baldwin asked.

'He is deeply spiritual,' Paul said in a slightly pained tone.

'Perhaps he would be more spiritual if he was more sympathetic,' Baldwin observed.

'You cannot understand.' The Annuellar gave a deprecating smile. 'It's the nature of our service.'

Smug little arse! Baldwin had lived under the threefold vows for fifteen years before this little puppy was born! But he swallowed his own pride. The lad meant nothing by it, and since Baldwin had no intention of confessing to his past as a Knight Templar, there was little point in beginning that discussion.

'I understand you found the body of the dead man in the Charnel Chapel?' he asked instead.

Paul hopped from one leg to another. 'Yes. I saw that the door to my chapel was ajar, and so I pushed it open. There was just enough light to see the body there.'

Baldwin eyed him. 'Are you all right?'

'It's just the cold,' Paul admitted.

'Let's find somewhere a little less chill, shall we?' Baldwin suggested. 'It is certainly too windy and cold here for thought.'

The Annuellar, nodded hastily as a gust of cold air blew around from the east. As Baldwin turned towards the welcoming door of the calefactory, he caught sight of the Charnel Chapel again, and his expression hardened.

Even to him, a warrior of some thirty-six years experience the chapel exuded an unwholesome atmosphere of its own.

If he were not so ill-disposed to superstition, he might have called it evil.

*   *   *

Udo was home again by twilight, and he was thrilled and not a little surprised by this sudden change in his circumstances.

He had walked into the hall and stood near the fire in his finery, picking his spot with care, knowing that the flames would sparkle and gleam on his new cote-hardie and the buttons of his gipon. Behind him, the boy with the basket was apparently overwhelmed by the appearance of the hall, and indeed it must have been an awesome sight to a poor, half-destitute youngster like him. The ceiling was high overhead, and the timbers were a pleasing light brown colour, since the building here wasn't so old as the exterior might have hinted. The roof was thatched, and the lowest, original layer was open to view; the lighter colour made the hall feel more cosy than its size should have permitted. Whoever built this hall knew what they were doing: the dais at the far end was not so high as to intimidate any guests, but was sufficiently higher than the floor to allow the master to keep all in his view when he sat at table. The fire was not quite central in the floor, but instead was a little closer to the dais, where it might warm the family; the window was less massive than some Udo had known, but that only meant that although there was less light to brighten the room, there was also fewer draughts, which was a cause of great relief on this chilly day.

Yes. Although Udo saw the shabbiness of the decorations, the scruffiness of old wood, the faded and chipped paint, he could still understand the poor lad's astonishment. It represented more wealth than a fellow like him could ever dream of. On entering, he saw the gracious figure of Mabilla rising from a seat near the window. She had been sitting there with some needlework, and now she hastily put her little workbox to one side, as though embarrassed to be found mending old clothing.

Udo smiled inwardly. If the poor lady must make do with old shirts and hosen, clearly she was in enough of a financial mess to be grateful for any man's rescue. 'My dear Mistress Mabilla,' he breathed in his suavest tones. 'Please allow me to offer my condolences. I have gifts brought – sweet cakes, *ja*?'

'Oh, that is kind of you, Master Udo,' Mabilla gushed. 'And my daughter loves *dowsettes* so much. That is really very good of you.'

'It is my pleasure.' Udo tapped his staff with an impatient forefinger. Where was Julia? He wanted to talk to her.

'My daughter,' Mabilla offered hurriedly, reading his mind, 'will be here in a moment. I know it is she whom you wish to see. A poor old widow is scarcely the same as a fresh young woman like her.'

Udo studied her closely. 'My lady, you are most sad, and this is not an appropriate time, perhaps.'

'Sir?'

'When you are in mourning, I should not come and intrude.'

'I was hoping that your visit would be no intrusion, but a welcome distraction, sir. My poor daughter would doubtless be happy to be diverted from her present misery. It is a terrible thing to lose a father . . . just as it is to lose a darling and devoted husband.'

She had some courage, this woman. Although her eyes gleamed with unshed tears, she wouldn't bend or bow to her grief, but sat bravely holding his gaze like a queen, and Udo was as impressed as she had intended.

'I know, my dear Mistress Mabilla, that before his death my relationship with your poor husband was not of the most cordial . . .'

'Yes. And you may yet sue us for the damage,' she said, and this time there was a faint break in her voice.

'My dearest Mistress Saddler, I should not wish to have to do so, but a man must shift for himself, you know. What would other men say of me, were I to allow this sum to be lost? I could have been killed, and then there is the matter of the expense to which I was forced to go. Because I was in bed, I lost a great deal of money.'

'And my husband would have wanted to make good your losses,' Mabilla sniffed, and put a hand to her brow. 'I shall see to it that we repay you, no matter what it costs us. But we should be glad of a little time, in order to overcome our sadness first.'

'Surely this is not the time to talk of such matters,' he said with his best attempt at kindness. 'Mistress, I should be attempting to amuse you and help you to forget for a little while the dreadful circumstances in which you find yourself, and here we are discussing a debt which . . . well, it is a lot of money, of course.'

'I know this. And we cannot afford to lose even a single ha'penny.'

'You will forgive my saying this while you are in mourning, but you will need a protector. A man who can keep you both. Your husband –

again, please forgive my bluntness – did he not provide for you after his death?'

Now she did break down. She put her face in her hands and sat silently sobbing, and Udo considered her with a feeling of admiration. All women had to dicker with tradesmen every day of the week, of course, but Mabilla was conducting this negotiation with all the skill of one who intended securing the most beneficial outcome for herself. Even the tears were splendidly timed. Not that he didn't believe she regretted the passing of her husband, but that didn't stop her using her position as a weak, lonely woman to best advantage.

He said gently, 'Perhaps I should leave you and return another day when you are more composed?'

'No, Master.' She wiped her eyes and gave him a bright, terrible smile. 'Please – do not fret. I shall be well in a moment.'

Udo cleared his throat. 'Perhaps before your daughter arrives I should discuss her with you, although it seems to me that it is a great insult to you both to haggle. Doubly so when you are still in mourning weeds.'

'Haggle? Over what?'

'Over your daughter's hand in marriage, Mistress. You have much to think of just now and I do not wish to add to your burdens, but I should like to know your feelings.'

'I cannot deny that there are many other things for me to consider now,' Mabilla answered, and for a moment her head hung dejectedly. 'Henry was a good man, Master Udo. A kind husband and father, and I shall have to travel far and wide to find such another.' She paused, then said passionately, 'Yet how else could I support myself? The city is expensive for a poor widow woman. The business is worth little, and the property, for all its advantages, is not in the High Street. My husband had a few meagre savings, but a widow with her daughter needs a protector. I fear we shall have to leave together and seek a new life.'

Udo nodded, with sympathy clogging every pore of his face. She was transparent, the hussy! Well, he didn't have too much to worry about here, then. 'Perhaps, if your daughter were to marry, at least that expense would be saved you?'

'My treasure?' Mabilla said. And her voice trembled with a passion that was surely not feigned. 'How could I think to dispose of her so lightly? My only darling, my little Julia?'

I am sure whatever you decide, Udo had thought to himself, you would not dispose of her lightly or cheaply!

And now, in the comfort of his hall, staring into the fire, his prized goblet of silver filled with wine in his hand, he knew the bargain. All living expenses for the mother to be paid, herself to keep the house in which she and Henry had lived for so long, and the threat of the court case to be dropped.

It was an expensive bargain, Udo told himself, pulling the corners of his mouth down. Very expensive. And yet as soon as the cost was named, as though she had been waiting at the door for her moment to enter, which no doubt she had, Julia walked into the room, and Udo felt as though the sun had suddenly landed on the ground before him. She was radiantly beautiful, even in her grief.

So! Udo was to become a married man.

Sara had stewed the meat with a handful of herbs and a little of the carefully hoarded salt she kept wrapped in a leather pouch. Every so often she glanced at the man at her table, wondering.

He was so vulnerable. It was curious: she was doubly bereaved, and yet he inspired a depth of sympathy as though his own pain and loss were incomparable. When he wept, she stared at him for a long while and then put her arms about his shoulders and rocked him gently, shushing him and remaining at his side until his terrible sobs eased. Then she kissed his forehead softly before preparing food. There was no need for words; both had needed and still needed comfort, and each had tacitly agreed to give it one to the other.

She hoped Saul wouldn't object.

The supper was almost ready when she heard the rush of feet outside, and the door was thrown open. 'Close it, Dan, it's freezing.'

Her son didn't move, but stood staring at Thomas. 'That's my dad's stool!'

'Thomas is tired,' she said. 'Look, he's brought us meat! Do you want some?'

'No! I don't want anything from *him*!'

She stared. His face was streaked with dirt, clear lines where the tears had run during the day, but he wasn't close to tears now. Instead there was a dreadful ferocity about him. 'Danny, be calm,' Sara entreated. She should have kept him here at home, not let him go out with his friends unwatched and unprotected. Something must have happened today to make him so angry. He sounded outraged just to see Thomas there in their home.

'I'll take nothing from him. Nothing!' Dan cried. 'He's a murderer!'

Thomas's head hung dejectedly. 'I'd better leave.'

'No, Thomas, please. Danny, he's told me. It was a terrible thing, but a very long time ago . . .'

'I don't know what you mean, Mother,' Dan interrupted. 'I'm talking about Daddy! That's the man who killed him.'

Sara gaped, and turned to Thomas to ask him what her son meant, but as she did so, he rose quietly and walked to the door. He opened it.

'No, you couldn't have!' she breathed, but even as she spoke, he turned to face her and she saw the terrible guilt in his eyes.

'I didn't mean to. It was an accident,' he said. 'I'd do anything to take his place.' Then he turned and fled from the room.

Sara had only enough time to sit down on her stool before the waves of darkness overwhelmed her. Her remaining son stood resolutely at her side, preventing her falling. She heard him sniff once, felt one tear strike her on the face after falling from his eye, and then she sank into the blackness.

Chapter Thirteen

Baldwin stood in the calefactory as close to the roaring fire as he could, while the Annuellar took a seat at the wall. Looking at him, Baldwin thought that he should have been out in the fresh air, riding and practising with weapons, not spending all his life sitting in chilly rooms or cloisters, while his fingers froze, his pallor and spots increased and his natural humours were subjected to slow decay.

He had once been like this lad, he recalled with a sense of shock. In those days, Baldwin had been impressionable, wary of others, and confused. His older brother, Reynald, was to inherit the manor of Fursdon, and Baldwin had the option of following a cousin into the Church or making his own way in the world. When he had heard of the disasters in the Holy Lands and the way that the crusaders were being evicted from God's kingdom, he had known that he must do what he could to help. Such, perhaps, was his destiny.

So he had taken ship and left from Devon's coast, a callow youth who had little to lose. He was supremely confident in his abilities and in the those of the other pilgrims at his side on that ship. They were Englishmen, knights and men-at-arms who could beat any force sent against them. The French may have succumbed to the heat and the fury of warfare in the Kingdom of Jerusalem, but that meant nothing. If the German warriors had been beaten, it meant nothing. One good English pair of legs with a stout English arm to wield a sword, and a man could vanquish any enemy.

That was his opinion, and the opinion of all the others on the ship as it set sail, and there was nothing to alter their view as they passed the hazardous tongue of land that led into the Mediterranean. One of the sailors was an older man, with a wealth of experience, and he pointed out the sights, the places where the Moors had tried to launch invasions, and the places where the Christians had thrown them from their lands.

When they passed a series of islands, he pointed out Cyprus, which Richard the Lionheart had taken when the the ruler, Isaac Ducas Comnenus, had tried to catch and ransom both King Richard and his sister. That rashness cost him dearly, because the wrathful King took the island by storm. There was nothing that a good English warrior couldn't achieve.

And then – then they'd arrived at the hell that was Acre, the last Christian foothold in the Holy Land, and the mood of the warrior-pilgrims grew more thoughtful. Baldwin himself had not been scared at the sight. Not yet. He was still too foolish and inexperienced. So he stood at the forecastle of the ship and stared at the columns of foul black smoke rising from the devastated land and felt only pride that here he and the other English would show their mettle.

It was at Acre that Baldwin lost the foolishness of youth and became a man.

Looking at Paul, Baldwin saw himself again. In his mind's eye he looked over the stinking, blackened corpses, their flesh desiccating in the awful heat, their fingers curling into claws, legs bending. Through the day, even when it was quiet, the sounds of creaking leather, the chinking of metal, could be heard as dead limbs tightened, pulling straps and mail into new postures. It was like listening to the armies of hell preparing to attack.

No, he would not have wanted to see this fellow put through the same appalling experience. And yet there was already a horror in his eyes. 'Was this the first dead man you have seen?' Baldwin asked him gently.

'No, sir. I have seen my father. He was stabbed too. It was a long time ago, though.'

'Yet a memory like that will remain with you.'

'Yes,' Paul said, and his eyes glanced away from Baldwin as the old pain was awakened. 'I found him, you see. It was during the famine, seven years ago, and some men entered the house to steal any food they could find. My father was there, and he tried to stop them, but one held him and the others . . . well, they beat him with cudgels, and then they stabbed him and left him there. I was lucky they didn't kill me too. So when I saw that man lying in the chapel, it made me remember, and I think I panicked a bit.'

'It is not surprising. A grown man may be shocked to discover a corpse where he had expected none,' Baldwin said understandingly. 'What did you see from outside?'

Paul shrugged. 'The door was a bit open.'

'Not wide, then?'

'No. Only an inch or two of gap.'

'What time of day was this?'

'Curfew. It was quite dark.'

'If it was that late, how did you see that the door was ajar?'

'I don't know. I could see, though.' Paul frowned.

'No matter. So you walked to the door? What then?'

'I walked up to it, yes, and I . . .' Paul suddenly had a vivid recollection. 'Yes! I remember, there was a faint glow from inside. It outlined the door itself, and I went to it wondering whether someone was in there holding a service – that was it!'

'You pushed, then?'

'Yes, but only gently. I wanted to see who was there. And as I pushed, I saw that there was a man on the floor . . .'

'Did you notice whether there was a candle in front of you?'

'I didn't see one,' Paul said with a glower of concentration. 'No, I don't think so. But there was something else . . . if a candle's snuffed, or if it gets blown out by a door opening, there's usually a smell of the smoke, yes? I don't remember that at all. Although there might have been the smell of some tallow or something.'

'Do you think that means that there *could* have been a candle alight, then?' Baldwin pressed him.

The lad shrugged.

'Very well. So you were standing in the doorway, and before you was the body. How was he lying?'

'He was on his face. His boots were towards me. I could see the soles of them. They were all stained with mud and dirt.'

Baldwin nodded. 'Face down, feet towards you. How were his legs? Were they straight, bent, together, apart? The same with his arms. And his head, how was that? Literally with his face down, or was it set to one side?'

'I didn't really look at his face that well. I was . . .'

'I understand – but his legs, his arms?'

'His legs were apart,' Paul said, his eyes closed as he tried to remember. 'And the left one was bent a bit, the right one straight. His feet were apart. His right arm was under him, I remember, but his left was beside his body, the palm up.'

Baldwin mused. The saddler could have marched in and been attacked by someone lying in wait, or someone could have been behind him and thrust the knife in his back as he crossed the threshold, perhaps clapping a hand over his mouth to smother his cries as he did so. Without having seen the body as soon as it was discovered, Baldwin would only be guessing based upon the boy's testimony.

'You ran and fetched the porter, I think?'

'Yes. I'd been locking up with Janekyn beforehand, and I ran back to him. I knew he wouldn't have finished there yet, and he's a good man to have at your side when you're a bit – um – worried.'

'I can imagine,' Baldwin said soothingly.

'He came back with me, and we hurried inside. It was so dark, we could hardly see a thing, and . . .'

'Yet you saw well enough before,' Baldwin pointed out sharply.

'Yes, but it was darker by then. Maybe it was the failing light.'

Or a man had been there with a candle when you first walked in, but he had left by the time you returned, Baldwin thought.

Joel gingerly touched the swelling on his jaw and grimaced. That was Will, right enough. The vicious devil had given him this blow just as he was about to leave Joel's house, slamming his bloody staff into his face as a goodbye gift. Good God alive! Joel had thought he was going to die at that point. The man had swung his weapon like a poleaxe, and Joel hadn't been able to move for some minutes, the pain was so intense. And then he found he had a mouth full of blood. One of his back teeth had chipped, because when he felt about there with his tongue, it caught on a piece like a razor up there. He had to go to his workshop and fetch a file to round it off a little so he didn't cut his tongue while eating.

Bloody William. He never even gave Joel a chance to talk. Just in, bash, and out again. Bastard! He hadn't changed much over the years.

Maud walked in just as he had set his file down, and she gazed at him with alarm. 'What on earth have you done to yourself? You look awful, Joel.'

'S'hank you, dear,' he lisped. His bottom lip didn't seem to want to work properly and he daren't open his mouth too much in case it hurt.

'What happened? Have you been robbed?'

Joel smiled lopsidedly. It was a constant fear of Maud's, ever since a friend over in Baker's Row was broken into some years ago. The thieves had entered over the wall to the yard, then got in by the rear door, ransacking the place, defecating on a chair, and generally ruining everything. And then, when the owners returned, they were attacked and beaten. The husband was so severely clubbed that he never fully regained the use of his right arm. They caught the villains and hanged them, but that didn't help the poor fellows who had been so badly wounded.

'No, maid. It's not that.'

'Then how did you do that?' she demanded. She had approached him, and she stood before him, peering at his jaw. 'Let me see . . . Keep still! If you jerk like that I'll hurt you.'

'Don't be so damn silly, woman, you already bloody have!'

'And none of that sort of language in my hall, Husband! Keep still, now, you're worse than a baby!'

'Woman, will you . . . *Will* you leave it!'

She ignored him, but started to roll up her sleeves and called to their maidservant. 'Bring warm wine and water, some towels and a cup. Oh, and ask Vince to come in here to help me.'

'Maid, I don't need to have this done. I've got customers to speak to.'

'Fat lot of good you'll be,' she said, peering with narrowed eyes at his wound, 'with your face like this, and unable to pronounce the simplest words. Keep still!'

'Woman, will you please . . .'

'Oh, good. Vince, pass me a cloth soaked in the wine, would you? Now, Husband, who did this to you?'

'I'll not talk while you're fooling around there, damn it. Ow!'

'Don't be so foolish. Now, who was it?'

'Good God! All right, it was William.'

She stopped and withdrew from him, staring at his face. 'William? Why on earth would he do this?'

'Jesus! Vince, get out. Go on, go!'

Maud was so surprised that she didn't argue, and Vince put the bowl down on the table beside her, then walked slowly from the room. He pulled the door shut behind him, and fully intended to leave the place, but . . . but didn't. It was an intriguing mystery, this attack on his master, and which apprentice could resist a tale like this? It was more than he could endure, to walk away now and leave the question of why Master Joel's old companion and friend had attacked him. Rather than scurry off to the workshop, he stayed, hand still on the latch and gradually, very gradually, his ear moved closer to the boards of the door itself, until his lobe actually touched the wood.

'I don't know why, Maud – the man's unstable. He said something about being attacked, but how should I know anything about it? He's mad; practically foaming at the mouth today.'

'Why should he think it was you?'

'I don't know . . . *Ow*! Are you trying to kill me, Wife? What was that for?'

'There's something about him, isn't there? What is it?'

'Oh, not again! Look, if I tell you, it's a secret. I don't want anyone else hearing about it, all right?'

'Very well.'

'And I want you to stop dabbing at me with that damned cloth. Just leave me in peace! No! Take it away, or I won't tell you. That's better.'

'I've stopped now.'

Joel's voice suddenly lost its warmth and power. Vincent thought he sounded like a man who had been hung over the edge of a precipice, and he had seen the depths beckoning.

'William was from Exeter originally. He left here many years ago after a crime. And he left to join the King because he knew full well that he'd be made to pay for that crime otherwise.'

'Why didn't you accuse him?'

'*Because*, woman, I was there too! It was the murder of the Cathedral's Chaunter – oh, nearly forty years ago. I was there, Henry was there, Will was there . . . we all were! We set upon the Chaunter as a mob.'

'You helped murder him?' she whispered.

He nodded glumly. 'It seemed the best thing to do.'

'What happened?'

'We all stood in the Close and waited. After Matins, the Chaunter and his *familia* left the Cathedral and walked to his house. That was when we jumped him. He nearly escaped, because one man was brave enough to try to save him . . . he came haring up before and shouted that there was an ambush, but one of the Chaunter's men thought he was a traitor, and struck him down instantly. And then we got to the Chaunter, and he fell.'

'Was he so badly protected?' she asked.

'He thought he was safe. I heard later that someone had told the Chaunter that there'd be an attack; the story was, the Bishop himself had heard of it and had placed men about the Close to protect him, so there was nothing to fear and the Chaunter believed the story. But it was a ruse. There was no one there to save him. The tale was a lie. So when we attacked, he was alone and defenceless, apart from a few weakly novices.'

'And one man died trying to call out to him to save himself?'

'Yes – poor Vincent. He was killed by Nicholas, who was one of the Chaunter's most loyal defenders. Nicholas himself was struck down and dreadfully scarred, and he left the city soon afterwards. I always thought he was dead, but recently he's been seen in the town again. He survived, and now he wears the Greyfriars' garb. Nicholas must have thought Vincent was running up to attack his master; he never realised he had killed one of his own comrades.'

Vincent stood back from the door and moved away slowly, his heart pounding. If what he had heard was true, then the man who had killed his uncle was in the city again. A man called Nicholas.

A friar with a dreadful scar, he repeated to himself.

As he silently tiptoed away, back in the room, Maud was thoughtfully washing her man's bruises again. 'I don't understand. Why should Joel think that you'd attack him because of that?'

'Because afterwards, I had a great idea,' Joel said. 'I was sick of apprenticing just then. I had three more years to run on my contract, and I wanted to see the world, not live here. So when the King came to hear the case, I decided I'd go and tell him about the escape. All the men ran from the South Gate, which had been left open.'

'I do remember, Husband,' she said tartly.

'Yes, well – I decided I'd tell the King and the court about it. I mentioned it to William because I was scared of him even then and didn't want him angry about my words, and he said it was a good plan. He thought he ought to do something like it himself, because he was irritated about his woman. She was clinging too hard to him and he wanted his freedom. But he had no money to leave Exeter. Well, I told him I could go on the morrow because I had a bag of coin I'd collected over the years. Then, the day the King came, I went to the court only to see William standing up and telling of the gate being open. And after the King had left, I looked for my purse, and it had gone. The bastard robbed me of my idea, my money, and my future!'

Maud stared at him long and steadily.

He hurriedly appended, 'Except I should be glad, for if he hadn't stolen them, I might not have met you, dearest . . .'

As soon as he had left Paul, Baldwin went to speak to Janekyn Beyvyn.

He found the porter to be a tall, rather morose-looking man. His face spoke of mistrust and scepticism – all no doubt useful qualities in a man set to guard a gate to such an important place as the Cathedral Close, but not ones to inspire confidence in his kindness or generosity.

'Master Porter, I should like to ask you about the body of Henry Potell, discovered in the chapel. It is my job to find out who was responsible.'

'I don't know.'

'But you were the man called by the First Finder, weren't you?'

'Paul asked me.'

'And you went to view the corpse with him?'

'He asked me. I went.'

Baldwin pursed his lips. This was like drawing water through a stone. 'Master Porter, may I tell you something? When I spoke just now to Paul, he spoke of a light that was in the chapel when he first found the body. When he returned with you, that light was gone. Did you see a light of any kind in there?'

Janekyn considered. 'No.'

'So there are two things to note. Paul had left you at the gate, clearing up. You are a most dutiful porter. You were here again when he hurried to fetch you. That means you are not only dutiful, it means you weren't in the chapel when Paul arrived there, and you didn't snuff a candle when he hurried off. In short, I do not suspect you. However, I do wish to know what you saw, because you, Master,' he paused and studied the man, 'you are older, wiser, and less likely to harbour superstitious nonsense about a darkened chapel late in the evening when all is quiet.'

Janekyn gave a shrug, then hawked and spat onto the ground near the wall. 'Would you like some wine?'

Baldwin's spirit quailed at the thought of drinking rot-gut with this man, but he forced a bright smile to his face and said, 'I should very much enjoy some wine.'

He followed the porter into the small lodge. Here Janekyn twisted the cork from a gallon pot and sniffed it with evident pleasure while Baldwin glanced around him.

It seemed that Janekyn had occupied this room for some years. There were little signs of his life. A palliasse which had seen much better days was rolled and tied with a thong in one corner. Above it hung a couple of thick blankets from a wooden peg. Where the bed would be unrolled, there was a stool and low brazier, which threw out a wonderful heat. There were two pots – one enormous one with three legs set in its base, which had plainly been well used over the years, to judge from the uniform blackness of its exterior. A second beside it was large enough for only perhaps a pint of food, and Baldwin assumed that the frugal porter would often cook his own pottage here. There was a table, two small benches, and a cupboard with one door which housed the porter's few belongings. Inside Baldwin could see many little pots and some reeds.

The walls were limewashed, but over time the wash had been almost entirely covered with pictures, mostly religious, but also others: portraits of jugglers in multi-coloured hosen and jacks; gaily dressed people walking among the tents and stalls of a great market at fairtime; bulls being baited by dogs; a man on horseback hawking . . . all these and many more were executed in a spare but precise style that rendered them utterly lifelike to Baldwin's eye. 'These are magnificent. Who painted them?'

'Me,' the porter said with a sharp look at him as though doubting the honesty of his words.

'They are truly excellent,' Baldwin said, entirely serious.

The porter gazed about him as though seeing the pictures for the first time. Then, '*I* like them.'

He set the jug down, took two mazers from a niche in the wall and poured the wine, passing the first cup to Baldwin, who took it with trepidation. For some years he had avoided strong wines. It was the effect of the training which he had endured in the Templars. He had learned that for him to fight with the strength and dedication owed to God, he should not partake of wines which tasted as though their primary constituent was vinegar. While learning his duties on Cyprus and after, he had come to appreciate that the worse the quality of the wine, the more severe the quality of the headache the following day. And he knew that porters were among the least well-regarded members of a religious institution. How else could they be viewed, when their whole life involved sitting on a stool and watching people walk past?

Taking a reluctant sip, he could *feel* the taste. It exploded on his tongue, a glorious, rounded, sweet wine. It was better than his own best quality. 'That is . . .' He looked at the porter. 'You are a man of surprises.'

'Just because I'm a porter doesn't mean I don't like good wine. I have an arrangement with the vintner. When I fetch my wine, he gives me good quality.'

'I see,' Baldwin grinned. He wondered what the porter offered in return. Perhaps an easy route into or out of the Cathedral's Close, if the vintner wanted to visit a young female companion, or was it simply that the porter knew something about the man? There were so many possibilities. Maybe the vintner had been blackmailed by someone else, for example, and had killed the saddler to stop news of his misdeeds escaping? Anything was possible – but speculation was no aid to a man trying to find the truth, Baldwin told himself.

'So tell me, what was your perception when you saw the body? I assume you wouldn't think that Paul could be the murderer?'

'Him? He'd crap himself if he was told to kill a rabbit,' Janekyn said contemptuously. 'No, I reckon the man who killed Henry was probably older.'

'Why?'

'When I got in there, the body was lying in front of the door, legs first, head away. Looking at him, I thought he'd just walked in and been killed from behind. That means someone who was sure of his attack. There was only one wound I saw, too. No practice stabs first. How I see it is, the saddler was with someone he knew and trusted, he walked into the chapel first, and soon as he was inside, the other man shoved his knife in his back. One push, into the heart, and that was that.'

Baldwin gave a shrug. 'Did you smell anything in there? A candle recently snuffed?'

Janekyn gave a sour grin. 'All I smelled was blood. I wasn't going to go and search for more. No, I sent Paul to fetch the Dean while I waited there with the body. That was that.'

'What of earlier? Did you see anyone in the Close who was acting or looking suspicious?'

Janekyn frowned. 'There was only the physician, Ralph. He was wandering about the place when Henry came in, and he asked for his money for treating the German. Henry just told him he'd bring it later, and hurried on. Ralph didn't look happy to be brushed off.'

'Was there anyone else?'

'Not that I saw, no. And Ralph didn't kill him   not just then, anyway. The two parted, and Ralph came back towards the gate. I was called by a man walking in just then and didn't see him actually leave, but he probably did. He doesn't live too far from here.'

'But he could have turned back and gone to lie in wait for Henry,' Baldwin commented.

'Aye. And he could have sprouted wings and flown to the chapel's roof,' Janekyn grunted. 'But it's best not to guess when it's a man's neck you're wagering.'

Although Baldwin questioned him on other aspects of the case, he could bring no further light to the affair. The porter had seen no one else talking to Henry that day, nor did he see where Ralph had gone, and there was no one suspicious who entered the Close. Baldwin left him as the light faded and stood outside the lodge, gazing at the labourers packing their tools amid the mess and chaos of the building site.

He scarcely noticed the man who hurried into the Close like one fleeing from the Devil himself.

* * *

Thomas hardly knew where to go or what to do. After he'd been accused by Dan, he'd run away from that hovel, up to an alehouse he spied from the top of the alleyway, but as soon as he reached the door, he turned and started running towards the East Gate, desperate to be as far as possible from Sara.

Ah, God! He'd never be able to forget the expression of horror on her face. There was nothing he could say in his defence. Nothing at all. It was true. He *had* killed her husband through his negligence; that meant he had killed her son and reduced her to abject poverty. It was all his fault. If his death could ease her mind, he'd kill himself, just to avenge the dreadful crime his slipshod work had caused. At least that way she might find some peace, and so might he, too. Since returning here, he had known little enough.

Standing in the Close, he felt his legs beginning to move towards the stark walls of the Cathedral. There was a ladder propped against the scaffolding, and he walked to it like a man in a dream. The last few workers were clearing up, most of them had already gone, and few noticed as Thomas stumbled over the ground, his face pale and preoccupied. Suddenly, he tripped over a loose rock and fell heavily onto a large shard of stone. The splinter was as sharp as a fragment of glass, and it tore a great rent in his hosen and sliced through his shin like a knife, but he didn't heed it. He righted himself and continued on his way.

At the bottom of the ladder, he stared upwards into the darkening sky. Turning, he saw the evening star gleaming, but then it was erased by a cloud, and as though this was the signal, he put his hand on the ladder and lifted his foot to climb.

'It's a little late for that.'

Thomas heard the voice and instantly his blood froze. His head was suddenly an awful weight, and he had to rest it upon the ladder's rung between his hands.

'Nicholas,' he breathed, but his voice was a moan.

Chapter Fourteen

Baldwin awoke feeling entirely unrested. There was a lethargy about him that was unusual for him. An old campaigner, he was used to taking his sleep wherever there was a dry place to rest his head, and normally he would be fully asleep in moments, but not now. Just now he felt as though his life was fraying, and he was distracted.

He had hoped that coming here to investigate a murder would allow him to forget his problems at home, but it had proved to be impossible. He had betrayed his wife, and that act of disloyalty must inevitably alter their relationship; perhaps even break it.

In his mind he saw Jeanne's face again when he had allowed his anger to show after her light comment about the peasant girl. There was such a depth of pain and hurt in her eyes, he wasn't sure how he could ever retrieve the situation. But retrieve it he must.

The room he had here at the Talbot Inn was large for a city inn. He always tried to rent this room when he needs must travel to Exeter, because he had a dislike, based upon too many years of sleeping in dorters with snoring companions, of sharing a room with other travellers. That was one thing that he would never miss about the life of a warrior monk!

Here he had a good-sized bed with a palliasse that was large enough to accommodate five men in a normal inn, but Baldwin had never yet been asked to share it. The master of this house had been a merchant until his profits from his excellent ale-brewing showed him that his talents were being wasted in providing ale only for his own household. He stuck up his bush over the door, and now his ale accounted for half of his business. A wealthy man, he was perfectly happy to accommodate Baldwin's need for solitude. In return, Baldwin paid rather more than the room would normally be worth.

Today he awoke early, and with a slight headache from a disturbed night's sleep. He was tempted to roll over and close his eyes again, but instead he lay back and stared at the cracked ceiling, trying to make sense of his feelings for Jeanne. Then, in despair, he pushed her from his mind and considered instead the murder.

This was one of those killings in which it was quite likely that no one would ever be brought to justice. There were cases of that nature – and although Baldwin knew that his own methods of detection were more successful than those of other men, still there were many murderers who committed their crimes and were never caught by him. Some men were too clever, others fiendishly lucky; most murderers were caught because they made mistakes or were too stupid to conceal their crimes. Baldwin had once found a man who denied the murder, but had cleaned his knife of blood by wiping the blade on his own jack. It was still fresh when Baldwin caught him, and although he claimed that he had killed a dog, he could not recall where, nor where he had put the body.

In a matter like this, though, there had to be a motive for Henry Potell's death. If he could discover that, he would be much further on in the enquiry. It was possible, of course, that the widow would be able to help in this, but all too often Baldwin knew that the wife was the last person to discover certain secrets. He put the sharp mental picture of his own wife to the back of his mind again as Jeanne leaped into the forefront of his thoughts; no, in matters of business many men would not tell their women all that had happened in a day. It was one of those basic differences between men and women: the men would prefer to leave their work and relax; women by contrast sought to discuss every aspect of their day in the minutest detail before they could think of relaxing. Or maybe that *was* their way of relaxing – Baldwin didn't know . . .

He woke to the sound of hammering on his door. Startled from a light doze, he was halfway out of his bed, his hand reaching for his sword when the door slammed wide. He grasped his hilt, swung it free with a flick of his wrist, sending the scabbard flying across the room, and span on his heel to face the doorway.

'Come on, Keeper, put the bloody thing down. You should be up by now, anyway.'

'Simon!' Baldwin gasped with relief and delight.

Then he scowled. 'Shut that door, Bailiff, before I catch a chill, and what is the meaning of this ridiculous noise? Are you so short of amusements that you must terrify a poor sleeping knight with your infernal row?'

'Yes, it's good to see you too,' Simon grinned.

It had been the right thing to do. Yeah, of course it was. Vincent swung his legs out of his little cot and sat there naked with his legs dangling. It was cold, so he dragged his blanket over his shoulders. He'd done the right thing, sure enough. It was only . . .

He'd been really horrified to hear his master say all that last afternoon. To learn after all this time that his master had been involved in that murder, to think that he'd been there on the night his old man's brother had been killed . . . well, it was really weird.

Rising, he pulled on his shirt and tunic and tied his hosen to the dangling laces. He had a thicker quilted jack which he pulled over the top, and then he tied a short strip of material about his throat. It was perishing cold out there in the yard and the workshop at this time of year, especially first thing, before anyone had time to build up a bit of warmth in their work. He tidied his bedclothes, put his blanket back on top, and patted the side of the cot. It was one of his first jobs when he was taken on as apprentice to Joel. His master had brought him up here and pointed to the small chamber. 'You could make a bed in there if you wanted. The wood's all outside.'

The first attempt had been embarrassing. He'd not known how to joint properly, and how to make the ends of the planks square so that they fitted together neatly was beyond him, but gradually as he learned his trade, he saw how to make the cot better. Each time Joel demonstrated a new joint or explained the principles of smoothing and chiselling, or how to square-off ends, Vince saw how to improve his work, until after two years he had a cot that was more prone to holding his weight, rather than falling apart every two months as wooden pegs worked loose.

His first real project, that bed. It was the sort of thing which he could knock up in a few hours now, but he was enormously proud of it. The cot had shown him that he was capable of doing this job, that he was right to be a joiner.

It hadn't been easy at first. The old man wanted him to follow in his own footsteps and learn the tanning trade, but Vince was determined to escape that trap. The idea of remaining his whole life with that stench was revolting. He'd been there long enough as a boy, before he managed to win the argument and come here instead. It hadn't been an easy fight, that.

The trouble was, his old man was determined to keep Vince with him so that he could protect him from the dangers of the city. Out on Exe Island, Wymond reckoned they were safe, free of the risks of politics and the disputes between the rich and powerful. The Church had regular fights amongst its different parts, between the Priory and the Cathedral, the friars and the monks. Wymond said it was only a few years before Vince's birth that the Cathedral had fought a bitter fight against the friars down at the southern wall, because the friars claimed the rights to some dead man or other and the Dean and Chapter stole the corpse to give it the funeral rites in the Cathedral. That was fine, but the man's estate was due to pay well for the funeral, and when the Cathedral later brought the body to the friars, they refused to accept it. The man lay there outside their gate for ages until the Cathedral shamefacedly sent someone to collect it.

Wymond wasn't an expert on Church law, but he believed that if a man was dead and his soul was at risk, it was the duty of men from the Church to see to his protection without worrying about how much money they'd receive. The behaviour of those churchmen was enough to convince him that a man was safer outside the city. Country people were more pleasant.

That was what he'd always said, anyway. And there was the other event, the one which had coloured his life so vividly. The result again of Church disputes: the murder of his brother Vincent, after whom Vince himself was named.

Over the years the memory of that dreadful night had faded in the city's memory. It was forty years ago: Wymond himself was only six-and-forty, but he remembered his brother with a fondness that bordered on adulation. When he was killed, it was like a bolt from heaven. And then the stories started to circulate.

It was just like the rumours which began over other events. If you have enough people together in one place, and you give them the opportunity of gossiping, some will inevitably come up with a theory that sort of fits the facts, without ever worrying about minor details like the truth.

So when there was the murder of the Chaunter, and some folks heard that Vincent hadn't been in the Cathedral with the others at that Matins, it was assumed that he had been outside in order to help the assassins. He had been one of the killers.

That, so Wymond had always said, was ballocks. His brother Vincent loved the Church, and he was a devoted member of the Chaunter's *familia*. The idea that he'd have betrayed his master, still worse taken part in his murder, was beyond belief.

Still, Vincent's complicity in the murder was assumed for many years. His death meant that there could be no defence, because the accomplices refused to talk about his part. In fact, the Dean and the vicars who were caught refused to discuss any part taken by Vincent – because they simply knew nothing. Other men had commanded the attack at the Cathedral's door; the Dean wasn't there, and the vicars were standing at other points of the Close. Only the men in the group who actually killed the Chaunter could answer yea or nay to Vincent's guilt or innocence, and they refused to admit their crime. The Mayor, Alured, didn't confess – so who else could speak for Vincent?

In the absence of any others, Wymond himself spoke of his brother's innocence and his devotion to his master, but that wasn't enough, and soon the whole city was convinced that the novice was an ally of the Dean, like so many others. His memory was polluted; his integrity slandered. That was why Wymond detested the city. It had allowed his brother, his wonderful, kind brother, to be turned into a traitor and killer.

Poor Uncle Vincent. The tale told yesterday by his master had come as a shock, because he had been content to consider that in those far-off days his uncle might have been persuaded to change his allegiance and join the men allied with Pycot; perhaps he had gone to murder the Chaunter at their side. Only now he had heard from a witness that the poor fellow had been trying to *save* the Chaunter, his master. He had been honourable to the very end, when he was struck down by the man Joel called Nicholas.

One thing Vince knew, and that was that his father ought to be told. So late in the afternoon, he had invented a ruse to take him out of the house, and he had fled down the hill to the tannery. Before long he found his father, stirring skins in the handling pits.

He was panting slightly, and he caught his breath, savouring the moment that he should explain to his father what he had heard. Wymond would be delighted to hear that his impression had been vindicated, he'd be over the moon to learn that there was a witness, a credible witness, who had confessed at last.

Which was why Vince was baffled when his father listened, and then walked away, head bowed with sorrow. Vince ran after him, gabbling that all was well: Vincent his uncle was cleared, but his father waved a hand for him to go. And as Vince went, he could hear the sound of dry, racking sobs. It completely mystified him.

Baldwin threw on his clothes, washed his face in the bowl of water provided, and then followed Simon down the stairs.

'You cannot know how glad I am to see you here,' he said as they sat at a table. The owner's daughter gave them bread and some cold slices of meat with a large jug of weak ale.

Simon gave a chuckle. 'Nice to know that I'm indispensable at last.'

'This affair is peculiar, old friend. A man suddenly appears in the Charnel Chapel, with a knife wound in the back. It's a strange place to commit a murder.'

'Perhaps. All I can say is, I am glad to be here,' Simon said.

'How is Dartmouth?'

Simon crumbled a piece of bread in his fingers. 'It's lonely, Baldwin. I hate living there without Meg and the children, and I worry all the time about Edith. What she won't do in order to get her way, I don't know, and it's not healthy for Meg to be looking after her on her own. They both need a man about the place to stop them fighting.'

'That's Lydford, not Dartmouth,' Baldwin pointed out.

'Dartmouth is a pleasant, fresh little vill. There's a great port and lots of ships,' Simon said drily. 'It's convenient, because it means that yesterday when I heard I was required here, I was able to be directed to a ship and board it to come here swiftly, rather than making the arduous journey on horseback.'

'You came by ship? That must have been a difficult transport!' Baldwin joked.

'You can smile, if you wish, Baldwin,' Simon growled. 'You won't get me on another, though. Damned thing. I had to stay up on deck the whole time to stop myself throwing up, and that meant I was soaked with spray and rain by the time I landed. Foul things, boats.'

During the year the two men had travelled to Santiago de Compostela in Galicia, Simon had learned that his belly was most uncomfortable aboard ship. During their return voyage, foul weather and pirates had almost killed both men, and the memory wouldn't fade from Simon's mind. He passionately detested anything to do with ships, and he intended to avoid them all his life. It was particularly galling to have to resort to a ship to come here now, when he had sworn only a matter of weeks ago, on their return, never to use that means of transport ever again.

'I am delighted to see you here, in any case,' Baldwin said, and explained what he had so far learned about the death of the saddler.

'So plainly we need to visit the man's widow,' Simon observed.

'Yes. It is unlikely to be a pleasant encounter.'

'A woman who's just been made a widow is hardly likely to be congenial, no,' Simon agreed. 'Does this mean you're getting to be a little less ruthless in your questioning, then? The knight who was always known for rigour bordering on callousness in the search for the truth is at last learning empathy?'

He'd only meant his words as a light jest at Baldwin's expense, and he was surprised to see his friend was offended. Baldwin half-turned his head from Simon, and when he spoke, his voice was a great deal quieter. 'There is nothing callous in my make-up, I hope. I try only to serve justice to the best of my ability.'

'I didn't mean . . .' Simon was unsure how to comfort Baldwin. 'Baldwin, I'm deeply sorry if I've given you offence. I wouldn't have dreamed of it, you know that.'

'Yes, of course. I'm just feeling rather fragile at present. It is the effect of coming here when I should be at home with my own wife.'

'I can understand that,' Simon grunted. 'In any case, my apologies if I've upset you, old friend. I'd never want to do that.'

'I know,' Baldwin said with a faint smile. 'And now, to our food.'

*   *   *

Mabilla was finishing her morning meal when she heard the bang on the door. Her heart sank as she heard the two voices. She looked down at her full board and hurriedly finished her dish of a tart and some apple.

This was a most inconsiderate hour to visit a lady, she told herself. At this time of day, civilised people returned from their early Mass to take something to break their fast, just as she had, and to turn up at a woman's doorstep now meant that there was serious business afoot. To her mind, that could only mean men who intended to demand money from her, supposedly because her poor darling husband owed it. Well, they'd soon learn the position, if they'd come here for that, damn them!

Hearing the knocking, Julia entered from the solar where she had been resting, and Mabilla felt her anger rising. Julia was looking particularly pale today. Usually such a complexion would be a sign of perfection in the opinion of most men, but today it was merely evidence, along with her red eyes, of her misery. She hadn't slept well last night again. Mabilla had heard her bedclothes rustling in the little truckle bed, and felt the floorboards move as she tossed and turned. Although she was being courageous about her marriage to Udo, it wasn't ideal, as Mabilla herself knew. If she could, she'd have tried to snare the man herself. She wasn't such a poor catch, surely . . . but he wanted a woman in order to start breeding his own line, and Mabilla's days of childbirth were behind her now.

Her poor, darling daughter. There was a look of resignation on her face as she entered the room, followed by a too-bright smile. She hadn't eaten anything yet today. Mabilla must make sure that she ate later. This starvation was all very well, but it'd be certain to weaken her.

Julia faced the door, and then, as she heard the voices, she threw a look at her mother in confusion. 'I thought . . .'

'It's not Udo,' Mabilla said as her maid walked in with two men behind her.

'Mistress, this is Sir Baldwin de Furnshill, the Keeper of the King's Peace, and Bailiff Simon Puttock. They want to talk to you.'

'Godspeed, madam,' said Simon, walking around the maid and looking at Mabilla. 'I am afraid that Sir Baldwin and I are here to speak to you about your husband's death. The Dean of the Cathedral has asked us to come to Exeter and investigate the murder. We're here to find his killer.'

Mabilla's attention went from him to the other man, the knight. He looked more stern, but there was something else in his face. He had dark eyes and a little beard that followed the line of his jaw. There were flecks of white in it, and a little dusting of more at his temples. A fine scar ran down his face, and it caught slightly at his mouth, twisting it up ever so slightly, she saw, giving him a very faintly cynical expression. Yet there was that little something else flickering in his eyes, she thought: vulnerability.

'We should like to hear what you can tell us about the day your husband died,' he said, 'but we also need to know anything else that might have a bearing. Did he have any enemies in the city? Was he involved in a legal dispute? Did he owe money? Anything at all may help us to find his murderer.'

'Julia, please leave us, would you?' Mabilla asked.

Caught off guard, her daughter nodded, and started to make her way to the solar's door, then suddenly she stopped. 'No, Mother. If it's to do with Father's death, I want to be here.'

'This is simply a discussion of matters which don't affect you.'

'You won't be discussing my future husband, then?'

'Perhaps,' Baldwin interrupted, 'you should both be present. There could be something which is relevant, which one may not realise, but which both of you together may see more clearly.' He motioned to a stool, and when Mabilla nodded her agreement, he seated himself on it, his sword clattering loudly on the stone flags. 'Ladies, please . . . even if it seems entirely unlikely that something could have a bearing on Henry Saddler's death, still tell us. It may help us to form an impression of the whole man, which could lead us to learn who killed him.'

'Do you have his business records?' Simon enquired. 'Perhaps I could look through them.'

Mabilla ordered her maid to fetch wine, and then she rose from the table and walked into the small room which had served as Henry's counting chamber. She had his key about her neck, and she opened the chest in there, bringing out his ledger. Returning to the hall, she passed it to Simon.

He opened it and began to peruse the figures. After the last few weeks with Andrew, he was more than capable of reading through the figures and seeing where there could have been any problems. He ran his finger down the numbers, the roman numerals slowly forming a pattern in his mind. 'His saddles weren't cheap!'

'My husband was a very accomplished craftsman. He used only the finest materials, and only the wealthy would buy them,' Mabilla said.

'I can believe that,' Simon said, his finger still running down the list.

'Perhaps first,' Baldwin said, facing Julia, 'you should tell me about your fiancé. You are clearly worried about him.' Baldwin sat very still and studied her.

She felt he was like an owl peering at a mouse across a field, knowing that there was no need to exert himself; the mouse would soon be his. The thought that he might look on her as mere prey made her hold her head a little more haughtily. She would not speak of her fiancé in front of this fellow. Udo was surely innocent of anything to do with her father. Why, only yesterday he had told her how highly he had esteemed Henry. The plain fact was, Udo was their salvation, and the idea that she should endanger that by discussing him with these two officers was unthinkable.

Mabilla didn't feel the same. Julia could see it in her eyes when she glanced at her mother. She was preparing herself to speak of him. She was going to betray him. 'Mother!'

'Julia, please leave us. I have asked you to do so once already. You have said your part. Sir Baldwin, you said you would prefer my daughter to remain. *I* should prefer that she leave us. I have some information that I should like to share, but it is not for my daughter's ears.'

'I won't go! You'll betray him, won't you?'

'Julia!' Mabilla blazed suddenly. 'This is very hard for me. Very hard indeed. It's a matter that doesn't concern you, and I want to discuss it in privacy. *Leave the room now!*'

Julia stared at her defiantly, but gradually allowed her eyes to drop to the floor. 'Very well,' she muttered, and made for the doorway again, pausing briefly at Mabilla's side to whisper, 'Udo is innocent of this. You'll only make him hate us, and then where will we be?'

Mabilla said nothing, but sat as still as a figure carved in stone.

Baldwin considered that often women would grow in attraction as they matured, and this woman seemed to have the dignity and poise of a queen, even in the midst of her grief. Until the door behind her was closed, she sat still and said nothing. Baldwin privately wondered whether her daughter was standing at the door and listening, just as any servant would when there was an interesting argument in prospect in the main hall, but then Mabilla took a deep breath.

'You will understand that I do not like to speak of this. My own honour is at stake, and that is a grievous heavy burden just now. You see, I fear *I* may be responsible for my husband's death.'

Simon heard the sudden silence after her calm, quiet words, and he looked up, his finger still on the vellum before him. He frowned. 'You don't mean you stabbed him?'

'Of course not!' she snapped, but then added introspectively, 'Yet perhaps I did, even though I didn't hold the dagger myself.'

'Please explain,' Baldwin commanded.

'Many years ago, long before I was married, I had a lover called William. I was foolishy attracted by his good looks, his dark moods, his aura of violence . . . I was young and my judgement unsound.' She paused and cleared her throat. 'Then, there was a fight in the Cathedral Close and the Chaunter died. My man was one of those involved, and he fled, leaving me behind. Henry and I got together later and I wedded him. And I don't regret it one moment! He was kind, good, and deserved my respect. I was graced with my daughter, and although I know Henry would have liked a son to carry on his trade, we were not so fortunate. Our boy-children both died soon after birth. Still, Henry never once criticised me or expressed himself disappointed. He only ever behaved affectionately and generously towards me, and for that I honoured him.'

'However, if this past lover were to have returned, you fear he might have grown jealous?' Baldwin enquired.

'He *is* returned. He lives as a corrodian at the Priory. As soon as I saw him again, I knew he wanted me for his wife. He couldn't remember that he had deserted me, and that I was left alone for nearly forty years! All he knew was, he wanted me and I should go running to him. He is entirely self-centred.'

'You think he could have killed your husband?'

'Oh, yes. He is a determined man, Sir Baldwin. A killer. He came here regularly to visit. Henry and he used to be friends, and Henry thought William was coming to talk to him about old times. He didn't realise that each time William was speaking to me and trying to persuade me to leave my husband. I felt such a *traitor*!'

It was no more than the truth. The way she had felt when William first appeared was a source of shame still. She had felt the familiar quickening of excitement to see William's old twisted grin again. He was always thrilling; even now at nearly sixty years old, he could make her blood race by merely shooting her a look.

Damn William! He had wanted her for years, that much was obvious. Even Joel still feared him, because of his taste for violence. And he hadn't actually denied killing Henry. No, the murderer must be William. An obstruction to his happiness – that was how he'd see Henry, as a pest who stood in his way. So he would crush Henry, thinking Mabilla would run into his arms again. Until he grew bored with her again, no doubt.

She covered her face quickly, turning away.

Baldwin felt his own heart lurch with sympathy. He could feel her self-loathing; it was much like his own. The heat of humiliation flushed his face.

'Do not blame yourself for the failings of men,' he said in a low voice. 'If this William did kill your husband, it is none of your responsibility, but his alone. Now! Is there anyone else you can tell us about who had a quarrel with your husband? Even a mild business dispute can lead to daggers being pulled.'

'No. No one at all.'

She spoke with determination, as one will when denying even to oneself a painful possibility.

As they were speaking, the Master Mason Robert de Cantebrigge was taking a turn about his works.

The buggers here were all bone idle, of course, and the loss of Saul was a pain, but at least the place appeared to be buzzing, even if the labourers were all sheep-fondling fornicators. Yes, the walls would soon rise again and then the roof trusses could be installed. They'd arrived a little while back and were all stored in the main shed while the walls were being finished. As soon as that was done, they'd be able to get the roof proper up, and then the interior works could be set in train. It hadn't been an easy task so far, but with luck it would grow easier.

Although Robert de Cantebrigge was by no means superstitious, he didn't like the fact that there was a dead man still lying in the chapel. He couldn't voice his concerns, but sometimes he felt he'd be happy to take his money and leave this Cathedral. Something was wrong here.

He had just come to this conclusion when he reached the walls of the old nave, and he stood there eyeing them contemplatively.

Much could be saved, he reckoned. The old stone could be reused in places, but he'd still have to order a lot of rocks from Beer and the local quarries. He'd already persuaded the good Bishop that they should make use of Caen stone in places, and Bishop Walter had agreed. Robert fancied that the latter wanted to be remembered for this great edifice. Well, if Robert had anything to do with it, Bishop Walter would be!

These walls must come down, probably as far as the window sills, maybe a little more – he would wait and see what condition the base of the walls were in before deciding – and then he could start erecting the new ones. Yes, he was looking forward to that.

There was a rope dangling nearby, and he tutted to himself. Ropes should always be neatly stored and carefully tied. If he'd told them all that once, he'd told them a hundred times. Following the line of the rope, he saw that it rose to a block, and then dropped into a space between some rocks and rubble thrown down from the top of the walls, not far from the north-western corner of the Cathedral. It seemed peculiar. He couldn't see why the rope should be lying over there; there was nothing to lift over that way. It was simply a pile of old stones from the walls which had to be sorted into those which were reusable and those which weren't.

He was frowning about this when Thomas walked to his side.

'Master, can I have a word with you?'

'Thomas? Aye. What have you done now, laddie? Killed off another bloody mason? You may not be at all bad at your job, son, but you'll end up doing it on your own if you're not careful.'

Thomas did not smile. 'It's nothing like that,' he said. 'I heard you were going to work on another building soon.'

'Yeah. I'm running four building projects right now, and it's time I went to check on the others . . . why? You bored up here?'

'Not bored, no, but I'd prefer to leave. I can only serve to upset Saul's wife if she sees me, and that's a sore grief to me.'

'His death was a sore grief to me, too. He was a good mason, sod it! I'll think about it, anyway.'

'Thank you, Master.'

'Now get back to work, will you?'

'Yes!' Thomas smiled. He grabbed a ladder and began to climb. As he did so, the master eyed the rope again. Giving it a tentative yank, he was about to leave it, when some instinct made him pull on it. It came fairly easily, although there was a dead weight at the other end.

'Christ and all His saints!' he bawled, when he saw what dangled on the other end.

Chapter Fifteen

'So on the night your husband died,' Baldwin said, 'did you know he intended to go to the Cathedral?'

Mabilla closed her eyes a moment. 'I did. I told him he should confess his sins, God help me.'

'Why? What were they?' Baldwin pressed her sharply.

She opened her eyes with resignation. 'He had participated in a murder many years ago. Have you heard of the death of Walter de Lecchelade?'

Simon looked at Baldwin with bemusement. 'Not me.'

Baldwin was peering at the floor with narrowed eyes. 'I believe I have! It was before your birth, probably, Simon. Wasn't it because of the murder that the Bishop was granted the right to build a wall about the Cathedral? I recall someone telling me of the tale when I was a lad.'

'A body of men set upon de Lecchelade, who was the Chaunter, after Matins one morning. Twenty of them. He was killed, and the men escaped. Later it was learned that the Dean of the time was responsible, and he was put in gaol. Well, the Dean wasn't alone. He hired men to do his work for him, and my Henry was one of those men.'

'I see,' Baldwin said. 'And the crime has been weighing heavily on his soul?'

'Yes. He wanted to confess. Particularly since . . . one of the men who was injured that night is now a friar called Nicholas. He was terribly wounded in defence of his master, Chaunter de Lecchelade.'

'So Henry's guilt was that he had conspired to help the Chaunter to be killed? Not that he had himself killed the Chaunter?'

Mabilla lifted her chin proudly. 'My Henry was no murderer. I don't think he could have struck a blow like that, even had he so wished. Perhaps he conspired, as you say, but he wouldn't have been able to kill a man in cold blood. He did tell me that many of his friends were involved. Maybe it was one of those events where people can be persuaded to join in against their better natures.'

'These others with him – do you know who they were? I should like to speak with them.'

'Henry always spoke of three companions in his past. There was William, whom I have already mentioned, then Joel, who is a joiner up in the High Street. You can't miss his workshop. It's a large place, with a good wooden sign over the door showing a carving of a carpenter with his adze in his hand.'

'Who was the third?'

She frowned. 'There was another man who was a close friend of Henry's before the Chaunter's death. I think Henry called him Tom.'

'Do you know where he lives?'

'I got the impression that he was dead, or that he had left the city. I have certainly never met a friend of Henry's called Tom in all the years I've known him.'

'We could ask at the Cathedral,' Simon said. He held his finger at another point on the ledger. 'Mistress Mabilla, there is an interesting entry here. It shows money being paid for a saddle by a Master Udo Germeyne of Bolehille, but then there is a large mark alongside it, a star. And I don't see where the money is supposed to have been paid in.'

'Udo has not paid for the saddle yet, that is all,' Mabilla said calmly, while inwardly she felt her heart quail. Please God, she prayed, let it be nothing to do with him.

No. In her heart of hearts, she had no doubt. Only one man could have killed Henry. It must have been William, because he wanted *her* back as his possession.

Matthew was one of the first to hear the Master Mason's cry. He followed Robert de Cantebrigge's pointing finger to see the body swinging in the breeze.

'Sweet Lord Jesus!' he exclaimed.

He and Stephen had just left the Treasurer's house and were walking to the Exchequer for their morning's review of the previous day's accounts when they saw Robert de Cantebrigge looking agitated. The two had hurried to his side, their black gowns flapping.

'Oh, dear heaven,' Matthew said with a wince. 'He is dead, is he?'

'With his neck twisted like that? Yes, I rather think he might be,' Stephen said caustically. 'Master Mason, send for the Dean. God only knows what he'll make of this, but we ought to give him fair warning, I suppose.'

'This is terrible,' Matthew said. Inside the leather cylinder gripped in his hand was the latest fabric roll, which detailed all the money paid and owed for the last couple of weeks' work. 'It's the last thing we need . . . the poor fellow, of course, but really, we should be trying to complete the Cathedral, and we can't wait for the Coroner to come and investigate *another* death!'

Stephen glanced at him sympathetically. 'I know how you feel, Matthew. I feel it myself. I adore this Cathedral, and would give much to see it completed so that I could revel in God's glory here on earth, but . . .' he drew a great sigh '. . . there is no possibility of that. We must simply do our duty as best we can, hoping that our successors appreciate our work.'

'But this will only slow it down more!' Matthew said tearfully. 'And it must cause great friction, Treasurer. Look at the fellow's garb. It is not the body of some saddler from the city this time.'

Stephen peered back. 'No? Oh, God. Is that who I think it is?'

Matthew nodded sadly. 'I am afraid so. It looks as though he was a friar.'

Sara came to when it was already broad daylight. Her son Dan was gone, but in his place was old Jen, who sniffed as she prodded the lacklustre fire with a stick and muttered to herself about the lack of food and drink.

'Where is Dan?'

'Gone to see if he can find something to beg, I reckon,' Jen said. 'I've got some pottage from last night here. You'd better drink it. It may warm you a little.'

Sara's stomach revolted at the thought, but she was grateful for Jen's help and hated to disappoint her. She allowed herself to be supported while Jen held a bowl to her lips. She took a sip. 'Thank you.'

'Don't thank me. I've done little enough, maid. Dan came running round saying he thought you'd died. Little monster was quite out of his mind until I told him you were only sleeping.'

'The man who came to bring food for me, he . . .' Sara began, and then her throat seemed to close up, and no more words would come.

'Dan told me all about it.' Jen patted Sara's shoulder, and rested her hand there in silent sympathy for a while. 'It must be terrible to know that the man you thought was a saviour was the cause of your trials.'

'He killed Saul! How could he come to my home and befriend me, knowing he was responsible for my situation?'

'And he helped you at the Priory, too, didn't he?' Jen said.

'Yes, he pulled me from all the bodies. He saved my life.'

'So he paid a little for his crime. Still, I hadn't heard that Saul was murdered. He was crushed, wasn't he, when a stone slipped?'

'I don't care whether he intended to murder Saul or not. He was the one who let the rock fall. If only it was him who died and my Saul had lived,' Sara said with a whimper. 'I want my husband back, I want my son back. I don't want to be widowed, I don't want Saul to be gone! I loved him! And I don't know anybody in this city, I ought to flee and go home!'

'Right, maid. First, you aren't fleeing anywhere. You can't. You need food and rest. Second, you know me here, and that's enough. Third – well, third, you know this mason too, and . . .' She held a finger to Sara's mouth and stared at her with a serious expression. 'Think of this, maid: he owes you much. He owes you a living, because that's what he took from you. He's no killer, is he? He's a good man, who was shocked to have an accident which crushed a man – *your* man – but accidents happen every week on building sites. If he hadn't killed your man, maybe someone else would have done so soon enough. But for you, unprotected and hungry, you could do a lot worse than find a man who wants to assuage his guilt by serving the victim of his offence. That means you.'

Sara looked at her, revolted. 'What – you think I should welcome him here in Saul's home?'

'At least he's the kind of man you could control,' Jen said, folding her hands over her ample belly. 'And a controllable husband is a delightful toy.'

Simon and Baldwin were walking up the hill towards the middle of the city when there came a pattering of feet behind them and Baldwin reached for his sword in an instant, whirling to meet their pursuer head on. As soon as he recognised the figure, he let his hand fall from the hilt.

'My dear maid, you shouldn't run,' he said calmly. 'You are already quite disordered, and your humours upset enough without pelting up the street in this way.'

'I had to speak to you!'

Julia stopped and caught her breath. These men were strangers to her, and yet they were committed to catching the man responsible for her father's death. She knew that they must be suspicious of her fiancé, but Udo can't have had anything to do with Henry's death. Why should he?

'My mother can be a little confused. Especially since Father's sad death,' she said, and the mere utterance of those dread words made her shoulders rack with sobs once more.

'I feel sure that she is as rational and sensible as a woman recently widowed could possibly be,' Baldwin said.

There was sympathy in his eyes, she felt sure, but there was also some cold intensity, as though he was prepared to think that even she could have killed her father. That was a scary idea, that someone could suspect her of such a foul deed.

'Sir Knight, I didn't hear what you discussed with my mother,' she said, which was true. They had spoken quietly, and what with the wind whistling past her in the chamber, and the constant rustling of drapes and tapestries, she'd not been able to hear much of what they'd said. 'But I want you to know what I think. My father's business has not been so good recently, and a customer who bought a saddle was hurt. The wooden frame was defective. Because of that my father threatened the joiner concerned.'

'He was Master Joel?' Baldwin confirmed. 'Yes, your mother told us of him. What else would you like to tell us?'

'Nothing. That is all I know.'

'Really?' Baldwin said. 'But I feel sure that there is more. Come, won't you trust us?'

'No, there is truly nothing else.'

'Very well, then. We thank you for your aid in this,' Baldwin said and waited until she had departed.

'What was all that about?' Simon asked when the girl was out of earshot and the two men had started on their way again.

'The woman and daughter are both trying to protect someone,' Baldwin said. 'I do not doubt that both loved the husband and father, but the wife sought to throw our suspicion upon one of her husband's friends, the daughter upon another of them.'

'Which means that neither is certain, so little of their beliefs can be trusted.'

'When *can* you trust the impressions of women like them?' Baldwin asked. 'They had a stable, secure life until their man was ripped from them. There has been little time for them to grow accustomed to their new situation.'

'They'll get used to it soon enough,' Simon commented. 'It's the way of things. Widows are so often ill-served by those who used to depend upon their husbands for their businesses and livelihoods. I wonder how the men of Exeter will look upon these two.'

Baldwin made no comment. The sight of the two women's misery had reminded him of his own wife. How would she feel, were he to die here, today? Perhaps she would remember their early days together, their mutual trust and delight, their love. But more likely, she would remember the more recent times, the sadness, the sense of loss when the man for whom she had prayed and waited had returned with a different temper. That was what Jeanne would remember.

They had reached the top of Smythen Street, and now stood at the junction with Bolehille. Baldwin was about to wander on to-wards the joiner's hall, when he noted that Simon was gazing down towards the great Southern Gate. 'The German lives down there, I think.'

It was a moment before Baldwin recalled who he meant. 'Ah – the one with the star against his name?'

'Yes. The widow was keen to say that he was only marked because he had not yet paid. Perhaps . . .'

'What, Simon?'

'I was merely wondering whether a man like him, a foreigner, might see it as an opportunity to avoid paying because the saddler is dead now. Some unscrupulous fellows are quite capable of doing that sort of thing. A widow can't afford to throw good money after bad by hiring a lawyer.'

'Where is this leading?'

'Should we visit him now and see whether he intends to honour his debt?' Simon said lightly.

Baldwin glanced up towards Carfoix. 'We should really carry on with our investigations. Perhaps later we can speak to him.'

Simon acquiesced and the two trudged up Cook Row before turning right along the High Street.

'Last time we were here was that Christmas with Jeanne and Meg, wasn't it?' Simon said.

'Yes.'

'How is Jeanne?'

Baldwin couldn't meet Simon's look. 'She is well.'

'Is there something the matter, Baldwin? Forgive me, but you don't seem yourself.'

'I . . .' He was at a loss for words. Simon was his closest friend, but he did not feel up to discussing his innermost feelings about his wife – especially not in the street. 'We can talk later. Let us concentrate on the matter at hand first.'

'Yes, of course,' Simon said, but he shot a look filled with curiosity at his companion.

The house was easy to find, as Mabilla had indicated. Over the shop's door was a great wooden board which hung from chains and upon which was carved the figure of a joiner at work, carefully painted and with gilt lettering proclaiming the man's trade.

Baldwin stood and studied the building while Simon banged on the door. Before long a man appeared, a thin, pinch-faced fellow with faded gingerish hair and the veins all broken about his lumpy nose. He did not look like someone who enjoyed great health. 'Yes?'

'We are here to see Master Joiner. Is he in his hall?'

'He is busy. I'll see if he can spare you a moment or two.'

Baldwin pushed past the protesting man. 'You will tell him that the Keeper of the King's Peace is here to question him. Go!'

The man scurried off, leaving the odour of sour wine behind him.

'I think,' Simon said, 'you've upset the bottler in the middle of his morning nap.'

'You may be right,' Baldwin said without concern. 'I feel terrible. Let's go and apologise to him.'

They went after the bottler into a large shop. There were many examples of the joiner's trade here, from small cupboards and chairs to a large table. Simon could hear voices coming from behind a wide-open door at the far end of the room.

'Tell them to go to the devil. I'm busy!'

Baldwin exchanged a look with Simon, then they both followed the sound of the voices. They passed along a short passageway, and then came into a large hall, spacious and bright. Sitting at his table on the dais, they saw Joel with a drinking horn gripped in his fist, a jug of ale on the table before him.

Simon's attention was taken by their surroundings. The hall was very tall, with the inner face of the thatch showing thickly overhead, and some of the timbers were very old and coloured by the smoke which perpetually hung in among the rafters. Yet many of them had new pieces of wood mitred in among them. These had rich carvings upon them, grimacing gargoyles alongside smiling saints. There was a dog cocking a leg at an ox, a cat sitting with paw outstretched to catch a bird that was a short distance out of reach, and two knights sleeping. The total effect was of a series of jokes by a master carver.

'You like it?'

Baldwin had been watching the man at the table while Simon stared upwards. The man motioned the servant away dismissively, 'You the Keeper?' he demanded. 'What's all this about?'

Simon wrenched his mind back to the matter at hand as Baldwin spoke.

'Yes, I am a Keeper of the King's Peace, and I am here because of the murder of your friend Henry Saddler.'

'Oh, him. Yes, it was very sad. I shall miss him.' Joel poured himself a top-up of ale. 'Poor Henry. He was my oldest friend.'

'Surprising how friends can fall out,' Simon noted.

'Who said I fell out with him?'

'We have heard that you supplied him with a poorly made saddle frame.'

'That means nothing. Sometimes things fail. One of my frames did, it's true, but that's no reason to fall out. Christ's Finger, we've been comrades for forty years.'

'So we have heard,' Baldwin said. He walked closer to the table. 'We would like to know all that you can tell us about the night the Chaunter died.'

'What makes you think I can help with that? It was many long years ago,' Joel said, and leaned back in his seat.

As he did, Baldwin saw the livid bruise at the side of his jaw. 'You have been attacked?'

Joel grunted and winced at a fresh pain in his chest. He wondered if it came from a broken rib. If it still hurt this much in the morning, perhaps he should go and see a physician. That man de Malmesbury seemed to have a good reputation. Not that he wanted to waste good money in seeking a man who would tell him he had been bruised – something he knew only too well already.

'It is nothing,' he lied. 'Now, how do you expect me to help you? All that took place back in the days when King Edward I was on the throne and I was a lad.'

'You were among those who attacked the Chaunter.'

'There were rumoured to be many involved,' Joel said evasively.

'You deny being a part of the gang which sought to assassinate the Chaunter?' Simon asked.

'Of course I do!'

'Mabilla told us that you were a close companion of Henry when he was a lad.'

'Hardly that. We grew up at the same time, and boys will often join forces when they have done so.'

'True enough,' Baldwin said. 'What do you know of Henry's other friend then – William?'

Joel looked away. He glanced at his horn, and refilled it. 'He's a corrodian at Saint Nicholas's Priory,' he said flatly.

'He was a companion of yours?'

'He wouldn't have many dealings with my sort, I fear. I was merely a skilled worker. He was a warrior!' Joel spat. 'After the assassination attempt, when the King came here to listen to the evidence, William told how the Southern Gate had been left open all night long so that the murderers could make good their escape. That was why the old Mayor was hanged, and the gatekeeper too. It brought William his fortune, though. For his evidence, the King rewarded him with a place in his household. I suppose the regard in which he was held is demonstrated by the fact that the present King has bought him a nice corrody at the Priory.'

'Was he involved in the murder of the Chaunter too?'

'How should I know?'

'We know that Henry Saddler was there. He was a close companion of yours, as was this William. There was another, too, wasn't there? Tom. Where is he?' Baldwin asked.

'Tom? Good God in heaven, there's a name I haven't heard for many a long year. Yes, he was a mate of ours, but again, he left the city soon after the King arrived, two years after the murder. I haven't seen him since.'

'You can tell us nothing then, about the attack on the Chaunter?' Baldwin pressed.

Joel had a clear picture in his mind's eye of Will wielding his great staff and slamming it into his face. 'No.'

'Perhaps we need to think of something you *can* tell us about then,' Simon said sarcastically. 'What of Henry's business? Was he doing well?'

'Henry Potell was one of the foremost craftsmen in the city. Everyone who could would buy a saddle from him. They were marvellous pieces of work.'

'Yet one of them broke recently. One that *you* had made.'

'Like I said, it can happen.'

Baldwin lifted his eyebrows. 'I have never had a good quality saddle break under me. Do your frames often fail?'

'I wouldn't still be in business if they did, would I?' Joel growled. 'No, I think that my apprentice made an error. There was some greenwood out in the yard, and I reckon he picked that by mistake. Nothing more than that.'

'How much would Henry have sued you for?' Simon asked.

'He said it'd depend on how much Udo expected to get from *him*.'

'We hadn't heard of that,' Simon said. 'Mabilla didn't mention him.'

'Maybe he's dropped the matter then. I don't know.'

'Perhaps he has,' Simon said. He didn't like the fact that the two women had mentioned nothing about Udo suing Henry, but then he knew that many men wouldn't discuss their business with their wives. It was possible Henry hadn't told Mabilla about being taken to court so that she wouldn't worry.

'Do you know what Henry would have been doing up at the Cathedral?' Baldwin asked. 'It was in the Charnel Chapel that he was found, and it appears a peculiar place for him to visit.'

'I wouldn't know,' Joel said.

'Is there anybody else in business in Exeter who could have felt a rage against him? A rage bitter enough to kill him, or to have him killed?' Baldwin said.

Joel looked up at him and in his eyes was a frank honesty. 'I don't think this has anything to do with business. Henry tended to pay on time, and he had a good reputation as a craftsman – why should anyone want to hurt him?'

'Why indeed?' Baldwin repeated thoughtfully, observing Joel with his head on one side.

He was about to speak again when there was some shouting from the shop, and the sound of urgent footsteps. Vince hurried in, a young novice from the Cathedral behind him.

'Master? The Dean has sent for the Keeper to go back to see him,' he panted. 'It's urgent, he said.'

Baldwin looked at the novice. 'Well?'

'Sir Baldwin, it's another body. Someone's murdered a friar.'

'Christ Jesus, not poor Nick?' Joel muttered, and Baldwin shot him a look as the novice nodded.

Chapter Sixteen

'What was the man doing here?' Baldwin wondered. If his voice was harsher than usual, that was because he felt scaffolding was precarious at the best of times. This lot in particular seemed to wobble alarmingly, and Baldwin was reminded of the story he'd heard that a rock had recently plummeted from the wall, through the scaffolding and crushed a man. He wondered now whether the labourers had put it back together again quite so solidly as they ought.

The others appeared unconcerned. They were staring at the body on the rough planking. It had lain in a rock enclosure, built as stones were piled at the base of the wall, and to remove it, the Master Mason had pulled it up until it could be lain down on the scaffolding, rather than manhandling it over all the rubble.

In life, Baldwin reckoned the dead man would have been a humbling sight. His back was badly hunched, his face disfigured by a dreadful scar that had penetrated one eye socket and ruined the eyeball itself, and his right hand was badly withered. His looks were not improved by the terrible, bloody burnmark that encircled his throat. Baldwin looked more closely. There was a lot of blood, he thought. Usually a man who was hanged would have bruising, perhaps a little blood where the rope had torn the flesh away, but not so much as all this. The fluid had soaked the rope itself, dripping down the man's neck and running into his old tunic.

'He could have been walking past the site, and when the rope was released to allow a stone to be taken down from the top, maybe he walked into it? The rope encircled his neck, and he couldn't do anything to get it off, maybe?'

This was the Annuellar speaking, but he was ignored by the other men. The Master Mason shook his head. 'This was no accident, I can tell you that much. He was strangled on purpose.'

'How can you be sure of – ah – that?' the Dean enquired.

'When I knocked off work last night, I came here as usual to take a last turn about the place. I always do, to make sure that there's no thieving bast— saving your grace, sir, no felons about the place seeing what they can take. It's been known before now. I once had a pair of anvils stolen from under my nose and . . . anyway, the fellow wasn't there then. He was killed later, I'd wager.'

The friar's flesh was thin, Baldwin noted. It was possible that a blood vessel had been ripped open when the rope tightened. He leaned down and felt at the greying skin, and then saw the nick under the ropemark. He nodded pensively. 'This rope. Would it have been up there yesterday?'

'Yes. It's one we use to bring mortar and tools up from the bottom. The heavy stuff is lifted on a windlass from a separate pulley up there.'

'His body was concealed down there, you say?'

'Yes, he was hidden in among those stones,' Robert said helpfully, taking Baldwin's shoulder and pulling him to the edge of a plank, pointing down. Baldwin closed his eyes and tried to quash the desire to knock the Master Mason's hand from him. It was very tempting to push the man away, even if it would mean his falling to his death many feet below. Swallowing hard, Baldwin peered down.

'There was no one working there last afternoon,' Robert said, frowning down into the abyss. 'He could have been throttled and just left down there.'

Baldwin could see what he meant. There below them was a large gap between slabs of rock. He would have been effectively concealed for as long as no one searched for him, but . . . Baldwin frowned. Surely the killer would know that the body must soon be spotted in daylight, as soon as someone climbed this scaffold? Had he hidden the body in a hurry, before some passer-by could see what he had done? 'So he wasn't hanging when you found him?'

'No. When I got here this morning, I found the rope hanging there for no reason, so I gave it a pull to see what was down there. Got the shock of my life!'

'I can imagine it,' Baldwin said, stepping back from the brink, he hoped not too hurriedly.

'So what now?' the Treasurer asked. He watched as Baldwin walked to the ladder and descended.

Baldwin didn't answer immediately. He reached the bottom with relief, and paused a moment before walking under the scaffolding to the pile of rocks.

Each of the rocks was a cube, the faces at least a foot square. There was a large pile of them in a rough horseshoe shape, the open edge facing the old wall. Baldwin squeezed around between the rocks and the wall. It was a tight fit, very tight, and when he was inside, he peered back at the gap thoughtfully for a moment.

The space in the horseshoe was only some six feet in diameter. Glancing up, he felt a vague sense of disquiet as he realised how high up he had been, standing on those warped planks. A noise behind him told him that Simon had joined him.

'What do you think, Baldwin?'

'I'm not sure. I don't like the fact that his neck seemed to bleed so much. When I looked, I think there was a cut.'

'Someone had opened his throat?'

'I think so. Just enough to bleed him.'

'Why put the rope about him, then?'

Baldwin walked to the Cathedral wall again. 'Could you have dragged a man in through that gap?'

Simon's face cleared. 'Of course. He had to lift the fellow in, so he threw a rope about him and raised him aloft, over the walls of this enclosure.'

'Which means this killer knew something about the works,' Baldwin said. 'He had to know that this space existed, and he had to know how to lift a body up and into this space.'

'It was a good hiding place,' Simon commented. 'The walls are high enough.'

'Yes, but men are working up there all the time,' Baldwin said, pointing up at the scaffolding. 'Why put him here, when the body must soon be seen? And then leave the rope about his neck? Is this killer so stupid that he wanted people to know someone was murdered?'

Simon shrugged. 'There's probably a simple excuse. He was going to slip in here and release the rope, cover the body with rubble or a strip of cloth or something, but then he heard people coming, so he bolted.'

'Perhaps,' Baldwin said.

'Or,' Simon said, warming to a fresh idea, 'he couldn't fit! What if he was large-sized, with a great paunch, and couldn't physically slip around the wall like you and me?'

'He'd climb over the top,' Baldwin said scornfully.

'If he was that fat, I doubt it,' Simon said. 'Anyway, if this friar's throat was opened, where is all the blood?'

'No doubt that lies where the friar was murdered,' Baldwin said with a sigh.

'Well?' demanded the Treasurer truculently. 'What have you learned?' He and the others had all left the scaffolding and were waiting for Simon and Baldwin in a huddle near the south-west corner of the Cathedral.

'Little enough so far,' Baldwin said. 'The friar had his throat cut, I think, Dean. The murder must have happened somewhere nearby. There will be plenty of blood at the spot.'

'So what do you want us to do?' Treasurer Stephen said more calmly. His face was set, Baldwin noticed. He appeared anxious.

'I would like you to order your lay servants to look for the place where the friar was killed. Meanwhile we need to know who was the last person to have seen this man. I don't suppose any of you did so last evening?' he asked, glancing at the Dean, the Treasurer and Matthew, who stood holding a leather cylinder for a scroll.

They all shook their heads, the Dean with his customary air of benign bafflement, the Treasurer studiously ignoring the Dean at his side; Matthew looked down at the man and shook his head too, as though reluctantly.

'I shall let you know as soon as we learn anything about either man's death,' Baldwin promised, and the Dean took hold of the Treasurer's arm and led him away a short distance to speak to him. Baldwin watched the two, so apparently at odds, and yet always managing to work together for the good of the Cathedral itself.

'Sir Baldwin, I know this is quite ridiculous, but . . .'

'What is it?' he asked, facing the man. 'You are Matthew, I believe?'

'Yes. I am the Warden of the Fabric, the Clerk of the building work. It's probably nothing, Sir Baldwin, but I did see the friar late yesterday afternoon. He was here with one of the masons, a man called Thomas.'

'Here? Where, exactly? What were they doing?'

'Thomas was at the foot of the wall, and the friar and he spoke together for a while. Then they moved away and I didn't see anything of them after that.'

'Thomas? That's interesting,' Baldwin said. 'Do you know much of him?'

'Not I, no. I had thought—' he frowned. 'But no.'

'You thought what?'

'It's ridiculous, but I thought he looked familiar.'

'He reminded you of someone?'

'Yes – a man who used to live here in the city many years ago. He too was called Thomas,' Matthew recollected with a slight frown.

Baldwin felt his mood lighten. If a man should run away for some forty odd years, and then desire to see the place of his birth again, what better method of doing so than coming to a building site like this? It was enclosed, so he need not face any of his old friends; he could remain locked within the Cathedral's precinct. If any man saw him, it was so long ago since he had lived here, surely he would be all but unrecognisable.

Except, should someone here realise who he was, and be afraid lest Tom reveal their part in the murder of the Chaunter, might not that same someone decide to kill in order to keep his secret silent? Baldwin thought he might.

'You say that the two were at the Cathedral wall. Where exactly?'

'There,' Matthew said.

Baldwin looked at the corner he indicated, and then found his eyes being pulled westwards again, to the rectangular block of the Charnel Chapel. 'I think I know where he was killed,' he said as he set off towards the chapel's door.

Simon hurried to join him. Matthew and the Master Mason stood staring at each other for a moment, until Simon glanced back and beckoned to them authoritatively.

Baldwin stood at the north-eastern wall of the chapel. From here, northwards there was the small circular house that held the conduit;

east lay the Cathedral and works. 'Where did you stand, Matthew, when you saw the two?'

'I was over there at the entrance to the Exchequer.'

Baldwin looked eastwards. The Exchequer lay beyond the tower of St Paul, the northernmost of the two Cathedral towers. 'Any man slipping down here would have been invisible to you, then; or a man who went behind the conduit?'

'Yes.'

Baldwin stalked to the conduit. The little building had its door facing east. 'If they had entered here, you would have seen them?'

'I think so, yes.'

Baldwin nodded, and he looked up at the Charnel Chapel once more, a feeling of leaden reluctance entering his bones. 'He was killed in there, I think.'

He led the way across the grassed cemetery to the steps descending to the crypt itself. His eyes spotted the tell-tale marks on the stone steps. 'Blood.'

He went down the steps into the crypt, pushing the door wide. It moved easily on well-oiled hinges, and Baldwin found himself in a dry, musty-smelling chamber as large as the chapel above: some twenty feet by forty. The floor was flagged, and there were thick pillars supporting heavy arches that formed the floor of the chapel. Baldwin could hear Simon's breath growing sharper, faster, and usually it would have alleviated his own sombre mood, but not today. Baldwin had a strange feeling that he had been leading up to this moment for a long time, as though the crypt was in some way a culmination.

However, while Simon's anxiety was based on the purest of super-stitions about bones, Baldwin felt that there was an aura of evil in this specific building. He had felt it generally upstairs in the chapel, but here in the crypt it seemed more potent. I do not like this place, he thought to himself, and even the thought itself felt dangerous, as though the spirit of the building might read his mind.

'Nonsense!' he muttered aloud, annoyed with himself for allowing the atmosphere to colour his mood. It was ridiculous! He could only assume that his guilt at his treatment of his wife had caused this aberration. With a renewed determination, he marched further into the crypt.

On either side were piles of bones, skulls nearest the door, thigh and leg bones further on, stretching over to the far wall. The skulls themselves were set somewhat haphazardly, unlike the tidily piled thigh and arm bones. They were stored neatly; respectfully. The skulls were not. Some had fallen from a neat pile, and one had rolled across the floor. Baldwin picked it up, gazing into the empty eye-sockets, wondering what sort of a person had once inhabited these ounces of bone.

'I don't know how you can do that,' Simon muttered from behind him.

Baldwin said nothing, merely set the skull back among the others, then studied the floor nearby. With a grunt, he removed the skull again, and then started taking away all the others too until he had cleared a space. He touched the bare flagged floor and rubbed finger and thumb together.

'He died here.'

'Could you take me to this man Thomas?' Baldwin asked when they were once more outside.

'My mason?' Robert asked. 'The clumsy one? Yes, I can take you to him. He was talking to me only this morning about leaving here and coming with me to another site. Can't settle.'

'I should be glad to speak with him,' Baldwin said, walking into the sunshine and taking a deep breath. In the crypt he had felt the onset of claustrophobia, and it was a relief to inhale the fresh air with the sound of birdsong in the trees, the wind soughing in the branches, and people shouting. In his distraction he missed the Master Mason's reference to clumsiness.

It took little time for Baldwin to tell the Dean what they had learned. 'This murderer tempted his second victim into the crypt somehow, and then stabbed him once in the neck. I think that the Coroner will find a stab wound in his throat on the right side. The rope burn was fortuitous, but wasn't intended to cover the stab, I don't think. When the man had killed the friar, he carried him over to the works, and put the rope about his neck, lifted him up and had him drop down into the hollow where the Master here found him.'

The Dean gave a firm instruction that the Master Mason should help

Baldwin and Simon in all that they required, and then left, his face grim. The Treasurer went off with Matthew to return to their work in the Exchequer, and Simon and Baldwin followed Robert de Cantebrigge over towards the breadhouse.

The odour of fresh baked bread was enough to set Simon's belly rumbling; they had been asking questions of people all morning, and soon they should think of a meal. Simon was used to the old mealtimes – a breakfast very early in the morning, dinner a couple of hours before noon, and a good supper in the mid-afternoon – and he found it hard to travel to places where the mealtimes were different. He knew that the Exeter canons tended to stick to the routine of monks, so they would have their main meal after Nones, or mid-afternoon, while their supper was after Vespers. Through the morning they survived on the odd hunk of bread and a little breakfast of weak porridge. It wouldn't keep him going.

As they passed around the tower of St Paul, there was an enclosure, and in it was a group of masons working on a huge rock. They were fashioning it into the shape of a column, cutting the top face smooth and setting rounded edges on the sides. A mason with a thick, bushy beard and long hair tied back in a pony-tail, was using a straight-edged stick to ensure that there were no bulges in the uppermost surface, while at his side was a large wooden mould cut into the precise curve that the stone should follow. Men would take this and measure the outer shape of the pillar to ensure that it would fit with all the other sections that would make up this support.

'Thomas!' Cantebrigge called, and the lead mason glanced at him, nodding. He put down his stick, and then seemed to realise that the Master Mason was not alone. His eyes flitted from Baldwin to Simon and back before he made his way to join them.

'This is Sir Baldwin de Furnshill, this is Bailiff Simon Puttock. They want to speak to you.'

Baldwin did not bother with any preamble. 'There has been another murder here last night. A friar was stabbed, and then hanged. Where were you last night?'

'I was in the city earlier in the evening, then I returned here and remained in the Close all night.'

Thomas was a brawny fellow with a beard as thick as a bramble bush. His deep-set eyes were distrustful and apprehensive, from what Baldwin could see of them, and his age was surely comparable with Henry's confederates. His heavy brow made him look a little slow of thought, but Baldwin reckoned that there was no dull-wittedness here.

'The dead man was a friar called Nicholas. Did you know him?'

'Why should I? Friars don't often come here to the Close.'

'You may know him because he was one of the men attacked forty years ago when the Chaunter was murdered here,' Baldwin said grimly. '*Did you know him*?'

'No. I wouldn't think so.'

Simon smiled. 'That's a lie, friend. You were seen talking to the man last night.'

'Perhaps the man who told you *that* was a liar,' Thomas said sharply.

'Your accent sounds just like an Exonian's,' Simon commented.

'I've been here a while looking to the rebuilding. Maybe I've picked up a little of the local way of talking.'

'Have you heard of the murder of the Chaunter?' Baldwin tried.

'Yes. It was after that the Bishop asked permission to be able to build his wall about the place, I think.'

'That's right. Because an armed band of assassins came here and slaughtered the Chaunter. We've heard that not many escaped that attack.'

'What? What's it got to do with me?'

'Be calm, friend,' Baldwin said, showing his teeth in a smile that held little humour. 'It is merely the oddness of this chain of coincidences: we've heard that the friar was one of those who was attacked with the Chaunter. He had been there that night and won his scars from those who would have tried to kill his master. He was brave and honourable. And there were others there that night. There was a man called Henry, a saddler. He lies dead now in the Charnel Chapel.'

'What of it?'

'How long have you been here working on the Cathedral?' Simon asked suddenly.

'Almost a year, I suppose,' Thomas said with a sidelong glance at the Master Mason.

Baldwin shot Robert a look and caught the brief pause, then the slight nod, as though he was considering and calculating before agreeing. 'Good. And these murders began a short while ago. Perhaps you would like to tell us where you were before that?'

'I have been all over the country. Immediately before coming here, I worked on the walls in London, I've been to the castle at Conwy, and I've helped with many churches.'

'Where were you born?' Simon asked.

'At Axminster.'

Baldwin knew the town slightly. Set in flatlands on the Devon and Dorset borders, not very many miles from the sea, it was a pleasant small market town. He had seen the place when he had visited Forde Abbey some years before. 'Was that where you learned your trade?'

'No. I left my home when I was not yet seventeen and went to Dorchester to learn this. There was a church being built there. I helped.'

'When was that?'

'I am six and fifty years old now, so it would have been forty years ago.'

Simon and Baldwin exchanged a look. Baldwin knew it was possible. Sometimes men were driven to leave their home cities in order to seek a better life. About forty years ago there had been the Welsh wars, and in the aftermath, men were taken from all over the country to go and build the King's new castles there; thousands of them. It was a massive undertaking, and it denuded the rest of the country of skilled masons. Many men who left their homes were snapped up by desperate town-dwellers who needed walls mended, new parish churches built, or even simply a new privy added to a hall. When Baldwin was a lad, he could remember his father complaining bitterly about the lack of workmen.

'It seems curious that there should be two murders in the Close just recently,' Baldwin said at last. 'Especially when both are associated with the murder so many years ago.'

'Why should it have anything to do with me?' Thomas asked.

'Because you bear the same name as one man who was there,' Baldwin said. 'A man called Thomas was involved in killing the Chaunter.'

'Then I would be foolish indeed to come here without changing my name, wouldn't I?' Thomas said, but without bluster. He sighed. 'Do you mean to arrest me? I've done nothing.' Except kill poor Saul, of course – and that by accident, he thought.

'It puzzles me that a man should say he saw you talking to the friar last night when you say you didn't.'

'Look – I was upset last night and went straight to my bed.'

'Why upset?'

'That's a matter for me. A woman,' Thomas said, glancing at the Master Mason in explanation and a search for sympathy.

Robert rolled his eyes. 'Wine and women will be the end of many a good building. Now, masters both, have you finished interrogating my man here? He has a lot of work to be getting on with.'

The Dean was in his hall alone when the two men went up and knocked upon his door.

'Ah, Bailiff, Sir Baldwin. Will you – ah – please come in and be seated? I shall ask for some bread and meat for you.'

In fact, when the door opened a short while later, there was more than the sparse repast indicated by his words. Three servants entered with trays held high. There were meats, cheese, wine and a thick, steaming pottage. 'I – ah – often feel the need for warmer foods at this time of year,' Dean Alfred explained. 'So, please, do you have any theories as yet?'

Baldwin spoke, looking to Simon for support as he described their visits to the widow and to Joel. 'So I think that there *is* a connection between the present two deaths and the murder of the Chaunter,' he concluded. 'Do you remember that night?'

'The night of Chaunter Walter's assassination? My heavens – um – no. It was many years before I came here. I only arrived when Bishop Stapledon was installed. Not because I was an especial ally of his, it just happened that way. Hmm. I'll have to see if there is someone who can help you with that. The Treasurer may have been here then. *Someone* must have been. Plainly it would have to be an older vicar or canon – a man who was then a – er – novice or chorister. I shall ask for you, Sir Baldwin.'

'It is certainly interesting that there were these different fellows who were all companions at the time,' Baldwin said.

'And a strange coincidence that the man who left was called Thomas,' Simon added.

'True, although the man's comment that he would have to be a merry fool not to have changed his name before returning was compelling enough,' Baldwin pointed out.

'Perhaps,' Simon said. 'Although . . .'

'What?' asked the Dean.

'It just occurred to me: if he had worked in other cities as a mason, he might have assumed that coming here, he'd meet men he'd worked with before. Changing his name might have seemed dangerous. Thomas is also, of course, a very common name. The chance of finding someone who recalled and cared about events so many years ago, was a risk worth taking.'

'A good point. Masons often go from one site to another expecting to meet someone from a past job,' the Dean commented. 'I – ah – know this myself. There was a need to find a new mason after poor Saul died recently, and one of the men suggested a fellow with whom he had worked before. Recommendation often works to recruit new men.'

'How did he die?' Simon asked. 'Was it an illness or an accident?'

'An accident,' the Dean said. 'The poor fellow happened to be walking along beneath the scaffolding when a stone fell and crushed him. In actual fact,' he added pensively, 'it was Thomas who was responsible for the stone slipping free.'

'Him again?' Baldwin said, his interest aroused. 'I should like to see where this happened.'

'I shall ask my Clerk of the Works, Matthew, to show you, if you like.' The Dean tilted his head, looking like a sparrow eyeing a suspect morsel of food. 'That – ah – doesn't mean Thomas is guilty, of course. These things do happen.'

'Yes, they do,' Simon agreed sharply, but there was a light in Baldwin's eye which Simon hadn't seen since he arrived in Exeter.

'What do you – ah – wish to do next, then?'

'We should speak to this curious corrodian, William,' Baldwin declared, sitting back with his mazer of wine resting on the top of his belly. 'And then perhaps, we should question this foreign gentleman as well – this Udo.'

'Udo Germeyne?' the Dean asked.

'You know of him?'

'By reputation. There are some who make their money solely by regrating and forestalling – that is, by buying all the stores in the morning and then reselling them later when they have a monopoly, or catching peasants on their way to market and buying in their produce before they reach the city, again in order that they control all prices. It is a violation of the city's laws, of course, but all the Freemen tend to do it to a greater or lesser extent, so the fines are – um – derisory. They are not enough, in my view, to prevent a man continuing.'

'So Udo is not a popular man with everybody?' Baldwin said.

'I do not think he is particularly *un*popular,' the Dean responded. 'However, I find such behaviour often indicates the character of the man. If he is prepared to be so mercenary in his business dealings, using money to create more money like a usurer, what else would he not be capable of?'

To Baldwin's mind, usurers were more evil than those who merely regrated and forestalled in a well-regulated market like Exeter's. 'I hope you don't think him capable of murder just because of his market trading?'

'Certainly his part in all this seems odd,' Simon mused. 'And the speed with which the two women sought to protect him was curious.'

'Let's go and speak to him first, then,' Baldwin said, rising. He drained his cup. 'Thank you, Dean, for our lunch. We shall see you again as soon as we have something to report. In the meantime – could you arrange for the mason Thomas to be watched? I should not wish him to suddenly disappear.'

'You think he could be the guilty man?'

Baldwin considered, staring through the Dean's little window out at the Cathedral Close. 'I do not know, but the coincidence of his name, the fact that he's about and Matthew says he reminds him of a man who left here years ago . . . It is better to keep him by than lose him.'

'Do you wish Matthew to show you to the place where Saul died now?'

'It will wait,' Baldwin said. 'If you could ask him to show me later, I would be grateful.'

They left the Dean's room and walked out into the Cathedral's grounds. Crossing the Close, Simon at first felt how chill it was compared with the warmth of the Dean's hall, but then there was a rift in the clouds overhead, and suddenly the area was flooded with warmth.

'It makes the whole city look more pleasant, doesn't it?' he commented idly.

Baldwin wasn't concentrating. 'Sorry?'

'I said . . .'

There was a rattling of hooves on the cobbles, and Simon looked up in time to see a knight wrapped in a thick black woollen cloak over a bright red tunic and green hose ride in through the Fissand Gate. The two stopped and eyed the man as he rode along towards them, and then, just as he was about to trot on past he stopped and threw back his hood. His gleaming bald pate had a fringe of golden curls now faded with the years, which looked like a baby's fluff on a middle-aged man's head. His mouth moved into a smile, and as it did so, Simon could almost hear Baldwin's hackles rise.

'Sir Baldwin. How pleasant to see you,' the man exclaimed. 'And Bailiff Puttock, too. I am delighted to see you both here.'

'Godspeed,' Baldwin said, less than entirely heartily. 'I am glad to see you, too, Sir Peregrine.'

Simon grinned to hear his friend lie. Baldwin had always cordially disliked Sir Peregrine de Barnstaple.

'I suspect we are here for the same reasons, but I shall have to speak to you later, if you do not mind, Sir Baldwin,' Sir Peregrine declared. 'I am weary, yet I still have business to attend to with the Dean and Chapter. Will you excuse me? Where can I contact you?'

When they had told the knight where they were staying, he lifted his eyebrows in apparent surprise, and then smiled sympathetically, as though their inn was far below his own standard before riding off towards the Dean's stables.

'What is he doing here?' Simon wondered.

'Sadly I am sure we shall soon find out,' said Baldwin. 'Come, let's get away from here while we can!'

Thomas was packing his meagre belongings and tools and preparing to escape. He had been very close to being uncovered when the two men had questioned him, and as soon as they left, he went to find the Master Mason, who was frowning at a plan sketched in charcoal on a sheet of vellum.

'Sir, do you think you could use me on your other sites?'

'No. If you want work, you can stay here.'

'But Master, I can't stay here, not now.'

Robert stopped his fiddling with the sketch and took a deep breath. At last he met Thomas's eye. 'If you've done something here, lad, that's your lookout. I tell you this: I didn't believe a word of your shite about some woman, right? And I didn't believe your tale of being born someplace else neither. No. You came from here, didn't you? And I reckon you're hiding something. No problem with that when you keep your nose out of things, but when it leads to the work being held up, that I do mind. And when men start to die, I mind that too, just in case I get to be the next one. Right? So as far as I'm concerned, you can stay here if you want, Tom, but you aren't coming with me anywhere else. Sorry, but that's the way it is.'

As he spoke, Robert's face was oddly devoid of compassion, as though he was talking to a man who was already condemned.

Perhaps, Thomas thought, he already was.

When he saw the knight approaching, John Coppe didn't bother to hold out his bowl. Sir Baldwin didn't ever give him alms. Still, there was a chance that he'd be more lucky with the strange knight's friend who was Bailiff, so he smiled, ducking his head as Sir Baldwin approached. Then John remembered that some little while ago, Sir Baldwin had been in the city with his woman, and she had been very generous. Perhaps she'd taught her old man something.

'Sir Knight, spare alms for a poor old sailor? Your wife was generous to me.'

Baldwin stopped and stared at him. 'Yes, I remember you,' he said as he fumbled in his purse. 'I haven't much . . .'

'That's enough, Sir Baldwin. Every bit is a help to me,' Coppe said with a lopsided grin. 'When you have as little as me, anything's useful.'

'Are you always here?' Simon asked.

'Costs me three shillings a year to take this spot, and I don't grudge it. I make enough.'

Simon nodded. The places at Tavistock were cheaper, but then the town was smaller and the chances of a beggar making as much money as Coppe could earn in a year were that bit more remote. He dug into his own purse and pulled out the first coin that came to hand, but then he held it up.

Coppe lifted his eyebrows. 'A penny? What are you after, Master?'

'Just news. You'll have heard about the friar killed out there in the Close? They found his body this morning. Did you see anything?'

'I saw him come into the Close yesterday, aye. It was late afternoon, and I remember because Janekyn was here, and as soon as the friar appeared, Jan slipped off so he didn't have to talk to the man.'

'Why was that?' Simon said.

'Jan was always a loyal Exeter man,' Coppe said dismissively, then threw a hasty look over his shoulder in case Janekyn was about. 'That friar, Nicholas, was guilty, in his mind, because he tried to protect the Chaunter against the men John of Exeter had hired to remove him. Daft, I know, but Jan feels strongly about that kind of thing.'

'You know him well?' Simon asked.

'Yes – and before you ask: he's no killer! Anyway, he was here when the friar went in and he stayed here. I was with him, so if you want to have him hanged, you'll have to hang me too. And that wouldn't be easy, lords, because you'd have to carry me to the rope on account of me not having the legs to walk there!'

Simon chuckled along with him, but didn't respond when Coppe held out his bowl expectantly. Instead he flicked the coin contemplatively. 'What about the other man, the dead saddler? Did you see him the day before they found his body?'

'He was often about here. You know, men like him, they'll come in here to do a bit of business before Mass, won't they? Actually, he was here with that man Udo, and they had a real shouting-match in the Close there. The foreigner threatened to kill him, in so many words.'

'Why was that?' Baldwin asked sharply. 'We hadn't heard this before.'

'Something to do with the saddler's daughter. Henry was saying something about the German not being allowed to marry her, I think.'

'Aha!' Simon said.

'What then? Was there a fight?' Baldwin frowned.

'No. A vicar ran up and stopped them before they could do that,' Coppe said regretfully. 'Could have been fun, otherwise.'

Simon flicked the coin again, and it rattled in his bowl. 'Keep your eyes open, and let us know if you see anything else.'

'My pleasure. Sounds to me like easy money,' Coppe grinned.

Baldwin looked at him, and then turned slowly. From here he could see the lean figure of Sir Peregrine crossing the Close with a vicar and the Annuellar behind him. He glanced at Baldwin without slowing his pace, and then made straight for the Charnel Chapel, disappearing behind the southern wall.

He had the look of a man who was involved in a busy and less than appealing task. Baldwin had not asked who the new Coroner of Exeter might be, and now he wondered with sinking heart whether this knight could be the replacement for the late Sir Roger de Gidleigh.

Glancing down at the beggar, who was happily fiddling with his coin, Baldwin shook his head. 'Be careful that this isn't the same as the easy money you were paid as a sailor, Coppe, on that last journey that cost you your livelihood and your leg.'

'Hardly likely!'

Baldwin nodded, but he found his eyes drawn back once more to that chapel. He felt a sick apprehension, and the worst of it was, he had no idea why.

Chapter Seventeen

William walked about the cloister at St Nicholas's Priory with his staff always in his hand, peering into the darkest places in the long corridors, while his ears strained for the hiss and clatter of a fine-pointed arrow striking the stones. When you stood in line waiting for the clash of arms, the first you would know would be the noise of the arrows whistling and soughing through the air, but something only a warrior knew was that when the thing was aimed at *you*, you usually wouldn't hear it until it hit. He knew that, all right. Jesus! He should do – he'd stood against the sodding things often enough.

It was why he was here, of course, because he'd wrecked his health fighting for the King and the latter was repaying the debt; but now William was prey to some worrying fears. If the King ever came to learn of his dishonest behaviour (even though this had occurred many years ago), that wouldn't stop Edward from demanding his corrody back, let alone heaping any other insults or curses he could upon William's head. And the King could heap an awful lot of shit on a man's head before he removed it.

Perhaps past loyalty would count. At the end of the day, that was all William had. He had done his duty time and time again – in battles from Scotland all the way across Wales and back. He'd been there in the bogs and marshes at Bannockburn to see the King's first setback, and he'd been a loyal supporter of Edward even after the Lords Marcher had ringed London and forced the King to exile the Despensers. He had been in the King's service when the latter himself took the offensive and headed northward, crushing the army of his cousin at Boroughbridge. Then there had been the fiasco of Tynemouth when he deserted his wife.

William had lost all faith in the King after that. As he sat in the boat, listening to the racking sobs of the Queen bemoaning her fate, her loveless marriage, and the death of one of her favourite ladies-in-waiting – a second died a little later – William had only one thought: this was the closest he had ever come to death. There would have been no escape, had he been caught there with the Bruce's men surrounding the place.

The King had just left him there. Him – *William*! Dumped like unnecessary baggage to be rifled and casually discarded by Edward's enemies. Sweet Mother of God, how could he do that to William? It left him with a very unpleasant taste in his mouth. And then the dizziness had started, and he knew it would soon be time to seek a quieter place to live.

He had been unhappy to leave his castle. Being in charge of a place like that, with so many squires and other men-at-arms under his control had been good. Far better than standing in a line of warriors, staring at a face only feet away, and swinging a sword.

That was battle. A man stood or fell by the power in his arms: his left holding up his shield and trying to avert blows from all directions; his right lunging with his sword, parrying, knocking aside when he could, prior to stabbing . . . and every so often the foe would fall, silently or shrieking, as his blood gushed like a fountain of bright crimson, drenching all those around him, or it might suddenly burst in a fine red shower. Then it was like the red mist which he had heard tell of so many times: that helmet of rage and hatred which encased a man so that, like a berserker, he could fly at his enemies with the power of ten men, scattering all before him.

Yes. Some men spoke of the honour of fighting, but Will knew better. Fighting was only ever a case of getting a good blow in first. Fuck the arse who decided to fight 'nicely', he wouldn't last long. No, it was better to slay all you could as quickly as you could, and stay with the other warriors behind the shield wall. Courage and honour had nothing to do with it. Will had stood in those lines at almost every battle the King had asked him to attend. Yet the bastard had left him there at Tynemouth to die, and it was only by a miracle that he'd escaped.

When he asked to be released from the King's service, the man had hardly bothered to talk. He'd simply indicated that Will should, 'Speak to our Steward of the Wardrobe.'

It had hurt. After all he'd done, to be dismissed like that! It was shameful.

Still, a man must shift as best he might. This Priory had accepted the King's money, but that wouldn't serve to help William, should news ever be bruited abroad that he had once lied to the King's father in order to be noticed. Whatever Edward's personal reaction, his sidekick Despenser wouldn't be amused. Despenser would want the money back, and he had none of the King's subtlety. He would come and take it back with a sword in his fist, and if the money wasn't all there, he'd ask where it might be, with that quiet, silky voice of his, while his blade was slowly sinking into Will's belly. He had no illusions: he'd seen the Despenser at work.

That was why it was vital that his part in killing the Chaunter was kept concealed.

He had hoped to enjoy a little more time with Mabilla. In fact, when she asked him to meet her that day in the tavern, he had hoped that that might be the reason for her request. How foolish of him! She'd simply gone ranting on about that simpleton Henry, God rot his soul. Obviously, now he thought about it, if anyone *had* known of his desire for her, they might realise that William had an excellent motive to murder the man, and a trained warrior like him could well kill without compunction.

The only person who really knew still was Joel, though. Just as Joel knew other things about William . . . and hated him, too. It was the man's own fault. He should have been quicker off the mark to tell the King about the South Gate being left open. Instead he let the opportunity slide, and William had grasped it. Of course he was jealous. And vengeful, too. He knew that the whole of Will's career had been built upon that lie at the King's court.

And then the corrodian had a most unsettling thought. It wasn't only Joel who knew these things – Mabilla did, too, and she was capable of hiring a man to shoot him down.

William gave a deep sigh, then set his jaw. He'd never thought that being involved in the murder of Walter de Lecchelade could possibly come back to haunt him like this.

Udo Germeyne was very content this morning. Some little while ago he had invested in a part share of a ship's cargo, and the proceeds from the sale had just come to him, exceeding by far his expectations. All his losses on the day he fell from his horse had been recouped, and he had also received a pleasing note from his fiancée which promised continued love and affection after their marriage. All in all, it was turning out to be a most satisfactory day. *Ja*!

The knock at his door made him beam. He was going to be married to the loveliest woman in the city. That was cause for delight, and he would welcome any man who entered his dwelling and offer them wine to celebrate his good fortune.

His servant walked in with two stern-looking men. 'Master Udo, this is the Keeper of the King's Peace and his friend Bailiff Puttock. They want to ask you about Master Henry.'

Udo's calm wobbled. 'Oh? Ah. So, how may I help you, Masters?'

Simon spoke. 'We should like to hear all you know about Master Henry Saddler, the man who was murdered in the churchyard.'

'Yes, I knew Henry. I had dealings with him recently.'

'You owe him for a saddle?' Simon asked.

'No.' Udo's face set firmly. 'He tried to make me buy a saddle from him, but it was lousy workmanship, and it broke when I first tested it. After that, I would buy nothing from him.'

'We had heard that his quality was excellent.'

'So it was, normally. Mine, that was not.'

'And you argued with him in the Close on the afternoon of the day he was murdered.'

Udo thrust out his lips. 'Was it then? I cannot remember.'

'It was a loud dispute, Master Udo,' Baldwin said. He was sitting at one of the merchant's stools, and had listened to their exchanges with interest. 'Others heard you.'

'Perhaps they were thinking of another man,' Udo said. Then: 'Come, let me offer you wine. I have so much to celebrate. It is sad to know that I have lost a father-in-law, but I am to gain a wife. That is cause to drink and make merry, is it not?'

'Who are you to marry?' Baldwin smiled.

'Why, the saddler's daughter.'

'Which is why she didn't want us to worry you about our suspicions,' Simon noted.

'What suspicions?'

'Oh, that a man might threaten to ruin a widow for his own profit. That a man might sue her and take her house.'

Udo smiled openly. 'Come, you suggest that? No, I have already told them that there is no possibility that I would sue them. It would be too cruel to sue a lady who has just lost her husband.'

'A man might kill, though, if he learned that his dearest wish to marry the woman of his choice was to be thwarted by her father,' Baldwin said.

'Who says so?' This time Udo's smile was a little more strained.

The servant came in with a pair of jugs and set them before Baldwin and Simon with two pleasant pewter goblets. Baldwin picked his up and studied it. 'These are pretty things. Must have cost you a lot of money.'

'They were not cheap, but you see, I am wealthy,' Udo said, waving a hand about him.

'A wealthy man might be righteously angry when another tries to fleece him,' Baldwin observed.

'A wealthy man would simply crush a fellow like that,' Udo said with perfect calmness.

'Perhaps. Yet if he was to try to marry into the family, there would be no point in impoverishing the fellow. Another means of punishment might be sought.'

Udo said smugly, 'Today I learned that a ship has entered Topsham Harbour with a large cargo, and a part of that is mine. I am worth so much money that I do not need to worry about such trivial matters.'

'You didn't know that the ship was about to come in when Henry died, though,' Baldwin stated.

'I have other sources of wealth,' Udo said.

'And no one with whom to share them,' Baldwin said quietly. He studied the rich German before him. This Udo was similar to how Baldwin had been before he had found his Jeanne. Jeanne, the source of his pleasure, the mother of his child; Jeanne, the woman he had betrayed. The thought made his tone bitter. 'You have been lonely for many years, looking at other men in the city and thinking: "Yes, they have wives and children, they have meaning to their lives. Yet I here have nothing. I am alone, with no one to mourn me when I die." That is right, isn't it?'

'But I am to marry!' Udo exclaimed. 'That is my joy, and the reason why I am celebrating.'

'It would have been terrible, then, if Henry Saddler had told you in the Cathedral Close that he would not have you as his son,' Baldwin finished sarcastically.

Udo pulled a moue. 'What? You think so? I would have persuaded him. Ach! How could he refuse me, one of the most prosperous men in the whole of this city? You tell me he would have maintained his rejection of me after he had had an opportunity to consider? No. I do not think so.'

'Even though you threatened to kill him?' Baldwin said.

'It was nothing. I didn't mean it.'

'What did you do that night? Did you remain out there, near the Charnel Chapel, and wait until he came past, meaning to discuss his daughter with him, only to learn that he was steadfast? Did you kill him because he wouldn't bow to your riches?'

'I went to a tavern, and then I came home.'

'Which tavern?'

'The Grapes in Broad Street.'

'That is very convenient for the Cathedral Close,' Baldwin sneered. 'You could have sat in there, gone to kill him, and returned.'

'Come, Master Keeper! With one breath you tell me that I was his enemy, saying that he would have nothing to do with me, and in the next breath you tell me that I was able to tempt him to talk to me in a dark alley!'

Baldwin suddenly felt the same strange sensation as he had experienced in the crypt – but this time it was worse. His palms felt clammy, his back sweaty. It was as though the walls were starting to lean inwards to crush him. There was a peculiar panic in his breast.

'You think you are clever, Master Udo, but I understand you! You wanted the girl, because she is a very pretty thing, isn't she, that little Julia? And the thought that her father might refuse to allow you to see her, that was like a lance-thrust in your flank, wasn't it? You'd have slaughtered the whole of the city rather than give her up, once you had set your heart on her. You still would, wouldn't you? She is beautiful, she's the sort of woman to whom a man could give his heart gladly. He'd offer to share all his wealth with her – even house her mother, if he had to. And here was her father, the bastard, who had done you no favours, selling you a cheaply made saddle that failed the first time you used it, and he was going to try to keep you from her. What would a man with blood in his veins do? Exactly what you did. You went to find him and stabbed him in the back at the first opportunity, didn't you?'

He had risen to his feet, and almost without realising it, had crossed the room and stood in front of Udo, who stared up at him with alarm. Baldwin shot a look at Simon, and saw the concern in the Bailiff's eyes. Only then did he realise how his anger had all but overwhelmed him. He half-turned to go back to his stool, but then he whirled round to face Udo again. 'Tell me it isn't true. Tell me you did not in truth murder her father. *Tell me!*'

Udo swallowed, then gulped at his wine. 'I tell you I killed no one. I did not wield the knife, and I did not order or pay or ask another to do so. I am innocent. If you want the killer, you must search elsewhere.'

'What was all that about?' Simon asked as they left Udo's house and meandered up towards Carfoix.

'I wanted to get to the truth of the matter, that is all,' Baldwin said defensively.

Simon touched his elbow. When Baldwin looked at him, Simon spoke quietly. 'Baldwin, we've known each other many years, and I've not seen you like that before. You almost attacked him. What came over you? Should we visit a physician?'

'No. I shall be fine,' Baldwin said. 'It was just . . .'

He stopped. He had never told Simon about the woman on the islands or his adultery. It seemed the wrong time to talk about it now.

'Baldwin, I can see you're upset. Come with me, old friend.'

'I am fine!'

'Let's find a tavern or inn where we can sit down. You don't have to tell me anything, but I can talk about Meg and try to remember what she looks like. I'd like to remember her,' he added wistfully.

Baldwin felt a strong pang of jealousy. Here he was, missing his wife and his happiness at his marriage, and here was Simon, who still held his wife's love, and who felt the loneliness of being parted. Baldwin would have given much to be in Simon's position, rather than in the dreadful place he currently inhabited.

He allowed himself to be led along the High Street, and in through a low doorway to a tavern. There was a small table in the far corner, and the two men went over to it. Baldwin sat while Simon beckoned a maid. Soon they were taking their first grateful swallows of mulled wine.

'You know I'll keep whatever it is a secret if you want me to,' Simon began, 'but there is obviously something worrying you. Perhaps I can help.'

'I don't think so, Simon,' Baldwin sighed.

'Is it Jeanne?'

'Why do you ask that?' Baldwin said with genuine surprise.

'Because of the way you reacted to a man who's announced his intention of marrying,' Simon said with a lopsided grin. 'There was a strong hint of jealousy in your response to him.'

'We are not getting on very well.'

'Can I ask why?'

'It is not her. It's me. I . . . I still love her, but I cannot . . .'

'Then you should make sure that she knows you love her,' Simon said. 'It's the only thing a man can do for his woman. Prove to her you love her.'

'How?' Baldwin asked simply. 'I fear I have squandered her love for me.'

'You have done nothing of the sort. You're feeling confused since returning from pilgrimage, that's all. It was a very different experience, Baldwin, especially for you. You have been to those places before, and you were revisiting your youth. You were excited, weren't you, when we were at Galicia? It was like rediscovering your past. I could see it.'

'I am home again now, though.'

'And she is the same, but you have changed a little. We suffered much on our journeys, didn't we? It changes a man. Perhaps you just need to relearn how good your wife is.'

'Again – *how*?'

'You trust her judgement, you like her intelligence. Make use of her. Why not bring her here now? Send a man to fetch her. Explain that you'd value her impression of things. You know she would never refuse you.'

'I can't!'

'Why not?'

Baldwin lowered his head into his hands. 'It would be impossible while that primped coxcombe Sir Peregrine is here.'

'Yes. I wonder why he *is* here,' Simon said.

'I have a deeply unpleasant feeling that we shall soon find out,' Baldwin said dejectedly.

Thomas thrust the last of his belongings into his small sack and bound his rolled blankets to it, before washing his hands, soaking the bloody rags to remove them.

Christ Jesus but they hurt! The left hand was marginally less painful. He'd grabbed the rope less hard with that, but the right was dreadful. Every time he moved that hand he broke the scabs again.

He rewrapped the linen bandages, flexing his fingers once or twice with a wince, and then threw his pack over his back and marched from his shed towards the Fissand Gate. He was going to get away from here *now*. There was nothing left for him here. The deaths of Nicholas as well as Henry would soon be laid at his door, and he had no intention of waiting around for that to happen.

There were some men lounging at the gate, and Thomas saw three of them eye him. So, instead of continuing, he walked round past the conduit and charnel, and then hurried along, concealed by the chapel itself, until he reached the Church of St Mary Major. There he stopped and hid, panting slightly, to check on what was happening.

Sure enough, the three men weren't lounging now, they were pelting along at full tilt, one of them swearing at losing 'that mother-swyving churl'. Thomas edged around the wall of the church as they ran down, one man yelling that he must have headed for the Bear Gate. Thomas immediately walked back towards Fissand.

This city was cursed, he thought to himself as he approached the gate. He stopped, turned and stared at the Charnel Chapel. It was a bleak, nasty building, he thought. Same sort of size as Lecchelade's house, but without the charm. It was not even built of good stone, but had been thrown up hurriedly. Anyone could see that the place was made as a gesture, nothing more. He wondered whether Dean John Pycot had ever cared about the building . . . but the daft sod had probably never seen it, had he? He'd ordered its construction as a reparatory deed, hoping that it might lead to his reassimilation into the Cathedral's

Chapter, but he had failed in that wish. He'd taken his punishment without demur and left to go to his monastery as a monk.

Thomas hefted his bag, and felt the tears prickle at his eyes. This place had destroyed him. His father, once a familiar face to all in the city, a man of honour and integrity who taught Thomas all he knew, had been hanged after the murder on the orders of the King. The shame and remorse which had overwhelmed Thomas when he realised how badly he had betrayed not only himself but also his father, had lingered throughout his entire lifetime. He had hoped it would be gone by now, but no. There was nothing but shame and destruction for him here. Those three men had proved that.

If he had taken the shortest road out of the Close, walking out by the Bear Gate and leaving the city by the South Gate, he might have missed the guards, but that would mean passing under the Southern Gate's arch again, and he wasn't sure he had the strength to do that. He'd be tempted to look up, and as he did so, see again in his mind's eye the body of his father swinging from his rope. No, rather than that, he'd thought he'd go out by the North or East Gates. In truth he hadn't decided yet.

At the Fissand Gate he threw a coin at the waiting beggar, then stood at the edge of the road, peering up at the High Street for a long moment before setting off. This city was not his any more. It was a foreign place, filled with danger.

The High Street was full as usual. There was a herd of cattle ambling along the way, two dogs snapping at their heels, a man behind with a great staff, whistling at them. For a moment Thomas wished he was also a drover – a man in control of his life, measuring each day in the distance travelled, knowing that there was an end to his journeying. That would be a restful life, far better than his present wanderings. And now he must set off once more. He had come here hoping that at last he might find some peace and rest, but there was nothing for him here but death and despair.

When the cattle had passed, he had to pick his gate, and although he turned right to face east, he never quite managed to set off. Instead, his eyes were drawn again to the north. It was in that direction that he would find more work, perhaps. The Master Mason had spoken reverentially of castles being constructed up there; the Despensers had

had several of their castles thrown down during the wars with the Lords Marcher, and there were opportunities there for a man with skill at hewing stone, so Thomas had heard.

It also meant he would pass close to Sara's house. That was in some way an appealing thought. He dare not see her, but just knowing that he was close to her one last time would be good. He couldn't imagine how she must be feeling today. Wretched to think that she had entertained her man's murderer? Perhaps even repelled by the thought that she had consumed his food and drink. The poor woman was probably distraught.

He recalled her face when her son told her: it became a mask of terror. In that moment Thomas knew that any affection she might have felt for him was gone for ever. He couldn't hope to win her, not when he had killed off her Saul. It was a ridiculous *dream*, nothing more. And in any case, what could he do here, in the city which saw his father hanged? Exeter held nothing for him, only memories . . . and memories didn't keep a belly filled.

Thomas glanced behind him. There was a figure running up around the corner of St Mary Major.

It was enough to persuade him to get moving. He set his face to the north, shrugged his pack more comfortably on his back, and started on his way.

In the Charnel Chapel, Sir Peregrine was studying the body of the saddler. 'You may remove him now. There's nothing to be learned in here, especially since there have been so many men walking about in here.'

'Yes, Sir Peregrine,' Matthew said. 'It has been terrible, what with this man, then the friar being murdered, and the stone mason too. What a time!'

'I shall wish to see those bodies, too,' the knight said. 'And we shall have to hold an inquest.'

'The friar has already been taken back to the Friary,' Matthew said. 'It's impossible for us to hold their dead for them.'

'Why? I'd have thought they'd be glad enough for you to hold their corpses until they were ready to take them and conduct the funeral.'

'Not they!' Matthew smiled. 'The friars have always been rather at loggerheads with us over death and burials. They have insisted on being able to bury people, but the Cathedral has the right to bury all the city's dead. We have an arrangement now, because the Friary started a ridiculous argument with us a while ago, demanding that they should be able to hold the funeral services for people whom they called their benefactors. Stupid, of course, but there it is.'

'Oh yes,' Sir Peregrine said absently. He was watching the three lay assistants to the grave-digger lifting the body. It was more than a little odorous now, even in the cool of the chapel, and Sir Peregrine was reminded of battlefields in autumn-time as he smelled the sickly sweet scent of rotting blood. 'I heard about that. It was poor Sir Henry Ralegh, wasn't it? He was taken by the Cathedral although he had stated that he wanted to be buried by the friars.'

'What he wanted really isn't the point,' Matthew remonstrated. 'A man who died in this city is the Cathedral's.'

'Absolutely! There is a lot of money involved,' Sir Peregrine said. 'And when the Cathedral had performed the service, you took the body down to the Friary.'

'But those dogs wouldn't let us take him inside,' Matthew declared with a shake of his head at such cruelty. 'How could they behave in such a manner?'

'And your men left the body to rot outside their gates when they barred them against you,' Sir Peregrine said mildly. Then he lanced a look at Matthew. 'You left him, a noble knight, to rot in the sun outside the Friary.'

'It was they left him there!'

'It was *you* who stole him away in order to win his money, Vicar! You played a contemptible game with a dead knight just for money!' Sir Peregrine stated.

His green eyes flared like emerald fire for an instant, and Matthew was careful to say no more. There was no way of telling how a knight might behave when roused, and this one looked particularly dangerous.

'What of this other body? Where is it?'

'The mason was buried ten days ago, Sir Peregrine,' Matthew said submissively.

'Really?'

'We could hardly leave the corpse sitting under a rock while we waited for a Coroner to arrive,' Matthew said with some asperity. 'What else could we do?'

'That is not for me to say,' said Sir Peregrine. 'All I know is that the body should have remained where it was until I could view it. That is the law. So perhaps the Cathedral will have to pay a fine for that misjudgement.'

Matthew said nothing. He was beginning to learn that this man was not the amiable sort of fellow who would listen respectfully to a vicar or even the Dean about matters which really pertained solely to the Cathedral and the Chapter. He appeared to think that he had a sole right to enquire about things here in the Cathedral. Perhaps the Dean should have stood his ground more.

The knight was already striding off towards the Dean's house, and now Matthew noticed that the Treasurer himself was standing near the corner of the Cathedral with a glower darkening his face as he watched the tall figure march away. Matthew sighed to himself and walked over to Stephen.

'How painful was he today?' Treasurer Stephen asked.

'It was a difficult meeting. I think he feels that the Chapter is lax in its works when a man dies. He wants to fine us for the burial of the mason now.'

'I did tell the Dean that we should stand our ground and insist on the man staying away. There was no need to call him. We are not part of the secular world.'

'I think that Dean Alfred felt we should not deny him entry in case it became common knowledge that we had deaths here which we sought to conceal. After all, not so long ago it was the Cathedral which had to ask the King to hear a case of murder here, even though it was a murder committed by clerics on ecclesiastical grounds. That makes it difficult to argue that we should exclude the King's officer now, surely.'

'The Dean shouldn't have allowed that man to come into our Cathedral,' Stephen said doggedly.

'Is there something the matter?' Matthew asked tentatively.

The Treasurer was startled by his question. 'What do you mean? What makes you ask that, Vicar?'

'I just thought you were worried, Treasurer. Nothing more than that,' Matthew said hastily.

'No, there is nothing wrong,' Stephen said. 'I just don't like to think that our work could be delayed while that man runs around, snapping at ankles and making our lives more difficult.'

Matthew nodded, but as the Treasurer turned and strode away, Matthew was reminded that the man who had ensured that his Chaunter, Walter de Lecchelade, had been murdered was also a Treasurer. John Pycot had only tried to claim the post of Dean when he already controlled the Cathedral's purse-strings. That in some measure was the reason for his popularity.

At least this Treasurer was honourable, he told himself . . . yet he couldn't entirely lose the frown as he watched Stephen hurry over the grass towards the Exchequer.

Chapter Eighteen

Baldwin and Simon left the tavern not long afterwards, Simon casting concerned looks at his friend as they walked down the road.

Clouds were moving swiftly across the sky, although here in the city there was little in the way of a breeze, and the shadows were growing. Simon could see that the alleys heading north from the High Street were already gloomy, and he thought they should return to the Cathedral to let the Dean know what little they had learned.

However, with Baldwin in his present black mood Simon wasn't sure that raising the lack of progress was sensible. He was growing a little anxious. It was so unlike Baldwin. The knight could spring back from the harshest knock without hesitation, usually retaining his good humour. It was rare for him to be so affected by anything, especially by this melancholy spirit.

'Baldwin, why don't we return to the inn and have supper? Then we can decide what we should do next.'

'We know what we must do next,' Baldwin said heavily. 'Speak to this other confederate of Henry's – the man called William who lives at the Priory. If we delay to fill your belly, we'll find the gates locked and barred against us, for the night.'

'I wasn't just thinking of my stomach,' Simon said, hurt.

Baldwin looked at him.

'Not entirely, then?' Simon said, with a small grin.

'I did not mean to offend you, Simon,' Baldwin said quietly. 'There is much on my mind, though.'

'I wish I could help.'

'I do too. I fear no one can.'

'Let's concentrate on the two murders, then,' Simon said.

They walked to Carfoix, then down past the Fleshfold on Fore Street until they came to St Nicholas's Lane, where they turned right. Soon they were at the Priory's gate. It was closed, but Baldwin was sure that it wasn't locked for the night yet; it was too early. He beat upon it with his fist.

There was a pause for some little while before shuffling steps announced the arrival of the porter. A wheezing could be heard at the other side of the gate, which showed that the man was undoubtedly of great age, and then a small hatch opened in the wicket. 'What?'

'I am Sir Baldwin de Furnshill, this is Bailiff Puttock. We have been sent on the Bishop's behalf to speak to a corrodian here, a Master William. Is he in?'

'Where else would he be, Sir Knight?'

'Please ask him to come here that we might speak to him.'

'I'll have to ask the Prior first.'

Baldwin's patience was running out. 'Then do so, and hurry! I do not have all night to wait here on your doorstep while you dawdle about.'

William's sole consolation as he followed the porter's pointing finger to the door, was that at least he'd got his revenge in quickly on Joel. The cretin must have gone straight to see the Keeper as soon as William had left him. He was obviously determined to get rid of William. He'd tried arrows and they had failed, so now he was attempting the legal route.

William stalked along the packed earth of the path around the little building until he came to the gateway. There he stopped, leaned on his staff and studied the two men. They had their backs to him, which he found annoying and disrespectful. He deserved better treatment.

Except, he reminded himself sadly, most of his power was gone now. 'I'm William,' he growled. 'What do you mean by coming here to a place of God and demanding to see me?'

'I am Sir Baldwin de Furnshill, and I would like to speak to you.'

'Why should I?'

'Because if you don't, I shall inform the Coroner that I think you could have killed two men here, and were an accomplice at the very least in the murder of another,' Baldwin said equably.

'I don't know what you mean!' William swapped hands, gripping his staff in his left while he rested his right hand on his belly, tucked into his belt. It was a comforting place to put it, reminding him that once he had worn a sword here. Now all he had was a small eating-knife which was little use in a fight.

'I think you do. You were worried about Henry, weren't you? He knew so much about you and your past. He'd have been a great threat to you, wouldn't he, if he'd managed to confess to helping kill the Chaunter all those years ago, because then your own part in that murder must surely come out into the open, and what would happen to your pension then? Your nice easy retirement could be all ruined, couldn't it?'

'Henry? He was an old friend of mine from many years ago.'

'As was his wife. And you could have her again, if you were only to get rid of him. It was probably just the thought of the threat he posed to you at first, rather than the idea of stealing Mabilla too, but that thought wasn't long in following, was it? And when you saw how to remove him, you took your chance. Why leave his body there in the chapel, though? What significance did that have?'

'None that I know of,' William said. He was intrigued that this man had learned so much about him and his history, but he had no intention of helping him in any way. Why throw him any titbits, when the man's talking was adding to his own understanding of how much had got out?

'How much were you paid for your murder of the Chaunter for the Dean? It must have been a handsome fee. This man was the Bishop's own friend, after all.'

'You are mistaken. I was the victim of an unpleasant campaign which sought to accuse me of participating in that murder, but it is untrue. What, should I become involved in disputes in the Cathedral Chapter? Why? All I ever did was support my King, as all subjects should.'

'So you betrayed your own accomplices?' Simon said.

William sneered, 'You ask me whether I betrayed anyone? I've never done that! I have been loyal to my word, and when I've been honoured for my service and have given my allegiance, that has remained to bind me. No man could say I've ever broken faith with another. What right do you have to accuse me of treachery?'

That barb struck home, he saw. The knight looked as though he had swallowed bile, and he looked away. The scruffy man at his side seemed less bothered, and said, 'Does that mean that you remained in the service of the Dean while you were taken by the King? I'd have thought that you'd find it hard to serve both masters.'

'I was never in the Dean's service. I only ever joined the King's.'

'So you say. Others tell us differently.'

'Then speak to them, if you don't like what I can tell you.'

'Where were you on the night of four days ago?' Baldwin asked. 'Were you at the Cathedral Close?'

'At night I have to be within these walls, Sir Knight. I'm a corrodian, I have to live by the rules of this House. What, do you think that I'd have broken out through this gate, broken in by one of the Cathedral's gates, killed a man, and then fled back, all without being noticed? I am not so young as I was . . . Perhaps I could do it, but I suppose I should be grateful that you *think* I could anyway. It shows how much respect you must have for me.'

'Where were you last night?'

'Where were *you*? You had more chance of getting out to kill someone.'

'The first man to die was Henry Saddler. We know you knew him, and we know he held your secrets for you.'

'Then call him to denounce me! Oh, but he's dead, isn't he? That makes it rather hard, doesn't it?'

'And last night,' Baldwin continued impassively, 'Friar Nicholas also died. He was murdered too – another man who could have accused you. He would most certainly have recognised you from that attack.'

'No, he wouldn't. And *I* didn't attack him,' William said. 'That was someone else.'

Baldwin faced William, hands on his hips. 'Master, this matter is too serious for me to bother about you. I look at you and I see an old man, withered and bent. You are not an ideal candidate for a murderer. To stand out in the cold waiting for a man to arrive, when it could mean you'd miss your curfew and get locked out . . . it is not likely. Whatever happened forty years ago is also not my concern. However, I have been charged by the Dean to seek the present murderer of Henry Saddler and this Friar Nicholas. It is possible that the murderer of these two has been here for many years, and his ire has only recently been encouraged by something. I will not seek to accuse you of past crimes, but if you can shed any light on this mystifying pair of murders, please do so.'

William looked at him steadily, then at the Bailiff. 'All right. I can tell you little enough, but what I can remember, I will tell.'

The three of them sat at a low bench nearby, and as the light began to fade, William told them his story.

'We all wanted John Pycot to be Dean. Everyone in the city was on his side. He knew Exeter, you see. You can't beat a man like that, who's prepared to fight for his own people. No, he was one of us, well enough. Then in comes this new Bishop, and he reckons to control everything in his own way. Quivil, his name was, and he sought to curtail some of John's efforts. See, John was a bit of a quick man to make a shilling or two. Always looking for the next profit, and that wasn't what he was supposed to be doing, was it? So Quivil gave him short shrift. Tried to stop some of his frauds. That was why he didn't recognise him as his Dean.'

'How would a Dean like him be able to fiddle the Fabric Rolls or the other Cathedral finances?' Simon asked. 'If the Treasurer was intelligent, it should have been difficult to pass anything remotely dangerous.'

'You could say John had an inside knowledge of the Treasurer's mind,' Will said with a chuckle. 'He *was* Treasurer. That was one of Quivil's points of disagreement with him. And then he lost the battle, because the Archbishop, God bless him, sided with John. I don't know why. Must have been they were old friends, or maybe John was going to share some of his profits or something, I don't have any idea, but the long and the short of it was, this Chaunter Walter was imposed on the Cathedral. If it was just the Cathedral, that'd be fine, but this lad wanted to restrict John's works generally, and we liked John. Like I say, men will support the fellow they can trust, and there's no one like the man you grew up with to instil trust, is there?

'John put together the force. There were about twenty of us . . . don't remember all the names and faces, but I do remember my lot. There was me, Henry, and some others. We all stood in the shadows up near that arch where Fissand Gate is now. There wasn't any wall in those days – it was the murder that led to Quivil petitioning the King for a safety wall. He realised that he was in danger from the city folk, I guess.

'We waited in the darkness until we saw the first chink of light from the door. See, the man who was guaranteed to be there was Chaunter

Walter. The Matins service was one of his own, one he had to participate in. He knew we hated him. He wasn't some idiot from London who'd think he could beat any number of *Deb'nshoir* churls without suffering pain, see. He tried to make sure that he always had a safe route home from the Cathedral. So he did that night. And we fucked him, we did!

'It was easy. We paid a man to tell him he was all right. That way the Chaunter reckoned he was safe, and he stepped out happily into our trap.'

'He was content to take the word of one man?' Baldwin asked dubiously.

'Yes, because the man told him it was dangerous!'

'What are you saying?' Simon snapped. 'Are you playing with us?'

'No, Bailiff. I'm telling the truth,' William wheezed, shaking his head with delight at the simplicity of the ploy. 'What we did was, we told the fellow to tell the Chaunter that there was a big ambush, but that his own men had heard, and they'd told the Bishop. The Bishop had his men all about the place, and they'd catch all the villeins trying to kill him. They'd be thrown into gaol and Chaunter Walter could have the pleasure of seeing them punished. Oh, he liked the idea of that, too, the bastard!'

'What he didn't know was that the man who told him this was in the pay of the attackers,' Baldwin guessed.

'Yes. After that, he sent a trusted man himself to tell the Bishop's men – the same man who had warned him. And then that man came back and let him know all was well; the Bishop's men would save him. I'm told he was still gazing about him, wondering where his rescuers were, when the mob cut him down.'

Baldwin pursed his lips. 'So who was this man?'

'Henry knew – he paid him. But I'll tell you another thing, sir. When it all went down, it happened really fast. We saw him at the door, then he was out with his boys, all of them walking to his house, which is where the Charnel Chapel stands now, and suddenly, one lad jumps past us all and hares off towards him. It was a novice, a boy called Vincent, who was utterly devoted to the Chaunter, and all he was trying to do was save his master's life. Christ's Balls, you could have cut me down with a nail-parer! I just thought, God's Teeth, this'll screw everything! I ran after him, and all the way he was shouting out to protect his master, yelling at the top of his voice that it was a trap, that there were men all about waiting to kill him. I think they all thought he was part of the ruse, though, and the first man he came to killed him on the spot.'

Baldwin leaned forward. 'Who was that, then?'

'Who stabbed him? It was a man called Nicholas. Funnily enough,' he added, 'it was the same Nicholas who's dead now. The friar.'

'This Vincent – where did he come from?'

'Oh, he was a local boy, I think, but not from inside the city. City men wouldn't have tried to save that arse Leechelade.'

'And afterwards?' Simon pressed him.

'Oh, after all that, we bolted. The gate to the south was open, and some men made their getaway through that. Others like me, Henry, and some friends, didn't need to try that. We knew our way in the city, and we just went home. The Bishop was furious, but no one would ever tell stories on us, not even when he brought up the idea of excommunicating us all. It didn't matter, we could all get absolution at John Pycot's door.'

'It must have made for a miserable time in the Cathedral.'

'I suppose so. The two camps refused to talk. The Bishop wouldn't acknowledge the Dean, and the Dean treated him with contempt. That lasted two years or so. In the end the Bishop petitioned the King, the King visited, he tried the city and found it wanting. He executed a couple of people, including the Mayor, and left. That was about it.'

'Why execute the Mayor?' Baldwin asked. 'Was he implicated?'

'Well, the gate was left wide, so the King saw that the city was complicit in this crime. He wouldn't slaughter every man, woman and child in Exeter, but he could at least kill the man who represented the city. So poor old Alured de Porta was hanged, along with the gatekeeper of the Southern Gate, because both were thought to have had a part in the ambush.'

He smiled at them both, a sly old man with the eyes of a fox. There was no need to tell these two bumbling fools who it was who'd told the King that the gate had been left open.

Thomas stood at the gate and stared out at the lands beyond. He hesitated for a long moment before coming to a decision.

He couldn't go, not without seeing her one more time. She was so pretty, so defenceless, and he was responsible for her plight. She'd not want him in her house, but perhaps he could pass by, just to see whether she was all right. And if she wasn't about, he could leave a gift. Nothing special – he didn't possess anything special – but maybe a little sum of money, or some bread. Anything to help her. It couldn't do any harm. Although the urge to commit self-murder had left him after last night, he held little value for his life now. All he had, he could give to her happily.

On the inside of the northern wall here was a street that led down towards the place where she lived among the poorer inhabitants of the city. It didn't take long to reach her home.

There was no sign of life. The door was shut, no smoke trickled from beneath the thatch, no cries or laughs came from within. It was as still as the grave.

This unwonted silence grated on the mason's nerves. The lad, Dan, he should have been making a row. It was what youngsters like him would do, shrieking and laughing, running about. Yet now, having lost his father and brother, maybe he simply sought to comfort his depressed mother as she descended into utter despair. A lad of eight or nine years having to cope with the anguish of a widowed woman was heartrending, and all the more so since Thomas was responsible. He had the blood of two members of her family on his hands.

Surely they were not dead? He had to know; he *must*. Taking a deep breath, he put his hand to the latch and licked suddenly dry lips before pushing the door wide.

The room was unchanged, a dark cell with few belongings. There was no food in evidence. On impulse, he grabbed his purse and untied the thongs that bound it. He'd need a little to buy food on his way, but she had more need of it than he. There was always work for a man like him; he'd easily earn more money. In the name of God, he had to do something to help this woman.

Pulling his purse open carefully so as not to hurt his hands again, he divided the full coins from the clipped fragments and left the whole ones in a neat pile on the table. All the bits and pieces he placed back in his purse and then he bound it tightly once more. He was refastening the thongs to his belt when there was a slight sound behind him. He didn't recognise it at first, but there was no reason why he should: the unfamiliar noise of a plank of wood whistling through the air, followed by a deafening crack as it struck the back of his skull.

As Vincent made his way down to his father's tannery the odour of faeces was clear in the cool evening air, and Vince knew that his old man had been preparing more skins. His poor little bastard apprentice must have been out with the scavengers again.

'Hey, Dad! Where are you, you old fart?'

Last night when he'd left his father, he hadn't been able to see Wymond's face, but he knew that internally, he was crushed and broken like a man who'd fallen under a mill-wheel. In one sense, to know at last what had happened to his brother, so long dead, must be a relief – but to hear that it was his brother's own comrades who had slaughtered him in the belief that he had become an enemy . . . that was a tough one to swallow.

Vincent was an only child, so the idea of losing a brother was hard to comprehend, but only last year he had lost a friend called Wat who drowned while fording the Exe in winter just to save the cost of the bridge's toll. Wat had been swept off his feet and sent tumbling two miles downriver. Hearing of his pal's death had put Vince in a spin. Joel had been good to him that day, too. He'd understood when he found Vince puking in the doorway after getting rat-arsed on cheap wine and rough cider.

'When I was about your age,' he had said, 'I lost a good mate of mine and I got out of my head in the same way. Just remember, a good friend is hard to find, and when you do find one, and he dies, he deserves all honour.'

Somehow that had helped. Vince had gone down to the horse trough at the end of the street and ducked his head deep, coming up blowing and puffing, ready to throw up again, but feeling better for having paid his proper respects to his old companion. Not that it helped over the weeks that passed. He was always aware of Wat's absence; whenever he wanted to go out for a drink, whenever he'd had a shitty day, whenever he'd had a brilliant day . . . or whenever it so happened that the sun was shining and the Church had declared that it was to be a feast day for a saint. At each event, he was lonely, and it still could make him sob in the depth of night, when he remembered his dear friend Wattie.

At the time Wymond had clouted him on the back and mumbled in that gruff voice of his, 'It's what happens as you grow up, son. Get used to it.' And then his eyes had clouded, and Vince knew he was thinking of his dead brother again.

'Oy – old man?'

He pushed the door open to the shack which his father happily called his home. The place was a mess. The table was on its side, his knives and tools all over the floor, as though someone had been in there and fought a bitter fight with Wymond. There was a bow and a quiver of arrows near the door, and Vince picked them up, a little worried to see such mayhem, but when he gazed about, he could see the barrel on its side in the corner of the room. The old twerp had been pissing it up again.

His father lay almost under the table, and although his mouth was wide, there was no snoring. Vince squatted at his side. 'Hello, Dad,' he said with a chuckle. 'How many quarts of ale did *you* drink last night, eh? Or was it gallons you measured them in?'

He grinned, and then grabbed his father's hand, only to drop it very quickly.

'If you're going to puke, do you have to roll in it?' he groaned, and then went out to fill a bucket from the river. With it full, he returned and stood contemplatively for a moment before upending it over his father's face and torso.

Blowing and cursing, Wynard rolled over, blessedly away from the pool of vomit and gradually came to grumbling under his breath as Vincent set about gathering some food. The bread was green; he took one look at it before throwing it out through the door. Even the rats would probably reject that. There were some tough old pieces of bacon, and an egg, so Vincent put fresh water into Wymond's old cooking pot, tossed in the meat and set it over the fire. There were some leaves; he shredded them with his hands and put them in too, adding the egg and mixing it quickly so it dispersed. Soon there was a broth with white strands of egg and lumps of greyish meat.

'Come on, Dad. Get some food down you.'

'I'm not hungry. I want more ale.'

'Forget it, fat man. You're getting no more ale until you've eaten something warm. What in Christ's name has got into you?'

'My brother, that's what.'

'I'm sorry,' Vincent said more quietly. He meant it. If he'd realised how badly his father would take the information, he might have kept it all to himself. Ignorance was bliss, after all. 'I thought you'd be glad to know that Uncle Vince wasn't dishonourable, that was why I told you about it.'

'Of course he wasn't dishonourable! All he wanted to do was protect his master, and they slaughtered him like a dog with rabies!' Wymond said hoarsely. He felt terrible.

'It's too late to do anything about it now,' the boy said gently. 'Eat up, Dad and then we'll have some ale.'

Wymond went outside, rinsed his face with water from his rainwater barrel, and wiped it dry with an old tunic. Feeling slightly better, he walked back inside again and sat at his table.

Looking at him, Vince suddenly felt a rush of affection. He would be lost without his father. Wymond was the solid rock on which his life was based.

'You never knew your uncle,' Wymond said sadly, lifting a spoon of the broth to his lips. 'He was a good man, a friend to any who needed his help, loyal to death. And that's how he died, of course.'

'I'd have liked to have met him.'

'You would have, if that murdering shit Nicholas hadn't killed him,' Wymond said. He snorted and shifted in his seat. 'My Vince should never have been cut down like that. A man who can do that deserves everything he gets . . .'

It was quite unlike his father, and it made Vin's blood turn to ice to see such ruthless ferocity on the tanner's careworn face.

Chapter Nineteen

Simon and Baldwin left William on his bench, and soon they were making their way back along Nicholas's Street to Fore Street, and then up towards the Cathedral.

'So you thought the same as me?' Simon said as they walked, his face wreathed in frowns.

To his secret pleasure, Baldwin's expression had lost its haunted look. 'If you mean,' he demanded acerbically, 'did I think that much of what that man said was true, then yes, I did.'

'You know perfectly well that wasn't what I meant,' Simon said musingly. 'I was thinking about the dead friar, Nicholas – the man who struck down poor Vince. If it's true that someone there was disloyal, it must have been Nicholas – and someone killed him for it.'

'You think that the whole affair could be due to a man who seeks revenge, all these years later?' Baldwin queried.

'It would make sense. The friar had struck down the only man there who was trying to warn the Chaunter. Surely *he* must have been the traitor.'

'That would seem true enough,' Baldwin agreed, 'but that hardly helps us. The two victims, Henry and Nicholas, seem to have nothing in common other than the fact that they were there in the Close that night. Henry was on the attacking side, and Nicholas on the side of the Chaunter . . .'

'Baldwin, you are slow tonight,' Simon said with a smile. 'They were on *the same* side. That's what I mean. I reckon Friar Nicholas was trying to shut Vincent up before the trap had been sprung; that was why he pulled out his dagger and silenced the poor fellow. And then the others, including Henry, attacked them.'

'But the friar was nearly killed,' Baldwin objected. 'Surely no man would agree to those wounds on his face and body just to add verisimilitude to the story of his loyalty?'

Simon shrugged. 'It was dark, they were in a mêlée, there was a racket of men shouting, weapons clashing . . . what else would you expect? Someone accidentally slashed at him, trying to hit someone else, and that was that. End of his good looks. If he was the cause of the Chaunter's death, he deserved it.'

'Perhaps so,' Baldwin agreed. Yet he still wore a puzzled frown. 'But who, in that case, could have wanted Henry dead?'

'Could Henry have been the man who planned it?' Simon wondered. 'His wife might know. We could return and question her.'

'I do not think that will be necessary. First let us go and speak to Joel once more. He might become more helpful when he hears that William has already spoken to us,' Baldwin said.

'In any case, Henry seems a likely man to have thought through the plan and left the hint that the Bishop was planning on using the Chaunter as a lure to draw the attack's sting.'

'Possibly, but it's more likely to have been a man of action like our friend William.'

'The man who took his opportunities,' Simon said drily.

'I did not warm to him either,' Baldwin said. 'My impression was that he was quite an astute fellow – he could be a good tactical commander of men in a battle.'

'Perhaps, but what was he like when he was a lad? Cunning and quick-witted no doubt, but to invent a ruse like the one used against the Chaunter would have taken more intelligence than he possessed,' Simon said. 'You know how people are: some will learn from experience, but others can imagine an outcome and put in place a plan to achieve it.'

'Why are you so convinced he's not like that?' Baldwin asked.

'Look at him! His sole ambition was to get to be a warrior, working for the King. That doesn't take brains, does it? No, I'd expect that sort of devious plot to come from the kind of man who'd get to be a master of the Freedom of the city.'

'Oh! You think it must have been Henry, then? Why not Joel or someone else?'

'I do not say it wasn't,' Simon frowned. 'But I think the murderer could reckon it was Henry, and might have killed him for that reason.'

'True enough,' Baldwin agreed. 'So who else should we suspect? We know of William and Joel.'

'And this fellow Thomas,' Simon pointed out. 'He would seem a likely candidate – especially as he was guilty enough to leave the city in the first place, and now since his return all those who could have known him have died. First Henry, now Nicholas.'

'And we have heard that Udo was angry about being refused the right to marry Julia Potell,' Baldwin recalled. 'It is possible, I suppose, that the friar was a witness to Henry's murder by Udo, and then Udo was forced to return to remove him too, although . . .'

'Yes, Baldwin?' Simon asked after a moment or two, but his friend shook his head.

'Nothing.' Baldwin could not confess to his strange loathing for the Charnel Chapel. There was something bad about the place, he felt. And surely that had coloured his judgement. 'I only think that the murder of the Chaunter could have something to do with this. Why else would Henry have been left in the Charnel Chapel, and why should Nicholas have been killed there, his body later moved . . .'

'Putting the body near the Cathedral would shove all the blame and suspicion onto Thomas,' Simon said musingly. 'It would be a shrewd move to distract us towards him.'

'Perhaps it would,' Baldwin said.

'So we have to consider William, Joel and Thomas because they were all involved in the original attack,' Simon concluded. 'And Udo because he had his own motives . . . Right! What shall we do now, Baldwin? Should we report to the Dean first?'

'All we have is speculation, so no, let's go to Joel first.'

'You don't want to see Sir Peregrine, do you?' Simon grinned.

'He would see me choose between the Lord Hugh de Courtenay and the King,' Baldwin protested, 'and I will not. I have enough allegiances already: my family first, my King second.'

'Sir Peregrine will try to persuade you otherwise?'

'Sir Peregrine is a loyal servant of Lord Hugh. He sees the King as a spendthrift and wastrel who will plunge the country into chaos if he is not restrained. The last few times I have seen him, he was trying to forge alliances against the King with the Marcher Lords, but now that they have been destroyed and the rebel leaders killed or exiled, I do not know what he plans. All I do know is, I do not wish to be thrown into a new plot against the King. He has shown his disdain for convention when he captures traitors. I'll have no part in that.'

'I don't blame you,' Simon said. 'Still, we'll have to see Sir Peregrine at some point. I think that we should go now.'

Baldwin grunted but did not argue further. He knew that Simon was correct, but Sir Peregrine was the sort of knight who could put a man in danger's path unintentionally, and a man who was forced into confrontation with the King was likely to pay for his temerity with his life, his possessions, his lands, everything. Baldwin did not value his own life too highly, but he did value his manor, and the fact that it represented the only means of support he could leave for his wife and daughter. He would not risk them.

Sir Peregrine de Barnstaple smiled as the Keeper and his friend entered the Dean's hall. Dean Alfred was talking quietly to Stephen and Matthew, studying their rolls of accounts, and he waved to Simon and Baldwin, motioning towards Sir Peregrine and the jug of wine.

Sir Peregrine sipped from his mazer, then rose to offer his hand to both. 'Sir Baldwin, it is a delight to see you again. And Bailiff Puttock, I am pleased to see you looking so well. I have heard from the Dean that you both undertook a pilgrimage. I congratulate you on the success of your journey. You must tell me all about it.'

The Bailiff did look well, in fact, Sir Peregrine thought, slimmer and with his face bronzed from the sun, although there was a new reticence about him. Still, that was to be expected. Sir Baldwin would have warned him off.

That idea made Sir Peregrine smile wolfishly as he took his seat again. The two were clever enough. Certainly Sir Baldwin was remarkably quick. Some reckoned he could see through a man's eyes into his very soul, and he was rumoured to be one of the most respected Keepers in the whole of Devon and Cornwall. Still, he didn't look so bright today. His eyes were duller, his posture a little stooped, as though he was feeling his age. No matter, he'd be an excellent ally for Lord Hugh, if Sir Peregrine could win him over.

There would be another war sooner or later, and there was no telling how many would die. The King's friend, Despenser, grew ever more voracious in his rape of the kingdom. The bastard had sewn up government to his benefit. No one could speak to the King without Despenser's approval, which meant paying him. Now it was impossible for any man who had been robbed by Despenser to win justice, because the Despenser refused to allow them to plead their case before the King.

This situation had been going on for years, but the mood of the country was growing restless. The man was a tyrant, and his reign could not last for ever. Since the Battle of Boroughbridge, at which the forces of Earl Thomas of Lancaster, the King's cousin, had been entirely destroyed, the knights who had been in his party chased through the kingdom and, when captured, slaughtered, their bodies separated and sent to all points to be displayed as the limbs of traitors, people had said little. There was nothing to be done against an all-powerful King, especially one who was prepared to wallow in the blood of his enemies; but now that the Despenser was ravaging all territories, he had succeeded in uniting the realm against the King. Even those who had not yet been on the receiving end of the Despenser's anger and demands for their lands or wealth, knew that it could only be a matter of time.

'Have you viewed the bodies, Sir Peregrine?' Baldwin enquired.

'I have seen that of the saddler. Unfortunately, the friar's body has been removed. I shall have to visit the Friary to see that. They insisted on burying him on their own lands. And the mason has been buried, too.'

'Mason?' Simon asked.

'Saul: the man we told you of. A rock fell on him while Thomas was up on the scaffold,' Dean Alfred explained. 'He was – um – squashed. A horrible sight. We could have his remains exhumed, of course,' he said, glancing at the Coroner, 'but it seems a little drastic. There were many witnesses, and all said it was an accident. Nothing was stolen from the man, and there was no suggestion that anyone had anything but praise for him. He never started an argument or any – ah – from of dispute. Never had a fight.'

'Who was there when the rock fell?'

'My Warden of the new Fabric here was on the scaffolding,' the Dean smiled. 'But he hardly knew poor Saul, did you?'

Vicar Matthew shook his head. 'It was a straightforward accident. Thomas was taking the walls down, and one stone fell. It utterly crushed Saul. But there was no reason for Thomas to want to see Saul killed.

And he has displayed the most clear and unambiguous proofs of his sadness to have caused the death.'

'That is true,' the Dean verified.

'Was it the falling rock that so damaged Thomas's hands?' Baldwin asked curiously, thinking of the linen wrapped about each of the man's palms.

'Yes. The rope stripped the flesh from his hands when he tried to stop it falling,' said the Dean.

'So he was holding a rope? It must have been a restraining rope,' Baldwin mused.

'Yes,' Matthew said. 'It was to stop the rock from swinging, and in order to be able to pull it away from the wall as it descended.'

'I shall have to see what sort of fine his burial too will require,' Sir Peregrine said with a smile.

'You must only recently have been made Coroner?' Baldwin enquired.

'Oh, yes. I was offered the chance of this job earlier in the summer. My predecessor died – but I understand you were there?'

In a flash, Baldwin saw Sir Roger de Gidleigh's face as the crossbow bolt slammed into his spine, the expression that burst across his face as he began to die. 'Yes,' he said more gravely.

Sir Peregrine saw how his face grew still, and regretted his levity. Fortunately the Dean also noticed, and asked Simon whether they had learned anything about the two murders. Sir Peregrine sat back and concentrated as Simon told of all they had heard.

'It seems that there are many who would have sought to kill the saddler, then,' he said when Simon was finished. 'And as many who'd like to see the friar dead.'

'Not quite as many,' Simon said. 'There were many who'd like both to die, from the frame-maker Joel to the King's corrodian William; but the saddlemaker had others who'd have liked to see him dead – the German, Udo, for example.'

'There may well be many more, too,' the Dean said. It was a proof of how deeply he was considering the matter that his speech was unaffected by stammering. 'The Treasurer, Stephen, remembers that time. He was here. It was before my arrival, of course, but I have heard that there was great dissension within the Cathedral.'

'We should talk to Stephen to see which of the men still in the

Cathedral were here at that time,' Simon suggested. 'We could then question them to see who else had a motive to kill these two.'

'You think that'll help?' Sir Peregrine said. He leaned forward, cupping his mazer in his two hands. 'If they are guilty of wishing Henry Potell and Friar Nicholas dead, they will hardly tell you. And most of them in any case would declare themselves wholeheartedly behind the Bishop, will they not? How could they admit they were once willing to stand against a Bishop and hope that the present incumbent would not come to hear of it?'

'We are a different – ah – Chapter now, Sir Peregrine,' the Dean smiled. 'Such things do not concern us any more. No, we prefer to see disputes openly aired and discussed. The old ways of bottling up arguments and then causing friction are gone for ever. We will not see them return.'

Sir Peregrine felt the Dean's eyes upon him and nodded graciously. 'I am glad to hear it, Dean. We'll speak to the Treasurer. While we wait, would it be possible for you to ask that the man who dropped the rock on the mason's head be called here? I should like to speak to this clumsy fellow.'

'Why? It was an accident. Many saw what happened.'

'I'm glad it wasn't another murder! In any case, I have to assess the *deodand* and ensure that it was not in truth a deliberate killing.'

The Dean was about to speak when he shrugged and called for his steward.

'The poor fellow will probably be in a tavern somewhere at this time of day,' he said when the servant had rushed from the room. 'He will likely be very tired, so please do not be too hard on him.'

'I shall try not to delay the building schedule, Dean,' Sir Peregrine said.

They chatted of other matters while they waited for the steward to return, but when he did, alone, Sir Peregrine was not unduly surprised. As the Dean had said, the man was probably drinking off a tiring day in the nearest tavern. 'He's left for the night?'

'Dean, I am afraid Thomas has fled,' the steward told him. 'The Master Mason tells me that all his tools are gone too.'

Baldwin shot a bitter look at Simon. 'We should have questioned him more closely!'

'I commanded that he should be watched,' the Dean said with a frigid calmness.

'The guards say that he looked as though he was going to escape through the Fissand Gate, but he saw them and ran back towards his hut. They thought he'd changed his mind. He didn't leave by another gate. They asked.'

The Coroner leaped to his feet. 'Show me this man's room!' he snapped to the steward and hurried from the room with him. Simon and Baldwin gave their thanks to the Dean, and followed him.

'So, Sir Baldwin,' the Coroner called over his shoulder as he threw open the door to the Close. 'It seems our killer might have been in the Cathedral after all! Even if he was only a mason, he would be able to kill with ease inside the precinct. And now he is trying to escape the city, since he knows we are on his trail.'

Peter, the acting Prior at St Nicholas, was sitting at his desk in his hall at the Priory when the rough knocking on his door woke him from a reverie.

Sitting here, he had suddenly imagined what it would be like to actually be recognised as Prior. If only he could take that position, and with it enjoy the power and influence it brought, he could work through to the end of his days with satisfaction. He would have achieved something quite fine. It would be enough to satisfy him.

The post was not all-powerful, but with an accommodating and compliant Abbot at Battle, and he and the new Abbot had always been reasonably close, there was every possibility that he might be able to wield a free hand. That would certainly be his hope. And then, what a life he would have! To be master of a Priory like this in a major city was to be the ruler of a small, self-contained principality. He would have complete control.

Yet the investigation into that idiot saddler's death was enough to bring the matter of Chaunter de Lecchelade back to everyone's minds, and then he'd be without a chance yet again. There was no possibility of his being able to survive the renewal of interest in all that. He'd be ruined.

He had just reached this conclusion when the knock came, and it explained his harshness of voice and manner as he recognised his corrodian. 'What is it, William?'

'That's no way to welcome an honoured guest in your Priory, is it?'

Peter eyed him like a King watching a poisoner in his kitchens. 'You may be honoured by others, but to me you are only a man I used to know, who made his way in the world by dishonesty.'

'Not dishonesty . . . just judicious use of the truth,' William said. 'But you and I need to talk.'

'Those two have rattled you?'

'They know more than I'd have guessed,' William nodded. 'They know about all of us. I suppose Joel told them. It means we're in trouble. It's likely to get out, unless we can shut them up somehow.'

'And how would you propose to do that?' Peter asked. 'Perhaps quieten everything by slaughtering the pair of them? That would certainly stop all investigations in their tracks.'

'Yes, it might,' William smiled.

Peter was about to snap at him when he realised that William was being honest. Speaking carefully, he said, 'I do not think that their deaths would succeed in stopping all debate. In fact, I feel that it might lead people to associate these recent deaths with that of de Lecchelade.'

'It may be a risk worth taking. Whoever comes afterwards to look into things will be likely to find an easier target than us. He could be more easily manipulated than these two.'

'You didn't think that you could persuade the Keeper and Bailiff to leave the matter?'

'No. They're committed to finding a killer.'

'Which means you'll not be able to remain here. Not if it becomes known that you helped kill de Lecchelade and then benefited from his death by throwing the blame onto de Porta and the gate-keeper of the South Gate. That wouldn't reflect well on you, would it?'

William looked at him but now the smile was wiped from his face like chalk from a board. 'It would not reflect well on a Prior either, if it came to be widely known that he was a convicted murderer.'

'All know of me, William. I submitted to the Church's justice and was exiled for many years.'

'Aye. And now you're back and want this Priory all to yourself, don't you?'

Peter made a dismissive gesture. 'I will never have it. That much is clear, and I have grown accustomed to the end of my ambitions. Nay, I shall remain here as a monk and pass on the power to my replacement and successor.'

'I won't leave! Not without a good fight first,' William swore.

'What do you mean?' Peter demanded. 'I won't have you committing bloodshed, Will. You are a corrodian now, man. You must not bring the name of this place into disrepute.'

'Oh, I won't let anyone know it's anything to do with the Priory, don't you worry, Peter,' William said. 'But I won't stand by and see my place here put at risk by these damned inquisitive fools. No one will take my pension from me!'

Simon reminded himself of the strange coincidence of the man's name and age, and wondered if it was in fact a mere quirk of fate. The mason had been surly and suspicious when they spoke to him. To learn that he had been responsible for another death, although it was apparently an accident, was still more curious. One coincidence was possible, but adding together the facts that a man like him had been involved with Joel and Henry all those years before, that he had been in the area when the friar had been murdered, and had even been seen talking to him, and the fact that he sounded like an Exonian even though he denied it, all added up to a suspicious chain of evidence, especially now that he had apparently fled the city.

'Did anyone see him go?' he asked when he reached Sir Peregrine and the steward at a small shack in the workmen's little shanty town.

The steward shook his head. He was a small, birdlike man with very bright brown eyes. 'No. The guard sent to stop him didn't see him go. About here, all those I've asked said they thought he was still here, but no one's seen him since mid-afternoon.'

The room in which he had lived was a rude hovel knocked up by a carpenter with little time for fripperies. It had plain beech walls that once had been lime-washed, a rough shingle roof of chestnut, and little by way of decoration. One stool, without even a table to sit at, and a wooden bench on which to lay his palliasse were the sole concessions to a man's comfort. It was a sad, bare little chamber.

'Nothing here at all,' Simon noted. 'He's clearly run.'

'And the gates are closed now,' Sir Peregrine commented. 'We should set off after him instantly . . . but it may be better to wait until morning.'

'Far better,' Baldwin said. 'But it would be worthwhile to send to all the gates to ask whether a man answering his description has actually left the city today. Could you arrange for that, Steward?'

'Of course.'

'In the meantime, perhaps we should go and take our rest,' Baldwin said. 'We shall be awake early.'

Sir Peregrine smiled coldly at that. 'I shall walk to the inn with you, Sir Baldwin. I am sure that we have much to discuss.'

Baldwin demurred, pointing out that Sir Peregrine had already been forced to ride a great distance that day, and suggested that they should all go to Sir Peregrine's inn. Accordingly they left his address with the steward for any messages from the gates, and then made their way to the Blue Boar, where Sir Peregrine was staying.

In the low parlour at the middle of the inn, Sir Peregrine sat and motioned politely for the others to do likewise. 'We have had our disputes in the past, but I am sure we can help each other now.'

'I am interested to know how the Lord de Courtenay could release you from his side. Surely he relies on your advice, Sir Peregrine,' Baldwin said disingenuously.

Sir Peregrine looked at him long and hard. 'My Lord de Courtenay feels that other advisors could be more suitable for the present climate.'

'Since the Despensers are now supreme?'

'Precisely,' Sir Peregrine said bitterly. 'He feels that the Despensers are likely to be in power for some years, and he would prefer to keep his head on his shoulders for the time being, rather than risk having them parted by the executioner's sword.'

'I heard that Earl Thomas was hanged like a common felon,' Baldwin noted.

'A shocking punishment,' Sir Peregrine nodded. He added drily, 'And it led my Lord to decide that the advice of his most loyal advisor might be suspected as biasing him against the King, so that advisor must leave his household. I was told to go.'

'Although you still owe him your fealty?'

'Of course. That was to death. Still, I was forced to seek a new employment, and when I heard that this post was available, I thought that it must at least keep me occupied.'

Simon could understand that. A knight had many calls on his time, what with managing his lands, protecting his serfs and, most of all, seeking to serve his master. If his master did not want him at his side any more, that reduced his workload considerably. Since Sir Peregrine, he recalled, had no wife and had lost his only lover some years before, he was plainly at a loose end. Finding a job like that of Coroner would be a relief to a man with an active mind; as well as being lucrative to a fellow who was corrupt, he added to himself, glancing at the Coroner. Fortunately he was sure that Sir Peregrine was not that kind of man. The bannaret was honourable.

'Does that mean you will no longer seek to persuade people to take a stand on one side or another?' Baldwin asked.

'I have no interest in doing so. In fact, I have been commanded not to do so by Lord de Courtenay,' Sir Peregrine smiled.

'In which case, let us discuss this strange series of murders,' Baldwin said more happily. 'Was there anything about Henry Saddler's body which struck you?'

'It was more a case of what *didn't* strike me,' Sir Peregrine said.

'Oh? In what way?'

'His hands weren't bound, his head and face unmarked so far as I could see, and there was only the one blow. It showed that he trusted his attacker enough to turn his back on him, and that he was not captured and later killed, but simply taken, or jumped on, when he was unawares. That means it's less likely a planned killing, more probably a spur of the moment attack.'

'Perhaps. Unless someone sent a message – for example, inviting him to meet a third person in there, and only when he entered did he realise someone was already there – concealed behind the door, perhaps? – who leaped upon him as soon as it was shut?'

'Possibly. This man Thomas could have been there on the scaffold, seen Henry enter the Close, followed after him until he entered the chapel, and then taken advantage of the situation and killed him.'

'It seems like too much of a coincidence. Why should Henry have gone into the chapel in the first place?'

'Thomas could have sent a message asking Henry to meet a man there. Perhaps he sent it in the name of William, since they knew each other.'

'But why,' Simon interrupted, 'should he go to the chapel? Surely Henry would be unlikely to trust a man like William at the best of times, and entering a quiet charnel with a man you don't trust would be folly.'

Baldwin nodded. 'But it could have been a message in the name of someone whom Henry would have trusted. We can check later. As a hypothesis it works – Thomas invented a message, sent it, waited on his scaffold from where he could see all the entrances to the Close, and then, when Henry entered the Close, Thomas descended and either walked inside first, or hung about until Henry was inside. Then Thomas walked in, killed him and left again, went straight back to his ladder and got on with his work. The others there might not even have noticed his departure.'

'What of the second killing?' Sir Peregrine asked.

'The case of the Friar, I confess, is strange. We think he died in the crypt,' Baldwin said and explained his reasoning about the movement of the body.

'That must mean that the body was moved to make it more conspicuous,' Sir Peregrine said. 'After all, it would be safer not to move the friar when he was dead. Why run the risk of being caught in the act unless there was good reason? And what was Thomas's motive to kill Henry?'

'I do not know. My suspicion is, like yours, founded solely on the man's sudden disappearance. Why kill the friar? Perhaps because Nicholas saw him kill Henry. And as for Henry – I cannot tell why that should have happened, unless there was a longstanding feud between them.'

'What of the mason Saul?' Simon asked.

Baldwin shook his head. 'I can only assume that he was another man who knew Thomas.'

'You mean that Saul recognised him from the past and threatened to disclose his identity?' Sir Peregrine demanded.

'I suppose so,' Baldwin said. 'Thomas may have feared the disclosure of his part in the murder of the Chaunter.' He frowned. 'Although dropping a stone on Saul's head would be an unorthodox method of murder.'

'But effective,' Sir Peregrine said.

'More lucky than effective, if he meant to murder,' Baldwin commented.

Simon was still considering the motive. 'Why would this Thomas suddenly fear recognition? The mason Saul was not a local man – so how could he have recognised Thomas? And Henry Saddler was an accomplice of his, so why should Thomas kill him? As for the friar – well, I suppose he could have seemed a threat, but what if we were right and Nicholas was himself one of the assassins? We thought he might have been in on the plot, didn't we? What could have made him so uniquely dangerous to Thomas? Also, surely the saddler himself, or the joiner, or even the corrodian, would have the same motivation? I do not understand why Thomas should have decided to enter this killing spree.'

'We may not understand until we have him in our hands and can question him,' Sir Peregrine said.

A short while later, Baldwin and Simon decided to leave. As Baldwin said, they would need their sleep that night, if they were to rise early to help a posse seek the missing mason.

As they walked along the road, Simon threw Baldwin a look. 'Were you persuaded by his protestations?'

Baldwin smiled. 'Am I *so* transparent, Simon?'

'Only to one who knows you, Baldwin!'

They were only a few scant yards from their own inn when they heard the scampering of feet, and Baldwin's hand went to his sword.

'Easy, old friend, it's only a lad,' Simon said.

'It is the sound of running steps; they always raise my hackles,' Baldwin admitted. It was not only the noise and the reminder that even here in Exeter there were footpads, it was the dislocation he still felt – the feeling that he was farther apart from his wife than ever – and the curious menace he had sensed at the Charnel Chapel.

The boy hurried past them and went into their inn. There was a sudden calming of the noise of talking and laughter, and in it, they heard the boy calling for the Keeper of the King's Peace.

Baldwin glanced at Simon, then pushed his way inside. 'I am Sir Baldwin,' he said. 'I am the Keeper of the King's Peace. What do you want, boy?'

'It's the man who killed my father – he's tried to rob us, and we need someone to come and take him,' Dan said, trying not to cry.

*   *   *

Udo had not enjoyed the talk with the Keeper of the King's Peace and his companion. He was not used to such treatment from strangers, and the thought that the men could have been so suspicious of him was worrying. As an outsider, he knew full well the risks he took in remaining here in a foreign country. If there was to be guilt attached to any man, the population would rather pick a stranger than a local man.

He could ride that storm, he hoped, but what about the assertion that someone had heard Henry rejecting Udo's offer of marriage? If that should get back to Julia, there could be only one course for her to take, which was to obey his last dying wish, surely? Udo must not let her learn of her father's words.

So he had the two problems now: the matter of his own guilt being decided by his neighbours in preference to their selecting someone from among their own, and the fact that Julia might discover that her father had set his face against her marriage to Udo.

And the two men, the Keeper and his Bailiff, were the interfering cretins who had exposed him to these problems. He could grow to dislike them both.

Chapter Twenty

Thomas came to with his head feeling as if someone had dropped a mallet on it from the top of his own scaffolding. As soon as he had opened his eyes he had to snap them shut. The light was too bright.

Where the devil was he? Then he realised: he was still in Sara's house. He was sitting with his back up against one of the two posts in the middle of the floor. The light came from a small tallow candle that smoked repellently over his left shoulder. His legs seemed to have gone to sleep, and he knew that he must move them. He had to get up and run from this place. Whoever had hit him could return at any time.

He tried to lift a hand to shield his face from the deadly beam of the candle, but his hand was stuck behind him. When he jerked his wrist, he felt the pain simultaneously in his palm as well as the wrist, and it was so sharp, it was like pulling against a razor. Giving a cry of pain, he started to topple to one side. To break his fall, he threw his other hand out, only to find that that too was securely bound. Cursing and sobbing, he slid to the side, his arms slowing his painful descent, until his head struck the packed earth of the floor, and he could lie there with the pain throbbing in both wrists, his heart pounding with fear and a feeling of sickness.

'You wait there,' came a harsh and unsympathetic voice. 'You try and rob a poor widow, you deserve all you get.'

'I haven't tried to rob anyone,' he protested, squirming to see who was talking. Peering over his shoulder, he saw that it was the woman, Jen, who had taken his wine on that first day when he brought news of Saul's death. 'Woman, why have you done this? I've never robbed anyone in my life!'

'You robbed this family of their father and husband. I'd say that was robbery,' she said equably. ' 'Tis a shame, too. You bought good wine,' she added, smacking her lips.

'Can I have a drink of something? My throat is parched.'

'Be glad you've got one. The boy would have cut it as soon as look at you. You're lucky I saved you and only sent him for the crowner.'

'The crowner?' he repeated dully. If the Coroner was on his way, there was little point in struggling. He was dead already – just like his father. He too would die on the scaffold and be displayed at the Southern Gate. Not for his own crimes, but like his father, for those of other men. 'Come on, maid, it can't hurt anyone to let me have a mouthful of water, can it? I'm dying of thirst here.'

'Then you shouldn't have come here to take her money, should you?'

'I didn't! I left her *my* money to try to help her!'

'I found you in here and clobbered your head with a stick, so don't lie to me,' she snapped.

'I'd taken the pennies from my purse to give to her,' he said with resignation, knowing she wouldn't believe him. 'I felt guilty about her man's death, and I wanted to give her something to help her get by. I was going to leave the city and find somewhere else to work.'

'They fired you, then?' she cackled. 'Not surprised, if all you can do is kill off their other workers.'

'I . . .'

Thomas was quiet as a shadow slipped in through the door. In sudden fear he recognised the quick movements of Sara's son, Dan. He couldn't see the boy because the door was behind him, but the shadow was terrifying, the boy's shape deformed and sly as it moved about the room until Thomas could see him. He saw the hatred in the lad's eyes: the fellow would draw his little pocket-knife at the first opportunity.

'Well, Master Thomas, I think you would have been better served to have waited for us at the Cathedral, rather than trying this frankly unorthodox approach to gaining our attention.'

'Is that the Keeper?' Thomas demanded. He was scared still, but less so by the looming shadow that now appeared in front of him.

'Lad, cut those thongs,' Baldwin ordered, walking around in front of the man and squatting. 'Now, Thomas, you are held under my authority and we are going to take you back to the Cathedral to the Bishop's gaol. When we are there, we are going to ask you some questions, and this time I want the truth from you!'

Thomas let his head hang. 'I will tell you everything.'

* * *

Matthew was surprised to be called to the Treasurer's hall so late in the afternoon, and he hurried there as soon as the summons came. As the Warden of the Fabric Rolls, he was largely responsible for the new Cathedral as it was building, and if the Treasurer had found a problem with his calculations or book-keeping, he wanted to know about it as soon as possible. It was the one thing about his job that constantly preyed on his mind, this fear that one day there would be a false calculation found in his work.

It wasn't very likely, of course. Most men, whether clerks or not, found it difficult to add and subtract the figures which had been passed down from antiquity by the Romans along with their venerable script for reading and writing. No man could argue that the Romans were not the most marvellous race of men so far created by God. They had built wonderful buildings, invented waterways and roads, and left a legacy of learning which was superior to any other civilisation.

'You called for me?'

The Treasurer's house was one of the smaller ones on the canons' street. It fronted the Exchequer, and suited the modest requirements of the man who was, after all, one of the most powerful men in the Cathedral.

'Yes, Matthew.'

He was looking old today, Matthew thought. Old and tired, like an apple left on the ground too long – not quite rotten to the core, but very close to it. He suddenly wondered whether the Treasurer would survive much longer. If he were to die, whom would the Dean select as his replacement from the members of the Choir? Surely it would be the man most attuned to the numbers which ruled the life of the Treasurer – the man who could understand the rolls and make the best of the money the Cathedral had allocated for this rebuilding. He suddenly felt a little light-headed.

'This old affair of the murder of Chaunter Walter is springing up once more. It is regrettable, but there is little we can do to cover it all up if it comes into the open. I wanted to warn you, Matthew. I know that the whole thing must be deeply distressing for you, but there is nothing I or the Dean can do to stop it, I fear. The dead saddler was certainly involved in the attack, and of course the friar was there.'

'Yes, I remember. Poor Nicholas. I was at his side when he won that terrible wound,' Matthew said incomprehendingly. 'But I don't . . .'

'Of course,' Stephen said. 'I wasn't in the Cathedral that night, but when I returned, you were still in a fever, and Nicholas was at death's door.'

Matthew nodded. It was odd how many men had apparently been out of Exeter that night. The Vicar of Ottery St Mary, for example, had been out of the Close; so had the Vicar of Heavitree. Both were later found guilty of being there at the murder, of course, and they'd paid heavily for their crime in the Bishop's gaol.

Still, he told himself, there was no point raking up old suspicions. No one really wanted to go into the matter again.

'If it were possible to ask these two men to hold their investigation, I should do so,' Stephen said quietly, gazing up at the cross that hung on his wall above the screens passage.

Matthew found his manner disquieting, but then he told himself again that it must surely be Stephen's great age. The man was exhausted, but he must carry on until he collapsed. That was the sort of man he was.

And then a more unnerving idea came to him: perhaps the Treasurer *had* been one of the men attacking – it might even have been him who knocked Matthew down on the night he so nearly died. A man who had done that would later make amends in any way he might. He could take a novice into his own department and see to it that he was well and carefully trained and nurtured, so that he would himself become indispensable.

Matthew found himself studying his mentor with a feeling of prickly nervousness running up his spine. This man, the one who had given him the better posts, who had looked after him in forty years of life at the Cathedral, had once been there trying to kill him just because . . . Why?

'Stephen,' he said quietly. 'Was it you struck me down?'

The Treasurer was still staring at the cross. He blinked then, as though the cross had itself stung him. There was a slight moisture at the corner of his eye, Matthew saw, and he felt the shock thrill through him before Stephen had even answered.

'The Chaunter was divisive,' Stephen said. 'He was a malign influence on the Cathedral – my God, anyone could see that!' His eyes were on the cross again, as though pleading his sincerity. Gradually his eyes fell, and he turned his attention back to Matthew. 'But I swear to you, Matthew, I never wanted to see you or anyone else harmed! Only *him*! He was evil, a man who would divert us all from our tasks and drive a wedge between the Bishop and his Chapter. Who could want to leave him in power when his entire efforts were dedicated to ruining us all? Any man who had a relationship, no matter how tenuous, with the Dean and Treasurer, was detested by de Lecchelade, and belittled and demeaned. No one who held the good reputation and honour of the Cathedral in his heart could tolerate his behaviour.'

'He was the Treasurer, wasn't he?'

'Dean Pycot? Yes. And perhaps he should have given that up earlier, but it's a man's nature to keep to the job he knows and with which he feels most comfortable. Dean John was like you, Matthew. He was excellent when it came to numbers; they held no secrets for him. It was possible for him to run a finger down a roll and when he reached the bottom, he could tell you the total. As fast as this,' he demonstrated, running a forefinger down a column. 'I could never emulate that, so I never thought I should take over from him.'

'He was your master?'

'I lived with him. I was Clerk to the Works at the time, and when Dean Pycot was made Dean I couldn't take over. I was too young, Matthew. Far too inexperienced.'

'It has been said that the Dean siphoned away a great deal of money.'

'Such accusations are easy to level against another man,' the Treasurer said dismissively. 'It is a great deal harder to prove that you are innocent.'

'So you took his part during that attack?'

'I swear I didn't hurt you, Matthew,' Stephen said. He looked at Matthew again with real fear in his eyes. 'I have wanted to tell you so many times in the last four decades, but there has never seemed to be the right moment. At first you were so badly beaten, it seemed ridiculous to add to your trials by saying I was myself one of those who might have hurt you; then when you were healed, it seemed foolish to risk my own position; more recently, it seemed madness to try to bring up long-dead history again.'

'But now?'

'The Dean has asked me who was here then. Who still lives at the Cathedral who was here forty years ago.'

Matthew understood. 'So you must tell him of my part. And that you too were here.'

'Yes,' Stephen said, and looked away with shame flooding his eyes. His voice was soft. 'I would have your forgiveness, if you feel you could be so generous towards me.'

He looked pathetic. Matthew was repelled by his tears and weakness. 'I forgive you,' he said, 'provided you were not the man who actually beat me and left me for dead. If it were not you, who was responsible for my injuries?'

'It was dark, Matthew. I think we'll never know. I was myself running to attack de Lecchelade, but I know I didn't hit you.'

'How can you be so sure?' Matthew demanded hotly. 'If it was so dark and you were so lost as to not know what was going on, how can you tell?'

'You were knocked senseless, were you not? I did not hold a club, Matthew. I had only a sword.'

Simon hauled Thomas to his feet. He stood like a man who has lost all his will to resist further, his head hanging, his expression utterly devoid of hope. There was only a grim fatalism in his eyes.

Simon had captured many people in his time. Some felons would wail and tear at their bonds, others would show no remorse, only a determination to escape any possibility of retribution. Seeing a man so hangdog was not unusual; it was a common attitude of one who had committed a crime in a flash of rage, only to regret his own behaviour later, especially when he was caught.

'Get a move on!' Simon growled, and the man stumbled slightly as he walked forward, his legs moving loosely and in a gangling manner, like one who was drunk or befuddled.

Baldwin was already outside, and Simon manoeuvred Thomas to the door just as Sara appeared in the lane.

'Thomas?' she said, glancing at him and then looking from Baldwin to Simon. 'Who are you?'

Baldwin introduced himself and Simon, and then nodded towards Thomas. 'This man was in your house to steal your money.'

'What money?' she asked with an expression of surprise. 'I don't have any.'

'There were some coins on your table,' Baldwin said. He beckoned to Jen. 'You have the coins?'

'Here they are,' Jen said, heaving her bulk through the door and holding her hand out to Sara. 'Look, this is what he was trying to take.'

'These aren't mine,' Sara said. 'I don't have more than two pennies, and they're here,' she added, hefting her purse in her hand. 'I wouldn't leave money in my house.'

'Then where did the pennies come from?' Simon demanded.

'I tried to explain,' Thomas said wearily. 'I put them there for Sara. When I decided to leave the city, I wanted to give Sara something to help her get by. I left her all the whole coins in my purse. That woman saw me enter and chose to assume the worst of me. When I was putting the coins down, she hit me.'

'And where did you come by all these coins?' Simon asked.

'They are the money I've been paid for my work. Since I've taken away Sara's husband, I thought the least I could do was try to help her.'

'It was kind of you,' Sara said. 'You didn't have to.'

'He's a *murderer*!' Dan said to Baldwin. 'Take him away from here, we don't want him or his money! You keep it, *murderer*!' he spat.

'Leave him, Danny,' his mother said quietly. She was exhausted, and although she had tried to seek work, she had failed through the day. All she wanted was a chance to fall onto her bed and sleep. 'Thomas was trying to help us. Sirs, he can't have been robbing us, so can't you let him loose? I won't accuse him of anything.'

'Mistress, we can't,' Simon said. 'He was involved in a murder many years ago, and he may well be the killer of two more men who have died recently. Until he's been questioned, we can't let him go.'

'If he was a murderer, he'd not have been so kind to me and Danny,' she declared.

Baldwin set his mouth in a firm line. 'I am sorry, but we do not know that. He must come and be questioned.'

'Sara, forget me. I hope the money will help you. Just be happy and find someone else to protect you,' Thomas said quietly. 'Take me away, please.'

Simon had him by the shoulder, and he directed the man away from the rough home, along the lane and then down the sloping road towards Fore Street. He glanced over his shoulder once, and saw the widow still standing in front of her doorway, her hands on her son's shoulders, gazing after the three men.

They soon reached the Cathedral, and Baldwin walked straight in through the gate.

'You made good time, Sir Knight,' Janekyn called. 'I'll be closing this gate soon. What have you there?'

'This fellow was trying to run from the city,' Baldwin said. 'The Coroner will want to see him in the morning, so we need to have him securely held in the Bishop's gaol. Who can open it for us?'

Janekyn eyed Thomas with some interest, and then led them to the part of the Cathedral where the gaol was, asking them to wait while he sent a novice to look after the gate for him, and then he disappeared to find the gaoler.

'I didn't do it, masters,' Thomas said.

'What?' Baldwin asked.

'I didn't kill the Chaunter, and I haven't killed anyone else. Henry was an old friend. I could never hurt him. And Nicholas . . . I gave him his wounds all those years ago, and I spoke to him to beg forgiveness. He did forgive me.'

'He forgave you those dreadful scars?' Simon said disbelievingly. 'And then what? He bought you a barrel of fresh ale?'

'No, only a quart of cider,' Thomas said.

'When?'

'The very night he died,' Thomas shrugged. 'He forgave me and we went to the tavern on the right as you go up beyond Fissand Gate towards the High Street. We were there for some little while.'

'Was there anyone there who could vouch for you?' Baldwin asked.

'I don't know. There must have been people there who'd recognise a description of the friar, though. They may have noticed me too.'

'We will check,' Simon promised. 'But for now, you'll have to remain here. The Coroner will want to speak to you in the morning.'

'He'll see me hanged.'

Simon was struck by his attitude. 'He may agree you're innocent. How could you be so sure that he'll want to have you hanged?'

'I cannot hide my guilt, Master. I was there on the night the Chaunter was killed, as I said, and I fled the city afterwards. I felt guilty and ashamed of my crime. And then, later, I heard that the South Gate had been left wide open, and those responsible hanged. Well, it wasn't fair or just, but it was a judgement of a sort. It was my father who was hanged. He died in my place.'

Simon gave a grunt of sympathy. 'I see.'

'I never thought to return here, not after hearing that. Especially now, though. I have learned who actually had my father killed. It was that devil, William. He told the King about the gate being left open and accused the city of complicity so he could worm his way into the King's favour. It was because of him my father was hanged.'

'Is that William the corrodian?'

'Yes. I was with him and Henry on the night of the killing, and I wish I'd taken the opportunity to kill him. If I had, I'd not be here now.'

Baldwin and Simon led him towards the cells as the gaoler and Janekyn returned. They passed him over, and Thomas walked with them. As Baldwin and Simon stood waiting, they heard the rattle of keys, then the slam of a heavy door being closed.

'So that is that,' Simon breathed.

'Yes,' said Baldwin. Then he sighed. ''Ach! Let us return to our inn and take our rest. We have little more to do tonight, and we don't have to do anything in the morning. There's no need to worry about haring off after Thomas now. Come, let me buy you some wine.'

'That sounds good,' Simon smiled.

They were outside the Charnel Chapel when Baldwin stopped and stared at it. 'Evil is not a word I use often, Simon, but I have been aware of a feeling about that building ever since I first saw it. It was built as a reparation for the murder of the Chaunter, but it brought nothing for the Dean who constructed it. Now it stores the bones of the dead, and yet bears an atmosphere of pain and fear. Do you know, old friend, I fear it myself.'

'And you used to accuse *me* of being superstitious!' Simon laughed aloud.

They walked past the chapel, up towards the flickering light of the torch in the arch of the Fissand Gate. And it was there that he heard it.

It was a soft, whirring sound, a little like a bird's wingbeat. For an instant, Simon wondered what it might be, and then he opened his mouth to shout while he threw himself to the ground. 'Christ Jesus!'

Luckily Baldwin had heard it too, Simon saw. He lay full length beside Simon, and the Bailiff frowned as he gazed about the place. There was no sign of the arrow. Now, lying on the ground, he wasn't even sure which direction it had come from. 'Did you see the man?' he asked softly. He might still be there, preparing to fire again. 'Baldwin? We ought to get away from here, find some cover.'

'Simon . . . Simon, help!' Baldwin's voice sounded strong enough, but there was a strange quality to it, as though he was a long way away and calling to Simon on a foggy day.

When he looked at his friend, Simon frowned. His mind didn't register at first. All he could see was the knight's suddenly pale face, the eyes grown huge, and then Simon saw the apparently frail stick, the fletchings quivering gently with the wounded man's every rasping breath, and he had to bite back his scream. 'Baldwin, hold on! It'll be all right, Baldwin – just hold on!'

Simon leaped to his feet and ran to him. Baldwin gave him a twisted grin as Simon knelt by his side, staring about them for a sign of the assassin, but there was nothing, no movement, no scurrying shadow-figure. All was still as he leaned down to Baldwin; he felt the skin crawling on his back, as though his very flesh was anticipating the next arrow to strike, but then he was studying his friend, and had no time to worry about his own safety.

The arrow had entered his back high, not far from his spine, and now protruded from his breast about three inches below his collar-bone. Baldwin's sword arm was all but immobilised, and Simon reckoned that his shoulder-blade was pinned by it. Still, as he helped his friend haltingly to his feet and pulled Baldwin's left arm over his shoulder, he was glad to see that there was no bright blood dribbling from his mouth. The lungs must be safe, and so high as it was, Simon was sure that Baldwin's heart was safe. He whispered encouragingly as he helped his old friend towards the nearest shelter, which was Janekyn's lodge at the gate.

'Janekyn? *Jan*! Come here now! Help me!' he bellowed as he approached the door. Baldwin was whispering urgently in his ear, but he ignored his friend's words. 'You'll soon be all right, Baldwin. You'll be fine.'

It opened as he reached the light of the torch still flickering under the arch, and then Janekyn, his face filled with alarm, helped Simon carry Baldwin through the door to a stool near the brazier. There they sat the wounded knight, panting, and Simon could see at last the wicked arrow-head. It was a modern 'pricker', a square-sectioned bodkin of some four inches long, designed to penetrate chainmail armour. The sight of it made Simon's heart stand still, but then he was ordering Janekyn to wrap his friend in a blanket and keep him warm, while he bolted for the Dean's house.

All the way, all he could hear was his friend's rasping breath, and those words spoken in his quiet, self-possessed manner.

'My wife. Tell her . . . Tell her I loved her. I still . . . love her.'

Chapter Twenty-One

That night was the longest Simon had ever spent. The Dean gaped, and then ordered that his steward should rouse the Mayor's household to ask who the best physician was in the city, and then bring him at once. Soon Ralph of Malmesbury was with them in Janekyn's little room, and he at once set about his work.

While the physician studied Baldwin's breast, Simon stood at his friend's side. There was no great effusion of blood, which gave Simon some hope, but he knew that the danger which threatened Baldwin would only become clear when the arrow was removed and the wound could be studied more closely. Ralph opened a small vein to release some of Baldwin's bad humours, and then started to work on the arrow itself. Baldwin maintained a steadfast patience, only showing his temper when the physician stood on his foot. 'Do you not think I have enough damage done to me?' he said weakly.

'I am at least experienced in this kind of wound,' the physician said. 'Stop your bellyaching. Most surgeon barbers would pull the arrow through one way or the other. At least there are no barbs on this bastard, eh? If there were, a barber would bend them back and try to yank it through you again. Me, I think that's daft. What's the point?' He took a pair of strong-bladed shears and rested them upon the arrow's shaft. 'Better to cut the arrowhead off like this. Are you strong?'

Baldwin gave a pale smile. 'As strong as I can be.'

'This may hurt,' Ralph said, and he threw a look to Simon. Understanding, Simon put his arms on Baldwin's shoulders and held him still as Ralph began to cut through the shaft, turning the arrow as he did so. 'This will be uncomfortable, but by moving the arrow itself, I free it up ready to be withdrawn,' he said. The process was slow, the shaft solid and difficult to cut. The grain was strong. Still, after some minutes, the shears were biting through the outer surface, and then sinking deeper and deeper. Although Baldwin grimaced, closing his eyes and grunting, he didn't cry out. Simon could feel his muscles tense, but then he slowly relaxed, as if he was growing accustomed to this peculiar pain.

'All done!' Ralph declared suddenly.

He was about to throw the arrowhead onto the floor, when Simon said, 'Put it on the table there. I shall want to look at it.'

Ralph glanced at him in surprise, looked at the bodkin in his hands, and shrugged. As though humouring the vill's idiot, he placed it carefully on the table before turning back to the arrow shaft. He cleaned its length with a mixture that he produced from a small bottle, smearing it over the shaft with a finger that grew crimson from Baldwin's blood, stoppered the bottle and rose. 'I need to stand behind him.'

Simon stood before Baldwin, and the physician rotated the shaft in his hand gently. 'This will hurt, I fear, but try to keep him still.'

Feeling the nausea in his throat, Simon took Baldwin's shoulders and stared deep into his eyes. Baldwin was in great pain, that much was obvious from his wan features. Simon had never seen him look so colourless, and if that weren't enough, the sight of Baldwin's white knuckles on the stool's seat was proof. Baldwin reached up as Simon took his shoulders, and put both his hands on Simon's forearms, gripping them tightly.

Ralph was watching almost absently as he turned the shaft slowly, and then he began to pull it out as though it was screwed, constantly turning it, while his gaze remained unfocused on a point over Simon's shoulder. Simon saw the cut-off end slip backwards until there was only an inch or so protruding from about three inches beneath Baldwin's collar-bone, and then it was gone. The dreamy-eyed Ralph remained there for a few more moments, slowly rotating the shaft, his fingers slick with blood, until the remaining section came free, and he glanced down at his hands with apparent surprise. 'Ah! All done.'

Simon felt Baldwin's hands lose their fierce grip, and then the wounded man sank into a merciful faint.

Baldwin was installed in Janekyn's bed, while the porter was removed to a room nearby to sleep on a bench. The Dean, who had come to see how things were going, tried to conceal a yawn.

'My dear Bailiff, do – ah – forgive me. You must be a great deal more tired than I am,' he said. 'I shall order that another bed be brought in here for you.'

'No, thank you,' Simon said. He was turning the bodkin over and over in his hands, frowning. Some blood still adhered to it, and his hands were growing stained, but he didn't care. 'If I sleep, the attacker may come back for another attempt.'

'You don't think that this was launched by a member of the community here?' the Dean asked.

'I don't know, but it's certainly possible, and I won't risk his life,' Simon said. 'The assassin could have been a foreigner who fled by the Bear Gate or the Palace Gate, but he may equally well be hiding here in the Cathedral's Close somewhere, and I won't take any chances that he won't try to murder Baldwin in his bed.'

'I see.'

'I was wondering where the arrow could have been launched from,' Simon said. He walked to the door. From there he could see where he and Baldwin had hurled themselves to the ground. Behind them at that moment had been the Charnel Chapel, with the black mass of the Cathedral beyond. 'It must have been either from the chapel or the Cathedral itself.'

He stared out. From here, the chapel blocked the whole of the Cathedral's front. When they had been out in the Close, a bowman on the Cathedral's walls would surely not have been able to see them – which meant the shot must have come from the chapel.

Simon was in two minds. He wanted to go to the chapel at once to test whether his theory was correct and the assassin had fired from there, but he knew that he would be better served to wait until daylight. Also, he feared leaving Baldwin in case he should need Simon – either because he had suffered a collapse, or because a killer tried again to dispatch him.

'Dean, I shall remain here all night to protect Baldwin. Could you arrange for a pair of men whom you trust to come and help me? Not so slipshod as the three told to keep an eye on Thomas, either. I shall also want to send a messenger as soon as possible to Baldwin's wife, to let her know about this attack.'

'Naturally,' the Dean said. He glanced back at Baldwin's figure.

'Bailiff, I cannot tell you how sorry I am, that this dreadful attack should have happened within my Close.'

'Dean, I am sure that Baldwin wouldn't blame you for one rogue, and I won't either.'

'Is there anything else I can do for you?'

'I should like a large flask of wine, and first thing in the morning, please arrange for Thomas to be brought to me from the cells.'

'Are you sure he is safe?'

'I think the idea that there could be two murderers running about the Close is far-fetched,' Simon said. 'Someone tried to kill Baldwin *after* Thomas was installed in the gaol, and that means it's unlikely he is the guilty party. Yes, I am happy to vouch for his safety.'

But who, he wondered as he again stared about him at the darkened Close, who will vouch for mine?

The night was a long and uncomfortable one for Simon. The Dean had been as good as his word, and sent two lay members of the Cathedral staff to stand at Baldwin's side; they were strong-looking young men, both armed with swords and knives, one with a club as well, and they exuded a general attitude of competence.

'You get some sleep, Bailiff. I can watch over him for you,' said one, whose name apparently was David.

Simon took a seat on a stool, but wouldn't sleep. He kept an eye on Baldwin, but most of the time he spent staring towards the doorway, wondering whether there would be another attack or not. It was hard to see how someone could hope to get past three men to kill Baldwin, but that was the least of his worries. What Simon wanted to know was, why should someone have decided to attack him in the first place? Was it because by some accident, Simon and Baldwin had come close to the truth of the matter?

And yet the bowman had only aimed at one of them – he had not fired a second arrow at Simon. Why not? Was it something Baldwin had learned which implicated the murderer, or was it simply that Baldwin's behaviour had upset the guilty man? Simon felt the possibilities flying about in his head all through the night, but when the first light started to brighten the cracks in the shutters at the windows, he was no nearer an answer.

But the answer itself could be damned. Just now Simon was aware of nothing but an overwhelming anger: he would find the would-be assassin, and make him pay. Simon vowed there and then to destroy the man who had made an attempt on Baldwin's life.

He looked at his old friend. The knight lay breathing stertorously, a deathly pallor on his gaunt cheeks. Simon prayed that the wound healed cleanly, and did not become infected. The next few hours were crucial . . .

As the night wore on, Simon found his mind wandering. He recalled how he had first met Baldwin in the torchlit hall at Bickleigh Castle, how Baldwin's face had shown such grim despair, and how over the last seven years that weary grief had eroded under the happy influence of his wife, the former Jeanne de Liddinstone. Recently he had seen how Baldwin's problems with Jeanne had caused him a renewed pain, and Simon was scared just now that Baldwin might not last the night and see her again. It made him grip Baldwin's hand and wring it, trying to force his friend to hold on, if only for as long as it would take Jeanne to arrive.

No messenger could leave until the city opened its gates, which would mean that she wouldn't know of this misfortune until the middle of the morning at the earliest. If she were to mount her own horse, she might, just possibly, be at Exeter at noon, but a little after that was more likely.

Simon could have marched to the gaol and demanded Thomas immediately. He could have started to learn all the mason knew, but to do so he would have to leave Baldwin with strangers to guard him, and that was not going to happen. Far better that he should wait until dawn. In daylight he would feel safer. All the murders so far had happened in the dark; during the day there were always too many people wandering about the Cathedral and in the Close for someone to be able to commit a crime of that nature with any hope of escape.

At full light, a man knocked at the door. It was the messenger who was to go to Jeanne, and Simon thought quickly. 'Just tell her that Baldwin has been injured, that he is not dead, but sorely wounded, and that he loves her.' He considered for a moment. A message like that would be sure to worry her . . . well, there was not much he could do about that. He didn't want to worry her, but she needed to be aware that

Baldwin was badly wounded. She should make the journey to Exeter to sit with him. Her presence would be a comfort to her husband. In the meantime, Simon wanted Baldwin's last words to be taken to her as well. They might prove to be soothing.

Soon after the messenger had hurried outside and clambered aboard his horse, a fierce-looking beast with hooves the size of small barrel-bottoms, and hurtled off through Fissand Gate towards the West Gate of the city, Simon found himself confronted with a canon who carried a tray.

'Bailiff. I was so sorry to hear of Sir Baldwin's attack last night,' Treasurer Stephen said. 'I trust that a little food would help to support him? Please give him these *dowcettes* to improve his strength, and send him my best wishes.'

'I thank you,' Simon said, and set the tray on a table. Just now he was unsure whom to trust, and although the Treasurer was no doubt a safe, fair man, he wanted to ensure that no harm could come to Baldwin. That meant treating all food with caution, keeping others away from Baldwin, and making sure that he was safe at all times.

The Treasurer saw how Simon eyed the food. 'It is good – do you want me to eat some of it in front of you?' he asked.

There was a plaintive tone to his voice which made Simon give an apologetic shake of his head. 'I must be cautious. Until the physician returns, I shall not be giving him anything.'

Stephen opened his mouth to speak, but was interrupted by the arrival of Thomas in the custody of a young layman. Simon did not notice how Stephen shot a glance at Thomas and winced, before looking away again, his face slightly paler.

'How are you?' Simon growled.

'As well as a condemned man could be,' Thomas replied caustically as Simon pulled out his dagger and cut the thongs that bound his hands. He stood flexing his arms for a moment. 'The Bishop's gaol is not so comfortable as a mason's shed, although I daresay it's better than some other prisons. Could I ask for some water to wash my hands? My palms are very painful still.'

'My companion was attacked last night and almost killed,' Simon said, motioning to the guard to fetch him a bucket. 'I will find out who was responsible, and to do that I need to know everything you can tell me about the murder of the Chaunter and what has happened since you returned here.'

'I've already told you all I can about the Chaunter's death. I know nothing more.'

'I know of Henry, Joel and William. Who else was involved?'

'There were many of us – but not all are alive now.'

'Well, who is, then?' Simon said harshly.

Thomas gave him a long, considering look. 'Very well.' He reeled off a series of names. 'As you can see, they are all members of the city's nobility. Those who were members of the Cathedral at the time have mostly gone.'

'Which ones haven't?'

'There are only two, I think. Peter, the acting Prior of St Nicholas, and one other: the Treasurer here, Canon Stephen.'

Simon stared at the Treasurer accusingly; the latter nodded, his eyes closed. Setting his jaw, Simon jerked his chin at the mason. 'There was one more, wasn't there? Matthew recognised you.'

'Yes, he was there, but he was one of the Chaunter's men.'

'That could mean that he wanted his revenge on those who'd had a part in the Chaunter's death.'

'I doubt it. He's been living here all these years alongside Henry Potell and Joel Lytell. What would make him suddenly become so lethal that he would seek to murder Henry and then the friar?'

'The same goes for Joel – and the Treasurer here,' Simon said. 'Was it the arrival of the friar or William that caused the murders to begin? Or your arrival, of course.'

'Mine?' Thomas said, startled. 'I've been here a year, in God's name. Why should someone wait so long before starting to kill?'

Simon nodded. His eyes were gritty, and his tongue felt as though it was made of felt. He needed a draught of good ale and some food. The guard was returned now with the bucket of water, and seeing how Thomas winced as he dunked his hands in the chill fluid, Simon made a quick decision. He said to the guard, 'Fetch us a plain loaf of bread and a jug of wine. Thomas, you and I need food. As far as I can see, you could have had nothing to do with the attempt on my friend and that makes you more reliable than many here. I'd like you to come with me.'

'You'll have to ask the Dean first. I think he wants me in his gaol.'

'The good Dean will do as I demand,' Simon said flatly.

Thomas had his mouth open as the scabs began to ease. His hands smarted and stung, but Simon's tone made him forget the pain. Looking at the Bailiff, Thomas was struck by the cold ferocity in his eyes.

'Perhaps you're right,' he said.

'I am,' Simon said, and then he turned to the Treasurer. His voice was harder now, like a judge preparing to command an execution. 'And now I want your story.'

Joel woke with his face aching a little less than the day before, and he was relieved to find that his breast was not so painful. Breathing was easier, and his first impression as he was helped from his bed by a servant was that he was healing quickly.

That was an notion quickly dispelled as soon as he stood. He coughed painfully, and had to grab his servant's arm to stop himself falling. Stifling the curses which threatened to burst forth, he tried to stay calm. Excitement caused the pain to increase, and he had no desire to enhance this in any way.

Dressed at last, he carefully went down his steps one at a time and then grabbed a staff to help himself down the passage to his hall.

Maud was already waiting for him at their table, and he forced a smile to his face at the sight of her, not sure how she would be after his gaffe of the day before. 'Not going to church today?'

She eyed him seriously. 'I have already been.'

He nodded, and hobbled across the floor to her, dropping into his seat with relief. 'I thought you'd waited for me.'

She nodded to the servant, who stood hovering at the doorway, and he began to usher in the other servants and apprentices. 'No, Husband. I felt the need to go and pray for you.'

'Now you know I'm a murderer, you mean,' he said bleakly.

Maud turned to eye him. 'Don't be even more of a fool than you already are, Joel. I married you for love, and I'd be unaccustomed to life without you after all these years. Foolish man, I love you still.'

He stared at her. Theirs was a marriage of easiness. They hadn't been fortunate enough to have children, but neither had blamed the other for that. As the priests said, it was God's choice whether a union would be blessed, and both had enough contentment in the company of the other for their mutual happiness. They only rarely expressed their love aloud. Somehow it seemed a little immature – and unnecessary. 'Am I such a fool?' he wondered aloud.

'Yes. For you've managed to upset that madman William while achieving nothing for yourself.'

'It's not my fault he's upset,' Joel grumbled. 'He assumed I must have launched an attack on him because of the way he treated me in the past. If I wasn't so important as I am, he'd have cut my throat and left me in a ditch. As it is, he's done enough, hasn't he?'

'Where is Vince?' Maud asked, momentarily distracted.

Joel's brows lifted and he glanced about the room. True enough, there was no sign of the fellow, and Joel felt annoyed. He disliked his apprentices behaving lazily; even if he himself were a little late for his meal, like this morning, there was no excuse for them to copy his example. Just when he was going to repeat the question, Vince walked in.

'You are late!' Joel called.

'Master, my apologies. My father was unwell last night, and I had to stay with him to tend him,' Vince said.

'You weren't with some whore from the Grapes, then?'

Vince held Joel's gaze with a cold contempt. 'I don't know that place, Master Joel.'

Joel felt sure that in a moment Vince would ask him what it was like inside, and he waited with the rage growing inside him, only to feel a curious blend of relief and annoyance when Vince curled his lip and looked away, striding off to wash his hands in the ewer.

'What was all that about?' Maud asked.

'I don't know. The boy's unhappy about something, though.'

'I shall speak to him, then,' she responded. An apprentice was much like a son, after all. If one of their fellows was unhappy or in trouble, the Master was responsible. She could ask more gently than Joel – especially today, she thought to herself, taking in her husband's wince and stifled gasp of pain as he shifted in his seat.

'Come along, then!' Simon ordered.

Stephen hunched his shoulders. He had refused to discuss the matter in the open Close, and had instead invited Simon to his own hall. Now he stood near the new fire in his hearth, gazing at the flames and wondering how to begin. While he hesitated, Thomas stood near Simon, lounging with his thumbs hooked in his belt. He looked every bit the labouring mason that he was, and although Stephen knew that he himself paid Thomas's wages, he felt unaccountably threatened by the man's presence here in his hall. More so than the Bailiff.

'It was before you were born, I dare say, Bailiff. I was a young novice, not yet old enough to take up responsibility for my own congregation, but with a voice that had broken. It was – it is – difficult for a fellow of that sort of age to move further up in the Church. One must be fortunate. I was lucky, I thought, because I had always had a propensity for numbers.'

Simon tried not to let his face show his revulsion at this thought. The idea of Andrew came unbidden into his mind, and he wondered fleetingly whether all clerks who liked playing with numbers were similarly prone to crime.

Stephen continued. 'The Treasurer was an engaging man. He was interested in me, and in all that the Cathedral could do to further the rebuilding works. It was largely due to my mentor, Treasurer John, that the Cathedral was placed on a strong financial basis. So when he began to help me and prove his desire to teach me all he could, I was flattered. I wanted to help him in return.

'He knew how to teach. If a fellow was confused about numbers and how to add or subtract, he would show infinite patience and kindness. He rarely if ever had need to resort to the strap or the birch, because we all respected him.

'Anyway, when the Bishop arrived, we all saw the difference in him. The Bishop took an unreasonable dislike to him, and would keep on at him all the time. The Chapter itself took the matter in hand, and at the first opportunity, they elected John to be their Dean.

'It drove the Bishop into a rage the like of which I have never seen before. The Bishop believed that men of the Church should not simply acquire riches, but should deal out such benefices as were won fairly and equitably. He felt that the Treasurer already had funds aplenty, and refused to let him take more. He insisted that Treasurer John should give up much of his wealth. The Treasurer refused, and so started the festering war that was to cause such bitterness and hatred.

'There were letters to the Pope, letters to the Archbishop, threats, shouts, rattling of weaponry . . . it was an awful time. And at the end of it, it grew obvious that one or the other man must go. I was in league with most of the Chapter when I chose the side of the Treasurer. We did not like this foreign upstart telling us what to do and when we could do it. We wanted a local man, a good fellow like the kindly Treasurer John. And so, when it was decided that we should destroy the Bishop's man, it was not a sudden decision by a small minority of people, but a firm resolution by all Treasurer John's allies. Me included.

'We laid an ambush after Matins, and when he came out, we killed him. That, I thought, was that. But no, now it is all coming back to haunt us.'

'Who was there with you?'

'Thomas there,' the Treasurer grunted, motioning towards the mason loitering at his wall. 'Myself, two vicars long dead, some townsfolk. I don't know how many exactly.'

'I know of Joel Lytell and Henry. Henry is dead and Joel has been badly beaten. Who would have done that? Were there any survivors among the Chaunter's men other than Nicholas?'

'There was Matthew, of course. Why?'

'Because so far Henry is dead – he helped in the attack – and so is Nicholas. I've already heard that someone told the Chaunter that he need not fear the ambush because the Bishop had been informed and had gathered together a force to catch all the assailants. But there was no such force. Whoever told that tale to the Chaunter was playing a cruel trick – and it worked. I am wondering whether Nicholas was the traitor.'

'I should not be surprised. I have heard similar stories, and I think that it is possible, although I'd have thought that the murders could have been committed for another reason. We killed the Chaunter forty years ago, Bailiff. Why should someone hold a grudge for so long? Why set out to do these things only now?'

'I don't know,' Simon admitted. 'But I will find out.'

Thomas said slowly, 'I remember another novice.'

'There were many of them?' Simón asked.

'Aye. Many enough on both sides. I myself attacked one whom I'd always called my friend,' Thomas said. He experienced the shame, but felt he had to admit to his crime. 'It was I who struck poor Nick. He'd always been my friend, but that night we were all mad, I think. I struck and struck at him in a fury, just because he was opposed to my Dean. And then Peter came up from—'

'Peter? Yes, Peter was there,' Stephen said suddenly. 'He might know something. He's the Prior of St Nicholas's now.'

Simon was still eyeing Thomas. 'You said last night you were the man who so injured the friar?'

'Yes. And my God, how I regretted it afterwards. I used to go to my church and apologise for it at every Mass afterwards, begging forgiveness. I confessed my sin to my priest, but he only said that a man who sided with the Bishop was clearly as good as an excommunicate and refused to give me a penance. I felt that very sorely . . . and then I saw how God punished me.'

'How, Thomas?'

Thomas had a vision of bodies swinging hideously in the twilight. 'He executed my father.'

Vince left the meal feeling sickly, wondering what had become of his father.

Yesterday, they had eaten and drunk themselves into a comfortable drowsiness after a meal, and his father had told him again all the stories he recalled of Vince's uncle, how decent and kind he had been, how honourable. It was dull, but Vince sat and listened, knowing that this constant repetition was his father's only means of exorcising the demon within him. His brother had been accused of taking part in a murder and had been denounced as traitor to his master. Now all Wymond could do was relive the good parts of Vincent's life as though by doing so he would somehow overwhelm all the lies.

It was that which had made his father renounce the city itself, Vince knew. That was why he was aghast when Vince told him he intended living in Exeter itself. 'You can live here with me, boy, you don't have to go up there. You can't trust folk in a place like that. They lie to each other, and if you're on the side of one man, his enemies will invent stories to insult you.'

But he had been adamant, and now he felt sure that it had been the right thing to do at the time, although now he wondered whether he could continue, knowing that Joel his master had taken part in the murder of the men in the Close.

His father had been dreadfully shocked by the revelation, he saw. That was why he stayed there through the afternoon when he should have returned to his master's workshop. He was worried about Wymond.

But there is something strange about older men. Those who have drunk strong cider and ale all their lives can sometimes drink more even than a young apprentice. Where Vince had intended to drink his father into another drunken sleep, he found last night that his eyes were growing heavy, his limbs incapable. He was laughing more than he ought, while his old man was resting back on his bench, eyes bright. At some point, Wymond picked up his bow and began to wax the string, protecting it from the wet by putting a thin coating of beeswax on it. Then there was a light oil which he used to buff the bow's wood. It was a simple yew bow, his, but Vince knew that it could propel a steel-tipped arrow through a half-inch-thick plank of oak. A fearful weapon, Vince couldn't even draw it to shoot one of his father's clothyard arrows.

Wymond had owned a bow since he was a young boy, and he'd practised with it at least once every week all his life since then. Now he used it to clear the rats and birds from his vats, so that they couldn't ruin his skins and leathers as they cured, and his eye was good for a shot of anything up to eighty yards for even a moderate-sized rat. On a good day, Vince had seen him fire that bow two hundred and fifty yards. They had paced it out afterwards.

And this morning, when Vince rose, his father was gone, and so was his bow.

Chapter Twenty-Two

Thomas sniffed, but without rancour. 'It's all a long time ago now. When I arrived back here, I was hoping to find a little peace and rest in my old city, but I hadn't counted on how the death of my father would affect me. He was a good man. He didn't deserve to be executed like some felon.'

'What happened?' Simon asked.

'I left the city after I so nearly killed Nicholas. I was disgusted with myself. There I was, supposedly a novice, readying myself for a life in the Church, and I had drawn a knife to murder my own best friend, purely because of the politics at the top of the Cathedral. That day I went home to my father's house and sat up until morning, wondering what had become of me.

'My father came down as he always did just as dawn broke, and he saw me there. He saw the blood all over my clothes and hands, and he went out and fetched me water, then crouched before me and cleaned me. Only when all the blood was washed from me did he ask me how I'd come by it, and I told him.

'He was very upset. I could see that. He'd always brought me up to be Christian, and here I was stabbing a man in a rage who was no enemy of mine. It was mad, and I saw that. And because of that, shortly afterwards, I left the city. I made no song and dance, but just packed some belongings and walked out. I eventually ended up in Winchester, and helped a stone waller, and began to learn my trade.'

'What of your father?'

'When I came back, I learned what had happened to him. The King came to hear the case when the Bishop petitioned him. He was told that the city's gates had been left open on the night of the attack. Because of that he ordered two executions. My father was one. While I walked away to find a new life, he lost his.'

'I've heard that there was another man there,' Simon said. 'A fellow called William.'

'I know him,' Thomas said. 'A madman. He would kill for the pleasure of testing his blade's sharpness.'

'And Matthew was there too, but on the opposing side,' Simon mused.

'Yes.' Stephen nodded palely. 'He was there. And I almost hit him with my sword, but managed to avert my blow when I saw who he was. I had always liked him. It was Peter who actually struck him down. At the time I remember thinking he was lucky. He fell so swiftly, all thought him dead and he was safe. Indeed, it was some weeks before he recovered from his wounds. Afterwards, when I was given ever better jobs, I brought him with me as a means of honouring his valour and integrity that night. He never flinched when all the men attacked. Others fled in terror, but not he. He stood his ground although he had no weapons on him, and was felled like a sapling under the axe.'

'Could he not have learned to hate the men who attacked and killed his master?' Simon asked.

'He is essentially a mild, kindly fellow,' Stephen said. 'I am sure that he would not do such a thing. And if he were to wish to do so, again, why wait so long? He has had the opportunity to kill his attackers many times over the years.'

'True,' Simon said. 'Which surely means that it's more likely that the murderer is someone like William, who has been away from the city for many years.'

'Or me,' Thomas said without humour.

'Perhaps,' Simon allowed. 'Except you forget that last night when Baldwin was attacked, you were safely in the gaol. I am sure that one man is responsible for the murders, and it's far-fetched to think that someone else attacked Baldwin. No, it must be the same man.'

'Not a woman?' Stephen asked.

'It was a good arrow struck Baldwin. The distance wasn't too great, but it would have been a man's bow.'

'It is always possible to hire a bowman,' Stephen said. He shot a look at Thomas. 'Even a man in gaol could command a hireling.'

'Maybe,' Simon said, 'but Thomas would have needed warning of his arrest. He thought he was escaping the city. Why order an assassin? And he had no idea that he would be arrested and in gaol just as the arrow flew. No. What of this Peter? He was loyal enough once, you say.'

'And was ruined by it. He was forced to take the threefold vows, just as John Pycot did before him. He is only here again because the last Prior was taken to the mother Abbey.'

'Then I shall see him now,' said Simon with decision. 'And I ask that you bend your mind to this affair, Treasurer. We have to learn who has been killing people here. If you can think of anyone, anyone at all who might have had a hand in these murders, you must tell me. Otherwise, there may be more blood spilled.'

'If I knew anything, I swear I would tell you,' Stephen said, and Simon believed him. The man's face was quite haggard. 'I had thought that this whole affair was left far behind me, but now it has returned to haunt me once more. I say to you, Bailiff, I would that none of this had happened, not the death of the Chaunter forty years ago, not the death of the saddler, and not the death of the friar. I regret the execution of the Mayor and of Thomas's father. Just think of all these deaths, all unnecessary, all repellent when men should be bending their minds to the building of this magnificent Cathedral. It is enough to make a man despair.'

'It is very sad,' Simon agreed caustically as he beckoned Thomas to follow him. 'Heaven forbid that the Cathedral should be delayed purely because of a few deaths!'

He was still angry at the Treasurer's attitude as he entered Janekyn's little chamber. Baldwin was still apparently asleep, and as Simon entered, the physician Ralph was at the wounded man's side. He looked up as Simon walked in. The physician's lips were pursed and he was very thoughtful.

'How is he?' Simon demanded curtly.

'He has no fever, which is a relief, but there is still time for it to come. The natural humours seem well-balanced, but I could wish for a little more pus from the wounds.'

Simon nodded understandingly. Everybody knew that the laudable pus would cleanse a wound, for it aided expulsion of the evil humours which caused men to fall prey to fevers and death. He watched the physician remove a linen swatch from Baldwin's chest and saw the wound, still leaking blood and red raw about the edges. Ralph leaned forward and tentatively sniffed at it.

'It doesn't seem to be foul, anyway,' he said pensively. 'It may be that he is already on his way to recovery. At this stage it is too early to tell.'

'Please keep a good, close watch over him,' Simon said.

'I will do the best I can for him,' Ralph sighed, replacing the patch over the wound and binding it in place with a bandage.

Simon nodded and tentatively leaned forward, patting Baldwin's forearm. 'Jeanne will be here soon, old friend. Godspeed, and get yourself better soon.'

'That is his wife?' Ralph asked. 'He has called to her in his dreams.'

'Yes. She should be here soon after lunch, I hope,' Simon said.

'Is it true that the scarred friar is dead?'

'Yes, why?'

'I was interested. I met him in the High Street a few days ago after seeing Joel Lytell. He was an interesting case.'

'In what way?' Simon asked, torn by a desire to demand answers from Prior Peter and remain here and learn all he could from a man who knew the friar in case his words could hold some bearing.

'Friar Nicholas was terribly cut about. A man had slashed at him and his wounds were dreadful. His face was only a part of his injuries. His back was deeply scarred, his arm withered and all but useless . . . It was a miracle that he lived.'

'You think that God was kind to him?' Thomas asked sarcastically.

'Who can tell what He thinks of men such as Nicholas?' Ralph said, standing back and surveying his handiwork before pulling the blankets over Baldwin's torso. He turned and looked at Thomas. 'I was talking to the man who used to know him, Vicar Matthew, and he said that the friar's features would be enough to make many a man confess his sins just to avoid the same form of punishment.'

'What sort of crime was the friar supposed to have committed?' Simon enquired.

'From what I heard, he had supported an evil man in the Cathedral.'

'That bears out what I thought,' Simon muttered, and then, 'Come along, Thomas. We must see the Prior and hear what he has to say for himself.'

*   *   *

Udo was finishing his preparations. A last glance in the big mirror in his hall, a dab of holy water to wish himself luck (a silly thing to do, for God would either bless his union or not), and then he left his house.

The distance was nothing. He strolled up the hill, turned left, then went up Milk Street and thence into Smythen Street, where he continued down the hill.

From here the view was magnificent. Ahead of him lay the river, shimmering silver in the sunlight through the smoke of the works on Exe Island, but beyond all was green. The land rolled most pleasantly, with low hills covered in trees all the way westward. Today, with the rains finished, he could see that there were many pools. They shone blue and grey, while the river itself was more torrential than he had seen before. Full from the rains, it raced past the city as though in an urgent hurry to get to the sea.

He stood enjoying the scene for a long while. It reminded him a little of his homeland, and that raised a small sensation of longing. As he set off again, he was reminded that it was many years since he last saw his home. Now, were he ever to see it again, he would see it as a married man.

At the door, he rapped loudly and stood waiting. The door opened and the maidservant showed him through to the women in the hall. He bowed and went to Mabilla first, although his eyes never left Julia.

She was as fresh as a flower in spring, he thought. Her skin was almost white, and it was so fine that he swore he could see the blood coursing at her temples and throat. She was dressed in a sombre dress with a girdle, her hair bound up in a net, and her eyes remained downcast, but for him that very correct modesty was itself wonderfully attractive. He could hardly believe that this marvellous creature was soon to be his!

'Sir, you are welcome in our house,' Mabilla said as he walked to the stoup and made the sign of the cross with the holy water.

'Mistress, I thank you. How is your daughter?'

Julia raised her chin, while keeping her eyes on the ground. 'I am well, sir.' She felt the fluttering of her heart like a caged bird, and desperately fought the blush that threatened to colour her face. 'I hope you are well too?'

This was not like other courtships she had witnessed. All too often, they were conducted without any involvement by the bride-to-be, but instead all aspects of the negotiation and contract went on in her absence until all was ready, and then she was presented with the agreement. Enough of her friends had become wedded for her to know that commonly the groom would be a man considerably older than his wife. Only last month two of her friends had been married, and both took men more than ten years their senior. An older husband was normal enough, because only when a man had finished his apprenticeship and acquired his own shop and business, could he start to think of the other necessaries of life. And a woman who preferred not to be a spinster or be forced into servitude would be glad to take a man with a profitable living.

No, Julia had no concerns about this man. He was a little pompous, it was true, but a good woman like her would soon be able to smooth off some of the roughness. And she would make him a good wife; she was determined of that. He was kind enough to take her and her mother, and right now she had a feeling of warmth and safety in his presence that was entirely lacking when he was gone.

Her only fear was that he wanted her purely as a prize; a trophy to ornament his arm when he walked abroad or invited guests to his home. She had heard of loveless marriages where the wives were bored and listless. They had little communion with their families or friends because their husbands were jealous of their companionship, or perhaps feared that they might speak to others in a derogatory manner of their lives. These were the sort of men she feared. If Udo were to become like that, she didn't know how she would survive. By merely thanking God that he would not live for too long, and when he died, he would leave her a wealthy widow, she supposed. It was a grim prospect, and one that scared her. But she had no choice.

'You are thoughtful, my dear?' he asked.

She could have sworn at herself for allowing her thoughts to become so visible. Colouring slightly, she said, 'I was thinking of my poor father. He would have been so pleased to see me wedded to so successful a merchant. But he will be watching over us, I am sure.'

'Yes,' he said, with a slight clearing of his throat. He appeared nervous for a moment.

'I do miss him,' she said.

Mabilla sniffed slightly and Julia saw her turn a little away. 'He would be very proud. I know that he was keen to have a respectable man for his only child, and he must have been as delighted as I am, Master Udo.'

'I thank you,' Udo said with a slight bow. 'And now, perhaps I should offer this? With your permission, Mistress?'

Julia saw her mother give a nod, for Mabilla was as thrilled to see what the man had brought as was Julia herself. Udo stood and approached her with a small leather purse. He weighed it in his hand with an anxious expression.

'My dearest, I have bought this for you, thinking that it would enhance your beauty, but now . . . I cannot but think that you are too perfect with nothing. I . . . I hope it is proof of my sincere devotion to you, and that you will look on me forever as a kind husband and master, who seeks only to make you happy. In all that I can do, I will seek your pleasure. I . . . Well, here it is.'

He suddenly thrust it out towards her and she took it. The purse itself was pretty enough, with small embroidery about the outside, but it was quite heavy, and she looked up at him with some doubt, wondering whether she should open it. He nodded encouragement, and she released the thongs at the neck.

From it spilled a necklace of gold, with a pendant that formed a cross.

'Do you like it?' he asked, and now the anxiety was all too plain.

'I love it!' she whispered, and smiled at him with tears of gratitude in her eyes.

The Priory's gatekeeper was reluctant to allow them entry, even when Simon used the name of the Bishop as his authority, but before too long the prior himself had arrived and he haughtily deigned to allow Simon and Thomas into the Priory's lands.

'What do you want from me?' Peter demanded.

'I have heard that you were one of the men involved in the murder of the Chaunter many years ago. There have been two murders since then, of Henry Potell and a Friar Nicholas. Both were implicated in the original plot with you, I understand.'

Peter looked at him and his upper lip lifted just slightly, enough to expose a tooth. It looked like an expression of deep and sincere contempt. 'I have nothing to say on the matter. And now you must leave.'

'I'm going nowhere, Prior. You may not like me or my tone, but that's not my concern!' Simon spat. His head felt light from lack of sleep, and just now his temper was close to boiling over. 'My best friend and companion was almost killed last night by an arrow. He may be dead now for all I know, and I want the murderer found before anyone else is harmed.'

'Your friend?' Peter said, his face suddenly still, as though he was thinking very quickly indeed. 'Why should that be?'

'I do not know, unless Baldwin's questions were bringing him close to the identity of the murderer. If that's the case, the killer should beware, because I intend to bring him to justice – and for trying to murder a knight, that will be a rope! I'll take pleasure in pulling it tight round his neck myself!'

'What do you expect from me?'

'Your help, and that means telling me what happened on the night that the Chaunter was murdered.'

Peter stared at him, and then gazed up at the sky for a long while, before giving a low sigh and clearing his throat. 'Very well.'

He told them all about the dissension in the Cathedral's Chapter. It was much the same as the story which all the others had told. 'It was simple, really. A fight between those who knew the city and had lived here all their lives. I was born here, only a short distance up from the main gates by which you entered this morning. I used to play ball in the street, bouncing a pig's bladder against the wall of this Priory. Sometimes we'd play football against the next parish, seeing which could take the ball into the opposing team's churchyard. It was hard work.'

Thomas nodded with a grin. 'I remember that. You used to gang up on my friends. We were in the parish of the Holy Trinity, while you were in St John's.'

'Yes. We used to play on festive days. Your parish, Matt in St Mary Major, Joel in St Mary Arches. And my team always used to win.' Peter smiled at the memory. 'We could be quite competitive. Especially Matt and William, as I remember it.'

'They were competitive about everything. The only time that I felt at risk of my life was when Matthew and William were betting on their target-shooting at the butts. Matt was winning as usual, and then I took a bow and fired one that beat them both! I thought they'd lynch me. William was furious,' Thomas recalled.

'What of Henry Potell? Was he there too?' Simon asked.

'Henry was born in St Kerrian's, as was poor Vincent.'

'He was the man killed when he tried to warn the Chaunter against the attack?'

'Yes. Some thought him a traitor, but he was honourable. He had given his word, and he lived in the Chaunter's house. That was the trouble, you see. When the Bishop arrived he upset a lot of people. He didn't understand how we'd grown up in the alleys and streets, forming our own relationships. It was as though he was deliberately pitting all those who were from the city against the newcomers. I can recall us all arguing about it in a tavern, some of us wanting to support the new Bishop and give him the benefit of the doubt, while others were determined to oppose him and force him to see reason.'

'What of the friar?'

'Aye, well, Friar Nicholas always argued for supporting him. He was a foreigner too, you see, and reckoned that the Bishop was always right.'

'But I thought you paid him to spread the story that the Chaunter needn't fear any attack?' Simon blurted out. He was suddenly aware of an appalling lassitude. The foundation of discovering the murderer was the fact that the prior had paid the traitor. If Nicholas wasn't the traitor, then what could be the reason for his death?

'Nick wouldn't have considered betrayal,' Peter said with conviction. 'No, it was another.'

'Who?' Simon demanded, but with less force. In truth, he was very tired now. 'It has been said that you were the man who paid a man to pass on the lie to the Chaunter that led him to believe that he was safe.'

Peter shrugged. 'It wasn't me,' he said. 'The man who paid was more deeply involved than me. I was only there because I sought advancement. I thought that if I was to help John Pycot get what he wanted, he'd see to it that I was well-rewarded. More fool me!'

Simon grunted at this sign of his self-contempt. 'You didn't get much from it, did you?'

'At least I am now the prior of this place, if only for a while.'

'Tell me about the attack again,' Simon said.

There was little to learn from him. The prior's story merely confirmed all that Simon and Baldwin had already heard, and Simon could discern nothing in it which rang false against all the other testimonies he had been given.

'I am still fascinated by the idea of the man who arranged for treachery. Who could have planted the lie so closely to the Chaunter? If a man were to behave so dishonourably, wouldn't he feel the guilt afterwards? Surely his crime would be obvious.'

'There are some who feel no such compunction,' Peter said. 'Look at my corrodian, William. He is a man of great resolve and determination, but if he finds another in his way, he will destroy the man. You have heard of his denunciation of the Mayor?'

Simon could feel Thomas suddenly stiffen, and Simon glanced at him as he said, 'What do you mean?'

'The Mayor was hanged because the King learned that the South Gate had been left open for the assassins to depart the city after their deed. While we of the Cathedral Close went to our beds and hid, the others fled the city through that gate. The watch was not efficient, and there was no means to check on who was in the city that night and who was not, so all escaped. Well, since that gate was left open, the first two people whom the King ordered to be executed were, of course, the gatekeeper and the Mayor. The city was complicit in the act, the King declared, so the representative of the city must pay. It was William who told the King of the gate being left open, so it is he who bears the guilt of the Mayor's death, yet you will see no shame in his eyes.'

'Why did he do that?' Thomas demanded.

'Because he sought advancement,' Peter said sarcastically. 'If a couple of deaths would lead to his being taken into the King's host, it was a trade worth his while. That was how he reasoned, and he was proved correct. He has lived to a good age in the King's service and now he can expect a long retirement.'

'All from a pair of executions so long ago,' Thomas said bitterly.

'I am sorry, Tom,' Peter said more kindly. 'I forgot the gatekeeper was your father.'

'Where is William?' Thomas said. 'I want to see him.'

'He left the Priory this morning quite early,' Peter said. 'I don't know where he's gone.'

William had, in fact, spent much of the morning in the Frauncey's Inn over near the East Gate. When the sun rose, he went out from the Priory with a desire to find a good pint of wine and drink it as quickly as possible. In a city like Exeter, with over thirty inns and taverns, that was no difficult task, and he had eschewed the first three he had come across on the basis that he had been to all of them before only recently. Today he wanted anonymity.

It was clear enough that Peter was not going to help save them. Someone was out there with a grudge against William and probably Peter too, and he could probably harm William, but Peter didn't seem to care, the bastard. He could rot in hell for all William cared now. The Prior just didn't understand how worried William was that his corrody could be endangered by the stories of his behaviour during the assault on the Chaunter. It meant everything to William! If it was bruited abroad that he had been in on the attack, the King could remove his corrody and leave him destitute. Entirely without a penny. What could a man do when he was faced with that kind of stern reality? There was only one route – become an outlaw and steal what was needed for survival.

William reached that conclusion at the bottom of his first pint of wine, and he set out to empty a second jug with a sense of increasing gloom.

It was not because he had a moral objection to the idea of life as a felon. That was no concern to him. After all, he had behaved that way before often enough. No, it was that with his recurring dizziness and headaches, the idea of life out in the woods was less than appealing. It could well spell his death. And he was not the warrior he once had been. In the past he had been as quick as a striking viper . . . now he was still fast, but . . .

All men had to admit to themselves when they grew too old to defend themselves against younger men, and William knew full well that his time was come. If he were to offer himself in the ring for combat, he'd not be certain to win. He had done so in the past, when he was a noted fighter, and he'd seen off several good swordsmen and sword-and-dagger fighters for good purses. Only a few had died in the ring with him. There was no need to slaughter them all; the audience got the pleasure of the battle without the need for an actual death.

Yes, in his youth and middle years, organising a prize-fight had been a profitable business. If he gained a scar or two, so be it if the purse was good enough. But nowadays – well, it was a younger man's game, that.

So with no prize, no corrody, the only life open to him was the harsh one of a felon, and that did not appeal to him. Living rough, always sleeping lightly in case the King's posse arrived to poke a sword or pike at a man's ribs, that was no way to live.

And then he had the idea flash in the back of his mind.

There was one other way to make a new life: find a wealthy woman who would marry him. Slowly his frowning concern left his face, ironed away by the brilliance of this new thought.

Mabilla would surely have him. She had wanted him. Oh, she'd said she hated him when they last met, because she blamed him for her old man's death, but that was hardly his problem. And just now she could help him. She must see that. She had enough money, too. All he had to do was marry her and then he'd become master of her money. The corrody would be unimportant, and he could thumb his nose at the King if he chose to steal it back.

No sooner had he considered the benefits of this course, than he had finished off his jug of wine, and stood. His head was a little dizzy, but no matter. He shook himself and sauntered from the tavern, making his way across the city towards Smythen Street, and then walked down the hill towards Mabilla's house. Reaching it, he banged on the door with his staff and stood back to wait. As soon as it opened he pushed his way inside and ignored the flapping maid who tried to keep him out. In the end he put an arm about her breast and shoved her ungently from his path.

'Mabilla, my love! I need to talk to you!' he called at the top of his voice as he left the screens and entered the hall, and then he stopped at the sight of the other man there. 'Who are you?'

Mabilla rose to her feet, her face cold and angry. 'You are not welcome here, William. What do you want here? I ask you to leave.'

'I'm not going anywhere, woman. I came to talk to you. Where's that little maid? Tell her to fetch me wine.'

'You are going to leave, Will. You aren't wanted here.'

'Woman, that's no way to speak to a future husband! I want to marry you.'

Mabilla's face froze. She looked like a statue formed of steel. Her voice, when she spoke, was harsh and grating. 'William, I would not marry you, were you the King of the lands. Now leave my hall.'

'Mab, don't be like that. You loved me before you married that foolish saddler. Come on. Give me a hug and say you'll be mine.'

'The lady asked you to leave,' Udo said.

Will turned with frank surprise that the fellow should dare to thwart him. He had looked a vain, foolish sort of man, not one to test a warrior of Will's mettle. 'I piss on you. If you're determined to have only one man here, you'd better go. Otherwise I'll make you. Either that, or shut up.'

'You have into this house of mourning broken, and now a riot you threaten?' Udo said, his anger making his urbane English falter. 'I would resist.'

William raised his staff threateningly. 'Try to resist this, you piece of German shit! I'll break your head if you get in my way!'

To his astonishment, the German didn't flee, but instead drew a solid-looking broadsword.

It was all he could do not to laugh. Will changed his grip and held the pole as a quarterstaff, with a quarter of the wood between his hands, the metal-shod end outthrust towards Udo like a lance. He might be old, but he had a staff, and a man with a staff would always beat a fool with a short lump of steel in his hands.

Moving slowly, he prodded with his staff, catching Udo in the breast. It made the German wince, and Will chuckled. Then he poked more aggressively, catching the German in the belly, in the shoulder, then the nose. He'd been aiming for the eye, but the effusion of blood was satisfying enough. Udo swung with his sword, but he couldn't get past the pole, and only when Will had backed him up against the wall did he lunge suddenly, cracking Udo across the head, and as the man slumped back, darting in to grab his sword. He stabbed once at the man's belly, then kicked his face, feeling that thrill again, to see a man beaten and at his mercy. It was tempting to hack at his head, but before he could do so, he heard the noise of men at the screens.

Turning, he saw the figure of a tall man. The latter bowed courteously enough, while keeping his eyes on William. 'My name is Sir Peregrine de Barnstaple. I am Coroner. You are arrested. Drop the sword.'

Chapter Twenty-Three

Simon and Thomas returned to the Close as the sun was just reaching its zenith, and were just in time to see a beautiful white Arab horse being led away from the porter's home at the Fissand Gate.

'Jeanne,' Simon breathed, and broke into a run.

He reached the door and wrenched it open, suddenly panicked that his old friend might have died during his absence, and it was with a feeling of relief that he saw Jeanne at Baldwin's side, one hand gripping his while the other stroked his brow. And then he became aware of the sword-point at his throat. 'Christ's Ballocks!'

'Sorry, Bailiff.'

Simon swallowed. 'Ah. Hello, Edgar.'

The tall, suave man at his side smiled and lowered his blade until its point rested on his boot-tip. 'I thought I should guard the doorway.'

'Not against Simon,' Baldwin said weakly. 'You can trust him, Edgar.'

'Yes, thanks to God there is at least one man here we can rely on,' Jeanne sighed. Then, 'What *have* you been doing, my love?'

Simon bowed his head to her respectfully. 'I am so sorry to have had to send for you,' he said, 'but I thought you should be here.'

'He seems to have a slight fever,' she said. 'Has he been seen by a physician?'

Simon nodded. 'Yes, the best in the city, so I'm told. Ralph of Malmesbury.' He motioned to Thomas to enter and stand by the wall. Edgar turned to keep an eye on him.

'Ask for him to be brought here, then. I shall need to talk to him,' Jeanne said. She was still wearing her cloak and an over-jacket against the cold, and she took them off now, laying them bundled on a stool while she pulled up the long sleeves of her dress. 'Simon, please fetch me a bowl of water. I shall stay here with him, as will Edgar.'

She returned to Baldwin's side and rested her hand on his brow, essaying a smile. He had a curiously vulnerable expression on his face, like a child trying to hold back the tears after a painful fall, and then she realised that she was herself weeping. The thought of losing this man was too terrifying. Even after his moodiness and ungracious leave-taking when he set off for Exeter, her love for him was complete. She knew that. If he were to die, she didn't know how she could herself continue living.

The messenger had arrived as she was finishing her breakfast, and Jeanne had instantly sent a man to tell Edgar. Once Baldwin's sergeant in the Templars, Edgar had been his most loyal servant ever since, and even though he was himself married now, he yet looked on his master as his first responsibility, and Jeanne was pleased to have the lean, wiry man at her side on the ride here, and to know that he was with Baldwin to protect him in case of another attack. Edgar would not permit any man to harm his lord.

But seeing Baldwin like this was terrifying. He was not so obviously knocked about as he had been after the tournament last year, but he was clearly very weak, and Jeanne prayed that he would not suffer from one of those terrible fevers which could kill stronger and younger men than he.

'Be strong, my love,' she murmured, and she was startled to see that his eyes were filled with tears. He said nothing, but his grasp was almost savage, as though he was holding on to her in the same desperate, fearful way that he was holding on to life.

Simon was soon back, Paul with him carrying a large pot of warmed water and some towels. Paul set it near Baldwin, while Edgar stood nearby, his sword still in his hand and a half-smile on his face that showed he was ready to use it.

'Jeanne,' Simon said in a low voice. 'Has he said anything?'

'I'm not dead yet,' Baldwin murmured with a trace of astringency in his tone.

'I just wondered . . . who could have wanted to fire that shot at you?'

'A murderer, clearly. Perhaps *the* murderer. Until we catch him, I won't know,' Baldwin said hoarsely.

'Why should someone have wanted to aim an arrow at you?' Jeanne whispered, dabbing at his brow with her cloth.

'Because I was getting too close to learning who the culprit is.'

Simon fretted, 'But I can't for the life of me think what we have heard that could have hinted at the killer.'

'No,' Baldwin agreed, 'but I think that you should go over it all, because this man is plainly determined.'

Edgar shifted near the doorway. 'Whoever it is, we'll find him, Sir Baldwin.'

'We need his confession first,' Baldwin said, his voice little more than a whisper now. 'I don't want you executing people without being sure of their guilt, Edgar, no matter how angry you are to see me like this.'

'When I find who did this, I will see him punished,' Edgar said imperturbably.

'I do not care for any of this,' Jeanne said, gently untying the bandages at Baldwin's breast. 'All I care about is your return to health, my love.'

Wymond had not enjoyed a restful night. He had left his son snoring at the table as evening turned to night, packed his bow and some arrows into his blanket, and set off into the gloom. He walked down to the Friary, then round their new wall to the fields near the Holloway. There he crossed over the river and found himself a seat on a hillock of turf.

He often came down here when he had to think. Bless his Vince, but the lad's inane chatter about other apprentices and the gossip at the joiner's shop was enough to make a man's brains turn to shit in his skull. No, Wymond needed to reflect, not sit in his house drinking wine until he fell over. Vince was not mature enough to be able to comfort a man like Wymond, who was nearly sixty.

It was the other Vincent whom Wymond needed: Vincent his brother, the boy who'd protected him as they grew, the kind companion who taught Wymond everything he knew, who used to chuckle at him when he hurt himself and somehow make the pain go away, the one who would always praise his triumphs. He was the person who, more than any other, showed him what it was to be a man. And then, just as he was entering adulthood, Wymond lost him. Some crazed bastard at the Cathedral took him away for ever.

Seeing a movement, he slowly unrolled his blanket, then gazed about him nonchalantly. There was no one on the road, and he took his old bow, stepping between the stave and the string. With the stave at his back, he reached up and pulled the upper portion over his shoulder, sliding the string up along it until it met the horn notch. He stepped out, took a quick look about him again, and selected an arrow. It had a tiny barb, this, ideal for small game. A last glance all around, and then he quickly nocked the arrow to the string, pulled it back so that the point of the barb lay just where the two ears forked up, and then gradually allowed his fingers to release. There was the familiar jolt to his arms, the single thrumming tone, and the fletchings scorched over his knuckle. He remained there a moment, his arms unmoving, until he saw the ears slam backwards, and then he let the bow down. Stepping inside the string, he quickly released it from the notches, allowed it to straighten, and wrapped it in his blanket again. Only then did he walk along the grassy pasture to the far end, counting his paces as he went. As he thought: a good fifty yards.

The rabbit sat transfixed, the arrow's fletching protruding from the side of its head, while the barb had gone straight through and into the earth behind. He pulled the rabbit from the fletchings, then took some grass to wipe the arrow and pulled it free from the ground, replacing it with the others.

The shock of the massive yard-long arrow penetrating its head had killed the rabbit instantly, and when he snapped its neck it was purely a precaution. He squatted and took out his little skinning dagger, paunching the cony and pulling out the entrails. He set these down with the head, and skinned it quickly, slipping his hand in between the pelt and the muscles and loosening it all about the body, cutting off the paws and slipping the skin over the little stumpy tail. Then he wrapped the body in a sheet of linen, and made his way to the river again.

He knew a little place where the river bent and where there was a short stretch of sandy beach; up above it lay a sheltered spot with a cosy little hollow. When they were lads, he and Vincent had used to come here to play, pretending to be outlaws. They would kill a rabbit, bring it here and cook it for their supper, sharing alike. Once they had stayed out all night when Vincent was debating with himself whether he should take up the post offered to him by the Bishop. He had not wanted to take it, knowing that it would alter his relationship with his family for ever, but in the end he had little choice. None of them did. A job at the Cathedral meant education, and that meant money. He could help them all if he won that.

So that was perhaps their last night together. The following morning, Vincent had left home and gone up to the Cathedral, and suddenly Wymond saw less of him. It was, in large part, the end of his childhood.

Now, as the light faded, he gathered up twigs and branches, and when he had a decent pile, he began to strike sparks from his flint and dagger. Soon wisps of smoke rose from the bonfire, and he settled back to wait.

It was a perfect evening. The soil was warm from the day's heat, the water rippled merrily, and the dying sun painted the trees and grasses with a golden hue. He jointed and cooked his rabbit, skewered on sharpened sticks over his fire, then sat back in the curve of the hollow, and let the warmth of his fire soothe his memories.

In his mind he saw the happy young face of his brother, then the broken, bloody body after that terrible night in 1283. He saw his dear wife's face, lit up and excited when she realised that she was pregnant, and then he saw her ruined body after the horse had knocked her down. The subsequent fever had taken her life, leaving him with his second Vincent, squealing and bawling in the corner.

These scenes were all so close, he felt he could hear little Vince's bawling again; he could smell the herbs and blood on his wife's body; he could touch Vincent's icy corpse.

Vincent was killed by the Cathedral. He had been destroyed because he was loyal to his master, and had tried to save him. A traitor cut him down. His wife had died because of the Cathedral, run down by a young fool of a clerk playing silly devils on a horse. The Cathedral had taken the two most precious people in his life.

There was no surprise in hearing from his son that Vincent was innocent of the accusation. Wymond had always known it. Yet the Cathedral had spread the news of his guilt as though it was established fact. Everyone knew that those raised in the city were against the Bishop, and that was enough to damn Vincent in their eyes. To many it seemed as though he was a hero, having stood up for his city, but Wymond knew that he was innocent. No, Vincent would never have betrayed his master. He had given his word to the Chaunter, and he would have guarded him with his life. As, indeed, he did.

Wymond fell asleep late into the night, struck with a strange melancholia.

It was long after dawn the next morning that he rose and stretched. He threw some water over his face from the river, dried it on his sleeve, and then picked up his package and bent his way towards the island. When he was close to the Friary he stopped, hesitated, and then carried on towards the city itself. He would go to the market and buy some bread.

Jeanne studied the wound. It looked like a tiny mouth with bright red lips. Now that the arrow was gone, it was smaller than the arrow's diameter as the flesh closed together. So small, it was hard to believe that it could do so much harm.

Simon peered closer. It was early days, but the wound didn't appear to have become too inflamed as yet. He prayed that Baldwin might survive.

Paul backed towards the door, his eyes fixed on Edgar's bright sword.

Watching him, Simon suddenly frowned. 'Have you seen the Coroner recently, Paul?'

The Annuellar shook his head quickly. 'Not today, sir, no. I think he went into the town.'

'What of the inquests? Has he said when he will hold them?'

'He has ordered the bodies of the friar and the mason to be disinterred so he can examine them. I think he means to hold all three inquests at the same time, and he has still to view all the bodies from the crush in the street outside St Nicholas's Priory.'

'I had forgotten all that,' Simon breathed. So many deaths in such a short time. The city was filled with distraught people. Everybody must know someone who had died recently. Yet there was nothing new in that. People died all the time, whether from brawls or illnesses or accidents. There was always somebody who was mourning for a child or parent or lover.

And there was one man who was perhaps mourning for people who had died here many years ago. Who could be so angry and bitter that he still sought to avenge that murder?

With that thought he was about to speak to Thomas when there was a noise in the gateway outside: the tramp of heavy boots and an angry voice shouting, 'Get your hands off me, you fornicating son of a diseased whore! What are you, you piece of shite! Brave when I'm bound, aren't you, but wait until I get a chance to pull a dagger on you, man, and we'll see how fucking brave you are then, eh?'

Simon glanced at Edgar, puzzled, but then he saw Thomas grit his teeth and suddenly recognised that furious voice. It was William again. Making a quick decision, Simon pulled the door open and walked outside. Thomas was immediately at his back, and Simon heard Baldwin's weak voice demanding to be able to hear what was going on. Edgar chuckled, and when Simon shot a look behind him, he saw the servant standing at the side of the doorway, his sword in his fist, the blade held at the ready across his body. No one would get past him to enter the room.

'Oho, Bailiff!' laughed Sir Peregrine. He was at William's side, holding onto a thong which bound the man's wrists. 'Here's a fine man. He tells me he is the King's corrodian, yet I found him attacking a poor merchant in his fiancée's house. A strange way to behave, wouldn't you say?'

From where he stood, Simon could smell the sour wine on William's breath. 'I wished to ask this man a couple of questions.'

'Please do so. I was about to take him to the city's gaol, but he claimed benefit of clergy since he's a corrodian, and I am on my way to ask the Dean what he thinks I should do with him. It cannot hurt to have him lodged here, I suppose – but I should prefer to see him in the city's custody if there is to be a fine laid upon him!'

Simon was uninterested in Peregrine's legal ramblings. 'William. You told us how you took part in the murder of the Chaunter all those years ago. You also implicated two innocent men, didn't you? You told the King that the gate had been left open, knowing that he would hang those responsible, and knowing that he'd reward you for your information.'

'If you know so much, what do you want from me?' William snapped. 'Get these damned thongs from me, you bladder of pus! Release me, I'm the King's man. Don't dare to hold me! Bailiff, release me. I won't stand here like a common felon.'

'You are worse than a common felon!' Simon roared. He shoved William, almost pushing him over. 'You lied to the King in his court, and committed perjury, didn't you? You denied taking part in the murder itself.'

'Why should I confess to something like that? Who says I was there?'

'I do,' Thomas said. 'I was there, and I accuse you, William. You were guilty. You stabbed the Chaunter's vicar as he lay on the ground, and you stabbed the Chaunter himself. I saw you. I accuse you of murder. You beat Matthew, too, and—'

'Wait!' Simon blurted. 'Matthew? You hit him? Why not kill him?'

'I deny this! It is all false! Release me!'

Thomas shook his head. 'We grew up together. I doubt he wanted to kill an old companion.'

'Sweet Jesus!' Simon moaned. 'That was it, wasn't it? Matthew was another like you, William. That whole dispute was between people from the city and people who were foreigners, wasn't it? The new Bishop, Quivil, was a stranger, and men like you supported the Dean, John Pycot, against him. All those who sought to support the Chaunter were from outside the city, weren't they? And there was one man in his *familia* who was from inside the city: Matthew. I've heard from the Prior Peter that he used to play ball with you and him. Matthew was a city man, so of course he wouldn't support the Chaunter or the Bishop.'

'Why don't you ask him?' William sneered.

'It was him, wasn't it, William? Matthew lied to the Chaunter and made him feel safe. Matthew wasn't an ally of the Chaunter. His loyalty was first to Exeter, second to the Cathedral.'

'I don't know what you're talking about,' William blustered.

'Matthew was no hero that day, was he?' Simon pressed. 'He lied to his master, deliberately, in order to persuade him to go out into the Close to his death.'

'Maybe he did, but that's got nothing to do with me,' William said.

'Except someone must have got Matthew to tell the lie.'

Peregrine was looking at Simon with the expression of one who is unsure what he is hearing. 'What lie was that, Simon?'

'This man told Matthew to take part in an attack on the Cathedral's Chaunter; he was to forewarn the Chaunter of the attack, but then lie, telling him that the Bishop himself knew of it and would position guards to protect him. The story was, they wanted to catch the assailants red-handed so that they could be tried for the attempt at murder. It was a good story, too, one which made sense – and it was invented by this man here, this shrewd fellow William. Afterwards, he also invented a story about the Southern Gate being left wide open, and caused the Mayor and the porter of the Southern Gate to be executed, solely that William could earn favour in the eyes of the King. And since then, he's been a contented member of the King's household.'

'Why is he here, then?' Sir Peregrine asked.

'The King bought him a pension at St Nicholas's Priory – as payment for his years of service.'

'It's all invention, true enough,' William spat. 'It's invented by *you*! Coroner, if you insist on holding me here, the least you can do is protect me from the misguided rantings of a fool like this. Are you going to put me in a cell or not?'

Sir Peregrine glanced at Simon. 'Are you sure of this?'

'As sure as I can be.'

'In that case, Corrodian, you are coming back to the city's lockup. I'll need to consider the case with the Justices of Gaol Delivery. After all, the King may like to hear about the matter. It sounds as though he has been rewarding you for years of deceit after committing a foul murder.'

'You can't be serious! I'm a King's man, damn your cods!'

'Which is why you're going to gaol,' Sir Peregrine said serenely.

'Wait! What if I admit? If I approve?'

Sir Peregrine and Simon exchanged a look. Simon said, 'If you become a King's Approver, the Justices may be lenient and save your neck.'

'I will approve! I admit my crimes, and I admit that I also persuaded Matt to tell the tale to the others, but it wasn't for love of the city – Matthew did it for money. He always wanted more money! That was why he agreed to help have the Chaunter killed. Joel helped, and Henry, but without Matthew, we'd not have succeeded.'

'So you admit your part in that murder?' Sir Peregrine demanded.

'Yes. I was one of the assassins. I helped kill the Chaunter and his *familia*. I did it to help the city, but Matthew did it from his lust for money. He was a mercenary.'

Sir Peregrine sucked his teeth. 'Bailiff?'

'I am content with that. I think you'd better take him to the city gaol now.'

'I don't want to go there!'

Simon looked at him for a long moment. 'William, you have the choice of an ecclesiastical gaol, where the gaoler will be interested in how you tried to thwart the word of a Bishop, or a city gaol where you will be looked after by men who may respect your protection of city men. The choice is yours.'

There was no choice. Soon William was being taken up towards the East Gate, and shortly afterwards, Simon was back in Janekyn's room. 'You heard all that?' he asked Baldwin.

The knight swallowed, and when he spoke his voice was a whisper. 'Very clearly. Where is the man?'

'He is usually to be seen on the scaffolding or in the Exchequer. I shall look there first.'

'Good. But Simon, be cautious. The man has a good bow arm. He may look like a feeble old clerk, but I am proof that his arm is strong indeed.'

'I shall be careful. Edgar, you stay here and guard your master and mistress. I will be back as soon as I know what has happened.'

Chapter Twenty-Four

The market was filled with people shoving and pushing, and Wymond allowed himself to be carried along with the general flow. At the outside were all the animals. songbirds in cages, kittens wriggling in larger crates, puppies tied to a post. There were stalls with sweetmeats, then the hawkers with apples and vegetables, and only at the top, nearer Carfoix, did he find the alley where he normally bought his bread. However, when he got to the shop he found that the boards were still up.

'He's been taken ill,' a neighbour informed him with that restrained excitement that another's misfortune will often bring out in a bystander.

Wymond chewed at his lip. There were other shops that sold bread, but he didn't want to go back to the market. Instead he continued up the lane, which led to St Petrock's Gate, a narrow way into the Cathedral Close. Intending to take a short cut up to the High Street, he went inside. A few yards from the church he suddenly saw the crowd of men. In their midst was William, a face he thought vaguely familiar, but the others were strangers to him. William was bound at the wrist, and Wymond wondered what he could have been accused of, to be tied up like that.

And then he heard the man's confession and his shocking revelation that Matthew had helped plan the death of the Chaunter.

Matthew. The Clerk of the Rolls was known perfectly well to Wymond. This man, who had been the sole survivor of the attack, who had been struck down at the beginning of the incident was himself guilty of causing the affray in the first place. He was one of the evil devils who had betrayed poor Vincent.

Wymond looked from William to the Exchequer, the building lay beyond the northernmost tower, and as he studied it, he saw the figure of a clerk among all the labourers on the scaffolding. The clerk was watching the group gathered at the Fissand Gate intently, then he slowly began to make his way along the scaffolding towards a ladder.

It was nothing for Wymond to walk idly down towards the Cathedral, around the wall of St Mary Major, along the line of houses, and over to the point where the ladder reached the ground. Once there, Wymond saw the clerk descend the last rung and then hurry along the paved roadway towards the Bear Gate.

Wymond gripped his bow more firmly and hastened after the man. He was certain now that this was his target. The clerk scurried along like a rat, his legs going all anyhow at speed, whereas Wymond could march steadily and cover a great distance with each stride.

At the point where the Bear Gate met the street, Matthew turned left, heading down towards the Southern Gate of the city; and now there were more people to block Wymond's sight, but he was sure of Matthew's direction, and didn't hesitate. By continuing to the gate, Wymond knew that soon he would be out of the city itself and back in the open wildlands where he had slept last night. Once through the old gate, there were fewer people, since all were heading *into* the city from the suburbs to buy their food, just as he had done. He sighted his quarry ahead, taking the Magdalene road, and Wymond felt delight stirring in his breast. This would be an easy shot!

Thomas couldn't wait while Simon and Peregrine split up their men, some to take William to the city's gaol, others to go with them to find Matthew. Instead he hurried across the Cathedral Close to the Exchequer and burst in through the door. He met Stephen's scandalised glare with an angry stare of his own.

'What is the meaning of this?' the Treasurer demanded, but Thomas merely snapped back, 'Where is he? The Warden of the Fabric?'

'Why, up on the scaffold, I believe. He likes to keep an eye on the men up there, especially since your clumsy killing of the mason. Why?'

'Because your lovely clerk is a *liar*! He helped kill the Chaunter. He deceived everyone.'

Stephen closed his eyes a moment. Then, 'You want him for that?'

'Yes,' Thomas said as he banged out. It was only later he wondered at the choice of words, almost as though Stephen had expected Matthew to be taken for something else. Still, just now he had no time to worry about the Treasurer's odd manner. He ran to the scaffolding and shouted up to the gang at the top: 'Where's Matthew? Have you seen him?'

'He was here a moment ago,' the Master Mason answered. 'He must have gone for a drink or something.'

Thomas chewed his lip. That did not sound right. The sun was nowhere near its full height in the sky; it was too early for Matthew to have gone for a drink. Perhaps a piss, but then he'd still be in view. No, he was gone somewhere else.

'Anyway,' the Master called, 'what're all those buggers doing over there? Matt was wondering – he said he knew the man in the middle. What's going on?'

Thomas swore to himself, and as Simon and a small force joined him, he shouted, 'He's gone! You've missed him!'

Baldwin had at last fallen into a light sleep, and Jeanne was able to release his hand; she stood, stretching her back. Just recently she had started to develop a mild back strain every so often, and hurrying down here to Exeter this morning had not helped matters. She missed her daughter Richalda terribly. Richalda would be fine, she knew, playing with Edgar's wife. Crissy and she always got on, the maid spoiling her daughter atrociously. Still, Jeanne hated to be away from Richalda for any time. Meanwhile, she was growing aware of an emptiness in her belly. She'd ridden here at such speed, there had been no time to pause for food. Looking at her husband, she reckoned that he wouldn't miss her for a little while, were she to seek food.

'Do you want something to eat?' she whispered to Edgar.

He looked at her and shook his head silently. She knew him of old, and she was happy that he would stand here by the door with that small smile on his face, watching over his master. That smile of his had won the hearts of many women until his wife, Crissy, had snared him. It showed his humour and essentially flippant, amiable manner. People little realised that it could hide a ruthless single-mindedness. This servant was a trained warrior, and he would have no compunction about using his weapons to protect his master. None whatsoever.

Walking from the room, Jeanne stood in the Close feeling the sun on her face, warming her body and making the earth smell fresh. It added to the all-encompassing joy she held within her, knowing that Baldwin was so pleased to see her. Her heart felt a renewed love for her man, and although she was anxious that he might suffer complications from this arrow-wound, she was at least content in the knowledge that Baldwin had rediscovered his love for her. She didn't understand his snapping at her over that maiden, and nor did she care. He had returned to her now.

She saw Janekyn and asked him, 'Where may I find some food and wine?'

'Don't worry, Lady, I'll get someone to bring you some,' Janekyn said. He gazed across the Close and saw a pair of choristers playing a game of catch around a tree. Lifting his chin and inhaling until his chest looked like that of a pigeon, he suddenly bellowed at the top of his voice, 'HAM AND ULRIC, COME HERE!' Turning back to Jeanne, he bowed slightly. 'Would a loaf of *paindemaine* and some wine with water be all right? I'll see if they can find some cold meats too, if you want.'

'That will be fine,' Jeanne said. She caught sight of John Coppe sitting on the ground by the gate and gave him a smile.

'Mistress, Godspeed,' he said, a grin twisting his awful scar.

'Godspeed, friend,' she said. 'I didn't see you before when I arrived here. I should have given you some coin otherwise.'

Coppe watched as she reached for her purse, and he felt a warm regard for her as she brought out a whole penny. 'Lady, I am very grateful. You are always generous to a poor beggar.'

'I try,' she said, but already her eyes were returning to Janekyn's door. She felt guilty to be out here when Baldwin was inside, so unwell. A thought prompted her to turn to Janekyn. 'Master porter, we have taken your room and bed. You must let me compensate you, too.'

'No need,' Janekyn said gruffly. 'Your man was ill, and it's enough payment to me to see him well again. No need for more.'

Jeanne's hand wavered near her purse for a moment, but then she nodded. 'I thank you, then. I—'

She caught sight of the expression in Jan's eyes, and when she looked over her shoulder, she saw Simon and Sir Peregrine marching back to them. Simon's face was grim.

'He's fled. Probably saw us from up there on the scaffold and decided to bolt before we could catch him. We need horses!'

*   *   *

Matthew's soul felt heavy with despair as he marched on down the road. Half a mile from the walls he passed over the Shitbrook bridge, glancing at the leper house that stood just over it, and then carried on, past the last houses and into the spare woodland and open fields that surrounded the city to the east and south.

Despair was the right word: it reflected his desolation, hopelessness, anguish, and desperation. All that he had ever done was gone. He had seen that as soon as the men started talking in their huddle, William in their midst. It was plain that they had spoken to him, and he was going to claim his rights as an Approver to protect himself. The King must listen to a man who had once been one of his own favoured servants, so there was nothing that Matthew could do to defend himself against Will's allegations.

Not that he could, in all conscience. Matt could hardly deny that Will was telling the truth. Matt hadn't had to lie about anything since that terrible night, and he wasn't going to risk his immortal soul by committing perjury now. No, he had been involved in that murder as a non-active participant, merely telling one untruth – and that not under oath. He was an accessory, perhaps, but plainly not guilty of the actual murder. After all, he was struck down only a moment or so after the attack was launched.

Yet all his life, all his efforts, had been built on the foundation of his integrity and honour, because people thought that he was the sole survivor of the murderous attack on his master. The Chaunter had died – and now everyone would find out that, instead of being a heroic defender of his master, in fact his master was slain because of his action. From being the hero, he must become the villain. He would be hounded from the Cathedral, forced to undergo humiliating punishments, and finally sent away to a monastery to live the rest of his life in penance. Sweet Jesus! He couldn't do that. The only reason he'd decided to join the Cathedral was because he had seen the easygoing life of the canons and reckoned that a civilised existence within the Bishop's enclosure, with good food, ale, and the ability and freedom to wander about the city, must be a great deal better than life as an humble apprentice.

Without his home in the Cathedral, he had no idea where to go or what to do. How could a mere clerk with training in controlling the Fabric Rolls be suitable for anything else? He had no money, no coin of any sort about him. He hadn't expected to have to run like this. He should have foreseen this situation. Damn those busybodies, the Bailiff and the Keeper! In his bedchamber he had secreted a small purse which was full of coins, but he had been forced to leave it all behind, so urgent had his escape become.

There was only one route open to him: to become an outlaw. Rob from others.

He stopped in the road, glanced about him, and then sank to the ground, his hands covering his eyes and weeping.

How could *he* become an outlaw? He was nearly sixty years old, he'd never learned how to fight, and his arms were feeble. There was nothing he could use as a weapon; all he possessed was a small knife, which was fine for paring nails, perhaps, but utterly ineffectual as a means of committing murder, or even threatening a traveller. Any merchant or carter would beat the shit from him for having the temerity to try such a thing.

Wailing, he rested on his knees in the dirt, staring about him with no idea what to do. His entire life had been ordered by ritual, by the seasons and dates, by the Feast Days of the saints, and the Offices of the day. The very concept of planning or fending for himself was alien.

One act so many years ago, and all his life was ruined. Now all must loathe him and look upon him with scorn. He was become a creature of contempt. How low could a man fall in his brothers' esteem? He couldn't live in the city any more, carrying that guilt with him.

He bent his head and wept again, just as Wymond slowly drew back the nocked arrow and let the barbed point rest on the bone that protruded at the top of Matthew's back, where the neck met the spine.

Jeanne was back inside the room when there came a knock at the door, and the tall, black-clad figure of the Treasurer peered inside. With him was a chorister with a tray that held bread and cheese and a large bombard filled with wine. Jeanne took the leather flagon from the tray to help the struggling boy, and set it down on the table. The tray was carried past her and placed beside it.

'How is he?' Stephen asked in a low voice.

'He is as well as can be expected,' she said. 'It is fortunate that the arrow missed any arteries and his lungs. It could have been much worse, although it is bad enough. A wound like this could kill a much stronger man. We must pray for him.'

'I am so sorry about it,' Stephen said. He made as though to approach the bed on which Baldwin lay snoring gently, but suddenly he was stopped by Edgar. It was his hand, rather than his sword, which ungently prevented the Treasurer from going closer, but Stephen was left in no doubt that were he to persist, the sword would soon be added to the argument.

'No one goes close other than his wife,' Edgar said with a smile.

Stephen nodded uncertainly, looking down at the knight's wounded figure. 'I am so sorry,' he repeated.

Jeanne said, 'It is terrible that such a thing could happen here in the Close.'

'It is a source of shame to us all,' he agreed.

'But the man responsible is soon to be caught. The posse will bring him back here, and then we can all rest easy in the knowledge that the whole matter is finished.'

'I hope so,' Stephen said. 'I hope that they can bring him back safely.'

'You care deeply for him?'

'He was from my own *familia*. I was his mentor. I taught him all I knew in order that he could become Treasurer in my place. Matt is so skilled with the numbers and controlling the works, much more so than most. He would have been an excellent Treasurer.'

'If he did this, he deserves death,' Jeanne said tightly, gesturing to Baldwin.

'Of course. Of course. Murder is wrong in any case,' Stephen said hurriedly. 'I shouldn't dream of suggesting otherwise. I was just thinking, if he were innocent of this terrible attack, and the murders, he would have been a good candidate.'

Jeanne said nothing. So far as she was concerned, the man who had done this to Baldwin deserved to pay with his life.

Stephen could sense her feelings, and went on: 'It is only that the Cathedral needs men who can serve the rebuilding, you see. Although we will never live to see the full beauty of our work here, will never see the fruition of all our plans, nevertheless we must work to ensure that God's House is completed. It is our duty.'

'God would scarcely want a murderer to work on His House,' Jeanne commented. 'No, Treasurer. There is nothing you can say which could possibly excuse the man. He is a low assassin, who tried to slay my husband in order to prevent the full story of his crimes becoming known.'

'Perhaps so.'

'So it is best that he be caught as soon as possible, and then caged or slain in his own time. There is no other way to deal with a murderer.'

Stephen looked at her sadly. She saw the desperate need for her understanding and compassion in his eyes, but she couldn't reciprocate. All Jeanne wanted to see just now, was the lifeless body of her man's attacker.

Simon had taken a horn from Janekyn to start the process of the Hue and Cry, blowing three times as loudly as he could. Before long he had a goodly crowd of men, all struggling and pushing.

Thomas tried to set off after them, but Simon grabbed his arm. 'No, Thomas. You can't leave the Close.'

'Why not? I couldn't have hurt the knight. You said so yourself!'

'I know, but you were responsible for other deaths, weren't you? You took a part in one many years ago, and you caused the mason's death too. You had best stay here.'

'I won't, I—'

'Man, you'll stay here!' Simon rasped. He had no time to argue. 'If you won't, you'll be set back in the gaol, understand me? I won't have you wandering the town in case someone takes it into their head to punish you for that, if nothing else! Now for God's sake shut up, before I shut you up myself!'

Leaving Thomas in the Close, Simon and Sir Peregrine went outside to organise their men. One group was to hurry towards the East Gate, checking the buildings and fields that lay about the Crolditch outside the city walls. The second, under Sir Peregrine's leadership, would take the Carter's Road that followed the line of the river down towards the estuary, while the third would take the Magdalene Street. Simon chose to lead this group himself. He had a feeling that Matthew would avoid the coast so near to Exeter, and would instead make for the east.

Simon had a horse, but many of his party did not, and he was frustrated by the need to hang back and wait for the slowest of the men. As was usual, the Hue and Cry had raised all those who were nearest and who were able to help. There were boys of perhaps thirteen, to look at them, and one toothless old man who must have been over sixty and had no place in Simon's team. Simon cajoled and swore at them all to make them move faster, but some of them could barely keep on their feet after only perhaps a half mile or so, just as they were reaching the Magdalene bridge by the lepers' hospital.

In the end his patience ran out. He bellowed to the two other mounted men to come with him, ordered the others to go home – since they would scarcely be necessary anyway, to catch only one man – and spurred his mount.

The beast was one of the Dean's own rounseys, and had muscles like corded rope. As soon as Simon gave him his head, he felt a charge of energy explode in the animal's shoulders and haunches, and then he was hurtling onwards, the air suddenly cool on his cheeks, the wind tugging and pulling at his clothing, his sword's sheath banging rhythmically at his side. There was little in the way of good road here, and although the sun had been out all day, the passage was rutted and muddy from the wheels of many carts bringing food and goods to the markets that made Exeter so wealthy. He thundered on, feeling the exhilaration that a powerful horse can give a rider when it obeys his commands.

He rode on with a keen delight. This was how he was born to live: riding a good animal quickly in pursuit. And today he had a more pressing desire than normal to track down the runaway. He must capture and punish the man who had tried to kill Baldwin.

The route grew darker as they came across a wood and sheltering trees, and there were twists and turns in the path, growing rapidly muddier and more filthy, until they had covered perhaps a mile and a half, and then at last Simon saw Matthew.

The Vicar was seated at the side of the road, his face hidden in his hands, back against a great beech tree's trunk. Simon allowed his mount to slow, reining in gently, and the rounsey gradually took notice, if reluctantly. When he was level with the man, Simon drew his sword and pointed it. 'You, Matthew, I accuse you of murder, and I will have you return to Exeter to answer to the judges.'

'I didn't mean to,' Matthew said brokenly. 'It was an accident.'

Simon felt his anger bubble, and he could easily have dropped from the horse and beaten the feeble cur. 'I suppose the bow leaped into your hands when you saw Baldwin there, did it? And the arrow flew and pierced his breast all on its own, eh? You are evil, man. Scum!'

'I believe him,' said Wymond, and Simon turned to see the grim-faced old tanner behind him at the other side of the road.

'Who are you?'

'Wymond. I live on Exe Island – I have a tannery there. This man, I thought, was one of those responsible for the murder of my brother when he tried to save his master, Chaunter Walter, many years ago. You've heard all about this, aye? Well, my brother Vincent was there. He called to the Chaunter to warn him, but a fellow cut him down, and over the years people in the Cathedral have tried to say that my Vince was as guilty as the others, that he was a traitor, involved in the attack, but he never was! It was those who *were* guilty, who passed that story about.'

'What's that got to do with this fellow?' Simon asked, indicating Matthew.

'He was the man who really betrayed his master, so he is one of those who put part of the blame on my brother and despoiled Vince's good name. I followed him here today to kill him in revenge.'

'But he's not dead.' Simon knew it was the right of any man to cut down an outlaw who ran and refused to stop.

'True. Because when I saw what manner of a man he was, it didn't seem to merit the use of force against him. Had he been a little more manly, I'd have killed him and not minded the danger of the law, but he looked so pathetic, I didn't want to waste a good arrow.'

Simon muttered, 'I wish he'd felt the same when he tried to kill my friend, Sir Baldwin.'

Chapter Twenty-Five

When Stephen had left the room, Jeanne sat at Baldwin's side again. She broke up the bread into pieces and when she saw that Baldwin was waking again, she soaked a little of the crust in wine and passed it to him. He sucked it eagerly and gave her a smile. There was a fine sheen of sweat on his forehead, and she dabbed at it with a spare piece of linen, smiling back at him as comfortingly as she could, and that was how she remained while he was awake. As soon as his eyes were closed and his grip loosened on her hand, she sat more upright, feeling the muscles in her back relax.

'My Lady? Are you all right? If you want to go and take a walk about the Close, I shall remain here with Sir Baldwin,' Edgar said. His tone was kindly, his manner respectful, but as compassionate as a brother.

She threw him a grateful look, but then her eyes went back to her husband's body. There was more sweat breaking out on his face. 'Do you think he'll survive, Edgar?'

He sniffed. 'I reckon he'll do. He's been wounded before, and I've seen worse than that pinprick. Yes, he'll live.'

Most servants would have been cautious in their responses to their mistresses, but Edgar was being honest.

He continued, 'I've seen men die from serious wounds about that part of the body, but usually there's more blood, either seeping from the wound or coming from the mouth and nose. He looks well enough. So long as the pus runs and cleans him inside, he'll be fine.'

'Yes,' she said thoughtfully. 'And that physician hasn't been here yet. Where is he?'

'We should send a messenger for him, perhaps?'

She nodded and glanced at her sleeping husband. He looked so vulnerable, so childlike. She said softly, 'In a while, perhaps. Not quite yet.'

*　*　*

It was hard. Daniel had stayed up late with her, trying to comfort her, but although she wanted the solace of his young arms about her, there was nothing that he could do or say which would ease her pain.

Her husband's death had left a hole in Sara's life that felt unfillable. Her man had taken her, a raw, foolish peasant girl, and seen something in her which no one else had. By marrying her, Saul had given Sara a very different life from the one she could have anticipated, and he had also given her himself. For that she would always honour him and his memory. Now, although others might say that they understood her feelings, they couldn't. Her life had ended that day when Thomas told her of her man's death.

The second loss was appalling, too: to lose a child was to lose a part of yourself. She had been one with this little boy for nine months, nurturing him within her womb. No man could understand how that loss must stupefy and devastate a woman. She had grown used to the idea that there would only be the three of them from the moment of Saul's death, and then God had taken her darling Elias too. It was too cruel! Then, for consolation, He gave her a man to soften the blow and save her from madness: Thomas. The man who had killed her husband.

How God could treat her so was a mystery. She must have sinned in her past . . . but for the life of her she didn't remember it. She had only ever tried to praise Him as the priests told her she must.

Thomas had murdered her Saul, and then arrived at her door to tell her; maybe it gave him some kind of gratification to see her pain. He was there again when she fell with Elias at the Priory's gate, as though God was sending him as a messenger of doom to oversee every misfortune of her life. Overtly a comforter, in fact he was only ever there to bring still more grief to her life. And then he had become a focus for her affection. She had learned that he was always about when she needed aid, and he had never sought to dissuade her from becoming attached to him, although he should have been consumed with guilt. He was the engineer of her misery. She must hate him!

Yes. She must hate him, just as surely as Daniel did. Her son was repelled by him, and even this morning as the first light had illuminated their room, Daniel had asked if she was also awake.

'Because when the Dean hears that man's story, we ought to be there.'

'I don't want to see him again,' she said.

'Don't cry, Mummy. Don't! We'll be all right. I'll get work and feed you. We'll be all right.'

'I'm fine,' she lied, wiping her eyes. 'I just don't want to think about him, that's all.'

'Well, I want to see him punished. I have to know that my father was avenged. Do you think the Dean will hang him for robbing us?'

She turned away. 'He didn't rob us, Danny. He tried to give us money.'

'Only because he was guilty! He killed Daddy and wanted us to forgive him.'

'Perhaps,' she said, but without conviction. If she were honest with herself, the sight of him in their home had shocked her. She'd thought that he wouldn't dare come back here again, but he had, to help with a parting gift. That had been kind.

'I want to go and see him pay,' Danny said grimly. He rose from their bed and began to pull his shirt on over his head.

It was one of Saul's, and many sizes too large. Seeing him there – little, thin, preparing for a winter without a father or secure supply of food – Sara could barely keep the tears at bay. The two of them might survive a while, but without a man they would soon know the anguish of hunger gnawing at their bellies as the money ran out.

She gripped him tightly against her bosom, rocking him back and forth as she prayed for help from the God Who had taken so much already, pleading that He wouldn't take her last son as well.

There was only Danny left for her to lose.

Matthew was weeping much of the way back to the city. His hands were tied with a thong attached to a long rein which Simon had bound to his saddle's pommel. The other riders were behind them, and the silent, thoughtful tanner marched on Matthew's right, his bow unstrung in his hands.

The weeping and wailing eventually got to Simon. 'Shut up that noise, Vicar!'

'One error, and my life has been ruined!'

'The error was your betrayal of your master, so don't expect sympathy from me!' Simon grated. 'You committed treason and saw to your master's murder.'

'It was for the good of Exeter and the Cathedral, though! I had no choice.'

'That was why you demanded money of William, was it?'

'That shit! Damn his heart! He persuaded me into it, and then fled the city himself. Made himself look good by telling the King about the gate, and took the King's money to go.'

'Much like you, in fact,' Simon said. 'You took all the advancement you could, didn't you?'

'Yes. Well, that wasn't my fault. I didn't seek advancement.'

'Oho! No, of course not!'

'I didn't! But if a man is offered . . . I mean, I didn't try to get new tasks and income, they just came.'

'Yes,' Simon scoffed. 'And none of them because of the respect in which you were held by your peers?'

'Perhaps,' Matthew said, and brought a sleeve over his face again. 'But I could hardly admit what I'd done. Bishop Quivil would have had me thrown into gaol and left there to rot, just like he did with John Pycot. I only ever sought to serve the Cathedral, nothing more.'

'And committed murder to protect yourself.'

Matthew sobbed again, head fallen forward, shoulders jerking spasmodically. For several paces he couldn't speak, and Simon was tempted to pull the long leash that bound his hands, but that would only yank the man off his feet and lead to another delay. Simon had no wish to pull him all the way to Exeter, and then present him to the Dean with the skin flayed from elbows and knees. Better to take the journey more slowly. Still, he was losing his patience rapidly, and he was about to ask the fellow to hurry, since Simon wanted to return to Exeter before old age saw off his friend Baldwin rather than the Vicar's own arrow, when Matthew started to talk again.

'It was terrible. My guilt is so clear and unequivocal, and I feel the shame of it every moment of every day. I cannot even confess properly! I tried to. I spoke to Paul at the Charnel, but I couldn't say the actual words, and when he caught wind of my crime, he said I must speak to one of the Dignitaries, not to him. He meant the Treasurer, of course. Stephen is my master. But how could I tell him, after all he had done for me, thinking that I . . .'

'That you were honourable,' Simon sneered.

'Not just that. Oh, how could you understand? You're just a Bailiff. You don't have the faintest idea what life is like in a cathedral or canonical church.'

Simon was again tempted to pull on the rein, but quashed the urge. 'You lived a life of falsehood because of the crime of your youth, and you hid that crime for forty years, taking all the advantages you could along the way, until at last you found that someone knew the truth – and then you killed him. Poor Henry knew what you'd done, did he?'

'No! I had nothing to do with his death, nor that of Nicholas.'

'Of course not!' Simon grinned disbelievingly.

'I didn't! But to my shame, I did kill the mason.'

'You say you murdered Saul?'

'I didn't *mean* to hurt him. What, do you think you can aim a rock from the top of a wall and hit a man tens of feet below you? Don't be stupid!'

His sudden vehemence surprised Simon into silence.

'No, that was an accident. Anyway, I was talking about Stephen, not Henry. He was the last person I could confess to: at first because I thought he believed me to be the embodiment of reliability and honour, and to tell him that I had deceived him would have hurt more than his mere pride, it would have devastated him and left him bereft.'

'You rate yourself highly, Vicar.'

'You don't understand! Stephen is too old to continue for long in his post, he is desperate to retire, and I am the only man who can keep control of the Fabric Rolls and see to it that the Cathedral maintains its progress. We have to make sure that the place survives and that the rebuilding is continued. My God! Do you have even the faintest conception of the amount of work involved in getting this sort of project completed? It is likely to take another fifty years to see it to fruition. That means four generations of canons since the work began. It is not some frivolous, ephemeral undertaking that can be started in a moment and idly set down a short while later. This is a crucial part of God's work. We have to see it through as best we can, each of us, and if the right man for a specific task is there, he must take up his responsibility. If there were another who could do the job so well as me, I would bow to him, and Stephen could hear my confession today – but there is no one!'

'Someone will be found,' Simon said. 'No man is indispensable.'

It was the tanner who had picked up on Matthew's words, though. 'You said you couldn't tell him "at first". What changed, Vicar?'

'Eh?'

'He's right,' Simon said. 'You said you couldn't tell Stephen initially. What changed?'

'He was another who was involved in the attack on the Chaunter,' Matthew sighed. 'He told me – and that meant I couldn't possibly tell him about my guilt. Look, all through our time together, he has brought me up with him, teaching me all he knows, giving me a good living, protecting me from the politics of the Cathedral Close . . . should I then, *could* I, go to him and tell him that his belief in me was all wrong?'

Simon frowned. 'He gave you honours and advancement through your life because he thought you were a man of integrity. Then, you learned that he had been guilty himself . . . I do not understand. Why should he not know that you too were guilty?'

'Because to a man like him, that would mean that the whole of his life had been in vain. He had tried to help me in order to expiate his own guilt. I was a symbol of his reparation, as significant to him as the Charnel Chapel was to John Pycot. How could I demolish his lifetime's act? I was there to take over from him; if he learned of my crime, he would see no means of continuing the rebuilding with me, and that must mean that the project would fail!'

'So you preferred to conceal your crime more effectively by murdering the saddler and Friar Nicholas and trying to kill my friend Baldwin,' Simon said nastily.

'No!'

Simon jerked the reins. 'And now you'll have to pay the price in full, Vicar, because we'll see you convicted in the Chapter's court!'

It was late afternoon by the time that Simon and his little group had reached the Bear Gate again, and they trotted into the Cathedral Close before leaving their mounts with a pair of grooms who promised to see that the horses would be well looked after and the Dean's taken to his private stables.

'So, Matthew. You've caused enough trouble already,' Simon said coldly. 'You can come with me now and see the Dean.'

'So there he is at last!'

Simon turned to see Thomas striding towards him. 'Hold on, Thomas! This fellow's coming to the Dean with me now. We'll see what Dean Alfred decides to do with him.'

'I have little interest in him. I just wanted to see his face one last time, to see what a man looks like who's lived a lie for so many years,' Thomas said sadly. 'If there's someone I want to see punished, it's William. He was the one who had my father killed.'

'Then come with us and hear what Matthew has to say,' Simon suggested, and they marched their prisoner along the Close, out to the Dean's house and inside to his hall, Wymond trooping along in their wake, his bow still in his hand.

The old tanner was feeling oddly disconsolate. After the excitement of haring off after this cleric, he had the sense that there was something amiss. He couldn't go home; not yet. There was some sort of unfinished business here, he felt, and he had to try to resolve it while he could. Perhaps this man's confession would make sense of Vincent's death on that black night in 1283.

Still, at least he had avenged his brother in some small way. His speed in capturing Matthew was deeply satisfying, although he'd have preferred to have killed the man on the spot, rather than see some protracted punishment. There was nothing that the Dean could do which would repay the debt so speedily as an arrow, so he'd thought.

It was only when he had the barbed tip aimed at Matthew's neck that he realised he couldn't do it. He couldn't fire.

All his life he had wanted to hate the men in the black garb of the Cathedral, because they represented the ones who had destroyed his brother, and later, his wife. It was they who had set up his Vincent and had him slaughtered in front of the Cathedral doors. If not for them, Vince might still be here now.

But Vincent had worn that same cloth, and Vincent in that clothing was the victim. In the end, it was impossible for Wymond to decide who was deserving of life and who deserved death. This man was, so far as he knew, guilty of having played some part in the death of Vincent – but what if he was wrong? There was a reluctance to shoot at a man who was in the same uniform which Vincent had worn. Looking at Matthew now, Wymond realised he could in fact have been an older, sadder Vincent. The thought had brought to his mind a picture of his brother: that happy, smiling face, the calm, generous spirit beaming from those bright eyes. The image for a moment obscured the reality of the snivelling Matthew, and made Wymond lower his bow. Killing like this was the last thing Vincent would have wanted, he knew.

Perhaps forty years ago Wymond could have released the arrow, but not now. Instead he had let Matthew see his bow, and had sat back to wait. The Hue and Cry couldn't take too long to find them.

And now the last stage of the tale was to be told. Wymond wanted to hear this. It might, perhaps, allow him to put aside all those feelings of sorrow and loss which had plagued him over the years.

Looking about him now at the richly decorated hall of the Dean, he realised that whatever the truth, there was little chance that he would ever be able to obtain any justice. This was a rich man's house, not the sort of place in which a mere tanner like him could hope for help or restitution.

Sara approached the Fissand Gate with a strange sense of nervousness. She wanted to know what would happen to Thomas. No matter what Daniel thought, he had been kind to her, and if he was truly a murderer, she must know why, and what his punishment might be.

There were rumours that he'd not only killed Saul, but that he'd killed two other men in the city as well – and tried to murder a third. He only failed because his arrow missed its mark in the gloom of evening, or so the people said.

The porter at Fissand was always helpful: he would give wine or bread to those who had need, and perhaps today he might be equally forthcoming with news or assistance, showing her where to go to hear of the case against Thomas. She had no idea when the Bishop's court was likely to convene, and the idea of waiting for days was very unappealing. She only hoped that, like most other courts, this would meet very soon and the sentence be imposed quickly. At least then she would know that justice of a sort had been served.

There was no porter evident. Instead she approached a vicar. 'Master? Can you tell me where—'

'I don't have time, woman!' The cleric to whom she addressed her enquiry was a tall man, quite old, and he threw her an anguished look. 'If you have questions, go in there and ask the porter!'

Feeling very small, she watched him stalk away. Sara didn't know why she'd bothered to come here in the first place. This was a man's world, not suitable for women like her. She was mad to have thought otherwise. She would have turned tail there and then, and returned home, but Daniel chose that moment to bolt, running over the graveyard towards the Bishop's palace, calling out that he'd find out where they must go.

At the wall was a beggarman. Sara had seen him about the city before: with his horribly scarred face and missing leg, he was hard to miss, but he'd never spoken to her.

'Maid, is there something wrong?'

The gentle tone of his voice nearly made her weep. 'I just wanted to know what's happened to the mason who killed the others here. Is he going to be put on trial soon?'

'What's your interest?'

'The dead mason, Saul, he was my husband.'

'Oh maid . . . I'm sorry.'

'Do you know what'll happen?'

John Coppe eyed her sympathetically, but closely. A beggar was quick to gain an insight into the feelings of others – it was an essential element of his make-up. He had to size up his market and grab the most money from those most likely to pay him. In his opinion this woman was close to her limits. She couldn't cope with any more shocks or alarms.

He said, 'Maid, I think Thomas, the man you're talking about, has already been proved innocent. Another man was attacked last night, while Thomas was in the gaol. So he seems to be innocent.'

'*Innocent*!' Sara felt as though her legs must fail her. Suddenly both knees began to wobble, and she teetered on the brink of collapse.

Coppe tried to lurch to his feet, but he was already too late, and all he could do was shout for assistance.

The door to Janekyn's chamber opened, and Edgar stood there, his sword ready in his hand, eyes flitting about the Close before they came to rest on Sara's figure and the desperate beggar at her side.

Others were already running over, and a number of men and women came to Coppe's side, lifting the woman up. 'Where can we take her?' 'What is it?' 'Ah, she's only fainted!'

Jeanne pushed her way past Edgar and peered at the huddle of men and women. Coppe saw her with relief. She was one, he was sure, who would look after a woman like this. 'Mistress, please help us! Can we put this poor widow in the room with your husband?'

'What is the matter with her?'

'She's fainted. It's her husband, he died here a few weeks ago. Crushed when a stone fell on him, and since then she's been . . . well, you can imagine.'

Through the encircling crowd Jeanne saw how young Sara was, and how vulnerable she looked. That one look was enough. 'Of course you must bring her in here. When Baldwin's physician arrives, I shall ask him to see to her at the same time.'

They carried her within, while Edgar stood at Baldwin's side, sword threateningly still in his hand. There was no need for him to wave it about to make a point. His apparent languid stance was enough to put fear into the hearts of all who eyed him. The crowd deposited Sara on a bench near the wall, and left.

As Jeanne stood over her, the woman started to moan softly, and Jeanne took her hand, pressing it. 'It is all right now. You are safe here.'

'How can I ever be safe?' came the bitter response.

'I am sorry,' Matthew said, his head hanging. 'I didn't think that my actions could cause so much grief.'

'You were happy enough to commit murder, though,' Simon said.

'I only did what I thought I had to.'

'Yes – you murdered Saul,' Simon said unsympathetically.

'No!'

'But you admitted it before,' Simon said. 'Out there, you said you killed him!'

'Not on purpose . . . but it was the same thing to God, though,' Matthew said with a pious shudder.

'What are you talking about?' Simon demanded. There was a noise of hoofbeats from the cobbles outside, and he turned to see Sir Peregrine ride in with his party. The Coroner threw himself from his saddle with the energy of a man half his age and hurried over to join them.

The clerk turned to Thomas and spoke clearly.

'I mean this: Thomas, I am sorry. I confess my sin, and I beg your forgiveness. I tried to kill you on the scaffold.'

Thomas gaped. He rubbed his hands against his thighs. The palms were sore again, but in some odd way the feel of roughness against his legs was soothing. It seemed to make the world more comprehensible, since the only feeling he was aware of at this minute was that of unreality. 'But the stone fell because of an accident.'

Matthew shook his head. 'I released the metal wedge that held the stone up. I thought that it might kill you.'

'What did you want to kill *me* for?' Thomas cried.

'Because I thought you knew about my part in the attack. I knew that William was aware, and I knew you were one of his friends. Henry and Joel had kept silent all the time I was being nursed after the Chaunter's death, but you I feared.'

'Why not William too?' Simon asked.

'Because, he was the man who paid me. If he betrayed me, he'd betray himself. As he did today,' Matthew said bitterly.

'So you let the stone fall?' Thomas said.

'You had a rope about your wrist. I thought that were I to release the stone, it must drag you down and kill you. I was panicked. I didn't know what else to do!'

'And Saul?' Simon said.

'He shouldn't have been there,' Matthew said resentfully. 'He ought to have been in the works, not hiding under the walls. I didn't know he was there, not until I saw the legs sticking out from under the rock and realised it had crushed someone.'

'So Thomas had no part in Saul's death?' the Coroner said.

'He was only the intended victim,' Simon agreed.

'Which hardly makes him culpable,' Sir Peregrine nodded. 'Very well.'

'Except we still do not know who was the murderer of Henry and the Friar, and the would-be assassin of Sir Baldwin,' Simon pointed out.

'Wasn't that him too?'

'No, I had nothing to do with their deaths. Saul's death was an accident, and you can't make me confess to the others. They were nothing to do with me!'

'And the sun doesn't rise in the east,' Sir Peregrine said, smiling.

*   *   *

Jeanne had called for some wine to help Sara's recovery, and she was glad to hear the steps at the door. It opened cautiously, and she saw Stephen standing there, holding a jug and some cups on a tray. He proffered the tray to Edgar, who glanced at Jeanne, busy with the sick woman, then set his sword at Baldwin's feet and took the tray. Even as he turned to take it to Jeanne, she saw the pale face of Stephen looking at Baldwin, not even shooting a glance at Sara, and she wondered why. It wasn't important, she told herself, taking a moment to reflect on the importance of Edgar in her life. Without him, her husband would certainly be dead already, because his trusted servant had been at his side in almost all the dangerous situations he had experienced during his life. Edgar was the most devoted, loyal and obedient servant she had ever known.

Which was why, as she saw the cudgel and guessed the truth, there was only time to gasp before the blow fell and Edgar dropped like a stunned ox. He collapsed on the shards of the cups, and when she saw the red liquid seeping over the floor by his head, Jeanne couldn't help but open her mouth and scream and scream . . .

John Coppe was still outside, thinking of little but where the next coin might come from, but when he heard that cry, he hoisted himself to his feet. Jan was nowhere to be seen, and there were few people walking about in the Close at this time of day, so John was unsure at first what to do, but he could identify the cry of a woman who needed help. He hobbled with his crutch over to the door, but when he pushed at it, it seemed jammed. Unbeknownst to him, Edgar's body lay against it and John couldn't gain enough leverage to open it.

Instead, he opened his mouth. John Coppe had been a sailor, and a man who has had to bellow over roaring wind and thrashing seas learns to make himself heard. He bawled the ancient call for the Hue and Cry at the top of his voice:

'Out! Out! Out! Help! Murder! Out! Out! Out!'

In the Dean's hall, Coppe's cries were just loud enough to penetrate the thick hangings and solid walls, and Simon set his head to one side as he listened a moment. His mind was still on the man in front of him, however, as he asked sarcastically, 'If not you, who else could have wanted to silence Henry and Nicholas and Baldwin?'

'How should I know? All I know is, it wasn't me!' Matthew wept.

Simon looked over at the Coroner; Sir Peregrine grinned at Simon. 'I've often seen this sort of thing before. A man realises he can't get away with his crimes and decides to surrender himself for a lesser crime. It won't work here, though.'

'It is a shame,' the Dean sighed. 'Matthew has been a good servant of the Cathedral. After all, that is what we do here. We are all servants of the Cathedral itself.'

Simon gaped at him in horror. Now he realised who was responsible for the murders! Even as his mind made the leap, he recognised John's hoarse bawling, and with a muttered oath he span on his heel and bolted from the room.

'What on . . .' Sir Peregrine murmured, and then grabbed Matthew's arm. 'Not you. You're going nowhere.'

Wymond was already hurrying after Simon, wondering what the screams might signify. He hurtled through the front door and gazed about him wildly until he caught sight of the Bailiff's sturdy body running off towards the Fissand Gate. He immediately set off in pursuit, wondering whether he should have strung his bow.

Jeanne threw herself over Baldwin's body with a fresh scream even as Stephen reached for the sword. As his hand touched the hilt, she grabbed at it and managed to catch the blade, pulling it from him. The brightly burnished steel cut into her palm, but she refused to acknowledge the pain, shrieking as loudly as she might to gather help. Somehow she must keep this fiend from her husband.

The sword clattered on the floor, and now Sara was screaming as loudly as Jeanne. Jeanne lunged for the hilt, but as she did so, Stephen swung a fist at her. His face was set in a white, determined mask. He looked petrified, but resolute. Jeanne felt the same, but seeing his own terror helped her to conquer hers. She ducked and his blow missed, but she also released the sword. It span away, out of reach beneath the table. They both went for it, Stephen on all fours, clambering over Edgar in his haste, while she scrambled across the floor, shards of broken pots and cups slicing her knees. A great splinter lanced up into the ball of her thumb, but she paid it no attention, her hand reaching out to take up the sword again.

This time his fist found its mark. While she stretched, oblivious, a blow thundered into the side of her head. It was like the first time she had been drunk: the very room appeared to whirl about her, and nausea bubbled in her breast, ready to spew forth. She tried to clear her head, but her arms and legs were formed of lead. There was a mistiness in the room, and a strange silence which made little sense. That was when his fist hit her in the eye.

Though the fog she could see Stephen. He stood near Baldwin, the sword held aloft in both arms, ready to strike, but his eyes were on Jeanne. Later, she thought he might have been pleading for forgiveness, or begging her to try to understand . . . but she could never be truly sure. He turned away from her, and prepared to deliver the coup de grâce.

But then she saw her husband's good arm rise up, and with the little strength remaining in him, Baldwin stopped the blow from falling. And as Jeanne saw that, she was aware of the door opening, juddering against Edgar's body, and Simon pelted in. He stopped and gaped for an instant as he took in the scene.

Behind him, Wymond, the experienced brawler of a hundred tavern scuffles, didn't hesitate. He shoved Simon from his path, then poked his unstrung bow like a pike into Stephen's face. The Treasurer gave a shriek of agony and dropped the sword. Wymond stepped to the side, and as Stephen's hands went to his ruined eye, he swung his heavy bow. It cracked across both Stephen's forearms, and he howled as an arm broke; then it swept back one last time, and smashed into his throat. Stephen fell to the floor, gurgling and thrashing as he desperately tried to take in air, but as he lay there, Edgar crawled to him, placed a hand on his brow, and ran a dagger over his throat. In the spurt of blood, Stephen's movements became more panicked for a while, but then gradually ceased.

At last he lay still, just as Thomas shoved his way in through the door and saw Sara, her face and torso smothered in blood. He gave a great roar of pain and grief, and ran to her, putting his face in the corner of her neck as he wept.

Chapter Twenty-Six

Udo lay back in his bed with a groan. His arm was exceptionally painful and his face was one massive bruise, while he could hardly breathe from his nose since its breakage by that madman William.

There were always some who were simply mad, no matter what the city or the environment. Udo had known some men in the highest courts in Europe who were absolutely insane; men who would whip off a man's head as soon as look at him. Yes, but they generally tried to behave within their own rules of courtesy. The trouble with a man like this William was that he was too lowly. He had no conception of the ways of his betters. That was why he ranted drunkenly before hitting Udo.

'My darling, are you all right?' Julia asked.

Udo grunted a response. If there was one benefit from all this, it was that Julia and he had grown very close. She had seen how he had leaped in to risk his own life and limb to defend her and her mother, and if she had held any secret doubts about their marriage, that act had immediately removed them. She adored him, and Udo had to admit, having experienced her devoted nursing for this past week, that she would be an ideal companion.

He looked at her now. She was sitting at his side, an expression of sweet kindness on her face, and he thought she could easily be the Madonna. Yes, he would be delighted to be married to her, and he would do so as soon as possible. For a while, perhaps only a little while, they would be man and wife, and when Udo died, she would have a goodly sum of money to protect her widowhood until she found another man to look after her.

It was good. She was lovely. He was enormously attracted to her. Her beauty would warm his heart, and he could adore her as he went about his business. Then in the evenings he could speak with her and instruct her in the ways of polite company. After all, taking on a child like her was rather like becoming a second father to her. It was a stern responsibility.

Except just now, he felt nothing remotely like responsibility. If he was honest, there was only one emotion uppermost in his mind: he loved her.

'I do not think that you should be walking about so soon,' Jeanne said as she helped Baldwin into a heavy cotte.

He winced as his arm was thrust into the sleeve. 'Damn this wound! It quite drains a man to have a hole in breast and back. I could return to bed and sleep for another week!'

'I don't think you should do that, Sir Baldwin.'

'I didn't ask *you*, Physician! You took so damned long to come and see me when I needed you, I see no reason to listen to you now,' Baldwin growled at Ralph.

Ralph smiled cynically.

It was one of the first things Baldwin had decided he disliked about this fellow: the complete lack of obsequiousness. At least most physicians had the decency to try to appear as though they cared a little for their patients, but not Ralph. He had one ambition, and that was to make as much money as possible.

Now he gave a little sniff, as though he was disapproving but not bothered. If Baldwin intended to kill himself, that was his own affair (so long as he was up to date with paying his bills, of course). Ralph would give advice, and that was an end to his responsibilities. 'It is up to you, but I have found that my patients survive better if they arise from their beds and indulge in some light exercise. Still, the corollary to that is that you should not overstrain yourself. I urge you to remain here, Sir Baldwin. It would be most unfortunate if you were to ruin the excellent progress you have made in the last week just for this one meeting. What good it could do you, I do not know. Far better that you should walk a little about the Cathedral Close, sit in the sun when it shines, and rest yourself.'

'Shut up, fool!' Baldwin snarled.

Jeanne took his arm, and the pair walked from the room. Outside Simon stood waiting, while Edgar sat on a bench nearby. His head was still very painful, as was obvious from his grimace as the sun shone full in his face, but for all that he was remarkably well recovered after his heavy knock. Seeing Baldwin, he stood immediately and the four of them set off.

Their path took them past John Coppe. Baldwin himself reached into his pocket and fumbled for a coin, throwing it to the beggar as they passed.

'That was kind of you,' Jeanne commented.

'He deserves better,' Baldwin said gruffly. 'If it weren't for him, you and I might both be dead.'

That was a sobering thought. She was silent for some while. Her black eye was still a glorious colour, with blues and purples fading to yellow at the edges. The whole of the battle in Janekyn's small chamber was hazy to her, and she was glad of the fact. She craved forgetfulness. All she knew was that her man was alive and recovering. With that she was well-satisfied. She thrust her arm through his. Unseemly, perhaps, to behave in so forward a manner in public, but convention be damned. She wanted to be like this for ever – close to her husband, secure in his love.

For that was how she felt. Ever since that appalling day of her arrival here, she had been convinced that her husband's love had returned. She looked up at his stern features with a sense of relief, tempered with the memory of that bleak time when he seemed to lose his affection for her. She dreaded it happening again and would do everything in her power to prevent it. She loved him: she couldn't bear to lose him.

Joel was already sitting in his chair waiting when they knocked on the door. He swigged back the wine in his mazer and rose to his feet as Vince led them into his hall. 'Godspeed.'

Baldwin nodded, and Simon managed a short bow, while Jeanne murmured her own greeting, dipping her fingers in the stoup by the door and making the sign of the cross over her breast. Edgar said nothing, but walked away from Baldwin to the wall not far from Joel. From there he appeared to be keeping an eye on Joel and on his apprentice, and Joel gave him a suspicious look. The man looked intensely threatening.

Joel was surprised to hear the next knocking at the door, and when he saw Vincent's father, his astonishment was reflected on his face. 'Wymond? What do you want?'

'My boy reckoned I ought to hear what you've got to say.'

'Vincent? What's this about?'

Baldwin interjected, 'Perhaps it will become clearer if you tell the story.'

Joel nodded. He contemplated the men in front of him as he began. 'I suppose you've heard all about the murder of the Chaunter?' he said heavily. 'Well, all I can say is, you don't understand how things were. It was hell in the city when that new arse came in.

'No one wanted Quivil. He was out to stop anything that made business profitable for us. The fellows from the city wanted someone who was more . . . *congenial*, but Quivil was determined to interfere, silly bastard! Sorry, my Lady,' he added, glancing at Jeanne.

'When the Treasurer managed to get himself the Deanship, that was like a red rag to Quivil. He went berserk, so they said. Ranted about the corruption eating at the Chapter, said John Pycot was a canker that had to be cut out, and the like. And then, to stifle any ambitions John might have had, he put that idiot Lecchelade in place to hinder him. Everything John tried to do, Walter de Lecchelade stopped him. Even refused him access to the Dean's stall in the choir. It was impossible. All business at the Cathedral was effectively held up by their antipathy. And what else could we do, but try to save the place?'

'By murder.' Baldwin's tone was flat and unemotional.

'Granted it wasn't the way most people would have sought to straighten things, but John Pycot had taken about as much as he could stand. He was at least a sensible bloke you could talk to, while the Bishop and his lackey wanted their own way and weren't prepared to discuss it.

'It wasn't just a few men in the city with an axe to grind, either. It was a whole mixture of people, many of them from the Cathedral. No one wanted this idiot Lecchelade foisted on us. There were vicars, men like Stephen . . . poor devil.

'So that night we all went to the Close and hung around until the end of Matins. That place where the chapel is now, that was where Lecchelade's house stood, and we knew we had to jump on him before he could go inside. It was William's idea, I think, to get the rumour to the Chaunter that there was going to be an attack, but that the Bishop had set up his own men to catch us in the act. It worked like a dream, too. The Chaunter couldn't tell what sort of counter-attack was being planned, because he was in the Cathedral running the service. All he knew was that Matthew, his darling boy, had said that all was under control. Matthew was so well-trusted by the Chaunter that his word wouldn't be doubted. And William told us not to kill him, so most of us guessed he was in on it.

'Stephen was with us, of course. From the first moment, he was in ahead of me. I think he had some other reason to hate the Chaunter, but I don't know why. Anyway, just before we could attack, a novice called Vincent ran up and tried to warn the Chaunter. The fool nearly messed the whole thing up. Luckily, Nicholas didn't realise. He had heard there might be an attack, and when Vincent rushed at him in the dark, Nick pulled out his dagger and saw him off.'

Wymond heard the words like a blow to his heart. Joel's matter-of-fact tone only added to the insult, to his sense of loss. He felt his son's hand on his shoulder, and forced himself to be calm. He wouldn't break down in front of an accessory to his brother's murder.

Joel continued, 'After that, we all piled in. Thomas slashed at Nicholas and did that damage to the poor sod's face, while the rest of us set to at the Chaunter and his gang. Someone knocked Matthew down – I think that was William – and the rest of us did what we could. Only later did I see William with the Chaunter. He was holding his dagger in the Chaunter's breast and twisting the blade. *He* was the murderer of Walter – I swear it.'

'What do you gain from telling us this?' Simon asked.

'Revenge! Afterwards I saw that there was some mileage to be gained from the fact that the Southern Gate was left wide open all night. When the King arrived, I decided I'd mention this, because the old King was quite generous. I told my *friend* William, but before I could speak to the King, I learned that William had already told him. Edward rewarded him with money and a place in the royal household.

'I was furious. I'd told William before, see – so that he wouldn't get angry with me. Even then he was a ruthless shite, and I didn't want him sticking a knife in my back for some supposed insult in later years. As it was, I wanted to get him instead. He stole my idea and my savings, and took my reward, the thieving git!'

'And that was that,' Baldwin commented.

'There's nothing more to tell,' Joel said. He looked tired now, as though he had worked hard at his tale. 'I wanted you to know the truth so that no lies could confuse the issue later.'

'Why did you choose to tell us?'

'Because I want William to pay for what he did. Look – I've had a good life. If I'd gone to the King's service instead of him, I'd not have met my Maud and might well be dead in a Scottish ditch somewhere by now. No, I reckon I've done better here than I would have, taking on the life of a warrior. But that doesn't mean that I'd happily see him rewarded for his murder. I saw him kill the Chaunter – it's wrong that he should live out his days with a King's corrody after that.'

Baldwin nodded, but in truth he was not very interested. His wound was giving him pain again, and the convoluted motivations of this man were of little import to him. He would prefer to return to his room and rest as the physician had suggested.

It was Simon who said, 'I don't think the King will take kindly to hearing that the man his father rewarded so well was in fact a murderer guilty of the crime he reported. The Corrody will probably be returned.'

'Good. I wouldn't want to think that the man was going to survive without punishment.'

'Do you not think others deserve some punishment?' Vincent burst out. 'After all, you yourself helped to get that man murdered, then sought to reward yourself as you could, reporting about the gate being left open, all for your own advantage and the devil take the others!'

'Be quiet, Vince. I didn't tell you to stay here, and I won't have you speaking disrespectfully in front of all these people.'

'You are a murderer and accomplice of murderers, *Master*,' Vincent spat. 'I can speak to you how I wish.'

'I've never committed murder,' Joel declared stiffly.

'You've plotted it, you've helped others kill, and you even planned to report the gate, which led to two men being wrongly hanged,' Vincent said hotly.

'Boy, be silent! I won't have you talk like this.'

Simon beckoned the apprentice to him. 'Joel, you know the man called Vincent whom Nicholas, so you say, killed? Did you never wonder that your apprentice had this fellow's name?' He put his arm about Vincent's shoulder.

'Vincent?' Joel said dully. 'You're related to him?'

'He would have been my uncle.'

'Christ Jesus!'

'So I think,' Simon continued, 'that you ought to agree that this young man's contract is finished. Vincent here wishes to set up shop, and it would be a right neighbourly thing for a boy's master to lend him the money to get him started – don't you agree?'

Thomas would never forget the sight of Sara, lying there on the bench, blood all over her. The mere thought could make the hairs rise on the back of his neck. In that moment, he thought he had lost her, and that he was the agent of a terrible fate.

Yet then he had reminded himself that the death of Saul was nothing to do with him. It was Matthew, trying to kill him, who had caused the rock to fall. Nor had Sara's little son Elias died because of Thomas. If anything, he had saved her life.

He sobbed as he huddled over her body, listening to the soft thudding of her heart. Dear God, soon she would be dead! While the men about him were carrying Baldwin and Jeanne from the room, Edgar tottering after them, Thomas knelt there, cradling Sara's frail body, until she gradually stirred and he felt her hand on his head.

He was convinced this was her death. She was going. He ought to demand that she confess her sins. It was his duty to a fellow Christian, and there was dispensation for a man to hear a Confession when there was no priest available. He pulled away from her, preparing himself to speak the *viaticum*, and then he saw her eyes open. There was a glazed look in them, and he burst out with more sobbing, only to hear her say, 'What's happened? Where am . . . *what is all this*!'

'You've been wounded.'

'Where?'

She sat up and he retreated, staring, still convinced that she must be about to die. The blood was so fresh.

It was only when he stumbled over the dead Treasurer's body that he realised the truth, and even then it took his brain some while to accept the glorious fact that she was fine.

Baldwin was clearly very tired, and Simon had to help Edgar support him on the way back to the inn where the knight and his wife were staying. Simon put Baldwin into his chamber, resting him on his bed, and then left Jeanne and Edgar seeing to his needs while he went about the city.

The murder of the saddler and the Friar was all but concluded, of course. There were only a few loose cords to collect together. And Simon had an idea of one man who could help him: Thomas, the man who had been trying to flee the place when they found him at some woman's house. Except no one seemed to have seen Thomas since the death of Stephen. His whereabouts were a mystery.

Simon pondered that for some while as he walked along Fore Street and then up the narrower ways to the old Friary. He turned the corner at the end of the road and continued until he reached the house with an old oaken door, upon which he knocked.

It was opened by a pale, drawn-featured woman with red-gold hair. 'Who are you?' she demanded suspiciously.

'I am a Bailiff; Simon Puttock is my name and I want to speak with Thomas the mason.'

'What makes you think he is here?'

'There's nowhere else he could be,' Simon said equably. 'Will you send him out here to be viewed by all your neighbours, or shall I enter and speak with him inside?'

Ungraciously she stood aside, staring hard at him as though daring him to bring any more misfortune into her dwelling.

As he entered, Simon saw the large vertical post that supported the roof, where Thomas had been bound last time he came in.

'Hello, Master Thomas,' he said.

The man seated at the table grunted. 'What do you want?'

'I've heard much about the killing of the Chaunter, but there's one thing I cannot understand: why did you choose to leave the city after his death?' Simon asked.

'Because I was repelled by it all. I saw what I'd done when I attacked Nicholas, and it made my stomach turn. I had become a butcher who would happily slaughter his own best friend for a little money.'

'Money?'

'Henry, Joel and I were promised coin for taking part. John Pycot wanted as many men as possible so that the Chaunter would have little means of escape. He paid lots of us to be there. That night I stabbed Nicholas, my oldest friend, and thought that I had killed him. Later, when I got home, I decided to leave and never return. I could only bring dishonour to my family, so I thought.'

'And you never came back until now?'

'Why should I? There was nothing here for me. I was an only child. My mother had died when I was a boy and thanks to the Chaunter's murder, my father was dead, too.'

'Dead?'

'Oh yes. That happened not long after I left. William, the devil, stood up and told everyone about the Southern Gate being open. Soon afterwards, my father was taken out and hanged.'

'He was the Mayor?' Simon asked.

Thomas frowned at him. 'Of course not! He was the porter, the man in charge of the Southern Gate. When William announced to the King that the gate was open all night, he chose to punish those who were responsible: the Mayor, because he represented the city itself, and my father, because he had left the gates open.'

'*Why* did he do that?' Simon asked quietly.

Thomas looked confused. He stared at the table-top, shaking his head slowly. 'I don't know. I think he must have guessed that I had a part in the killing, because he found me the next morning, and I suppose he opened the gate to make it look as though someone from outside the city had committed the assassination. But it didn't work, of course. It was a mad idea. Even if it was true that he had allowed the murderers to escape, he'd then have relocked the gates, not left them open all night.'

Simon nodded thoughtfully. 'I see. What of your companions? Were you so very friendly with men like Joel and Henry and William beforehand?'

'William wasn't someone I'd have kept in touch with. He was always ruthless – not a pleasant character. Henry and Joel were good fellows, though. I always enjoyed a drink or a game with them. And Nicholas, too. He was a laugh.'

Simon felt his instinct had failed him. 'So you didn't see much of William, then?'

'We went about a lot together. He stayed at my home, and I stayed in his, when we were younger. It was only when we got older that I saw what he was really like, and I started to avoid him.'

'He knew your home, then?'

Thomas looked up at him. 'What are you driving at, Bailiff?'

Simon stood with decision. 'Nothing. Don't worry about me.'

He bowed slightly to Sara, then turned and left. As soon as he was gone, Thomas looked despairingly at Sara.

She saw his expression and said, 'Don't worry, Tom. I don't mind.'

'It's just going to keep reminding you, that's all,' he said thickly.

Sara rubbed at her eyes tiredly. 'No, Thomas. I don't need reminding. Saul's always here with me.'

'I'm sorry. I'll go soon and leave you.'

'You can't stay?'

'I won't be arrested, the Bailiff said so after the Treasurer was buried. He reckoned that there'd been enough death resulting from the Chaunter's murder.'

'So you could stay if you wanted?'

'I can't. I'm a reminder to you of your loss.'

'All I know is, I'm happy while you're here.'

He was staring at her, dumbfounded, when there was another knock at the door. Thomas rolled his eyes. 'What now, Bailiff?'

Jen poked her head around the door. 'So you *are* here, then. I just wondered. Suppose you haven't got any more of that wine, have you? No? Right, well, never mind. Well done, Sara. I said you ought to snare him. You look after her, fellow. She needs understanding, that woman does. You be careful with her, all right?'

She withdrew her head and Sara and Thomas exchanged a baffled look. Gradually she began to smile, her lips twitching. 'You realise that means everyone around here will know you're here?'

'I am sorry. It will give you a reputation.'

She nodded, her smile gone. 'I would not have my husband's memory besmirched by gossip over my behaviour.'

'I . . . it would be impertinent to ask,' he stammered. 'But I think . . .'

'What?'

'It would mean upsetting those who believe you should honour your dead husband for a period.'

'Do you mean—'

'Sara, I'd ask you to be my wife.'

She stared at him. In her mind were all the little events since Saul's death. The day that this stranger appeared in front of her house to tell her Saul was dead; the day that she and Elias were pulled from the mound of corpses before the Priory; the day he brought her meat; the day he left money for her . . . waking from her faint to find him kneeling at her side weeping. He cared for her. There were few men whom she could trust as deeply, nor for whom she felt such an attachment. Saul was only recently dead, but there was nothing in the Priests' laws which said a widow couldn't remarry as soon as she liked.

'You could at least ask properly,' she said tartly, and then she gave him a sweet, shy smile.

Dan would take time to understand. He would find this man's presence hard to accommodate. But she was lonely, and perhaps, given time, even Dan could grow to appreciate his kindness and honour. She hoped so. Because she needed Thomas and she wouldn't risk losing him.

Chapter Twenty-Seven

A week later, in the gaol, William sat and fulminated.

It had cost him good money, but he'd been removed from the stinking pit that was the general gaol and been brought up here to this more civilised cell with a view over the eastern landscape from the slit window. From the north he could see the castle on its mound, but he preferred to avert his eyes from that dread building. There was every chance that he might one day be tried in there, and that would not be a pleasant occasion. With luck, he might only lose his Corrody; and that was better than a lingering death hanging from a rope while the crowds laughed and jeered.

His money had brought him a table, two benches, and a room with a few rushes scattered. It was less noisome than other places he had lived when he was free, so he didn't complain, although the gaoler charged dearly for his food. William couldn't survive much longer at this rate.

Better to live well while he could, though. That was a principle he had learned early on, and one he intended to maintain.

There was a rattling of keys outside, and then the door swung slowly open to show Simon and Sir Baldwin in the company of the gaoler. Simon slipped a coin in the gaoler's hand, and the man ushered the two inside, locking the door behind them.

'Well?' William snapped. 'What do you two want? Haven't you done me enough harm already?'

'We have done you no harm,' Baldwin said. 'All we have done is uncovered the harm you have done to yourself and to others. Do not seek to blame us for these present conditions.'

'I am innocent.'

'You were the man who told the King about the gate being left open after the Chaunter's death?' Simon asked.

'What of it?'

'It seems peculiar that the keeper should himself have left the gate open,' Baldwin said. 'After all, it must lead to the King realising that he was involved in some way. A more open declaration of complicity would be hard to imagine.'

'He was an old fool. Maybe he didn't think.'

'Or maybe he was a fool enough to trust a young lad. Maybe he thought that his son's friend couldn't do any harm in his home.'

William shot a look at Baldwin. 'What do you mean?'

'Only this. You sought to profit from the gate being opened. I simply wonder whether you could also have been guilty of opening it yourself. I don't believe that a man as respected as a gatekeeper could resort to leaving the gate wide in that way.'

William shrugged. 'It was nothing to do with me. The man must have thought it was a good idea.'

'Did he often leave the gates open, then?' Simon pressed.

'No, of course not.'

'Quite so,' Baldwin said. 'And yet he left them open that night, or so you would have us believe.'

'I don't care a fig for what you believe, masters!' William hissed, snapping his fingers at Baldwin. His anger was fired now, and he half-stood. Simon moved a hand towards his sword hilt, but William didn't care. 'You want to rake over that shit from years ago? Well, you do so. It's no concern of mine. All I know is, Joel had an idea and I took it from him. Since then he's hated me. So what – I don't give a toss. Me, though, I've been treated abysmally. I have been shot at, almost killed, and you treat me like a common draw-latch. Well, I'm not going to suffer this longer than I have to.'

'Who attacked you?' Baldwin enquired.

'As if you care!'

'But I do. Who was it – do you know?'

William studied him for a moment, assessing his honesty. Then he sank back onto his bench and shrugged. 'I can't be certain. I thought it was Joel, so I went and thumped him, but he denied it and I believe him now, in retrospect. He was always a good bowman. These two arrows were close to me, but not quite near enough to hurt me, and they were fired from not far away. The bowman was lousy, unless he just intended scaring me.'

'You should be glad that it was not the tanner who shot at you,' Baldwin said, remembering the dead rat on Exe Island.

'If you say so. I assume it was the same man who shot you. Stephen must have had the same fear about me as he did about the others. He thought we would expose him as being part of the Chaunter's murder, and since his position depended upon his integrity, he thought our evidence would destroy him. So he tried to kill them, and me, and then you.'

Baldwin nodded. 'I expect you are right,' he said smoothly, and a few moments later he had paid another small coin to the gaoler and was walking with Simon towards the East Gate and the High Street.

'Why didn't you tell him?' Simon asked.

'What – that it wasn't Stephen who tried to kill me? It didn't seem important. The fact that Matthew did so might possibly lead to William deciding to take his revenge at some point, and there's little point leaving a potential cause for further feuding.'

'William will be released, you believe, then?'

'I expect so.'

'What will you do about Matthew?'

Baldwin smiled. 'I shall speak to the good Dean.'

'And what of the Southern Gate?'

Baldwin glanced at the sky speculatively. 'A good question. I think that William might have slipped into the porter's lodgings and taken the chance of opening the gate when he could. Then announcing it to the King detracted from his guilt. But there is no proof if he refuses to confess.'

'Do you think he will?'

With a sigh, Baldwin shook his head. 'Stranger things have happened, I suppose.'

Dean Alfred was in his hall when they arrived. He had been celebrating Mass, and then had to attend the Chapter meeting at which many issues were discussed.

'But without any – ah – advantageous conclusion,' he sighed as he motioned to the visitors to sit.

Baldwin groaned as he sat. Each time he moved his shoulders, arms or torso, it felt as though a fresh stab wound was opened in his breast.

Much as he disliked the physician, he acknowledged that Ralph's ministrations were helping; however he couldn't sit still for as long as Ralph recommended. At least the wound appeared to be healing well. Even Ralph himself expressed approval with Baldwin's progress. If only it were not so painful.

'Sir Baldwin? Some wine?' the Dean enquired solicitously.

As soon as Baldwin and Simon were seated comfortably with large mazers in their hands, Alfred sipped at his own, shaking his head. 'I don't know what to do. There is no one in the Cathedral's Chapter who is remotely capable of taking over Stephen or Matthew's work. No one can make sense of the figures in their rolls.'

'Were they really so indispensable?' Baldwin asked.

'Without a doubt. There was no – um – false modesty about their assertions that they were irreplaceable. I fear for the rebuilding.'

'Then why should Stephen have put all that at risk by setting out on this murderous spree?' Simon asked.

'I think that – er – is easily answered,' the Dean said. 'It was simply his attempt to prevent what has in fact happened. He tried to – ah – stifle any suggestion that he was involved in the murder of the Chaunter so that he could continue with the rebuilding work and bring Matthew up to his own standard. He hoped that the works would not be – um – compromised. You must try to understand, Bailiff, that this fellow lived for the Cathedral as he hoped it would one day be. It was never a part of his design to kill a man and damn his soul, but he was so desperate to see the great plan go ahead unhindered, that he was prepared to try anything to protect it. Even kill.'

'Yes, I confess that his attack on me was a surprise,' Baldwin murmured.

'But logical. He realised you had learned that there were others involved in the murder of the Chaunter, and he thought that removing you would remove the threat of that becoming common knowledge. Ironically, it was the realisation that you were approaching Matthew that led him to take such a course of action.'

Baldwin smiled and shook his head. 'That is intriguing, but I don't think it likely. The arrow that hit me was a clothyard shaft. What use would Stephen have had for that? No, that was not him. Stephen only attacked me in Janekyn's room. Stephen was acting for the best, as he saw it. He reckoned that Matthew was in danger, but he thought that I was the one who would, as you say, put the case against him. To protect Matthew, Stephen decided to destroy me.'

'I don't understand. You – ah – say that he didn't fire at you, but he did.'

'Matthew tried to shoot me because I realised that he was the killer of Saul. It occurred to me that aiming a rock from a Cathedral wall and hoping to kill a man so many yards below was a foolish method to use. But Thomas was up there on the scaffold . . . surely a rock falling could sweep him away with it, especially if he foolishly tried to stop it from plummeting to earth. Yes, Matthew reasoned that I was too close to the truth, and he tried to remove me in order to protect himself.'

'What use would Matthew have had for a clothyard arrow?' the Dean asked. 'You say that Stephen had no use for one – why then should Matthew have one?'

'Matthew was a keen archer when he was younger. William told us how competitive he and his companions all were at football and other games, and Peter and Thomas recalled shooting at the butts. Thomas said how Matthew always used to win at archery. And at the butts men will use a standard clothyard shaft, will they not?'

'Why then did Stephen choose to kill you when Matthew failed?'

'Because Stephen had protected Matthew all through their lives. It was an ingrained habit from the last forty years,' Baldwin explained. 'For all that time I think Stephen protected Matthew because he thought Matthew was honourable and deserved to be defended. It would be hard for him to change his attitude overnight. Although perhaps,' he added thoughtfully, 'his own terror that I was about to bring up his past led to his deciding to remove me. That would also make some sense. Whatever, I am as sure as I can be of the relative guilt of the two.'

'It is a terrible thing when a man of God decides to turn his skills to evil,' the Dean said. 'Especially when it leads to the Cathedral being without a decent Warden of the Fabric.'

Simon smiled broadly. 'Dean, I feel sure that I can help you there.'

Peter reread the letter with astonishment, but at each reading the words jumbled up and he had to try again. In the end, he called in one of his assistants, who humbly took the sheet of vellum and read out the message, his brow furrowed with the effort. Then he put the roll back in Peter's hand and congratulated him.

'Me!' Peter gasped as the fellow left his room. 'Me!'

At last. After so many years, he was actually going to be permitted to take it on! He felt his heart swell. This was his first opportunity to show what he was made of – a chance to demonstrate his skills and his honour. He would make this Priory the most efficient in the country. His monks would be seen to be the most chaste and obedient, the length and breadth of the land. Before long, he would be able to hope to rise to a small abbacy, perhaps, and then . . .

No. Nonsense. The fact that his dear Abbot had decided that he was a safe master of the Brothers here in Exeter was a proof of his faith in Peter, but Peter needn't grow above himself. He was probably here to stay, and to die here in the city where he had been born was no shame. It was a good city, and he could do some little to make life better for the population here. He had a duty too, to guard all the people here, the living and the dead, with his prayers and the prayers of his Brothers. They should all seek to save the souls of the men and women of Exeter.

Yes, that was enough for him. He had reached his zenith. As Prior he was now at last recognised as having paid for his crime forty years ago.

He puffed out his cheeks with relief to think that his other crime, so recently attempted, had failed so abysmally. Otherwise he would now be forced to obtain forgiveness for William's death, when he had tried to shoot him down before he could make clear Peter's involvement in the Chaunter's murder. In a curious way, it was actually rather amusing to reflect that William's excellent suitability as a felon was making the crimes of others invisible in contrast.

His job done, Simon took a leisurely journey homewards, refusing to accept the generous offer of a ship to carry him to Dartmouth. In preference, he hired a horse and took a long sweep through Dartmoor and thence down south towards the coast. It was a delightful journey, relaxing and soothing to his nerves, although he still missed his wife. He must soon arrange for her to join him. He couldn't continue like this, with Meg living so far from him.

The first day back at his work was probably the most enjoyable he had spent there in the company of his clerk.

'Andrew, I am afraid I shall have to lose your company. There is a new task for you in Exeter, a much more important one.'

Back in Exeter, Sara and Thomas exchanged their oaths at the door of St Olave's, while Daniel watched sulkily and planned his escape into an apprenticeship.

At the same time Vincent was packing a small bag with some food and a cloak, and swinging it over his back. He walked down to the Western Gate, and there he met his father. The two of them set off, following the river southwards, walking as the sun set in the west, down to the little cave-like corner of the river, where they built a fire just as Wymond had done forty years before with another Vincent.

But this time, he was sure that he was not going to lose his son, and later, when Wymond sat back with his belly filled with meat and wine, he felt more content than he had for many a long year.

Baldwin rested at the inn while he waited for his wound to heal. Edgar remained with him, as though distrusting any others to look after his master, and Baldwin was as glad for his companionship as he was to have his wife with him still. Matters could only have been improved by the presence of his daughter Richalda. He missed her dreadfully. If he was forced to remain recuperating here much longer, perhaps he could arrange for her to be brought to Exeter to be with him and Jeanne?

Jeanne had flourished. While Baldwin was still sometimes tweaked by guilt at his betrayal of her while he was returning from pilgrimage, his guilt was oozing away under the influence of her careful attention. He was coming to appreciate her again, rather than seeing her as a reminder of his shame, and with that realisation came the renewal of his love for her. Perhaps not so complete and untainted as before, but no less warming to his soul for all that.

The Dean found him sitting on his bench there one morning while Jeanne was out at the market. 'Sir Baldwin.'

'Dean. Please, take a seat.'

'Thank you. Yes – hmm – I shall, thank you.' The Dean sighed as he sat, and rested his head against the inn's wall. 'That is better.'

'You came all this way to rest against my wall?' Baldwin asked with a grin.

'I came to – ah – tell you of William. He has confessed to his deceit in telling the King of the gate being open, and now he admits that he himself opened the gate and left it wide.'

'Did he explain why he wished to admit?' Baldwin asked.

'I think that he – ah – felt he might as well admit to all his crimes since he's little to lose. Apparently he already has a letter of pardon from the – um – King in honour of his service over the years. Not that it'll help him much, for the punishment is more cruel than we might think. The man has no money, the Prior of St Nicholas refuses to have him live there, and he will be forced to resort to begging.'

Baldwin shook his head slowly. 'A hard way of life for a man of his age.'

'Perhaps he has a friend who can help him. I do not know,' the Dean said. 'So long as he leaves Exeter soon and our lives can return to their even tenor. Oh – ah – yes, and there was the other thing: Matthew. He has confessed to trying to kill you. It was only the darkness, he said, that saved you, for otherwise he would have aimed true.'

'Did he shoot from the Charnel Chapel?'

The Dean glanced at him, hearing his tone. 'Yes. Why?'

Baldwin shook his head. There was no possibility that he would leave himself open to accusations of superstition by admitting to his strange feeling of fear at the sight of the chapel. 'Nothing.'

'It's curious, though,' the Dean said. 'He did mention that he regretted standing on the chapel to fire. He felt quite sickly and weak up there, as though the building itself was moving under him when he released his bowstring. I think he must have been drunk.'

Baldwin smiled and nodded, but in his mind he wondered. 'The chapel was built because of one clandestine murder. Would it be so surprising if a man involved in that murder felt the earth move beneath him when on that same spot, he tried to kill again?'

'Hah! You think he was weak in the head?'

Baldwin smiled, but as he closed his eyes, he had a notion that he would not feel so anxious at the sight of the Charnel Chapel again.

Still, he was determined that under no circumstances would his own body be buried here in Exeter. He would be buried in Cadbury or Crediton. He did not want his bones to rest in the chapel of bones. He wanted nothing to do with the place.